PRAISE FOR THE OTHERWORLD NOVELS

"Spectacularly hot and supernaturally breathtaking."
—Alyssa Day, *New York Times* bestselling author

"Erotic and darkly bewitching . . . a mix of magic and passion."
—Jeaniene Frost, *New York Times* bestselling author

"Simmers with fun and magic."
—Mary Jo Putney, *New York Times* bestselling author

"Yasmine Galenorn's imagination is a beautiful thing."
—*Fresh Fiction*

"Galenorn's gallery of rogues is an imaginative delight."
—*Publishers Weekly*

"Otherworld is one truly exceptional series."
—*RT Book Reviews*

"It's not too many authors who can write a series as long-lived as this one and make every book come out just as interesting and intriguing as the last, but Yasmine Galenorn is certainly one of them . . . Her books are always enchanting, full of life and emotion as well as twists and turns that keep you reading long into the night."
—*Romance Reviews Today*

"Explore this fascinating world."
—*TwoLips Reviews*

Shadow Rising

An Otherworld Novel

YASMINE GALENORN

JOVE BOOKS, NEW YORK

THE BERKLEY PUBLISHING GROUP
Published by the Penguin Group
Penguin Group (USA) Inc.
375 Hudson Street, New York, New York 10014, USA

Penguin Group (Canada), 90 Eglinton Avenue East, Suite 700, Toronto, Ontario M4P 2Y3, Canada
(a division of Pearson Penguin Canada Inc.) • Penguin Books Ltd., 80 Strand, London WC2R 0RL,
England • Penguin Group Ireland, 25 St. Stephen's Green, Dublin 2, Ireland (a division of Penguin
Books Ltd.) • Penguin Group (Australia), 250 Camberwell Road, Camberwell, Victoria 3124, Australia
(a division of Pearson Australia Group Pty. Ltd.) • Penguin Books India Pvt. Ltd., 11 Community
Centre, Panchsheel Park, New Delhi—110 017, India • Penguin Group (NZ), 67 Apollo Drive,
Rosedale, Auckland 0632, New Zealand (a division of Pearson New Zealand Ltd.) • Penguin Books
(South Africa) (Pty.) Ltd., 24 Sturdee Avenue, Rosebank, Johannesburg 2196, South Africa

Penguin Books Ltd., Registered Offices: 80 Strand, London WC2R 0RL, England

SHADOW RISING

A Jove Book / published by arrangement with the author

PUBLISHING HISTORY
Jove mass-market edition / November 2012

Copyright © 2012 by Yasmine Galenorn.
Excerpt from *Haunted Moon* copyright © 2012 by Yasmine Galenorn.
Cover art by Tony Mauro.
Cover design by Rita Frangie.
Map by Andrew Marshall, copyright © 2012 by Yasmine Galenorn.

ISBN: 978-0-515-15116-9

JOVE®
Jove Books are published by The Berkley Publishing Group,
a division of Penguin Group (USA) Inc.,
375 Hudson Street, New York, New York 10014.
JOVE® is a registered trademark of Penguin Group (USA) Inc.
The "J" design is a trademark of Penguin Group (USA) Inc.

PRINTED IN THE UNITED STATES OF AMERICA

10 9 8 7 6 5 4 3 2 1

ALWAYS LEARNING   **PEARSON**

Dedicated to:

My readers.

Because without you, these books wouldn't be a success.

ACKNOWLEDGMENTS

Thank you to my beloved Samwise—my biggest, strongest, and sexiest fan.

As always, huge thanks to my agent, Meredith Bernstein, and to my editor, Kate Seaver—thank you both for helping me stretch my wings and fly. A salute to Tony Mauro, cover artist extraordinaire. Thanks go to my assistant, Andria Holley; Scotty Talley, my Otherworld wiki organizer; and to Jenn Price, who answers my fan mail. Love to my furry little "Galenorn Gurlz," LOLcats in their own right, who keep me company during the long, isolated hours of writing. As always, most reverent devotion to Ukko, Rauni, Mielikki, and Tapio, my spiritual guardians.

And the biggest thank-you of all—to my readers, both old and new. Your support helps keep the series going. You can find me on the net at Galenorn En/Visions: www.galenorn.com. For links to social networking sites where you can find me, see my website. If you write to me snail mail (see website for address or write via my publisher), please enclose a self-addressed stamped envelope with your letter if you would like a reply. Promo goodies are available—see my site for info.

The Painted Panther
Yasmine Galenorn
February 2012

By the pricking of my thumbs, something wicked this way comes.

—SHAKESPEARE, *MACBETH*

Life is neither a good nor an evil, it is a field for good and evil.

—SENECA, ROMAN PHILOSOPHER

Chapter 1

ﾠ✦ﾠ

I hadn't been home to Otherworld in a while—not for any length of time. As we stepped through the portal into the barrows near Elqaneve, the Elfin City, the brilliance of the night sky hit me, untainted by the light pollution running rampant in Earthside cities. Over there, even in the country, the stars sparkled more faintly, muted and dim. But here . . . I stared up at the heavens, stunned.

Had I really been away long enough for me to forget how beautiful my home world was? And yet . . . and yet . . . the Earthside city lights that watched over the nighttime landscape called to me. The hustle and bustle of Seattle had worked its way under my skin, and I wasn't so sure I wanted to return home for good, even should we be offered the chance.

We arrived in Otherworld just shy of seven P.M., and the darkness of the spring evening was spiraling over the sky. My sisters were relieved to see the chill weather begin to break, but I preferred winter, when the sun set earlier and rose later. During summer, the long sleep of daylight claimed too much of my time. But the wheel must turn, and now spring held sway. The vernal equinox was due in a week, and along with it, my promise ceremony with Nerissa.

We still hadn't settled on details for the ceremony, and time was running short. As was my girlfriend's temper. It irked her that I couldn't come up with ideas for a concrete plan. My continual stream of "whatever you want" was wearing thin, but the truth was, I had no clue what I wanted. When Dredge had turned me into a vampire, I'd let go all hope and plans for love and weddings, and now I couldn't remember what I had dreamed about before I'd lost my life.

But thoughts of Nerissa and home and rituals drifted to the back of my mind as Trenyth approached. The advisor to Queen Asteria, he was meeting us to escort us back to the palace in the center of the Elfin city.

"About time he got here. I'm freezing," Delilah mumbled as she blew on her fingers.

Camille jabbed her in the ribs with an elbow. "I'm cold, too, but be nice. He probably got held up by something important."

"He can't hear me from over there." Delilah glared at her, then shrugged and jammed her hands in the pockets of her jeans.

"Don't bet on it. Elves have extremely sensitive hearing."

"Shut up, both of you. Whining about the cold won't do anything to warm you up." I felt a little guilty barking at them. After all, I was immune to the chill. Vampires didn't feel much in the way of weather changes unless it was extreme, one way or the other. I knew my sisters and our escorts were freezing, but I didn't want Trenyth's feelings hurt.

We'd divided up the manpower, making some of the guys stay home. Accompanying us were Trillian, one of Camille's husbands; Shade, Delilah's half-dragon fiancé; Chase, the human detective with a touch of elf in his background; Rozurial, an incubus; and Vanzir, a demon who worked with us. That left us with a fighting contingent, but still enough manpower over Earthside to protect the house. And protecting our home there was an absolute necessity, especially now that Iris and Bruce were back from their honeymoon, and Iris was pregnant.

Trenyth looked tired, and for the first time, I noticed a few tiny age lines around his eyes. Elves seldom showed their age. Time passed for them differently, leaving them untouched and unperturbed. And most exhibited a patience that defied understanding. Unlike some of the more volatile denizens of Otherworld, that Elfin quality seemed to grow with the centuries.

Standing medium height, Trenyth was thin but not gaunt, was elegant to a fault, and carried himself with a regal air. Decorum incarnate, his manner wasn't a façade, as it was with some members of the royal courts.

"Welcome back to Elqaneve, girls." He sounded rushed and kept glancing back at the carriages behind him.

"Trenyth!" Delilah apparently had forgiven him for letting us stand out in the cold. She stepped forward to give him a hug.

Trenyth blushed lightly, awkwardly returning the embrace. "Delilah, blessings to you and your house." He turned to Camille and held out his hands. "And you, my lady. How are you doing?" A look of concern washed over his face as she took them and pressed them to her heart for a moment before letting go.

"Are you . . ." His words slipped away.

Camille ducked her head. "It's going to take a while, but I'm making progress. I don't think I'll ever be the same. You can't be, not after something like that. But it helps that Hyto is dead and that I saw him die." Her smile turned to ice. Camille had become harsher since her ordeal, darker in nature, but it seemed to suit the transitions through which she was going.

"Camille's right," I said quietly. "What she went through with Hyto . . . what *I* went through with Dredge, traumas like that change you forever. But it doesn't mean you can't find happiness, or grow stronger than before." Life had a way of forcing you to either take charge or knuckle under, and neither my sisters nor I were the knuckling kind.

Trenyth nodded. "And the two of you have gone above and beyond what I'd expect of anybody, under the circumstances. Now, come, please. We have much to discuss—events are transpiring that you must know about. And although spring is on the way, the night is still cold and the carriages are waiting for us."

And, quick as a cat, we were tucked into the carriages with blankets spread over our laps and heading toward the castle of Queen Asteria.

Elqaneve was a city of cobblestoned streets that wound through beautiful gardens, surrounding low-rising houses. Windows glimmered, illuminated by the soft glow of lanterns. The town was simultaneously elegant and cozy, and while I appreciated its beauty, it felt too gentle for me. Though perhaps *gentle* wasn't the right word. Elves weren't gentle. They could be dangerous and terrifying when roused. No, perhaps the word I was looking for was *subtle*.

The Elfin race wasn't known for being in your face, and that's exactly the type of person I was. I hadn't always been like this—*take no prisoners, my way or the highway.* I'd been a loner when I was younger, and only in the past twelve or thirteen Earthside years had I turned into the fury that I could become.

When I'd become a vampire, I'd come out of my shell . . . once I managed to climb back *into* my mind. Sanity had been sporadic for the first year—I didn't remember much from that year—and it had taken the Otherworld Intelligence Agency a lot of patience and training to teach me how to function in society, and *not* turn into the monster Dredge had planned for me to become.

I glanced over at Camille. She seemed lost in thought, gazing out the window, leaning her head against the side of the carriage. Trillian sat next to her, holding her hand, stroking it lightly with one finger. The jet black of his skin glowed against her pale cream, and for a moment I thought I saw a swirl of silver race from his fingers to hers.

Chase sat next to me, and he, too, stared quietly out the window. Delilah, Shade, Rozurial, and Vanzir were with Trenyth, in the carriage behind us.

"Hey, you get lost somewhere in there?" I spoke softly, but Camille's eyes flickered and she shook her head.

"No, not really. I'm just wondering what Queen Asteria wants to see us about."

She was lying. I knew it. Most likely, she was thinking about our father. It was hard not to, now that we were back in Otherworld. He'd disowned her, and as a result, we'd disowned him. Everything was convoluted into a horrible mess, compounded by his lack of sensitivity. At this point, we could probably qualify for an Otherworld episode of *The Jerry Springer Show*. No doubt *that* would thrill Delilah to pieces, as long as the ringmaster himself hosted it.

With another look at her face, I let the subject drop. We'd hashed and rehashed the family drama to the point of no return. It was moot. Father didn't approve of Camille's choice in husbands—Trillian in specific—nor her pledging herself as priestess to Aeval's Court. But she'd had no choice. Love doesn't always give you a choice, and neither do the gods.

As a result, we had said "buh-bye" to both Dear Daddy and the Otherworld Intelligence Agency, and now we worked for Queen Asteria.

"Why do you think Queen Asteria summoned us? And why ask me to come along? I almost never interact with her—that's more yours and Delilah's department." Being able to come out only after dusk had its drawbacks.

"I was wondering why she asked me to come along, too." Chase frowned.

"You *are* a distant relative of hers, you know." I gave him a poke in the ribs, careful not to shove too hard. Sometimes I forgot how freakishly strong I'd become. It was easy to hurt my friends and family if I wasn't careful.

"Doesn't track. She made it a point to invite me, and I doubt familial bliss has anything to do with it." He played with the buttons on his new blazer, fastening and unfastening the bottom one until I thought he was going to rip it off. "You really like my new jacket?"

Camille and I exchanged looks. This had to be the twentieth time that he'd asked since we started out for the portal at home.

"Yeah, it's nice." I wasn't good with diplomacy, but Chase

was nervous and I didn't want to hurt his feelings. Unfortunately, the pseudo-military look didn't suit him at all. However, since Sharah—his elfin girlfriend and the future mother of his child—had given him the blazer, he was better off pretending he liked it. Humans had *nothing* on the elves or the Fae when it came to pregnancy-hormonal mood swings. It was in his interests of self-preservation to lie to her.

But that didn't mean I couldn't needle him. "So tell us, in the privacy of the carriage, you really think you can rock that look?" I grinned at him. His expression when he was under fire was priceless. And by now he knew when I was serious and when I was just blowing smoke. Though it *had* been more fun when I could scare the crap out of him just by tickling his neck.

He squirmed. "Do *not* do this to me, Menolly. Don't put me on the spot." But his eyes twinkled and he laughed. "Only you would force me into a corner."

"I only torture the people I love." With a snort, I folded my arms and leaned back in my seat. "Don't answer. I can tell you don't feel comfortable in it. But we promise we won't tell Sharah. Or her aunt. *The Queen.*"

That sparked another ripple of fear in his expression. Queen Asteria happened to be the aunt of his girlfriend. And therefore, the great-aunt of his child. I had to admit, I wouldn't want to be caught up in the web of politics Chase was facing.

Another thought struck me. "Does Asteria even *know* Sharah's pregnant?"

Camille swiveled her head, glancing at Chase. "*She doesn't*, does she? You'd better come clean, because you don't want us saying something stupid to her."

Chase shifted uncomfortably. "Um, well . . . the truth is . . . *no*. She doesn't know. Sharah wanted to wait. We haven't decided what we're going to do yet. I've asked her to marry me, but she turned me down." He sounded morose. "She said we aren't ready."

"You *aren't* ready." I stared at him. "You know that. She knows that. Why rush it?"

"She's carrying my child—" He paused, then let out a

long sigh. "I guess I'm thinking about it from Earthside morality. I'd be a scumbag if she wanted to get married and I said *no*."

"She isn't asking you, though. And she's not cutting you out of the baby's life, either." I cocked my head. "Wait. She hasn't cut you out, *has* she?"

"No, it's not that. Sharah said I can be as much a part of the baby's life as I want." He looked so uncomfortable that I couldn't help but wonder what the root of the problem was.

"So tell me again what's the problem? You in love with her?"

He blushed this time, and Camille broke in softly. "Perhaps the issue is that Sharah offended him by insinuating he might not want to participate."

Chase shifted in his seat, and glowered. "Exactly! *I'm not my father. I'm no deadbeat and I'm not going to vanish on my kid.* And since she's choosing to have the baby, I damned well plan on being there to make sure the child knows his— or her—heritage."

The words poured out so fiercely that at first I thought he might be pissed, but the hurt that flashed across his face spoke volumes. Chase was afraid someone would even *think* he might consider abandoning his child. He couldn't take being seen as a carbon copy of his missing father—the father he'd never known. His childhood had left him with deep emotional scars. The situation with Sharah must be triggering fears and resentments from his own past.

I sheathed my fangs. "We know you'd never abandon your child, Chase. And Sharah knows that, too. Nobody who knows you would ever think you'd bail."

I was about to reach over and pat his hand but stopped. I simply wasn't the comforting type, and he knew it. I opted for catching his gaze and holding it. I silently focused on him, willing him to relax. It wasn't polite to use Fae glamour on our friends, but sometimes we chose to do what was necessary over what was ethically correct.

After a moment he relaxed, breathing softly, and leaned his head back against the rocking carriage.

"Don't think I'm unaware of what you just did," he said softly. "But thank you. Delilah knows that Sharah hasn't told anyone yet, so she won't say anything, either. We talked about it last night on the phone."

Chase and our sister Delilah had been involved in what was a downward spiral of a relationship. Now, they were both with other people, both a lot happier, *and* they'd saved their friendship.

At that moment the carriage shifted and Camille peered out into the evening street. "We're nearing the palace." She smoothed her skirts and pulled out a compact, peeking into the mirror to make sure her makeup was set.

"Me, too?" Not for the first time, I wished I could check my own damned makeup, but that wasn't ever going to be a reality, so I sucked it up and asked for help. She leaned close, brushing my face with a quick sweep of powder.

"You're good to go. You look great." She winked. "Not that the Queen's going to care, but . . ."

"But it isn't politic to visit royalty looking like a slob." The carriage lurched to a stop and the door opened, the driver reaching in to help us down. "I guess we'd better see what bad news is in store for us now."

"I don't even want to know." Camille flashed me a wry grin as the driver put his hands on her waist and swung her down from the carriage step to the rain-slicked path below. "But I guess we don't have a choice."

Once Delilah and the others stood next to us, Trenyth led us into the palace to meet the Elfin Queen.

Overhead, the stars glimmered. They were beautiful, but all I ever saw were the stars and the moon and clouds against the night sky. Sometimes it seemed like sunlight had become a myth—a dream I'd once had, a dream that was beautiful but fleeting. For me, only the starlight existed.

The palace of the Elfin Queen rose in gleaming alabaster. Simple, elegant lines mirrored the symmetry of the city in general. Amid a flurry of gardens, the royal courts were clean, quiet, and decorous. They were nothing like the Court and Crown of Y'Elestrial—our home city-state, which was a hotbed of lush opulence and debauchery.

The cul-de-sac ended in front of the entrance to the palace, and as we quick-stepped up the path behind Trenyth, Camille sighed happily.

"What is it?"

She clasped her hands under her chin and whirled around, her skirts swirling in the breeze. She stared up at a tall tree. The faintest hint of green leaves were beginning to show among tiny starlike white flowers that covered the branches.

"The scent of the untahstar tree . . . we're really home." A catch echoed in her throat as she gazed up at the vine-laden tree that grew only in the northern reaches of Otherworld. I could see the war waging within her. She loved being Earthside, but this was her home. She was more wistful now than ever, since Father had exiled her from Y'Elestrial.

Delilah followed her gaze and smiled softly. "It smells like childhood, doesn't it?"

Our father's home—the house of our youth—had two untahstar trees growing in the front yard. Their branches had wound together and Mother used to joke that the trees reminded her of their marriage. Two trees, on opposite sides of the path, reaching together across a void.

I allowed myself a quick breath. I didn't have to breathe and by now I was out of the habit, but when I wanted to smell something, I could force my lungs to take in air, to hold and catch the scents riding the wind.

The spicy floral fragrance swept me back through the years, to days long gone and dreams that belonged to my former life—the one I would never, ever be able to reclaim. Disconcerted, I shook them off, not wanting to be caught up in memories. Memories were dangerous for me, even now.

Trenyth motioned for us to get a move on. We followed him into the alabaster palace, leaving old dreams and lives behind.

Asteria, ancient queen of the Elfin race, wore the tire tracks of age on her face—which meant she was probably older than anyone we would ever meet with the exception of the dragons, or the Hags of Fate.

She had been queen before the Great Divide, before the Great Fae Lords split the worlds apart and Otherworld was forcibly shifted away from Earthside. She had been old when Titania and Aeval were young and new to their thrones. As she swept into the throne room, she ignored the throne hewn of oak and holly and crossed to a marble table standing to the side. As we waited, she gave us an impatient look and motioned for us to join her.

Trenyth's mood had gone somber. It was clear we weren't here for a potluck or a game of Monopoly. Something bad had gone down, and whatever it was, the fallout filled the throne room.

Camille gave me a cautious look. She shook her head and mouthed, *Bad.*

Delilah edged her hand into Shade's as they glanced around the room. Trillian, Vanzir, and Rozurial moved in closer. Even Chase seemed ill at ease. As for me, the tension set me on edge to the point where my fangs descended in a rush, in auto-defense mode, breaking the skin of my lip.

Camille curtsied while the rest of us bowed. "Your Highness, we came as soon as we received your summons. Something is wrong, isn't it? What happened?"

Asteria looked at us, one after another. Tension rode her face. Even in the darkest circumstances, I'd never seen this much stress on the Queen's face before.

"Sit. There is much to discuss and we have little time."

As we slid into the chairs around the table, Trenyth motioned to one of the elfin guards who'd been standing nearby, holding a long scroll. He brought it over and rolled it out on the table. A map of Otherworld, it filled the table, and we rolled it out and held it flat as Trenyth picked up a long pointer. Serving maids quietly offered us food and drink—they'd even filled a goblet with blood for me, though the girl's nose wrinkled as she handed it to me.

Head down, Queen Asteria closed her eyes, her arms crossed across her chest. She looked like she was gathering courage.

After a moment, she looked up and said, "We have dire news."

Delilah let out a little gasp. "The spirit seals are missing, aren't they? We feared—"

But before she could get out any more, Camille silenced her. "This is worse, isn't it? This is far worse."

Inclining her head slightly, with a pained voice, Asteria answered. "Yes, far worse. Although, it *does* have something to do with the spirit seals. At least, the two that Shadow Wing has managed to steal away from you."

Silence followed as we waited for more news of death and bloodshed and panicked plans to descend. We'd been embroiled in this war for months now, going on a year and a half, and there was no easy way out.

"Telazhar has returned to Otherworld, the first time since we exiled him. And he's brought the war with him."

Her words hung like crystal in the air, then shattered into a thousand shards, raining down on us.

Telazhar . . . the ancient necromancer who had led the Scorching Wars up from the Southern Wastes against the northern cities. Telazhar, who had been banished from Otherworld to live with the demons in the Subterranean Realms. Telazhar, whom we had done our best to kill, but who had slipped through our fingers. And now, he was here. *Back in Otherworld.*

Everybody started talking at once, but after a moment, I jumped up on the table and, putting my fingers in my mouth, let out a shrill whistle.

"Shut up! It's not going to do any good if we all talk at once." In the lull that followed, it occurred to me that my spiked heels might not be the best thing for the marble table, but the queen gave me a soft smile as I leaped down and took my seat again. "You know this for a fact?"

"Thank you, my dear. I'm too weary to whistle and shout on my own. And yes, it's true. Shadow Wing is behind it. Telazhar, wearing one of the spirit seals, has been spotted in the Southern Wastes. From what our informants say, he's inciting the sorcerers to align with him. He's rallying them to war."

"The Scorching Wars." I stared at her, barely able to comprehend what this meant for Otherworld, beyond one hell of a bad party.

"Yes. He seems to be planning to create another series of wars as bad as—or worse than—the Scorching Wars. Only this time, the sorcerers have a Demon Lord at their back. While Shadow Wing can't gate over here, *yet,* Telazhar can raze half the world for him and then open up the portals if he can get hold of the spirit seals we have hidden here. I'm afraid that, very quickly, Otherworld will be embroiled in such turmoil to make the recent battle in Y'Elestrial look like chicken scratch."

We sat, silent, digesting the news. This was far worse than what any of us had been imagining.

Camille shifted. "Will the sorcerers follow him? Do we know the extent of his influence?"

Queen Asteria moved back and Trenyth took over. He pointed to the city of Rhellah, the last city before a long stretch of desert in the Southern Wastes, where rogue magic played free and easy on the winds, bonding with the grains of shifting sand.

"We're readying a trio of spies. They'll head to the south, first to Rhellah to discover what's actually going on. From there, they will infiltrate the desert communities. The cities farther south—down in the heart of the Southern Wastes— are dangerous and wild and filled with slavers and sorcerers. We don't dare just barge in. Our spies must proceed carefully. They can acclimate to the weather in Rhellah while planning out the next step."

"How long have you known about this?" If this had been going on for a while, then we had wasted valuable time.

Trenyth looked straight at me. "Lady Menolly, we first learned about this development four days ago. We dispatched a runner to check out the rumors at their source—over in Dahnsburg. The rumors *are* true. And our runner was caught. He managed to escape and made it home. Missing an arm, his tongue, and one eye."

I shut my mouth, suddenly pissed at myself for questioning him. Although we couldn't accept things blindly and we had to question, I also needed to remember, the elves were on our side. We were all in this together. Queen Asteria wouldn't have stirred this in her cup for weeks before summoning us. No, if anyone was to blame for anything, this was *our* fault. We'd let Telazhar—and another spirit seal—slip through our grasp.

Delilah must have picked up on what I was thinking, because she leaned her elbows on the table and rested her chin on her hands. "We're to blame. We didn't take him out when we had the chance at the Energy Exchange. We failed."

"Bullshit. We were overwhelmed and, if you'll remember, Gulakah, the Lord of Ghosts, just happened to be there. Along with Newkirk *and* all of their cronies." Vanzir slammed his chair back against the wall and rested one ankle across the other knee. He pounded the table with his fist. "We did what we could. Nobody's to blame except Shadow Wing and his fucking delusions. He's fucking insane."

"Vanzir is right." Camille cleared her throat. "We simply didn't have the manpower to take them all on. And we aren't going to do anyone any good by moaning over what we did—or didn't—manage to accomplish. We have to focus on *now*. On what's going on this instant."

"Well said, my wife." Trillian slid his arm around her waist and kissed her brow. They made a striking couple, and when her other two husbands were in the picture, a formidable quartet.

"Then, the question becomes, what do we do next?" Rozurial said, playing with the belt on his duster. He had an armory stashed in his coat and was forever delighting in finding new toys to replace ones he grew tired of. He made Neo from *The Matrix* look like an amateur.

Queen Asteria crossed to the throne. "That's where our spies come in. I want you to meet them, because you will be working together from now on. You must exchange every scrap of information that you have about Telazhar. They will remain in contact with you while on their mission."

As she settled into the chair, the queen arranged her skirts and let out a sigh that I heard halfway across the room.

"You're tired, aren't you?" I didn't mean to speak aloud,

but my words cut through the room and I cringed, realizing what I'd done.

Asteria merely crossed her hands in front of her. "Yes, young vampire. I am weary. But that does not negate my power, nor my determination. It merely means that I wear my crown a little heavier now, and lean on my staff a little harder." She motioned to the serving woman for a glass of wine. "War is thirsty work."

"Have you any allies here? Besides us?" Trillian let go of Camille to take a closer look at the map. "Have you talked to King Vodox?"

"As asked, so answered. As I prepare my armies for war, so do my allies. King Uppala-Dahns of the Dahns unicorns and Tanaquar have pledged to arm their soldiers in my service. I have sent messages to King Vodox, and to the kingdom of Nebulvuori. We wait for their response. And . . . another ally has pledged her service. Derisa, the High Priestess from the Grove of the Moon Mother."

Camille nodded. "Truth. My order would be obligated to join you. The sorcerers and the sun god are our nemeses. I wonder . . . will Telazhar approach the temple of Chimaras? The sun brothers are still looking to start it up with the Moon Mother's Grove, from what Shamas tells us."

Queen Asteria brushed the gnarled arms of her throne. "Shamas? What does he know of this?"

We had protected our cousin's secret since he told us the truth a few weeks ago, but now, any information he had might come in handy. "Shamas was studying with a sorcerer in the Southern Wastes. A Tregart named Feris, who was bent on waging war on the Moon Mother's Grove. Shamas spilled the beans on him at risk of his own life."

"Tregarts? The Tregarts were over here a year ago? Why did no one inform me of this?" Queen Asteria leaned back against her throne and cast a long look to Trenyth. I had a feeling there was a discussion going on to which we were not privy.

Trenyth sprang into action. "We have no time to spare. We must send our spies out in the morning via the portals.

They can travel as far as Ceredream and from there, walk afoot to Rhellah." He moved to the side door and opened it.

Three figures stepped in. I didn't recognize any of them, but Trillian and Camille both gasped as one of the figures let out a low chuckle. He was a Svartan, ruggedly handsome with the same blue eyes and silverish hair as Trillian. But rather than mirroring my brother-in-law's smooth metropolitan look, this man's eyes were wild and he felt slightly uncivilized. He was also far more muscled than Trillian, who was no slouch in the buff department.

"Darynal!" Trillian was around the table before they'd cleared the door, hugging the man, who clapped him on the back. Camille joined them, giving him a kiss on the cheek.

"*Lavoyda* . . . it's been too long. Bound by oath, bound by blood." The Svartan held out his hand and he and Trillian performed some sort of intricate handshake.

"Bound by oath, bound by blood, my brother." As Trillian broke away, Darynal turned to Camille and bowed low.

"Your woman, she is looking good. Camille, lovely to see you again."

She offered her hand and he took it, kissing it gently. She reached out and stroked his face, brushing a stray curl out of his eyes.

"My husband's brother . . . it's so good to see you again."

And then, I remembered who he was. Darynal was Trillian's blood-oath brother. Pledged to back each other to the death, they weren't lovers, but brothers on a level that was almost soul-bound.

"*Lavoyda* . . . I'm glad to see you here and healthy. But what are you doing with the elves?" Trillian suddenly stopped, as if aware all eyes were on them.

Camille brushed him on the shoulder. "We should let Queen Asteria tell us," she whispered, and they positioned themselves near Darynal as the three newcomers took their seats.

Queen Asteria favored them with a brief smile. "I knew that you would be surprised, Master Zanzera, but I chose to let Darynal's appearance speak for itself."

Trillian cocked his head and winked at the queen. Shaking my head, I repressed a snicker. He was incorrigible, but he'd come a long way from the arrogant bastard to whom Delilah and I had taken an instant dislike. We'd been wrong about his character, for the most part. Our prejudices had blinded us.

Asteria gave no sign whether she noticed the wink, but instead, she motioned to Trenyth, who introduced the others in the trio.

"Darynal is our lead scout in this mission. You know his background, you know he's a skilled mercenary, so allow me to introduce the others. This is Quall, an undercover agent for Elqaneve for many years. He's an assassin."

The tall, lithe Fae stood. With pale blond hair barely cresting his shoulders, he was almost albino except for his eyes, which shimmered a startling green against the pale cream of his skin. He almost looked anorexic, but upon a closer look, I saw the tightly wrapped muscle molded beneath his skin.

Assassins were an odd breed, especially those employed by governments. They danced to their own tune, made their own rules, and usually ran outside the law in almost every way. As I looked into his eyes, I knew right then how much Quall enjoyed his job. He enjoyed the hunt, and ten to one, he enjoyed the kill. He caught my gaze and held it, an insolent sneer lurking behind the brief nod.

The third member of the team was average height, cloaked so heavily that I couldn't tell exactly what race he belonged to. Only his eyes gleamed from within the fiery red robe.

"This is Taath. He's one of our sorcerers."

"*Your* sorcerers? But . . ." Camille looked confused.

"Yes, my dear. We have our own sorcerers. After the Scorching Wars, we vowed Elqaneve would never be caught unprepared again." The Queen leaned forward. "Sometimes the only way to fight fire is with fire. Sometimes the only way to fight hatred is with violence. Often people think the Elfin race a passive one. We are not. We think first, but when we act, we do not hold back."

"I'm starting to realize that." Camille said.

"Perhaps now is the time to tell you. Your beloved Moon Mother trains her own sorcerers, although she will not call them that. They wield dark Moon magic . . . *death magic.* Why do you think Morio's magic comes so easily to *you?*"

Camille gasped, staring at her, but said nothing, although I could see the wheels churning in her head. None of us did. That was a revelation we'd address later.

After a moment, Asteria turned to me. "I asked you here because we will need all of your talents soon. Your father requested that all of you come to Otherworld." She held up her hand, putting a stop to any outbursts before they could happen. Delilah and Camille looked like they wanted to say something but kept their mouths shut. As for me, I could be very petty when I chose, and so I refused to ask what he wanted.

Queen Asteria looked my way. "He asked for all *three* of you. Do not enquire as to why. When you finish here, you will travel to Y'Elestrial, and there you will meet with your father."

"But—" Camille sputtered, but the queen stopped her in her tracks.

"*Camille,* give me no mouth. We align our powers. War has come to Otherworld, on the wings of demonic forces. The same war you are fighting over Earthside. There can be no more borders. No more division."

The room fell silent. We were facing Shadow Wing on two fronts now. I'd been waiting for the other shoe to drop, and now that it had, I realized that I'd never expected us to wrap this up easily.

From the first time Shadow Wing claimed a spirit seal, I knew—*absolutely knew in my gut*—that we wouldn't make it out unscathed, or without a long, bloody battle. We'd had collateral damage so far, but this . . . this was a full-scale attack. The war had only just begun.

Asteria and Tanaquar might be able to stem the tide of sorcerers. But those who would join the sun brothers, the goblins and ogres and other malcontents, would ensure that a bloody swath would mar the landscape. Otherworld had existed in relative peace for centuries with only minor skir-mishes. But that peace had been a fragile veneer. And now it was crumbling. Once again the sounds of battle would fill the air.

I stood, the ivory beads in my hair breaking the silence. "Tell us what we need to do and we'll do it." And just like that, we jumped from the frying pan into the flames that were brewing down south.

Chapter 2

My sisters and I originally signed up for the Otherworld Intelligence Agency because we were raised by a guardsman. Serving the Court and Crown was as natural to our lives as breathing. It wasn't until the fiasco with our father disowning Camille that we had broken away, even though the organization had treated us pretty shabbily over the years, from Camille's boss sexually harassing her, to them sending me into Dredge's lair without backup, to keeping us from advancing just because we were only half Fae.

Our mother's human heritage left us the odd children out, taunted by both children and adults alike. They called us Windwalkers, nomads with no roots or home. They called us far worse things.

Discrimination is everywhere, even in Otherworld. But life has a way of working out, if you let it. Or, at least, I tell myself that. The elves appreciate us, and my sisters and I have no quarrel working for the Elfin Queen.

I'm Menolly Rosabelle D'Artigo, half-Fae, half-human, all vampire.

I used to be a *jian-tu*—a spy/acrobat for the Otherworld

Intelligence Agency, before Dredge got hold of me. He tortured me, and raped me, and when I was a bloody mess, he forced me to drink from his wrist. Then, and only then, did he kill me. Apparently that wasn't enough play for him to get his rocks off, because after I rose as a vampire, he sent me home to destroy my family. Thanks to Camille, that plan went awry.

I spent a year in intensive rehabilitation with the OIA. They brought me back to sanity, teaching me to coexist with society and my family. It was a hard, uphill battle, but I mastered my nature, and when they felt certain I wasn't going to go on a killing binge, they let me go home. This time, I didn't terrorize Camille and the staff. And this time, I didn't break my sister's arm in my attempt to destroy her and turn her into a vampire.

After a petition from my father, the OIA allowed me to keep my job.

Dredge went underground until a little over a year ago, when we found out he'd crossed over Earthside. My sisters and I managed to track the son of a bitch down. I staked him *real good*, forever freeing myself from the nightmare that he might come back for me.

My sisters are my go-to girls.

Camille—the oldest—is a witch. Her powers go astray at the wrong times, but the Moon Mother has called her into the Priestesshood and she's now studying with the Earthside Fae Queens. She's got a figure that could rival the pinup girls of old and is married to three husbands. Somehow, their quartet works for them.

Camille's always been the rock for our family, ever since our mother died. But now she's letting go of some of that control. A recent run-in with her sadistic dragon father-in-law left her nearly as raw and wounded as Dredge left me. She'll be okay, but she's no longer trying to shoulder the whole load for everybody. And that's a good thing. She's working death magic with her youkai-kitsune husband, and she's developed a taste for the darker arts.

Delilah, born in the middle, had a twin who died at birth—Arial. A two-faced Were, she turns into a golden tabby, especially when she's stressed, and a black panther. Delilah was naïve and trusting until we crossed Earthside. The demons ensured that her rose-colored glow faded all too quickly.

Called into service by the Autumn Lord—one of the Elemental Lords—she's also training as a Death Maiden and is becoming a formidable opponent. She's engaged to a half dragon, half shadow walker, and is growing into a striking woman.

And me . . . as I said, I'm Menolly D'Artigo, and I'm in love with a werepuma—Nerissa. I'm also the official consort to Roman, the son of Blood Wyne, the vampire queen.

Our lives have become complex, and our family of choice, rich and varied. There's always too much going down, but we manage to make life fun even in the midst of all the blood and guts, and we watch out for each other. We're family.

There's an old Chinese curse and it fits our lives all too well: *May you live in interesting times.* At least we aren't bored. But sometimes, I think boredom would make a nice change of pace.

"I can't return to Y'Elestrial—" Camille started to say, but the Queen raised her hand.

"In time, child. We will discuss this in time. Trenyth and I have some minor business to attend to. In the meanwhile . . ."

"In the meantime, get to know one another. You'll be keeping in close contact through the next weeks so you'd best develop some sort of rapport." Trenyth gave me a warning look and I read it clearly—*Get along, or else.*

The Queen and her advisor exited the room, leaving us alone with the trio. Trillian and Darynal were already buddy-buddy, but the other two seemed reserved to the point of snobbishness.

Camille, Delilah, and I waited for someone to break the ice. We were itching to discuss what our father wanted with us, but it didn't seem prudent to do so in front of strangers. Finally, I decided to take charge. Camille was scowling at

Taath, and Delilah was frowning as if she were trying to think of something to say.

I caught Quall's gaze. "So you are headed to Rhellah? By what route?"

He pointed to a city on the map. "First, we travel through the portals to Ceredream and then work our way down to Rhellah on foot. There's less chance of being fingered that way. Plus, the desert burns. We need to acclimate ourselves before we march into that heat."

I squinted, trying to figure something out. "I'm puzzled. You are obviously albino. Why send you into the desert? Won't the sun scorch you almost as surely as it would me?"

"I'm no *vampire*."

Okay, the sneer was insult number one. I ignored it and pointedly stared at him, waiting.

After a moment: "I am not truly albino, although I suffer from a distinct lack of pigmentation in my skin, and yes, the sun is most certainly a danger for me. However, I'm the best and Queen Asteria knows it. Not only am I one of the most highly ranked assassins running free from any guild, but I was posted to Ceredream for some time, emerging to do business at night and holing up during the day. I know the customs of the Southern Wastes in an intimate manner." He crossed his arms and stretched out his legs, reminding me of Vanzir when we'd first met him.

"How did you make it this far without a guild? I thought they had a chokehold on assassins. Thieves can get away with running independent, at least as long as they remain petty thieves and don't make themselves noticed. But assassins are watched in all the major cities by the big guilds." I'd had to infiltrate one of the major guilds many years back, and barely escaped alive. But I'd learned a great deal about the way the assassins' hierarchy worked. And they weren't kind to those who ignored their summons.

Quall's eyebrow twitched and he cocked his head. "So you have done your homework. Being the Queen's pet has its perks. The guilds up here know enough not to bother me. And I have forged credentials that keep me out of trouble when I'm out on a mission."

He glanced at Chase and snorted. "Now, answer a question of mine. Since when do vampires, Windwalkers or not, play buddy-buddy with an FBH?" Addressing Chase directly, he added, "We don't see many of *your kind* around here."

Chase bristled but kept his mouth shut. Before Delilah or I could speak, Camille leaped to her feet.

"Listen, *dude*." She stood, hands on hips, looking ready to thrash Quall. "Hotshot assassin or not, mind your fucking manners. We were in the OIA for years before switching over to working for the elves. We may be half-human, but you'd better start showing some respect for us—*and* for our friend here." She motioned to Chase. "Chase is one of the bravest, most helpful allies we have, and if you don't back off, you're going to find out how we've managed to take out several demon generals. The hard way."

"You *really* think you're my equal?" Quall had barely gotten the words out when Camille was halfway over the table, her eyes flashing. Trillian grabbed her back as the assassin pulled out a blade.

Trillian wrestled her back, pinning her arms behind her as she tried to free herself from his grasp. "Camille—come on. Let it go. Let it be." His voice was smooth, like honey. After a moment, she stood there, panting heavily, looking in a murderous rage.

I turned to Quall, fangs down and glistening. "Apologize. *Now.* Don't ask why, don't bother objecting. Just do it. I can suck your blood faster than you can load an arrow." I knew why Camille had lost it—Hyto had said something eerily similar to her, just before he raped her. Some triggers, you never could disarm.

Quall caught my gaze as I waited, neither blinking nor moving. He shifted with the faintest of hesitations, then a barely visible shudder.

"Accept my apology. I spoke out of line."

Of course he didn't mean it—his heart wasn't behind the words, but that didn't matter, at this point. The snide look disappeared and he took a deep breath, letting it out slowly.

I glanced at Camille. She was fuming, but she was out of the fight-or-flight mode. She shot him a look of disgust but took her seat again. Trillian kept his hand on her shoulder and flashed me a grateful look.

I sized up Quall again. I didn't like him. I *really* didn't like him. But that didn't mean he wasn't loyal to the core when it came to Queen Asteria. Personal trust was a different thing than professional trust, and we could work with him, if he learned to keep his mouth shut.

Sidling a glance at Taath, the sorcerer, I tried to gauge his reaction, but it was near impossible. His eyes gleamed from within the robe, but without seeing his face, I had no clue as to what he might be thinking. Darynal, however, looked pissed out of his mind. I didn't expect him to speak up, and was pleasantly surprised when he turned to Quall.

"Show these women and their companions some respect, or I *will* speak to Queen Asteria about replacing you. Your skills are worthless if you alienate our allies." His voice was riddled with threat, and he leaned forward, his eyes a pale flurry of ice. I'd seen Trillian with that look once or twice, but Darynal had perfected it and magic oozed off him. The Svartans weren't called the Charming Fae for nothing—they could mesmerize with a kiss, hypnotize with a look, if they really wanted to. And they could menace just as easily.

Trillian arched his eyebrows, but said nothing. The flush in Camille's cheeks faded as she relaxed.

After another tense moment, Taath let out a low whistle. "Assassin, we need you. Do not let your pride cloud this mission."

"Sorcerer, I'll do as I see fit." Quall grimaced, as if he'd just swallowed a frog, but he shrugged. "Very well. Let us move on."

"See that you mind yourself. You may be an assassin but you know nothing about the Svartans' abilities to inflict suffering." Darynal gave him another long look, then turned to us. "Tell us everything you know about Telazhar. We have the records from Queen Asteria, but it's been over a millennium since he walked the sands of the Southern Wastes, and much can change in that time, especially with him locked away in the Subterranean Realms."

And so, we put aside our quarrel and shared all the information we had, from when we first suspected that Telazhar had gated in Stacia Bonecrusher over Earthside to our discovery that he was working with Gulakah.

In return, Darynal promised to tell us everything they found out about what was going down in the Southern Wastes, which—as of now—wasn't much.

"Our operatives in Dahnsburg heard from another agent sequestered down in Rhellah that the sorcerers are uniting again, under an ancient necromancer. They did enough research before contacting us to verify that it's Telazhar, but since he's keeping himself hidden in the Southern Wastes, there isn't much that Queen Asteria, King Uppala-Dahns, or Queen Tanaquar can do about it. The former two were among the primary triad who had ousted him the first time around."

"What about Vodox?" Trillian cocked his head. "Queen Asteria mentioned she'd sent word to him. What says the King of Svartalfheim? And the dwarves? Is the court of Nebelvuouri pledging arms?"

"Both are listening with open minds, but neither has taken a stance yet. We expect Vodox to take our side before the dwarven court makes up its mind. Since Svartalfheim has lately returned to Otherworld from the Subterranean Realms, our king chooses to cooperate."

For a long while, the city of the Svartans—Svartalfheim—had existed in the Subterranean Realms, among the demonic forces. But when Shadow Wing took over, the entire city packed up and moved back to Otherworld, causing a major stir in both realms.

They had not used the portals—they could not, since the portals to the Sub-Realms were still sealed—but since they were not demons, their most powerful wizards had been able to transport the entire city, lock, stock, and barrel, with only minor damage. King Vodox had feared that the Demon Lord would turn his eye toward the growing power of their people and use it to tear open the portals. Whether their wizards even *had* that ability didn't matter. Either way, Shadow Wing would have torn them—and the entire city—to shreds.

Though the Svartans were technically shadowy cousins

of the elves, they were often lumped in with the Fae, because of their chaotic natures. It was all very confusing, and I personally believed that, if we dug back far enough into the past, we'd find both elves and Fae had common ancestors.

"So you are certain it's Telazhar?" Delilah asked.

"Without a doubt." Taath leaned forward, still cloaked within his robes. "He means to win as many over to Shadow Wing's side as possible and we think he knows that the spirit seals are here, in Elqaneve. They will try to assail the city for them. The more backing they have, the easier it will be when the Demon Lord attempts to break through the portals."

It made sense. If no one was answering the front door, go around and try the back to see if it's unlocked. "He's clever. He hasn't had much luck Earthside. There are too many divisions among Earthside countries to win over a majority."

"Yes, where here, in Otherworld, the south is a hotbed of unrest. It always has been. The sorcerers chafe at the restrictions they're under when they come north, and they've been left to their own devices since the Scorching Wars ended. Sorcerers have always valued power and strength." By the tone of his voice, I had a feeling Taath admired this aspect of his comrades in magic.

Camille spoke up. "In some ways, I think it was a mistake to banish them from the northern cities. Keep your friends close and your enemies closer, that sort of thing." She leaned forward, clasping her hands on the table. "So, what's next?"

Darynal stood and, hands behind his back, paced. "We infiltrate the Southern Wastes. You return home and do what you can to find the next spirit seal. Shadow Wing has two of them. We know he's outfitted Telazhar with one of them, but he'll be looking for the last two, in order to further increase his power."

"How long do you think it will take you to find the information you're looking for down there?" I'd never been to the Southern Wastes, and they were definitely on my do-not-visit list, but even I knew they were vast, sprawling plains of sand, with rogue magic blending into the very landscape. The Wastes were a dangerous and volatile place.

"As much as I dislike it, the reality is we'll probably be

spending at least one moon cycle worming our way in."
Darynal shrugged. "There's nothing to hurry it along, either.
We dare not push too quickly or we'll draw unwanted atten-
tion to ourselves."

A pensive look on her face, Camille turned to Delilah and
me. "I hate to suggest this, but . . . do you think Shamas
would be helpful to them?"

"No, he wouldn't." Delilah scowled. "Don't forget, our
cousin nearly sacrificed himself to warn the high priestess of
your order. The sorcerers he trained under aren't going to
forget that anytime soon. And they probably spread the word
through the guilds about him."

"She's right. We can't offer him up on a platter." I shook
my head. As angry as we'd been with Shamas when we
found out he'd been training in the Southern Wastes, we
weren't going to hang him out to dry. He'd turned himself
around and was trying to contribute to both the household,
and to the Seattle Fae community.

Camille heaved a sigh of relief. "I'm glad you think so.
As nice as it would be to have our own operative working
with Darynal's group, I really didn't want to stick Shamas's
neck on the chopping block. I was still pissed at him, but you
know what? I think I need to get over it."

"He'd be chopped all right, head first." I pushed my chair
back. "So Darynal . . . I suppose we've covered all there is to
cover? Send us whatever you find out, even if it seems like
nothing. We'll do the same."

"We will." The Svartan stood, bowing to the three of us.
He reached for Camille's hand, again, kissing it gently.

But we were saved awkward good-byes with Quall and
Taath when Trenyth reentered the room.

"You are finished talking?"

"Yeah, for now." I wanted nothing more than to corner the
elf privately for a little tête-à-tête about their choice in agents.

"Then, Darynal, Quall, Taath, you may retire for the evening. Rest well. You will need it. Girls, please remain here
for a moment." He waited until the three men left, Darynal
hugging both Trillian and Camille before he sauntered out
of the room.

Once we were alone again, Queen Asteria joined us. "What do you think of our scouts?" It didn't sound like a rhetorical question.

I decided to be upfront. "I don't like Quall. I'm wary of him, and my alarm bells are going off. Camille, what do you think?"

She raised her eyebrows. "You *know* what I think. A testosterone-laden macho jerk . . . but he's good at his job. I can tell."

"He is." Delilah said. "But I don't trust him."

"We *have* to trust him." Trenyth crossed his arms, looking dour. "Darynal is good to his word. Taath was trained by our own techno-mages. He's a sorcerer, yes, but he's one of us. Quall . . . there are extenuating circumstances as to why he is on this mission. He'll be accepted more readily than the others down in Rhellah. We need him."

"Why will they accept him over others?" I sensed one of those announcements coming—the kind you really don't want to hear.

"Because he's the son of the high commander of the city. When Quall was young, his mother fell out of favor with his father, who killed her and sold the boy to raiders. The raiders grew tired of toying with him and left him in Dahnsburg."

"I'm sensing Lifetime victim-of-the-week movie here," Delilah said.

"Truly, Quall was a victim of circumstance. In Dahnsburg, he was enslaved by a roughshod orphanage. He managed to escape a few years later by hiding in a caravan headed for Elqaneve. He was still very young, but resourceful."

"But how did he come to be in Queen Asteria's service?"

"He was caught stealing a loaf of bread and turned over to the Youth Guard, where he showed an aptitude for bowmanship and scouting. He eventually struck out on his own when he came of age but returned to the Guard and offered his services a decade or so ago. He feels a debt to the Crown, for feeding him and giving him a home and a good start."

I frowned. "He became an assassin."

"Not, mind you, the most ethical choice of careers, but he's good at it and we must face facts—assassins are necessary, as are scouts and rangers and soldiers. Every government has its own elite arsenal of fighters. Quall belongs to us, and we make use of him when we have the need." Trenyth slid into the chair that the assassin had vacated.

"And you approve of having assassins in your employ?" Delilah cocked her head. "I thought elves wouldn't approve of the darker routes."

Trenyth shrugged. "Elves hold honor in high regard. However, that does not mean we eschew common sense, nor vital military tactics." He leaned forward and rested his elbows on the table.

"But you don't like it," I said softly.

"No. I long for the days when Elqaneve was isolated, when we kept to ourselves. But that was long before the Great Divide, and time waits for no one, be they elf or Fae or human. Politics do not make good bedfellows with honor, and try as we might, there can never be a return to the days of glory, where we wandered through the forests, silent in our thoughts, singing of heroes long lost and battles shrouded in the mists of time."

It was, perhaps, the longest statement we'd ever heard Trenyth make, and it left me unsettled. For a moment, I caught a glimpse of the days during which the worlds had been one, when time had still been young in the way of sentient beings, before progress had come to both Earthside and Otherworld.

"You were young then, weren't you? Before the Great Divide?"

He gave me a faint smile. "Was I *ever* young? Ah . . . yes, my dear, beautiful *vampyr* . . . I was young, and the Queen was in her glory days. I entered her service and gave my life to the Crown."

"And your heart," Camille whispered.

Trenyth jerked. "What are you talking about?"

But rather than tell him what we knew, rather than put him on the spot, especially in front of Queen Asteria, she just smiled softly.

Trenyth waited for a beat and then, seeing that we had run out of steam, brought the conversation back to the present day. "Quall is under orders to infiltrate his father's inner circle. His father is a known sympathizer to the sorcerers."

Delilah voiced the question running through my mind. "What if Quall takes a notion to change sides when he meets his father? He may have grown up in Elqaneve, but if he's a desert raider by birth, what's to say that blood won't out and he'll return to the fold?"

"There's never a guarantee that something like that won't happen," Queen Asteria said. "Anyone can go rogue at any time. However, remember—his father sold him. There's no love lost there. And despite his demeanor, Quall is one of the most loyal hires we have. He's been on a number of missions and come through with not a single smirch on his record." She gave us a quiet look, indicating the matter was settled. "We have to trust him. He's our best chance at finding out just what Telazhar is plotting. We know *what*, but we don't know *how*."

We'd have to be satisfied with that.

"And now, I must attend another matter. Trenyth will see you out. Thank you for answering my summons so quickly." The aged queen swept out of the room, still a fountain of power.

"Then we wait for Darynal to contact us through the Whispering Mirror," Camille said. She glanced at me. "How long before morning?"

I closed my eyes. "A while yet. It's barely past midnight."

"Your evening is far from over. As we told you earlier, you must go to Y'Elestrial." Trenyth sighed, pushing himself back away from the table.

"Yeah, about that. You mentioned that our father wanted to see us. But that's not possible. Camille's proscribed from setting foot through the gates. And didn't you tell us some time ago that our father and Tanaquar are on the outs?"

He grimaced. "Your father is muchly changed this past month. He's become withdrawn and silent, and while he is still working for Queen Tanaquar, he confided to me that he made a grievous mistake when he did not stand behind your choice, Lady Camille."

Her lip trembled. Father's denouncement had cost her a

price far more than any she had ever paid. It had cost all of us. We'd always done everything to make him proud, but he was quick to judge. He'd judged me since the day I came home a vampire—he hated vampires, and I knew it took every ounce of self-control he had to remain civil to me. But I didn't care. Not like Camille.

"He truly wants to see us?" A flicker of hope lit up her voice, but I heard doubt behind it. And fear.

Trenyth pressed his lips together, a gentle smile playing across them. "Yes, my dear. He truly wants to see you."

And so, without another word, he bundled us back in the carriages and we were on the way to the portals, to travel to our home. For the first time in several years, we'd all be together at home again.

Chapter 3

❦

As we were on the way to the portals, Camille pulled her cloak around her shoulders and shivered. "Is it just me, or does it feel colder than usual out here?" She rubbed her temples. "I have such a headache. What the hell are we supposed to do? I don't want to go but we don't have any choice."

"We *do* have a choice. We can go home. We've been obedient all of our lives, but this time . . ." I'd had it. I'd had it with everything. "We can still fight the demons, but on our terms. We aren't beholden to Tanaquar or to Father anymore. We work for Queen Asteria."

"Yes, we work for her and she gave us specific instructions to journey to Y'Elestrial." Camille kicked a pebble on the street and watched as it bounced over to the gutter. "But if he so much as raises his voice to me . . ."

Trillian caught her hand. "My love, you will do as you always do—follow your heart, and follow your gut. I'll always back you up." He raised her fingers to his lips and kissed them gently.

Chase cleared his throat. "Maybe your father has come around. Why else would he send for you?"

"Any number of reasons. But perhaps he's actually sorry."
Even as I said it, I wasn't sure I believed it.

Father was a stubborn fool, and once he made up his mind,
he stuck to his guns. Camille took after him, and they'd been
butting heads since we were young. He'd expected more out
of her than out of Delilah and me, and she'd chafed at his
demands. She wasn't cut out to play mother, though she
tried, and while she'd become our rock, it had—in the long
run—hurt her.

Delilah and I had been freer to make mistakes, to go our
own ways. In some ways, I knew it was because he'd loved
Camille most, but his love came with a price that was too
high for me to ever want to incur.

I stared into the night as we passed through the streets.
We were going home. To Y'Elestrial. To the place where we
were born and raised. To the town I'd renounced the day we
went Earthside.

A trip through the portals is the wildest roller-coaster ride
you've ever been on. Toss in a bungee jump, skydiving, and a
few hallucinogenic drugs to the mix, and you might come
close to what it feels like. You get yanked apart in one place
and thrown back together somewhere else. And you remember everything in between those frozen seconds when you're
noncorporeal and shimmering in between the worlds.

We arrived in Y'Elestrial, expecting the Des'Estar—the
formal guard of the Court and Crown—to meet us, but all
we ran into were a couple of louts trying to persuade the portal guards to give them a free ride. It wasn't working, save
for one drunk bitch who had hiked up her skirts and was
fucking the lot of them, two or three at a time. We stared at
her for a moment, then, shaking our heads, turned and
walked into the streets.

During the day, Y'Elestrial was gorgeous, bustling and
filled with the cacophony of street vendors and open markets
and the lush shopping districts that attracted visitors from
hundreds of miles around. It was probably one of the most
beautiful cities in Otherworld; gleaming domes with spiraling

minarets topped the city buildings, and marble retaining walls surrounded the upper-crust gated communities where the nobles and Court favorites lived—those who weren't quite popular enough to reside within the Court itself.

But at night . . . at night, Y'Elestrial took on a darker edge, a dangerous and glittering appeal that filtered into the streets in the sweet, cloying scents from the opium dens and the raucous music that came from the brothels and night-clubs. The shadows were filled with thieves and thugs, with assassins and slavers and gamblers looking for an easy mark.

I looked around for a carriage, but there were none in sight. "So Father didn't send an escort for us. That figures. But if he wants to see us, he can jolly well pony up for trans-portation. It's a good two miles and while that's not all that far, I would think he'd have better manners, since he was the one who sent for us."

Delilah glanced around. "I don't like this. Why aren't they here?"

Camille let out an exasperated sigh. "Fuck this. We need to get moving. There are gangs in this area that could take us on and win, even with all our firepower." She glanced at Roz and smiled. "You do have your arsenal under that duster, don't you?"

He slyly flipped it back, flasher-style. Metal and wood and magical bombs glinted out from within the folds, under the eye catchers that floated through the streets. "I've got what you want, babe."

Trillian snorted. "You're lucky I'm not Smoky."

Roz snickered back at him. "As much as I admire the thought of being in your shoes, when it comes to Camille, I wouldn't trade places with you for a million bucks. Sharing a woman, no problem. Sharing a woman with a testosterone-laden dragon whose temper has a flashpoint of zero—not so much. And I've already been on the receiving end of that temper."

"If you've finished discussing this scintillating matter, I suggest we get a move on." With a *hrmph*, Camille pushed past the two men. I swung in beside her, and Delilah took the other side. The guys fell in behind us, as we headed down the cobblestone street in the direction of the palace.

The scent of opium wafted out of the buildings by which we were passing, and then, with a little gasp, Camille stopped, staring at one of the nightclubs.

"The Collequia." She turned to Trillian, who slid his arm around her waist.

I leaned against the stone wall of the opium den. So the old joint was still up and running, and probably still owned by our father's friend, Jahn.

"It seems hard to believe it's been thirteen years since we first met here." Trillian gently pressed a kiss on her lips. "Do you want to go in?"

She stared at the door for a moment but then shook her head. "Too much water under the bridge. I'll always remember the first time I laid eyes on you, but it wasn't because of the club. It was because you were . . . the most striking man I'd ever seen. And you came to my defense when I needed you. We were meant to be together. You're my alpha."

Without a word, he swept her away from the door, and they began walking down the street again. We followed.

Chase caught up to me. "Is that where . . ."

"They met? Yes. Camille was on assignment. This city holds our past, Chase. It guards our secrets and dreams. Our childhood and our memories."

"Where were you when . . . I mean . . . I suppose I shouldn't ask but . . ." He floundered for words but I knew what he meant.

"There's a cave not far outside of the city limits. Dredge kept his nest there. In Y'Elestrial, vampire nests are forbidden to have more than thirteen members before they have to hive off. But Dredge defied the order. He was attempting to set up a Vampire Court—which is against the law within the city-state. Since the land the cave's on is Y'Elestrial territory, he was breaking the law. And I was sent in to spy on him, so we could raid them."

"Have you ever gone back?" Chase's question hovered in the air, and if I had been breathing, I would have caught my breath. As it was, I stopped in my tracks. I guess the look on

my face was either terrifying or terrified, because he quickly
began to backpedal. "I'm sorry—I didn't mean anything
by it—"

Not wanting to scare him, I forced myself to speak. "No,
I've never been back there." A wave of horror swept over me
at the thought of setting foot back in the cavern. I'd thought
myself over the fear. Dredge was dead. I had staked him. I
was free. Or, at least, I thought I was free.

"I'm so sorry. Menolly, I should never have asked. I'm so
stupid." Somehow, Chase's contrition was worse than the
question he'd asked.

"It's not your fault." I hurried to reassure him. He'd asked
a simple question. The fact that the question had hit me so
hard worried the fuck out of me.

The others had noticed our conversation and stopped.
Camille and Delilah surreptitiously moved to stand behind
Chase, and I realized—again, with a touch of horror—that
they feared I might attack him.

Feeling both mute, and muted, I shook my head. "I'm
okay. Just . . . I never . . . nobody ever asked me that before.
I've *never* thought of going back. *Ever.*"

Camille stepped back. Delilah, more slowly. But Chase
didn't flinch. He just stood there, his gaze softly fastened on
my own, and held out his hand. I stared at his fingers, warm
and pulsing with blood, and a thirst welled up in me that I
didn't like.

"Take my hand. I trust you." His words hit like a ton of
bricks, and I realized he was offering me something that few
mortals would ever dare. Trust that I wouldn't hurt him, that
I wouldn't fall prey to my nature.

I swallowed my thirst and tentatively took his hand,
entwining my fingers in his. I didn't like touching people—
or being touched unless it was on my own terms. But this
was important. He squeezed my hand and I returned it,
though cautiously. I could crush his fingers with one quick
grip.

And then the moment passed and the tension lifted. As I
let go of his hand, I gave him a silent nod, and he smiled.

"You can never go home again." Delilah looked at me.

"But that's not what we're doing. Even if we go back to the house, we're not going home. We're going to . . . the place we were born."

Shade slid his arm around her waist. "You have a home Earthside. And if you return to Otherworld, you'll build a new home." And then, everything was normal again, and we continued down the street.

But something still felt off. I sidled over to Camille. "Use your senses. Something's wrong."

She stopped, and I could feel the swell of magic as she started to close her eyes. But before she could do anything, a crash broke through the night as a large group of men emerged from the shadows of the nearby alley.

They weren't Tregarts, they were Fae, but one look at their faces and I realized that they wouldn't be any picnic to deal with. Armed with long knives, they were dressed in black to cloak themselves within the shadows. The leader, at least I *thought* he was a leader, was slender, with long dark hair pulled back in a ponytail, and a silver bandanna wrapped around his head. Silver chains draped around his neck, and in his hand, he circled a nasty-looking serrated blade at us. But that wasn't what made me nervous.

As he approached, I knew what he was. There was no mistaking the grace and fluidity with which he moved. A rogue *jian-tu*. Which meant he'd be more flexible and quicker than anyone in our group except for me. He and his group arced around us in a half circle, cutting off our path.

"Hand us your valuables, my lovelies, and we'll let you go." His voice was light, and though it had been some time since I'd spoken our home tongue, it was familiar and smooth on the ears.

"I advise you to let us pass. You have no clue just whom you're dealing with." Shade spoke up, pushing beside Delilah.

"A group of class acts, I imagine. A group of well-to-do's. You're obviously not from the crusty side of town, so perhaps you'd penny up your goods and we'll let you go without further harassment." The leader let out a throaty laugh.

"Really, then?" Quick as a cat, Delilah's dagger appeared

in her hand. At the same moment, Trillian pulled out his blade, and Camille backed up, sucking in energy. By now, I could tell when she was working up a spell. Vanzir had blade in hand, and Roz was holding something small but, no doubt, deadly. Shade disappeared in a puff of shadow and smoke.

I just smiled, letting my fangs descend. "Are you sure you want to take us on, pretty boy?"

"Crimsy, they have weapons." One of the henchmen backed away a step, but the others—about twelve in all—moved forward.

"Leave my name out of this, you dolt." The leader—apparently Crimsy—took one leap and landed in front of De-lilah. His blade swept around and she barely had time to duck.

"He's a *jian-tu*. Be careful!" I leaped, flipping head over heels to land by his side. Crimsy whirled around, and his eyes lit up.

"Well met—another *jian-tu*, and a bloody girl at that. Come on, let's do it, love." He gestured to me with his dag-ger, and I circled him around, away from Delilah, who was already beset by another one of the gang. I knew better than to take my eyes off him. I remembered my training, and chances are, he did, too.

"You're going to find out just how bloody." I launched myself into the air and flipped over his head, landing in back of him. As I hit the ground, I whirled to send one stiletto boot heel into his back, knocking him forward.

Crimsy rolled into a front somersault, springing to his feet. He immediately tricked into a back flip with a twist, spinning as he hit midair so that he landed facing me. As he tossed his dagger from hand to hand, his gaze never left mine.

I licked my fangs as the scent of blood filled the air and a scream rang out, cut short. I didn't recognize the voice, so I assumed it was one of them rather than one of us and kept focused on my own fight. Crimsy didn't flinch, either.

"Seriously, you should have targeted a different group." I gave him a cold grin and then was down, my right hand touching the ground as I spun like a break dancer, my foot gliding in front of me to slide behind his heels, catch hold of his legs, and bring him down.

Crimsy landed flat, his hands reaching above his head to push himself up again, and within seconds he flipped back to his feet. He did a flat spin, scissoring the air with his legs, and managed to clip me in the nose. Startled, I tripped backward and rolled to my feet as he landed, coming for me, dagger aimed directly for my heart. The fun was over; he was intent on killing me now.

I'd had enough play as well. I leaped on him, all finesse gone, and took him down, slamming him to the ground. The surprise that filled his eyes told me he had never tangled with a vampire before, and I had a momentary flicker of doubt.

He was an elegant opponent, and I'd seldom met someone who could match me move for move in the air. But then reason took hold again, and I quickly yanked his head to the side, the bones shattering like a string of firecrackers. With one last breath, he was gone, and I jumped up, turning to survey the rest of the fight.

Three men were down—all Crimsy's men. Delilah looked like she'd taken a few cuts, as had Trillian. Camille was staring at one of the men, who lay there, a blackened mess. Spellwork. She'd managed to take him out with her lightning instead of having it backfire on her.

The rest of the gang, seeing their leader dead, began to back up. I realized they still didn't understand I was a vampire, so I opened my mouth to show them my fangs, hissing.

"Run away, little boys, unless you want to be my dinner." I grinned as they turned tail and vanished into the alleyway.

"Everybody okay?" I glanced over them.

"Yeah, I took a few cuts but there wasn't any poison on the blades as far as I could tell." Delilah shrugged, wiping a trickle of blood off her forehead. "They were an easy lot, compared to some we've tangled with."

"No poison," Trillian said. "I recognized the crest on their tunics. They belong to the Asa Tone Asa gang, and they have an honor code that forbids the use of poisons and venoms. But we'd better be going. They'll head back to headquarters and report what happened. And then, the big boys will come out to play. These were penny street thugs. Their masters won't be so easy."

"Let's get moving then—" I paused as the sound of horse hooves clattered down the street, a large carriage pulled by a quartet of Friesians. Not as grand as the noblas stedas, the gorgeous Earthside horse had been imported to Otherworld. Their black coats gleamed in the light of the eye catchers.

The carriage stopped in front of us and the door opened. Out stepped a man, a little taller than Camille, who looked just like her. Sephreh ob Tanu. Our father. He glanced at the bodies on the ground.

"I apologize for my tardiness. I was held up by official business. Please, get in. We have little time and much to discuss."

Without a word, we climbed into the spacious carriage that was made for large groups. I looked at Father as he settled in beside Chase, but he said nothing as the door shut, and we were off, once again, into the night.

But Father didn't take us to the palace. Instead, we headed for a smallish building on the outskirts of the Court. A step down, definitely, from an office under the Queen's watchful eye, but also providing more freedom.

As we pulled up to the building and clambered out of the carriage, my father lingered at the door, reaching up to help the three of us girls down. I looked at his hand, ignored it, and leaped lightly to the grass. Camille stared at him, then took Trillian's hand and stepped gracefully down the steps. Delilah bit her lip, but then accepted Father's hand, for only a moment, and let go the minute her foot touched the ground.

"So, is this where you're working now?" Somebody had to break the ice and though I was willing to let it stay frozen, for Camille's sake, I decided to take the bull by the horns.

Sephreh nodded. "Yes, these are my new headquarters." He paused, then let out a long sigh. "You're going to find out soon enough. I'm no longer the Ambassador. As of yesterday morning, I'm now back in the Des'Estar, but I've been promoted to special ops. I'm the liaison between the OIA and the Des'Estar."

"Congratulations?" I wasn't sure what to say. Being demoted from the status of advisor and ambassador couldn't feel good, but this was a major promotion in the Guard, something Father had worked toward for years. They'd passed him over time and again because of Mother's human heritage.

Sephreh perked up. "Thank you, Menolly. I've waited a long time for this. As to the position of advisor, it was an ill fit, shall we say. And before you ask, the Queen and I are no longer . . . involved." He didn't look all that upset. I had a feeling their breakup hadn't left him heartbroken.

Camille gave him a long look, then swept into the building, Trillian behind her. Delilah hesitated, then followed her, along with Shade, Vanzir, and Roz. Chase glanced at me. I nodded for him to go in. After my father and I were alone, I leaned against the wall and crossed my arms.

"You going to apologize to Camille? Because if you don't, we might as well pack up and head home." It was time for straight talk. No more pussyfooting around. Camille wouldn't talk to him, and Delilah couldn't bring herself to confront him, so it was up to me.

Our father tilted his head, giving me a mirthless smile. "You were never one for subtlety, were you? You always were independent. But I never expected Camille to disobey my wishes."

I snorted. "I have no use for diplomacy. Not in situations like this one. Face it, Dad. *You fucked up.* You cast aside all of Camille's love and devotion, and everything she ever did for you. *For us.* You left her out in the cold. And when she was captured by Hyto, you were a total prick."

"I realize I made a mistake—"

"*Mistake* my fucking ass. Do you *know* what happened to your daughter? Do you know what that pervert did to her? He ripped her heart to shreds, and bruised her body along with it. Her own father-in-law raped her, humiliated her, and beat her senseless. *But she survived.* She survived like *I* survived what Dredge did to me."

"Please, don't—" He held up his hand, but I wasn't hearing any of that bullshit.

"Oh no! You don't get off that easy. You made a *mistake*?

Well, *pity you*. We've paid for your mistakes. You may not like the fact that we're independent, and that we make our own choices, but motherfucking know this: *You raised survivors*. You raised women unwilling to knuckle under. Unwilling to take it lying down. You raised us to believe that family matters. Well, the three of us are family—we stand up for each other. Did it *really* surprise you that we turned against you when you turned against us?"

Sephreh leaned his head back, his ponytail trailing down his back. "No," he said after a moment. "No, it doesn't surprise me. Believe as you will, but I'm more proud of being your father than of anything I've ever done in my life." He sucked in a long breath. "It's hard for me to admit this, but yes, I was wrong. I was wrong about Trillian. I was wrong in my actions toward you. Toward Camille. I have been blind." Tears flickered in his eyes. "I wish I could take it all back. That I could have the chance to start again."

"Earthside, we call it getting a do-over. But there's no way to pretend this never happened. All you can do now is haul your ass in there and beg Camille for forgiveness. And apologize to Trillian for the way you've treated him. And then, maybe, we can talk." I gave him a long look. "You burned your chances with me, but if they forgive you, I'll go along with them and we'll play nice-nice again."

Sephreh winced. "I am sorry. I have a gift for you—it's not finished yet, but I truly want you to have it. I think . . . I think you'll like it."

"Prove yourself. Do everything I said, and then . . . maybe I'll accept it." And with that, I turned. Leaving him in the dark, I swept into the building. Let him know what it was like being left out in the cold, alone. Let him struggle with his conscience for once.

As I entered the hall, I realized that Tanaquar had basically cast our dear father into the likes of Siberia. Oh, it was luxurious, by many standards, but by the standards of the Court and Crown, it might as well have been as spartan as a cell with bread and water. Tanaquar really *was* pissed with him.

The hall was about the size of a grand ballroom, with several doors leading off to each side. And a stairwell led up both sides of the room, leading to a second level that over-looked the main floor. More rooms were up there. The décor was simple—blue and gold, the colors of Y'Elestrial. No velveteen drapes, no gold leaf, no marble statues, just a few simple pillars running from floor to the high ceilings. But the marble was polished to a high shine. And the hall felt clear and open.

"This is nice." Shade looked around. "I like it."

Sephreh glanced at him. "In our city, it would be consid-ered a slum by the Queen. She has one thing, at least, in common with her sister Lethesanar. A love of luxury."

He turned to Camille and went down on one knee. "I'm sorry. I was wrong, about you, about Trillian, about your path. I can never apologize enough, but I beg your forgiveness. Give me a chance to earn your trust again. I wasn't there when you needed me. I can never make it up to you, but if you'll allow me, I'd like to try. Your mother would have been ashamed of my actions. As am I."

Camille sucked in a long breath. She glanced over at Tril-lian, who wrapped his arm around her shoulders.

"Trillian, forgive my blindness. You have treated my daughter with the love and kindness that *I* should have given her. You are the better man. I was wrong about you. And, if you'll allow, I would like to formally welcome you into our family." Sephreh broke down then, tears trickling down his face. "My Maria, she would have handled this so much bet-ter. She would have kept me true to myself rather than letting me get mired in politics."

It was then that we all realized how much he still missed our mother. He'd never let go of her, never been able to say good-bye.

Camille slowly stepped forward, one hand still holding Trillian's. "Do you mean what you say?"

Father nodded. "With all my heart. You, my daughter, have withstood my tirades and demands that you take over for your mother, that you be perfect. And no one, not even my beloved Maria, could have filled the shoes I tried to make you wear. Even my beloved wife could not have competed with the ghost of her memory."

Camille cocked her head, looking unsure. But then, her face clear of tears, she placed one hand on his heart. "I hold you to your oath. I hold you to your words. I will give you a second chance, but only one. Break my heart once more, and you will never hear from me or see me again."

Trillian pulled her back, gently. "Lord Sephreh, don't take her threat lightly. As for me, I will abide by my wife's wishes. I will eat at your table, treat you with respect, as long as it cuts both ways. But know this: I will not stay where I am not welcome, nor suffer my wife to do the same."

And with that, a truce was born. I watched, silently standing by Delilah. We couldn't just forgive and forget. Too much water had passed, too many land mines had gone off. But maybe, perhaps . . . just perhaps . . . we could move forward from here and find some common ground.

After tentative hugs and kisses, we gathered around a central table. I was beginning to feel tired, and I *seldom* felt tired. But the emotional war with our father and the stress of coping with Quall and his cronies had set me on edge. Give me a rumble with a gang like Crimsy's men any day over the drama-queen flurry we'd been through.

Father called for food—including a goblet of blood for me. The blood was fresh and sweet, Fae blood . . . not human. I didn't ask where he'd gotten it.

"We have a serious problem, and Tanaquar instructed me to approach you. She thought I'd be the best intermediary. First, we're prepared to offer you all your jobs back. Full reinstatement with back pay."

Bomb number one. None of us had seen *that* coming, that was for sure. I glanced at the others, who looked just as confused as I felt.

"Based on what Queen Asteria has discussed with Tanaquar, we think it in everyone's best interests to have you girls working for both sides. Queen Asteria is aware of our offer." He stopped, giving us time to think.

"If we *were* to entertain such a thought, what conditions might we expect to be working under and to whom would we

report?" If they wanted us this badly, they could jolly well
ante up for us. The OIA had been our home for many years,
but it had also tossed me into a vampire's nest and kicked
our butts Earthside when we didn't perform as expected.

"And what about the fact that I'm pledged to Aeval's
Court? That's suddenly okay?" Camille still sounded bitter.

Sephreh rubbed his temples. "It would seem that Tanaquar
is no longer concerned about that."

"What about you?" She leaned forward, waiting for an
answer. "How do you feel about me working with the Earthside Fae Queens?"

Leaning back in his chair, still rubbing his forehead, he
glanced across the table at her. "I admit, I'm not entirely
thrilled with the idea, but I won't stand in your way. Nor will
it be a problem with us working together."

"*Us* working together?" I saw where this was going.

"Since I am the liaison between the OIA and the Guard
Des'Estar, and in charge of covert operations . . . and since
you are my daughters, Tanaquar decided that—should you
decide to work with us again—you will be reporting directly
to me. I will be your superior."

Vanzir, who had managed to keep his mouth shut all this
time, let out a snicker. "Oh, that's lovely. The family that
slays together plays together?"

"Shut up, demon." Contrite or not, Sephreh was still our
father. "Please, take the assignment. We need you. We have
trouble and have pulled back all other OIA operatives, so we
need you Earthside, especially now."

"What trouble?" Delilah pulled out her notebook. She
was so used to taking notes that she acted as our secretary
without being asked.

"Your friend, Andrees? He was sent Earthside on a mission to discover what you are up to. But he's vanished. We
have no clue of what happened to him, no idea of where he
might be. We need you to find him."

Andrees. He'd been in the OIA training class that the
three of us had taken. We'd studied together, and he'd never
treated us with anything but respect. Delilah had developed
a crush on him, but he'd never known. He'd trained as a

scout, and the OIA had originally planned for him to spy on
Dredge, but he came down with a fever and had been laid out
for a good month. So they'd pawned the assignment off onto
me. He'd avoided me ever after that, and I could see the guilt
in his eyes. I'd always wanted to tell him that it wasn't his
fault, but never had the chance. Maybe now, I would.

"We'll deal with the fact that the OIA was spying on us
later." Camille straightened her shoulders. "Where did they
send him?"

Sephreh thumbed through a folder of papers. "Somewhere
in . . . West Seattle. White Center area. We had a small store
there, a massage parlor on Roxbury Street, owned by Iyor,
one of our operatives. We sent Andrees there to connect with
Iyor, and from there, he was supposed to work his way over
to see what you were doing. We haven't heard from him
since he crossed over."

"You sent Andrees to *White Center*? To a *massage parlor*?
You know that's a *brothel*?"

"A brothel? No—a massage parlor." Father looked confused.

"Trust me, in that area? Doesn't mean what you think it
means."

Sephreh blinked. "Well, our mistake again. But the massage parlor has closed and we can't find our agent Iyor,
either."

"I can guarantee that if you guys don't have contact anymore with your 'masseur,' either he's dead or he went rogue
and is turning tricks or dealing drugs or working with the
gangs. And as far as Andrees . . . a newbie-to-Earthside OIA
agent walking around there alone? Without being prepared?
What time of day did you send him?" *Please don't say
"night" . . . please don't say "night" . . .*

Sephreh tossed the folder across the table. "Night. I
assume a stupid move, as well? So, will you take the job?
Will you work with us and help us find Andrees?"

I glanced at Camille and Delilah. They both gave me
slight nods. "Fine, but on our terms, and with raises, full
back pay, full reinstatement, and a free hand. *We* run the
Earthside operations and *we* set up an OIA headquarters

over there the way it was meant to be. If you can agree to that, we'll knock out a deal. But we have to work fast. I need to get home."

Sephreh coughed as both Roz and Vanzir began to laugh.

"They'll get you every time, dude," Vanzir said. "Just jump on the deal while it's still on the table, man."

Sephreh gave him a faint smile. "I have no doubt you speak wisely, Master Vanzir. No doubt at all." He turned to me. "You have a deal. Whatever you want, you get. Andrees has been missing for three days. What do we do?"

I pushed back my chair and stood. "First, we knock out details of our agreement. Second, we head home to look for Andrees. And we'd better get moving because I don't have long before I have to be in my lair, before sunrise."

As the others stood and stretched, Father began to hand out dossiers and called in a secretary. We had a lot of work to do and very little time in which to do it. And that didn't count keeping tabs on Darynal and his crew. Somehow, I had a feeling that we were going to be in for a busy week. Or month.

Chapter 4

———

We finished hammering out details ninety minutes before dawn, declining the invitation to spend another day and night there so we could visit our home. The night had evoked too many emotions as it was. By the stunned looks on Delilah and Camille's faces, they needed a break. Hell, *I* needed a break. None of us were drama queens, and the whole night had been like one long angst-ridden Dr. Phil show.

Besides, we wanted to get a start on looking for Andrees. He'd been a good sort, and to think of him wandering around in the Roxbury area made me nervous as hell.

We headed outside. The nearest portals leading Earthside were about a mile away, and the carriage would take us there. But as I stood outside, looking up into the sky, I realized that—for just a moment—I wanted to focus on what was right with the world. I was in love with a wonderful woman. I had a sexy vampire consort for the times when I needed to cut loose without hurting my lover. My sisters and I were still in one piece, regardless of the enemies we faced. We were being paid by both the Elfin Queen and the OIA. That had been one of the stipulations I'd insisted on—double payment.

And, tucked away in Camille's robe, we also now officially held the deeds to the buildings housing the Wayfarer Bar & Grill and the Indigo Crescent bookstore. When we'd first been sent Earthside by the OIA, they'd set me up as bartender at the Wayfarer and Camille as a bookstore owner. Delilah had a small private eye agency ensconced above the Indigo Crescent.

Shadow Wing and his cronies had kept us so busy that we weren't able to spend as much time working at our cover jobs as we had when we first came over Earthside, but we'd all grown very fond of our businesses. I'd hired Derrick Means, a werebadger, to be the bar's manager, though I still went in at night a lot. And Camille had Giselle, a demon, working for her.

"Are we ready?" Camille's breath puffed in the air, frozen wisps. Nearing spring or not, it was still chilly.

Sephreh stood near, along with two guards, keeping watch. We'd said our good-byes inside. Now, only time would tell whether the truce would hold. I thought it might, but didn't want to jinx it, so kept my feelings to myself.

Chase was standing near me. "A lot of changes going on." He thrust his hands in his pockets and stared at the sky. "I don't think I've ever seen so many stars. Or smelled air quite so clear. It's unsettling."

My boots made a scratchy noise as I scuffed the soles on the gravel. I lifted one leg, balancing on the other, to check the heel. It was a little loose. I'd have to have it repaired when we arrived home.

"So, Johnson, this is the second time you've been here. What do you think of Otherworld?" It wasn't a rhetorical question. I was curious as to what he thought of our home world.

Chase paused, mulling over his answer. "Otherworld is beautiful. Haunting. Elqaneve is strangely familiar, while Y'Elestrial . . . I'd have to call it exotic." He let out a long stream of breath. "And speaking of Y'Elestrial and the OIA . . . your father, do you think he's blowing smoke?"

I shrugged. "I doubt it. Father has the subterfuge of a slug. He's always worn his heart—and his pride—on his sleeve. His emotions run close to the surface. But whether his apology is too little, too late, remains to be seen."

As the carriage rumbled up, Chase touched me lightly on the arm. "May I ask you one thing?"

"What is it?" I could see in his face that he'd been thinking about this for a while—whatever *this* was.

"Do you think I could manage over here? Do you think I have what it takes to make the transition? Just in case Sharah wants to come home to live?"

"Why are you asking me? Why not Delilah? She knows you better."

"I'm asking you because you'll tell me the truth. Camille would be diplomatic, and Delilah might lie to make me feel better. But you'll give it to me straight."

He was putting his fate in my hands. I didn't like the responsibility, but Chase was a friend and he needed something concrete to hold on to. And he was right. Delilah would lie and tell him what he wanted to hear. Camille would play both sides of the fence. I was the one who never prettied up the picture, who painted what I saw, rather than what I wanted to see, or thought someone wanted to hear.

"You want to know what I think? I believe you'd fade here, Chase. You don't have enough elf in you to ever be accepted by the other elves. While they might seem all cozy with you now, the long-lost son and all—trust me, discrimination is rampant over here in Otherworld."

"I wondered about that." He shook his head. "Your world isn't much better than ours in some ways."

"Damn straight. Each has its trade-offs, but no matter whether you're in Otherworld or over Earthside, people are people and a lot of them are jerks."

"I keep thinking about how much I'd miss."

"While you might enjoy the difference at first . . . I think you really would miss home too much. After a while, you'd have to leave, or you'd wither like a blossom in the frost. If Sharah *does* return home, I think you should limit yourself to visits. Maybe on weekends, or for a week every few months. But I promise you, as much as I can promise anything, Sharah will make certain you get to see your baby, and more than just once a year. She has too much respect for you to do otherwise."

"You really think so?"

I nodded. "I know so. She loves you, Chase. Even if she's not ready to get married just yet. And you love her."

He ducked his head, smiling. "Yeah . . . I do. I really, truly do. I never expected it to work out like this, but Sharah . . . I think . . . I've found out what it really means to be *in* love. And the thought that she's having my baby scares the hell out of me, and yet it's so absolutely right."

And then, we were scrambling in the carriage, and off to the portals, on the way home.

The house was bustling by the time we burst through the door. Iris and Bruce were back—and since their house was still a ways from being a reality, Bruce was now living with us, too. We'd slowly enlarged our extended family to the point where we were now a freaking commune.

As we walked through the front door, Smoky caught up Camille and planted a kiss on her as he swung her around. Morio was helping Hanna clean up a patch of wet finger paint that had managed to take out one of the roses on the handwoven rug. Hanna looked flustered and Morio was trying to calm her down.

"It's okay. She gets away from all of us at times. Don't worry about it."

"I did not see her run! She's picking up speed from the time I get here." Hanna had come to us from the Northlands. She helped Camille escape from Hyto. She spoke English now, and though she was still a little awkward around us, her heart was in the right place.

Iris trailed out of the parlor, a very colorful Maggie in her arms. Our baby calico gargoyle was in the toddler stage and she'd be there a very long time, much to our consternation. She was getting into everything, and that wasn't likely to change for the foreseeable future. Her fur was matted with blue and red paint, and she was giggling as she watched Hanna and Morio.

"Maggie—no! You were a bad girl. No playtime tonight for you. You can just take a time out and think about what you did." Iris caught sight of us and let out a sigh of relief. "I'm so glad you're home. Tonight has been one disaster after another. But Menolly, you don't have long before sun-rise. You're cutting things close—" She stopped, looking at our faces. "What happened? I can see something happened while you were over there."

I was about to tell her to gather everyone in the kitchen when a loud whistle sounded. Smoky immediately set Camille down and she raced for the kitchen, with Trillian on her heels.

"The wards! They've gone off." Her voice echoed from the kitchen, and, giving Iris a helpless shrug, I took off after Delilah and the guys. Iris let out an exasperated sigh in the background.

"I swear, can't we have one evening in this house where we're left in peace?" The talon-haltija muttered loudly, and then I heard her say, "Maggie! You stop that—I do not need a bright blue nose, thank you very much!"

As we gathered around the table where the grid of quartz crystals sat, forming the alarm for when our land's wards were breached, Camille and Morio examined the pattern, sorting through the energy coming off the grid.

"Not Demonkin." She glanced up at Shade. "Can you tell me if it's what I think it is?"

He held his hands out to the crystals. A crackle charged the kitchen as a faint bolt of purple lightning jolted from his skin to the smooth crystals. Jerking his head up, he nodded.

"Ghosts. But why would ghosts set off the wards? Spirits walk the world all the time." He bit one side of his lip.

"These aren't Casper's kin. Ghosts won't set off the wards unless they're baleful. These aren't run-of-the-mill spirits—they're out to hurt us." She paled. "How are we going to find them? I can ferret out Demonkin energy, but . . ."

"I'll be the bird dog." Shade turned to the door. "Assign posts. Morio, you'd better stay here. You can deal with Neth-erworld creatures better than anybody except me. Who else is coming outside?"

"Me." I stepped forward. "Camille, you stay with Morio. Trillian, you stay with Camille and Morio to protect the household. Iris, I know you're pregnant, but get your spells prepared, just in case. Hanna, I want you to take Marion, Douglas, and Bruce in the parlor and stay there. Keep the door to the living room open, and take Maggie with you. Delilah, you come with us . . . Smoky, Vanzir, Roz, you're also with us."

And so we split off.

Delilah had Lysanthra, her dagger. Roz had his arsenal, and Vanzir was armed as well. Shade, Smoky, and I all were weapons in our own right. We headed out the kitchen door to the backyard.

The rain had started—a light drizzle, and mist drifted along the ground. Wind ruffled through the tops of the trees, setting up a ghostly susurration that whispered through the yard.

Our three-story Victorian, with basement, was on five acres in the outskirts of the Belles-Faire district that lies north of Seattle. We weren't exactly out in the country—there isn't really an "out in the country" in this area for miles—but we were as rural as we could get for being in Seattle. Our five acres buttressed up against Birchwater Pond, and beyond that lay a patch of wetlands no one could develop. We'd talked about buying up the wetlands to ensure they wouldn't come to risk, but we hadn't quite reached a decision.

The outer reaches of our backyard were overgrown and wild. We let it go, for the most part, because we found the energy revitalizing, and the overgrowth encouraged strangers to stay away.

As we looked around the part of the lawn we actually kept mowed and clear for the vegetable garden, I motioned for Shade to take the front. I couldn't sense ghosts until they made themselves known to me. Some minor Demonkin I could suss out, but the spirits of the Netherworld? Not so much.

Shade held out his arms, palms forward, and closed his eyes. He began to slowly turn in a circle, one step at a time. A faint cloud of shadow began to emanate from his body as he moved, tendrils of smoke, wisps coiling out from him. The shadows began to form into winged creatures, no bigger than a canary, that went flying out from him. There was still so much about the half dragon, half Stradolan—shadow walker—that we didn't understand. And like all dragons, he wasn't about to give up his secrets easily.

Delilah crossed to stand beside me, crossing her arms. "This scares the hell out of me," she said, as quietly as she could. "I don't want to think about ghosts again."

"Me either." Our last encounter with ghosts had left Morio almost dead and all of us shaken to the core. An entire area of Seattle had been inundated by hungry ghosts, and though we hadn't licked them, I'd thought we had the problem somewhat under control. But with the appearance of Gulakah, the Lord of Ghosts, I wasn't so sure. Then, he'd vanished, and I'd hoped that—with the spirit seal in his possession—he'd gone back to the Sub-Realms and stayed there.

"Do you think Gulakah's in town?" Delilah shifted to her right foot. She was tall—six one—and athletic as hell. Compared to her, and to Camille's five seven of voluptuousness, I might as well be a shrimp. Barely five one, I was small-framed and small-breasted, and when I'd died, I'd been slender, so I always would be. But tiny or not, I could tear through the toughest of enemies. Well, most of them. My size belied my vampiric strength.

I glanced to the side. Shade was so focused he didn't appear to hear us at all. "Ten to one he's back," I said, reluctant to admit it. "I'd hoped that stealing that spirit seal from us might buy us some time, but now . . . I don't think it did. Shadow Wing is on a high. He's hyped up from claiming another of the seals. He sent Telazhar to Otherworld. Chances are Gulakah's back. And if so . . ."

"If so, the ghostly activity around Seattle is going to soar." Delilah winced. "I hate that."

"Me, too."

A rustle of wings, and the shadow creatures came rushing back to Shade. He held out his arms and they made a beeline for his chest and vanished into him. The moment they'd reentered his body, Shade turned abruptly.

"They're near the rogue portal. And they're headed our way."

"Any idea of *what* they are?"

He paled. "I don't know, but I *can* tell you they're nasty. And they're on the move."

"How the hell can we fight them if we don't know what they are?"

He shook his head. "Delilah, you and Vanzir head back to the house and send Camille and Morio out here in your place. We need their magic to go up against these things because I haven't the faintest clue if physical attacks will work on them."

Delilah gave him a swift nod as she and Vanzir turned tail and raced back to the house. Meanwhile, Shade started toward the patch of woods where the rogue portal had opened onto our land. We had guards watching over it but none of our efforts—or those of Queen Asteria's mages—had been able to close it. As for where it went—the destination changed every so often, and there was never any guarantee where it would lead. Which was why we tended to avoid it.

Roz and I fell in beside Shade. We'd gone only a few yards when the energy thickened and I could hear Roz's sharp intake of breath. The beating of his pulse beckoned me, and my fangs descended, but I pushed the urge out of my mind. I didn't feed on friends, not even when they invited me to. More than one person had offered their services, but I had never taken a bloodwhore and I wasn't about to start.

We slowly approached the sparkling light that filtered from between the trees, and Shade parted a tangle of vines that thrived in the area. Even in the early spring, they coiled, tendrils burgeoning forth to cover the walkway.

I debated whether to call ahead to the guards, but hesitated. I'd alert the spirits if I yelled. But if I didn't, the guards would be in danger—

"Crap." Roz's voice cut through the night. "Look."

And then I saw them. Bodies, prone on the ground. Two elven guards, and they looked terribly, horribly dead. There was no blood, not even a whiff, but they were pale as snow, pale as a clean sheet on a cold morning. I glanced around but couldn't see anything else out of the ordinary. As I knelt by the corpses, Shade, Smoky, and Rozurial kept watch.

There didn't seem to be any wounds—no marks, nothing to indicate why they died, except the extreme pallor of their skin. That might indicate a vampire, but there were no fang marks that I could see, and something else felt off, but I couldn't pinpoint just what.

"I want a Corpse Talker." I glanced up at Rozurial. "We need to know how these men died. They're Queen Asteria's guards, and something killed them—either coming through the portal or . . ."

"Trying to go through it to Otherworld?" Shade asked.

I shrugged. "Six of one, half dozen of the other. Or we could be off base. Keep on your guard while I call Yugi down at headquarters and see if he can get me a Corpse Talker out here."

"We could help, if you think one would travel through the Ionyc Seas?" Smoky took up guard directly in front of the portal. I pitied anybody trying to make it through him. Dragons were notorious for being cruel to their enemies, and Smoky was no exception.

"A Corpse Talker? You're kidding, right?" Corpse Talkers were reclusive and dangerous. But the more I thought it over, the more sense it made. "I have no idea. I really don't even know *what* they are. Nobody really does."

Corpse Talkers could give voice to the dead. They would ask questions, and the souls of the recently departed channeled through their lips. Nobody ever saw their bodies or faces—just the luminous steel-gray eyes that gleamed from within the dark hood. Only the women of their race could become Corpse Talkers; the males were sequestered below ground in their villages hidden beneath the forests of Otherworld.

"If they will allow, I will bring them." Smoky looked rather disgusted, and I knew that he didn't like to have much to do with the dead.

I put in a call to Yugi and gave him our request. "I think Chase is on his way to the station, by the way. He took off the minute we got back to the house."

"I'll see what I can find out and call you right back." Yugi was a Swedish empath who was Chase's right-hand man. He was a good man, and while I wasn't sure just how Chase used his abilities, Yugi was trustworthy.

I knelt by the bodies again. "Shade, can you check on the ghosts again? Are they near us now?"

Shade nodded, stepping back, once again holding out his hands. The shadow creatures emerged from his fingertips and zoomed off into the night.

The next moment, a force slammed into me, knocking me forward to sprawl on the ground. I rolled, coming up on my heels in a crouch, looking around for whoever had shoved me. But there was no one in sight.

Roz shouted as he went flying across the field to land at the base of the portal. He'd been picked up and tossed like a child might toss a pebble across a pond. "Crap! What the fuck?" He was on his feet the next second and was reaching into his duster.

Next, Shade took a hit, but he stayed on his feet. His shadow creatures came swooping back to him and rushed into his body. With a grunt, he shook off the impact and turned to me.

"They're all around us. I can see them—but I doubt if you can."

I shook my head. So did Roz.

But Smoky let out a hiss. "I can see their forms." He let out a long guttural sigh and turned, his nails lengthening into talons as he reached out to swipe at something. A horrid scream cut through the night, and a brilliant flash of light appeared at the area where Smoky had struck.

Roz lit a round, golf ball–sized bomb and threw it on the ground. As it exploded, the glowing sparks outlined our attackers, giving them form. I counted eleven of them.

"What are they? What can I do to them?" Frantic, I stepped back as two of the spirits began to crowd in on me. Three were after Shade, four after Smoky, and two more after Roz.

Smoky bellowed and sliced at the air again. "I don't know—I have never seen these beings." Another shriek and the spirit vanished. "I don't know if I killed it or just made it go away."

Shade caught his breath and let out a low sound that sounded almost like a howl on the wind. A chill ran down my spine as I watched him. He began to transform, right there, in the middle of the tree-crowded wood. Smoky let out a low growl but backed away as Shade's form rippled. He began to grow, but unlike Smoky, instead of a majestic white dragon, what appeared was a terrifying, haunting form of a skeletal dragon surrounded by shadow and a violet smoke. He looked almost fossilized.

We'd never seen Shade in his natural form before. I wondered if Delilah even knew what his dragon form was. We'd all assumed he'd look like Smoky, but with black skin instead. Nobody had expected this.

I backed up and ran straight into Rozurial, who steadied me with one hand. "Helluva way to find out what he looks like," he whispered. "Ten bucks say Delilah's going to freak."

As I watched the coiling, serpentine dragon whose wings were as skeletal as his body, I couldn't help but think otherwise. "She's never seen him like this, but don't forget, Kitten's a Death Maiden. She's not the gentle tabby she began this journey as. I actually think my sister likes playing in the dark more than she's willing to admit."

"Maybe, but I'm not hedging my bets until she's actually—holy crap. Look at that." Roz broke off. I'd never seen him so unnerved.

The figures that had us surrounded were focused on Shade now, and they rose in the air and dove toward him, flames to a moth. He lashed out with his tail and front feet, and as he connected with one of the spirits, it let out a howl that echoed through the yard and a purple flame washed through it, leaving only a thin flicker of ashes.

The others backed off. As one, they turned toward Roz and me, aiming like swift, ghostly arrows, as they barreled our way.

"Fuck!" I leaped out of the way as one skidded past me. Deciding to give it a chance, I spun in the air and kicked it with the heel of my boot. Though my foot passed through it, there was still a shudder as energy connected with flesh, and for a moment I felt dizzy but managed to land in a crouch. Leaping to my feet, I let my fangs down. So I could actually touch these things, but whether I had any sort of effect, I didn't know.

Next to me, Roz pulled out a bottle and splashed water on

one of the incoming spirits. It hissed and a wisp of flames sizzled. Then it redoubled its efforts against the incubus.

But I didn't have time to focus on what was going on with anybody else. I was surrounded by a circle of the grasping creatures, and every time their ghostly auras reached out to swipe at me, a jolt shot through my body.

I wasn't sure if they were doing any damage to *me*, but next to me, Roz let out a shout. I turned to see him fighting off one of the spirits. It had managed to latch onto him. I couldn't get a good look, but from what I could see, it looked like its mouth was pressed against his forehead. Roz was screaming in earnest now.

I tried to leap on the spirit's back and ended up going through it, taking both Roz and myself to the ground. But my attack was enough to startle the ghost, and it dislodged itself from Roz.

"Smoky! Shade! Where the hell are you? We need help!" I didn't realize I was screaming until Roz winced and covered his ears as he struggled to his feet. I helped him up and tried to push him behind me, but the spirits were still circling us and no matter which way he faced, he'd be at their mercy.

Just then, an icy wind blew through. It froze the ground, frost forming in a lacework beneath our feet. Smoky was causing it—the wind rolled out of his hands, along the ground, as it dropped the temperatures to a bone-chilling degree. The spirits began to back off us as they headed in his direction.

But before they could reach him, Shade's coiling neck swooped down and the purple flame raced through their midst. Another three of the ghosts went up in flames, their cries piercing the night.

"*Mordente!* The blades of death, they come for you!" Camille's voice severed the air, slicing through the chill. She and Morio were on the move, hand in hand, coming our way.

The ghosts halted and turned toward them, and for a brief moment I caught a flicker of their nebulous faces—greed, and hunger. Envy. They spiraled toward the pair, but as Camille and Morio reached out—her left arm and his right— a circle of glowing purple light began to whirl around them, like the blade of a circular saw.

The energy flickered faster and faster. Morio and Camille looked like feral creatures, their eyes gleaming in the night. Camille's violet eyes were almost silver, and Morio's were a glowing topaz, and the wind whipped her cape and his kimono into a frenzy. This wind wasn't coming from Smoky or the air around us, but from the magic itself. The wheel of light began to keen, wailing louder as they pushed it forward.

The spirits paused, as if they were uncertain, and then one tentatively dove forward toward the pair. The moment it came in contact with the whirling blades of energy, it flared, screamed, and was gone.

Camille laughed, wild and throaty, and Morio joined in. They were enjoying the hunt, reveling in the energy that whipped around them. The spirits tried to withdraw, but they wouldn't allow it. They drove forward faster, herding the ghosts, and then Shade was there to meet the spirits with his flames.

That was when I realized that Shade's purple flames ran on the same wavelength as Morio and Camille's magic.

Together they boxed in the spirits between them, and before the ghostly figures could head to the sides in an attempt to get away, they pushed their magic together, taking our enemies from both sides. The carnage was an energetic gorefest. Sparks flew as the spirits exploded, and the screams that filled the air hurt even my ears, they were so sharp and pained and full of fury.

And then, we were standing there, alone, with not a body in sight except for the guards, who were still terribly dead. I stared at them, then glanced back at Camille and Morio, whose eyes were still glimmering even though they'd lowered their ring of energy.

Shade was still in his dragon form and Camille stared up at him, a look of awe on her face. Morio grinned at him and I had this weird feeling that the three of them were in some secret club the rest of us couldn't access.

A noise through the trees startled me, and I whirled around as Delilah came rushing down the path. She skidded to a halt, staring openmouthed up at Shade. I froze, waiting for her cue.

But instead of panicking, she began to laugh and rushed

over to his side. He towered above her, though he was only about two-thirds Smoky's size. As she walked around him, marveling at his form, my sister—who only a year ago would probably have run shrieking—reached out and began to touch the bones of her lover's body.

Roz cleared his throat. "You win."

"Yeah, but I didn't think she'd be so delighted. I give up," I whispered under my breath. "I have no clue of what to expect next."

"The unexpected, love. The unexpected." Roz was shaking his head, leaning against a nearby tree.

I was about to answer him when my phone rang. Yugi was on the line.

"Menolly?"

"Yes. What's going down? Did you find out anything?"

"Yeah. A Corpse Talker will come to your house. But, and this is the interesting catch, she'll only allow Shade to bring her through the Ionyc Seas. Not Smoky. If you want her there, you'd better hurry. And Chase said he's on his way back to your place."

"Yeah, I doubt that will be a problem. Call you back in a moment." As I hung up and turned back to the others, it occurred to me that we were in for a long, terrible fight. If Gulakah was truly back in town, and this was an example of what he was bringing with him, I wondered if there was any way we could defeat the next onslaught.

But all I said was, "Shade, get your ass down to the Faerie-Human Crime Scene Investigation's headquarters now. You need to bring back a Corpse Talker *stat*. Because I need to head inside in forty-five or fifty minutes. And I want to be here when she talks to the dead."

The next moment, Shade was back to his usual form, and then gone with barely a word. I looked at Delilah. "So what do you think of your boyfriend now?"

She wrinkled her nose. "Fiancé. And he's cute. Like a living fossil. I think I should nickname him Spot when he's in his natural form. In honor of the Munsters' pet dragon."

And with that, I dropped to the ground, laughing until my stomach hurt.

Chapter 5

❧❧❧

Delilah went back to the house to check on everybody there while the rest of us speculated over what kind of spirits the ghosts could have been.

A sour tang rang through the air—the scent of overturned soil and mold and fungus. I glanced at Morio. His eyes were still glowing, and a sudden hunger ran through me. We'd formed a bond, an unasked-for, unwanted one. He'd been given a transfusion of my blood to save his life. Ever since then, we'd been pulled toward one another, though I was dealing with it a lot more easily than he was. Camille knew about it, and while she wasn't thrilled, she tried to ignore it.

His gaze latched onto mine and he licked his lips, his long, black nails digging into his hands as he made a fist. I could feel the slow breath as his chest rose and fell, and the sound of his pulsing blood stirred my hunger. I turned, pulling myself away, before I did something we'd all regret.

"I need to feed," I whispered. "I need to drink deep." I had bottled blood in the refrigerator, but the thought of it sounded gross. I wanted hot blood, fresh, spurting from the vein onto my tongue. I wanted Roman here with me, but there wasn't time to call him.

Roz was suddenly beside me, pulling me off to one side. He pressed me against one of the trees. "I know what you need. You can drink from me. I can handle it."

"I don't drink from friends."

"And you don't want to drink from your sister's husband, either. Menolly, listen to me." He forced me to focus on his face. The usually serene good-natured look he wore was replaced by an intensity I couldn't ignore. "I'm a demon—an incubus. You know I can handle it. You can drink from me and I doubt if you can do anything worse than leave a hickey."

"But . . . *you know* I'm pledged to Nerissa and consort to Roman—" I'd fucked Roz once, but though it had been fun and good, it wasn't meant to be a long-term thing. I knew it in my heart.

He shook his head. "I'm not asking for sex. I want to help you get out of the bloodlust before that Corpse Talker comes back. Before the sun rises and you go to bed hungry."

I bit my lip, one of my fangs piercing the skin. A few drops of blood trickled down my chin. A glance over my shoulder told me that the others were busy, wrapped up in speculation about the spirits. I hated being at the mercy of my bloodlust, but it was no different from Camille's pull to the Hunt and Delilah's inability to withstand the lure of the moon when it was full.

"What the fuck," I moaned, suddenly so horny and thirsty that I could have fucked an ogre. Roz bared his neck and I licked my lips, eyeing the beating pulse of his jugular. "I'll make it feel good . . . I promise. I won't drink much."

"Just fucking do me." Roz sounded excited, and as I pressed against him, I could feel his erection through the front of his tight black jeans. His long curly brown hair tickled my face as he leaned down for me to get a good angle, but I pushed him back against the tree, hovering at eye level. I could make my victims feel every single pain tenfold, or I could take them to ecstasy. And this . . . this was *not* the time for pain. As I lowered my fangs to his creamy skin, they

slid in effortlessly, slicing through the flesh with one, seam-
less, movement.

Roz moaned and I turned on the glamour. Even though he
was an incubus, he was geared for sex so my glamour played
off his and I suddenly found myself in thrall to him, so hot
my pussy was burning up. I wanted Nerissa. I wanted Roman.
I wanted both of them. At once.

Roz's blood tasted sweet and rich and thick in my mouth
and it flowed down my throat, making me ache for more. I
coaxed it out with my tongue, drop by drop, the crimson
nectar pulsing with his life, with his energy. And then, I
could feel it—his sensuality rushing over me. I moaned, biting deeper, sucking harder, wrapping my legs around him as
I pinned him to the tree. He gasped, his hands cradling my
ass, and began to whisper things, dirty things, hot, sexy,
wanton things, into my ear.

"Take it in baby, take it in. I want to fuck you, to lay you
down and drive my cock deep into your cunt, you delicious,
redheaded wench. I want to fuck you till you scream, till you
come . . ." His voice was ragged.

I ground harder against his crotch, reaching down with
one hand to unzip him. I wasn't going to fuck him here, not
right now, but I grabbed hold of his cock and fisted my hand
around it, holding it tighter than he'd probably ever felt in his
life. Even than when we'd fucked the one time before.

He began to pant as I drank deep, spiraling into the
energy, catching the pre-cum on my hand to lubricate his
penis.

But then, something—I don't know what it was—perhaps
a voice of reason, or maybe just my conscience, whispered,
"Stop . . . you can't drink him down . . . he's your friend."

I realized Roz was becoming too pale, even in the moonlight splashing between the clouds, so I pulled my fangs
out, but the energy was riding us and he kept hold of me,
pulling behind the tree so the others couldn't see us. My
mind was warning me—there might still be ghosts lingering, but they didn't seem to be bothering us if they were,
and I was pretty sure that the death magic Camille and
Morio had been running had wiped them out, Shade taking

out the rest. Rationalizing my desire any way I could, I let Roz take me down to the ground, on a bed of wet and molding leaves.

He slid off his duster, revealing a mesh tank top over rippling abs and gorgeously toned pecs and biceps. The man was gorgeous, like a long-haired Hugh Jackman, and he knew it and used it.

The next moment, my jeans were down around my knees and he was plunging into me, his cock filling me up as he groaned with delight. I rolled him over, riding him like a bucking bronco, pulling up my sweater to cup my breasts as he watched, his eyes growing wider. I leaned forward, rubbing my clit against his cock, feeling so full of his blood that I might burst, and the warmth of it made me feel alive again, like I might have some shred of my mortal self left.

As we rose and fell in the dark night, I looked up and there, I saw my sweet Nerissa coming toward us, her eyes glowing with lust. She licked her lips and I held out my arms to her, beckoning her in. She dropped her robe and, naked, stepped toward us, a dangerous and wild gleam in her eye. I wondered if she was about to shift into her werepuma form when she let out a low laugh and the ground seemed to shake beneath us, everything rippling like rings on a pond.

As she knelt beside me, cocking her head to the side, her shoulder-length blond hair coiled out toward me. And that was when it began to filter through my lust-crazed brain that something was deathly wrong. I did not make a habit of fucking my friends in the woods when we were in danger. Nor did I drink from my friends—I'd broken one of my sacred oaths to myself.

I looked up into my lover's golden eyes, only to see them darken and sink into pits, deep sockets of emptiness. And within that void, I could see shadows flying, shades moving, as her hunger reached out to encompass both Roz and me.

Roz began to scream and I leaped off him. I yanked up my jeans and aimed for the creature's head. This wasn't my betrothed. This wasn't her at all. And the moment I hit her, I could see only a gray, alien figure with a rounded mouth filled with a row of sharp teeth, and dark eyes with no pupils.

Rolling away, Roz staggered to his feet, looking weak. I'd drunk too deeply and he was having a hard time recovering quickly.

"Help! Camille!" I might be small but my lungs could rattle the house. Even as I shouted for help, I landed a kick in the creature's stomach. My foot slammed into it, knocking it back against a cedar.

If it had actually been my lover, I would have killed it with that kick, but the creature shook off the blow and grinned, a dark, filthy, tainted smile. I whirled again and slammed the other foot into its face, fully expecting my stiletto heel to pierce the nose. But it was like kicking solid stone. My heel didn't survive, though I wasn't hurt.

"Fuck! What the fuck are you?" Furious now, Roz's blood pumping through me, giving me strength, I launched myself at it, knocking it to the ground.

The thing let out a garbled laugh but said nothing, merely reaching up to wrap its bony hands around my throat. It couldn't choke me to death, but it could break my neck and put me out of commission for a while. As I struggled to free myself from the iron grip, Smoky appeared, along with Camille. They took one look at the situation and Smoky rushed over to help me out while Camille supported the struggling Roz, guiding him out of the area as he leaned on her shoulder.

Smoky motioned for me to move and I tried to roll away, but the creature held tight and I couldn't free myself. Smoky flexed his fingers as his talons sprang forth. With one quick swipe, he sliced through one of the creature's arms. As it let out a garbled roar and let go of me, I took the opportunity to get my ass out of the way.

Letting out a rumble, Smoky punched her in the gut, all talons front and center. As he ripped through the flesh, the creature struggled to get away but then, with one slow motion, toppled forward. Smoky jumped out of the way as it landed on the forest floor, still twitching.

"Not dead yet?" Morio asked, coming into the picture. He glanced at me, and then his gaze flickered back to the body on the ground. "Doppelganger. Summoned by a powerful necromancer."

I managed to catch his gaze and hold it. "Or the Lord of Ghosts?"

He nodded. "Yes, Gulakah."

I watched the figure writhe on the ground. "Can we talk to it?"

"Nope . . . it has no will of its own. Or mind, really. It follows instructions, and it's hungry. It feeds off energy and flesh. And they have a natural charm that creates hallucinations in their intended targets." He turned away. Over his shoulder, he added, "The Corpse Talker has arrived. I suggest you dispatch this thing now."

Smoky gave it one more blow, and then he let out a long sigh. "You all right?"

I checked the heel of my boot, which was truly broken now. "No, not really. But I guess I'll have to be. I just hope I didn't fuck up Roz too bad."

"The incubus will live. Come, we'd best go interrogate the dead before they refuse to give up their secrets." And with that, he motioned for me to go first, and we slipped back through the trees to the clearing where the dead elfin guards were lying.

Shade was there, with the Corpse Talker. A faint blue glow emanated from within the folds of the cloak, and those luminous steely eyes peered out of the hood. I swallowed my revulsion—they really were squirrelly, but they had their place and were very useful.

Camille stood to one side, Roz sitting on the ground beside her, looking dazed. Moon Witches and Corpse Talkers weren't the best of friends. In fact, something about their energies produced a volatile mix and the result could be a nasty implosion, explosion, or some kind of 'plosion. And Delilah didn't like Corpse Talkers. So I'd be the one in charge of this little venture.

I stepped up to the shrouded figure, who was around my height. "Welcome, Speaker of the Shrouds."

There was a rhyme we'd chanted in childhood, a charm to keep the bogeymen at bay.

Lips to lips, mouth to mouth,
Comes the speaker of the shrouds.
Suck in the spirit, speak the words,
Let the secrets of the dead be heard.

But bogeys were as real as the Corpse Talkers, and not nearly as worrisome as the speakers of the shrouds. Corpse Talkers were an unknown factor in so many ways, and there were rumors of them going rogue, wandering the wastelands of Otherworld, sucking souls from the living. How true it was, I didn't know, but I didn't really want to find out.

The Corpse Talker nodded. "Has the body been touched?"

"I checked them over briefly to look for a cause of death. That's why you're here. I couldn't figure out why they died. But I didn't touch them much."

"Move back." The order was direct, blunt, with an expectation of obedience.

We all shifted, moving away from the dead elves. I didn't relish telling Queen Asteria that two of her guards had died on our land, but it would help if we could tell her why. They were noble men; they were honor-bound and would have put up a struggle if it had been any normal foe, so I had the feeling that we weren't facing anything in the way of normality here.

The Corpse Talker knelt beside the first body and leaned down, pressing her lips to the lips of the elf. It was disconcerting watching her kiss the cold body, but then—who was I to talk? Nerissa kissed me, and technically I was dead. Well, *undead*. Vampires walked two worlds—we were truly the living dead, but at least we were sentient and still had our souls.

After a moment, the Corpse Talker raised her head, and again, all we could see were the gleaming steel eyes, but there was something else—a nimbus around her, a mist swirling. It was the spirit of the elf, which she had drawn into herself with her kiss. She stood and turned to me.

I bit my lip, trying to think of the first question. I'd have anywhere from one to five questions before the spirit would speed away.

"What killed you?"

"The soul sucker." The voice that emanated from the

Corpse Talker's lips was a rattling breath, leaves quivering in the wind.

I frowned. *Soul sucker.* That didn't give us much of an answer. There were any number of creatures who could suck out souls from the living.

"What did it look like?"

"A flash in the night. A swirl of flame and light. There was no body, only a ghostly apparition."

I turned to the others. "I need more questions, now. What else should we ask?"

Shade stepped forward. "Spirit, tell us, how were you attacked?"

The Corpse Talker inhaled sharply and the voice of the elf fluttered through once more. "It ate away the magic in my soul." And then—with a whoosh—the elf's body jerked on the ground. The connection had been severed and his spirit had left to the Land of the Silver Falls, to join his ancestors.

As Camille murmured our prayer for the dead, I shook my head. We didn't know that much more than we had at first, except that some ghostly creature had attacked the elves before they could defend themselves.

The Corpse Talker knelt by the second body but shook her head. "This one has departed already."

"Then take your payment."

The Corpse Talker pulled up the shirt of the body of the elf she'd communed with, then took out a thin, sharp blade. She deftly sliced a thin line down the elf's chest, and then, with fingers cloaked in the shadow of night, reached into the cold cavity and withdrew the heart. How she severed it so quickly from the body, we couldn't see, but she placed it in a small box and shut the lid, then ran her hand over the wound and it pulled together again.

I stared at the elf's body. I'd never seen a corpse after the Corpse Talker took her payment, so I had no clue that they were able to mend up the wound like that. The dead elf would return to Otherworld seemingly intact. And the Corpse Talker would take his heart and eat it, in a bloody communion.

She stood and turned to Shade. "I will return now." Without a word, Shade stepped forward and the Corpse Talker allowed him to loosely wrap his arm around her waist, and they vanished into the Ionyc Seas.

Camille let out a long breath. "What could have attacked the guards? I don't recognize that description of any ghosts I know about. It wasn't a revenant. But maybe, a shade?"

Revenants weren't as dangerous as shades; they could suck out all the warmth from the body and leave you frozen, but shades . . . a single touch from a shade could give a human a heart attack, and they could do nasty things to the Fae, too. But I didn't think they were responsible for these deaths.

"No, I just . . . don't think so. Shades don't appear in a fiery vision, either—they're usually hidden in the shadows and attack without any warning."

"These attacked without warning." Camille turned to Morio. "What do you think?"

He shrugged. "I've been racking my brain but can't think of anything. We've got some research to do."

"What do we do about the body of the doppelganger?" Smoky motioned toward the patch of woods where I'd almost lost it.

I blushed. "About that . . . I have no idea of what went on. Roz . . ." I didn't even want to get near him. I was afraid I'd damaged our friendship for good.

But he managed a wan smile. "Enchantment. Morio said it could put out a form of hallucination—make you see what you want to see. A type of charm, so that's what happened. You'd never take advantage of me unless something triggered it like a spell. And . . ." He flashed me a slow wink. "It wasn't all bad, was it?"

I didn't want him to be nice to me. I constantly had to guard against my predator nature. Vampires were high up on the food chain, and it was too easy to lose sight of perspective and begin viewing everybody as your own private blood bank. I never wanted to fall into that mindset—the mindset of a monster. But for now, I accepted his forgiveness. We needed to find out who had sent the creature our way. The *why* was apparent—we had enough enemies that there was no need to ask why. But the fact remained that we'd been attacked in our own home again.

"No, it wasn't bad at all." I smiled at him gently as he struggled to his feet. "We should get back to the house. I need to get my ass in my lair before long. It's nearing dawn."

"Yeah . . . Morio and I will stay out here and reset the wards. Smoky, will you stay with us in case anything else comes through?" Camille leaned against him. At six four, Smoky towered over her, but a strand of his hair rose up to gently stroke her face and she smiled at him, a glowing smile—one filled with love. Morio leaned over and pressed a kiss on her shoulder, and the three of them headed off toward the driveway where the first batch of wards were hidden.

Roz, Shade, and I trudged back to the house. I motioned for Roz to hang back a moment, and Shade moved off to the side to give us some privacy, still within sight, but studiously ignoring what we were saying.

"I'm truly sorry." I motioned for him to show me his neck. My fangs had left a deep wound, and dried blood encrusted the holes. "I should never have done that. I was looking at Morio and the next thing I knew, the bloodlust came over me. It's not an excuse, but damn, I'm usually in better control than this. Do you really think it was the doppelganger's charm?"

"I don't know, but I'll tell you one thing. We're being targeted, and we're being watched."

He grimaced and rubbed his neck. "I'll admit, as sensuous as you made it, I don't think I ever want to feel your fangs again. The rest . . . well . . . I'd be happy to take another go. And you know with me, it's all play. I can't settle down. It's not my nature. If it was . . . to be honest, I'd probably have swooped in and tried to break up Iris and Bruce. If you haven't guessed, I have a distinct fondness for that house sprite, and she's gorgeous." He grinned again. "But don't worry. I'm not mad at you, Menolly. This wasn't your fault and I'm thinking it wasn't really my idea, either. However, we'd better figure out what the fuck is going on and we'd better figure it out as soon as we can."

"I have to sleep, but I may be able to do something even then. Roman's been working with me, teaching me to lucid dream. While I can't do much in the dream state, I *can* talk to him and control my dreams to some extent. I haven't had a nightmare for several months."

My dreams had been filled with fire and pain ever since Dredge had turned me, and while I'd slept better after staking my sire, still the memories caught me up at times—especially when I least expected it—and I'd relive the experience, unable to wake out of it. Now, thanks to Roman, I usually could divert the nightmares before they became too intense, and they'd transform into nebulous wanderings through the dream state.

Roman had taken me in hand and begun to teach me things that only an ancient vampire would know. He was sharing with me the secrets he'd learned through the centuries, and I was his grateful student.

I clapped Roz on the back and held out my arm. "Come on, dude. You're weak. I drank way too much. You need to rest for a while."

As we headed back to the house, Shade fell in behind us.

"I'll heal up fast. I'm demon, remember—even if I am a minor demon. I could have staked you if I thought you were in danger of killing me. You know I keep stakes in my duster." He opened the jacket to reveal a couple of wooden stakes hanging off two of the numerous hooks inside his coat, amid a flea market of weapons including a mini-Uzi, a magical stun gun, a blowgun and darts, knives of all sorts, a wooden hammer, and who knew what else the fuck he had in there.

"How the hell do you carry all that?" But I knew the answer—he was an incubus. All demons had superior strength. "Doesn't that get annoying, clanking against your body?"

"I'm used to it," he said. "And it gives me a feeling of security knowing that I have so many weapons at my fingertips. I like weapons. I like collecting them." And then, with a darker edge, he continued. "And I like *using* them. As much as I'm happy you took out Dredge, hunting him kept me going. It was my only reason for living for centuries. I chased him like a dog, sniffing him out, only to see him slip through my fingers time and again, and the failures fueled my desire for revenge. When he died . . . all of that focus vanished with him, leaving me empty. So now, I've replaced the hunt for Dredge with the one for Shadow Wing and his cronies."

That explained a lot. I knew why our lovers were fighting alongside us, and I even understood why Vanzir stayed with us . . . but Roz—I hadn't fully figured out why he cared so much about Shadow Wing.

Dredge had hurt *me*, but he'd wiped out Rozurial's family when Roz was a child. And Roz had watched every sordid detail, hiding and praying he wouldn't be found. That moment had turned him into a tracker. A few centuries later, after Zeus and Hera had destroyed his marriage and turned him into an incubus and his wife into a succubus, Rozurial's hunt for the Scourge had only intensified.

"Well, your help is invaluable. And if I ever do cross the line . . ." I paused and looked at him. "I've asked Camille this, but I'd also ask you. If I ever cross the line like Sassy did . . . if I ever turn into the monster I do my best to keep at bay . . ."

His voice was gruff, but I could hear the tears it muffled. He rubbed his hands across his eyes. "You've got it, Menolly. I'll do you proud. But it's not going to come to that. You're going to age gracefully, like Roman has. You're going to keep control of your nature."

"I hope so. But today scared me. I made an oath to myself that I won't feed on friends. Roman—yes, because he's a vampire and we can take it to the extreme. But not my other friends. Not my family, or my love. I never want to break that oath again."

Roz slipped his arm around my waist and for once, I allowed the touch. Nerissa was usually the only one who could get away with it. I just didn't like to be touched, especially by breathers. The hunger flared in the oddest moments and I didn't even want to give it a chance to tempt me.

But now, I rested my head on his shoulder. Roz understood what it was like to have your life totally disrupted and turned inside out. All of us did, but he more than most of them.

By the time we reached the house, I was twenty minutes away from needing to be downstairs. Iris must have heard what had happened because she drew me aside. "Do you need anything before you sleep?"

I shook my head. I was full, thanks to Roz. "No. I assume you heard what happened?"

She nodded. "Yeah, Camille warned me on her way through to grab some supplies to replenish the wards. Menolly, it sounds like you were under a spell."

"Yeah, but now I'm scared because that thing took the shape of Nerissa, and if I didn't know she was safely off at a conference in Bellingham, I'd be tearing over to her place to make sure she was okay."

"It probably was able to play on your weaknesses—you saw the person you trust the most." Iris smiled. "However, I called her to make sure when Camille told me what happened. Woke her up, but she's fine. You can rest easy on that."

A wave of relief swept over me. "Thank you . . . you always look out for me, Iris. I don't know how you find the energy."

"It's just what I do. Now you should get into your lair and sleep." She yawned.

"Yeah . . . listen, tell the others to do whatever research they can today. When I wake up, we'll figure out what to do about finding Gulakah. I'm certain he's over here now."

"You're probably right. But go—it's nearing dawn and you must be tired."

I was. The rise of the sun didn't just mean danger for vampires; it also meant that we were pulled into a dizzying sleep, one from which we could not awaken until dusk. The rise of the sun sent us into a deep somnambulance, and even a nuclear attack would not wake us. Mortals were safe from us during the daylight hours—there was no way we could attack them. Although ancient vampires like Roman could sometimes resist the pull for up to a half hour or so, even they were slaves to the light.

I raised her hand and kissed it. "Thank you, little mama. How's your morning sickness?"

Iris's morning sickness had struck her 24/7. She rolled her eyes. "Oh, simply *lovely*. I *wanted* to live in the bathroom. But it should ease off after the first three months. Or at least I keep telling myself that. Oh—before you go, I might as well tell you. I'll tell the others after they've had a rest. Bruce and I are renting a trailer and putting it out back. It should be here today. We'll live there until our house is built. I love this house, but there are just too many people living here now for comfort, and Hanna deserves her own room."

I wanted to argue, but I knew she was right—the house was getting too crowded. And she and Bruce would be just steps away.

"That's probably best. But we'll miss having you in here, and you'd damned well better let Camille and Morio set up wards. With his help, her magic shouldn't backfire. And now, I have to sleep."

My eyes were beginning to close and I was finding it hard to ignore the magnetic pull of the sun. Part of me longed to peek out the window, to watch dawn break. I could, but I'd be cutting it close and there was just too much at stake to make a mistake.

I opened the bookcase in the kitchen and unlocked the steel door behind it. After locking it behind me, I descended the steps to my bedroom and stripped, dumping my dirt- and bloodstained jeans and turtleneck into the laundry basket, which sat just inside what passed for a bathroom.

Well, it was a bathroom, but I never needed to use the toilet. We'd installed it in case the others needed to use my lair for a panic room. But the shower—a wide walk-in affair—was perfect to stand in, hosing down after feeding or fighting. And even though I didn't notice the hot or cold unless I chose to, I did enjoy feeling clean, and I liked standing under the spray of water.

I let the water wash over me as I lathered up with a raspberry-scented body wash. As I rinsed and toweled off, I thought about Roz and what had happened. There had to be some way to ensure that this remained the only time. I had to find something to keep me from ever being susceptible to charm again. Because I could not live with myself if I killed one of my friends—or one of my sisters.

With these thoughts on my mind, I slid under the green toile cover and turned out the light, and let the sunrise sing me to sleep as I hid in the dark.

Chapter 6

❦

I found myself walking in a fog. Everywhere I looked, a mist rose around me and the world seemed hazy, all shades of gray. And then, as I adjusted to my surroundings, I began to run.

Long ago, Camille had asked me if vampires dreamed. I told her yes. We walked the Dream-Time in our sleep, locked away from the waking world, caught in our own private universe. We could never go out of body, but we could wander on the ether in a somnambulant daze. Sometimes we walked the past, reliving the days from our lives, and sometimes we walked the present.

But I had always welcomed the nights when I slipped into obscurity, when my mind shut down and left me to rest in the blessed darkness. It was a relief, to be free from the constant edge of hunger that lurked within me. For all vampires were predators, and we were all capable of turning into wild beasts, the monsters of legend and lore.

But tonight, I wanted to talk to Roman, and so I called out for him as I ran, searching for him on the Dream-Time.

A faint bluesy tune reached my ears, and I blinked.

Roman was near, all right. He always made an entrance—one impossible to ignore. The music—I recognized it as the Gorillaz' "Every Planet We Reach Is Dead"—swelled and I felt a rush of anticipation. Though I didn't like to admit it, there were times I simply needed to be around other vampires who understood what it meant to be a bloodsucker.

And then, the mist parted, and I was standing in his parlor. Well, not really, but I might as well be. My mind had reached out and touched his. My spirit couldn't leave my body, though I could travel physically to the astral. But my thoughts could project outward. It was a complicated matter, and I wasn't even sure that I fully understood my own nature.

Whatever the case, there he was—all five eleven and one hundred sixty pounds of him. Roman had been turned by his own mother—Blood Wyne, Queen of the Vampires, thousands of years ago. He'd been in his prime, a warrior set to conquer, and he looked as good as he had the day he'd died, if not better—the vampiric glamour that we developed heightened our best attributes and muted our flaws.

"Roman." My words caught in my throat as the repressed thirst and passion that had been aroused during my tryst with Roz flared to life again. Even though I was here only on a mental level, I could release it—safely.

He heard the hunger in my voice and a sly, cocky smile stole over his lips. He reached back and freed his hair from the leather thong that held it back in a ponytail and dropped it to the side, then opened his silk blouse and was standing bare-chested in black leather pants.

I swallowed hard and looked down. I realized I wasn't wearing anything. I'd been running through the Dream-Time naked. But I didn't care. All I cared about was Roman's touch—and letting my predator free without worry that I'd hurt my partner. As he slowly reached down to unzip his pants, I tumbled into the fire.

We were together, growling, hissing, rolling across the floor like wild dogs. He'd taught me how to play rough while still keeping myself safe. I rolled on top of him, pinning him down by his wrists as I straddled his cock, plunging down on the shaft in a fury of lust. He broke free and reached up to massage my breasts, pinching the nipples as I rode him up and down like a carousel horse.

I let out a throaty moan and then we were up again, and he was carrying me, his hands under my butt, over to the glass doors. Without blinking, we were outside, in the rain and the mud as lightning streaked across the sky. Here, it was still dark. Here, we were safe, riding the howling winds that played around us.

He pinned me against a tree, thrusting into me again and again, cradling me with one hand while, with the other, he worked his finger into my ass. I let out a low moan as he fucked me, the bark of the cedar rubbing harshly against my back. But I didn't care. All I wanted was the feel of him driving into me as I forgot my worries, forgot my fears, and gave in to the primal lust.

I growled again and bit him, deep, in the chest. He howled, not in anger or pain, but with joy, and bit me back, on the nipple, digging deep with his fangs. The exquisite agony rocketed through me and I swooned as he sucked both nipple and blood from my body, continuing to fuck me as hard as a ramrod, as hard as steel. But I could take it. I was made for the rough stuff, like he was.

His fingers reached down, pinching my clit, then rubbing me into a frenzy, first harsh, but then milder till he was tickling me. I wanted to scream, to tell him to stop—his touch was so light it was painful, but then the ecstasy took hold and I began to climb. I wrapped my legs tightly around his waist and we rolled to the ground, with his hips swiveling as he sought to go deeper, seeking out my core, the light deep within the darkness.

I latched my lips onto his and we kissed, fangs raking against each other. The feel of his tongue against mine, the smell of his scent, the silver of his eyes that had grown so pale with the millennia . . . he was the glittering man who had for so long been more than a man. And now, he drew me in, bathed me clean with his blood. In our fury, we created a sacred union—the dark gods rising, the son of a vampire queen and the daughter sired by a demented sadist.

And then, a shimmer beckoned, and I rode it high. It was

almost like seeing the sun, and it engulfed us in a warm, brilliant glow as I willed it closer. Roman rode me faster, urgent now in his driving thrusts, and as he let out a long howl, his head drawn back, fangs out, he plunged them into my neck and I came, hard and high and spiraling into the light that we'd created together. Soaring on the orgasm, I felt him drive into me one last time, and rest, his cock pulsing in my cunt.

The music that had steadily risen in intensity began to fall away, and after a moment he pulled back from me and helped me sit up. We were both bruised and bloody and beaten, but we'd recover, especially since this was all on the Dream-Time. But meanwhile, my need had been quenched.

Roman draped an arm around my shoulder and pulled me to him, kissing the top of my head. "Rough day, love? I heard you call. You needed me and so I came. What happened to cause such urgency?" He tilted my chin up and gazed into my eyes, his own gaze aloof and cool again. But I'd come to realize that beneath the clouded iciness of his stare, he hid a multitude of emotions.

I thought I'd be able to talk about it without worrying, but when the words rose to my lips, I stumbled over them and hung my head as they came out in whispers.

"I drank from a friend today. Something was able to charm me and I drank from a friend to prevent something even worse." I winced, the remorse flooding back as I told him about what had gone down in Otherworld, and what we'd come home to. When I told him about Roz and the doppelganger, Roman's cool look vanished and his nostrils flared.

"Not a good thing. I know you too well to believe you did this willingly. But if something can charm a vampire, we need to know what it is. Doppelgangers don't have that power innately; someone had to empower it when they summoned it into this plane and gave it a face. Do you have any idea of who it was?"

I bit my lip. How much I should tell Roman about what we were facing was always an uphill battle. Oh, I knew that he'd dug around enough to have at least some idea of what was going down, but that didn't mean I should just open up and discuss things that might be better off left silent. The spirit seals could be used by vampires, too, and it would make for an incredibly powerful being if one were to get hold of it.

While I trusted Roman—for the most part—to be sane enough not to covet one, I wasn't so sure about his mother. I'd never met Blood Wyne, but her record of conquest was daunting, and while I appreciated that she had come out of seclusion with the intent to unify the vampire community, her methods were often severe. If vampire nests didn't fall in with her rules, she systematically destroyed them.

"We think we have an idea. But . . . let me find out for sure before I say anything. But I wanted . . . I guess I wanted reassurance that I'm not slipping."

"Trust me, if I thought you were slipping, I would deal with the situation. I will not have rogues running the streets in my territory. Especially now that Mother has ascended to power again."

I wasn't sure just how secure that made me feel, but I nodded. "Thank you. Meanwhile, we have another problem. A friend of ours—an old friend from the OIA—was sent over Earthside and he's missing. His name is Andrees, and the idiots in charge sent him to the Roxbury Street area, in White Center. I gather there was a covert OIA outpost stationed there, as a massage parlor of all things. A *real* massage parlor, not a hooker joint."

Roman let out a laugh. "Your people don't do their research very well, do they?"

"Apparently not. Anyway, Andrees is missing and we're afraid something happened to him. We're going to investigate, but would you put the word out to your men to let me know if they hear of anything?"

Roman tickled his fingers over the back of my neck and I closed my eyes, reveling in the feel. "Of course. I will be happy to help however I can. But do you have the time right now? You and your lover—your fiancée—are planning your nuptials."

I groaned. "Yeah, we are, though we had another fight over the ceremony the other day. I'd be happy just saying a few words in front of family, but Nerissa's right, this is an important event and we need to do something special. I just don't know *what*."

"I wish you would invite her to join us. She sounds positively delicious." Roman leered, and I shivered.

"No drinking off my girlfriend. She's my love, and I won't let you hurt her." I didn't think Roman would harm her, but then again, he was ruthless in his assessment of issues and how to take care of them.

When he first told me he thought he was falling for me, I'd warned him to backpedal. My heart belonged to Nerissa, no matter how much I enjoyed playing with boys. My heart and body were hers, first and foremost. Anybody else was icing on the cake. And we'd already made ourselves exclusive when it came to other women—the ones who could pose a threat to our stability as a couple.

"But it would be so much fun. Not to drink, and I promise I would never hurt her. But to play. To watch you and your lover touching, kissing, fucking . . . you know I'd like that." He whispered in my ear and I shivered again. I wasn't monogamous, but something about the proposal scared me and I wasn't sure what it was. "I would join only if both of you asked me to, and I would make sure she was treated with respect and that she enjoyed herself."

"I'll think about it." The conversation was starting to irritate me.

But Roman turned my chin so that I faced him and gazed down into my eyes. His fangs were gleaming sharp and dangerous in the mist that rolled around us. "*Do* . . . think about it. You are my consort. It is only fitting that your lover and I should be friends." And with that, he stood and offered me his hand.

I stared at it, thinking at first to ignore him, but then wisdom won out and I accepted his help even though I didn't need it. Roman hadn't reached the age he was without good reason. He could be as cold and ruthless as they came, and he was also smart. While I trusted him, my trust was within reason, and I knew that if I really pissed him off, he'd make me regret it.

"I'll talk to her. But if she's not interested, you'll drop it, right? And you won't hurt her?"

Roman inclined his head. "I would never harm her. She holds your heart, and if I were to break her pretty neck, you would hate me. So no, I will do my best to protect her, and I will never make her regret your association with me."

I watched as he smoothly strode through the rising mist.

And then, he turned, stopping to look over his shoulder. "Oh, Menolly, there's a meeting of Vampires Anonymous tonight—well, what will be tonight. You will attend? I will be there and, of course, you will appear as my consort."

"Of course." And there was nothing more to say.

When I woke to dusk's sweet summons, I was almost relieved. The meeting with Roman had unsettled me. While it was all done on the Dream-Time, it was still as real as if we had met in person. My body showed none of the scratches or bites that he'd given me, just as his would show none of mine. While we healed fast, any damage that happened on the Dream-Time stayed there. At least I'd gotten the bloodlust out of my system without hurting anybody.

I dressed, trying to sort out my feelings, but decided to leave them for later. Right now, I wanted to find out what the others had discovered while I was sleeping. I slid into a pair of black leather jeans and a crimson cowl-necked sweater, then picked up my stiletto boots and scampered up the stairs.

The kitchen was a blur of motion. It seemed that everybody had descended for dinner. The table was huge. Smoky had bought one that filled the available room, and we'd already planned to put an expansion on the kitchen this summer, after Iris's house was built, to create a huge formal dining room. The men would take care of that. They were as handy with saws and hammers as they were with swords and daggers.

Iris was sitting in the rocking chair holding Maggie, while Hanna and Trillian handled the dinner preparations. Delilah and Bruce were setting the table. I smelled chili and toasted bread and my mouth watered.

Sometimes I hated the fact that I could only drink blood. Food would make me sick—the moment it went down my throat—and so would any other drink save for blood. But bless Morio, he'd managed to find a way to enchant blood for me so that it tasted like some of my favorites and—as he saw me glance at the bubbling pot on the stove—he grinned and held up a thermos.

"Chili-cheese flavor."

"Seriously, dude, you rock! You should go into business with this stuff. You could make a fortune." I grinned at him. "Why don't you come to the VA meeting with me tonight and take a few orders? Do a few for free and get them hooked. How hard is it to make this?"

Camille laughed as she pulled the salad out of the refrigerator and handed it to Delilah. "That's not a bad idea. It would be a handy sideline and could become very lucrative. Or you could teach others how to do it—franchise the concept out."

Morio scratched his head. Even though he normally wasn't my type, he was gorgeous, really—all of Camille's men were. His shoulder-length black hair was shiny and straight, caught back in a ponytail most of the time. He was of Japanese descent, and the shortest of her husbands, but in no way less handsome or dangerous. He was dressed in a green tank top and a pair of black jeans, and his muscles gleamed in the dim light of the kitchen.

"That's an idea, actually. I don't have a lot of spare time, but I could take a limited number of orders each week." He grinned. "I could become a gourmet blood dispenser."

Smoky harrumphed. "No offense to you, Menolly, but we really don't need a lot of vampires hanging around the property." His ankle-length silver hair shimmered as it rose to thunk Morio lightly on the head.

I snorted. "I tend to agree with you. Morio, if you're serious, you should take orders at the meetings and then have them delivered, by vampire messengers. No use in taking a chance on setting up some poor delivery person for being somebody's dessert. So what did you find out today?"

Morio shook his head. "Wait till dinner so nobody misses it. Shamas will be here in a few minutes. We've brought him up to date on what's going down in Otherworld."

Camille was foraging in the fridge for salad dressing, butter, and all the usual condiments. "He took it hard. The guilt about his foray into sorcery is exacerbated by the news about Telazhar."

I nodded. Shamas was our cousin, and he'd escaped our former queen's wrath by using sorcery to wrest energy away from a triad of assassins who were out to kill him. He'd teleported himself out of the dungeon, and later we'd been reunited and brought him Earthside.

Shamas was the spitting image of our father and Camille. He and Camille had feelings for each other when we were younger, but she was long over him. However, Delilah and I privately believed that he was still in love with her, though he tried to deny it.

"He'd better get over that guilt. What happened, happened. He fucked up and he knows it, but the best thing he can do now is to use what he learned to help us instead of trying to repress it." I frowned, looking around. "Is Nerissa home yet? That fucking doppelganger has spooked me and I won't rest well until she's back from her conference."

Delilah grinned. "She called an hour ago. She'll be here any minute. I asked her to come directly over instead of going back to her condo first. I figured we might want to go with her to check it out and make sure everything there is safe. She won't make it here by the time we start dinner, but she'll be here soon."

Relieved, I jumped up and gave her a hug. "Thank you. I was worried about that. The demons have broken into our house before. Our enemies could easily get into her condo. I wish she'd just come here . . ."

"Speaking of houses, Bruce and I got word that our trailer will be delivered tomorrow. So there will be a little more breathing room in here, though I'll still be here all day. But Hanna will take over making supper for me. I'm starting to tire a little quicker now." Iris patted her belly. "The bun is extremely active."

"Do you know whether it's a girl or a boy?" Trillian glanced over at her.

Iris blinked like a deer in the headlights. "Actually, yes, I do know. And I have some news. I saw the midwife today and she did a scan—think of it as a magical ultrasound that my energy and nature won't interfere with. Um . . ." She paused. "Bruce, honey, sit down."

Bruce, the curly-haired leprechaun she'd married who looked like a slightly older Elijah Wood, gave her a long look. "You are all right, love, aren't you?"

"I'm fine. Fit as a fiddle. But we're having twins." She blushed and ducked her head. "A girl and a boy."

Bruce blinked. "We're what?" Then, with a laugh that belied his stature, he slapped his knee. "Oh, girl, that is too fitting. Twins run in my family and I'm not *at all* surprised. We're off to a good start, my love."

I grinned at them. "Twins, huh? You're determined to make up for lost time, aren't you?"

Iris snorted. "I know very well what a handful they're going to be. But I've waited for this for a long time, girl. And I intend to enjoy every moment I can. Except for the morning sickness—that can go away, especially since it lasts all day long." She sighed. "I'm just sorry it means I won't be able to help out more."

"You're part of the family. We'll be helping *you* for a change." Camille walked over and took Maggie from her. "Here, Smoky, will you feed her while we finish getting dinner on the table?"

And so, for the next few minutes, the chatty bustle continued. Smoky took Maggie and put her in her specially designed high chair, feeding her the cream drink she so loved, but only after she agreed to eat a few bites of the ground lamb Iris had prepared for her.

Maggie was starting to eat the meat she needed in order to grow, but it had been a fight to get her to give up several of her bottles in exchange for solid food. She'd still get her cream drink three times a day—morning, evening, and right before bed, along with three meals of ground meat and other foods she needed for growth.

Our little gargoyle would be a baby for a long, long time, but we were seeing the gradual changes in her as the weeks went by. While she wouldn't grow out of toddler stage for a good fifty years or more, she was gaining more balance, using more words, and learning.

While Smoky fed her, Iris helped Hanna with the last of the dinner and everything was ready by the time Shamas walked in. He washed up and joined the fray around the huge oak table, looking grim.

"What's wrong?" I thought it was the trouble in OW, but when he spoke, I realized I'd missed the mark.

"We have a problem down at the station. There's some new movement going on, and while we don't think it's going to be as dangerous as the Brotherhood of the Earthborn, we're not quite sure what it is."

"Not another hate group?" Delilah slumped, looking glum. "I would have thought with Andy Gambit dead, we might be free from some of that."

"No, not that. We're not sure just what it is, though. In the past three days we've gotten reports of both teens and adults running off from their families to join this . . . cult." Shamas flourished his napkin and laid it on his lap as the rest of us gathered around the table.

I took my usual place, hovering up above them with my thermos of chili-cheese-flavored blood, to leave space at the table for everyone who could actually eat real food.

Delilah passed around the biscuits. "Is there a name for this movement?"

Shamas pulled out a notebook and flipped it open. "Not that I know of. But there's every indication it involves several ghost hunting groups, a few of the FBH covens, and even some of the Fae organizations that have sprung up are vaguely connected to this. We haven't been able to dig up much info yet, but Chase is concerned enough to ask that we look into it."

"*We* as in . . . ?" Smoky piled his plate high with biscuits, sliced ham, sweet potatoes, salad, and everything else that was on the table.

"You guessed it." Shamas accepted the bottle of wine and filled his glass, then handed it on to Vanzir. "We as in—*us*, meaning all of you. I have to investigate it while I'm off duty. Chase can't do anything officially because there's no sign that anybody is truly missing. But at least four reports of family members withdrawing their life savings to give to the organization and breaking all ties have come in during the past few days."

Once we were all settled and the food had been passed around, we began the discussion. Everybody had been filled in on our trip back to Otherworld, and we all knew what had gone down last night with the ghosts. I took notes to free the others up for eating.

Morio started. "I stopped in to talk to Carter. While he's not an expert on ghosts, he was able to verify what we feared. Gulakah has made his headquarters somewhere here in Seattle, and we don't know where."

The silence was deafening, the only sounds those of people chewing and sipping their wine and milk.

I jotted everything down on my steno pad, along with Shamas's news and the facts we'd learned about Telazhar being in Otherworld. Things were going from grim to grimace worthy. After a moment, I cleared my throat.

"We knew he would be. So let's just check that off as a verified expectation and move on. So, we have the Lord of Ghosts living in our backyard and we now have to deal with his freak show agenda. We can talk about that in a while. What next?"

"I did some digging into the delightful world of freaky-assed ghosts," Camille said. "I still can't figure out what we were facing last night, but I did find out more about doppel-gangers. While they have trouble speaking actual words, other than a laugh or a scream, they don't need a sorcerer or necromancer to summon them up. Their ability to mimic is innate. However . . . the charm thing? Not so much in their league. Therefore, it's likely that the one last night was under control of someone."

"Sorcerers?" I jotted the information down.

"Actually, no." She consulted her notes. "You know, the screwy thing is that most people don't realize that doppel-gangers are part of the Netherworld. They're not spirits per se, but they are creatures that—when they journey to the physical realm—need to take the form of a person here. They often just mimic whoever they were last in contact with until the next meal comes along."

"What happens if they don't feed?"

"They'll fade back to the Netherworld after a while. So when they're summoned here, it will usually be by a necromancer. But when they're charmed, they appear to their targets as the object of their desire. In other words, if I'd been out there last night, I would have probably seen the creature as Smoky or Trillian or Morio."

Trillian coughed. "Yeah, that makes me feel better."

"Could Telazhar have empowered it? But he's over in Otherworld." Vanzir stabbed another biscuit with his fork and bit into it.

"Think about it," I said. "Gulakah was originally from the Netherworld, until he got kicked out. I think the Lord of Ghosts might just be into necromancy in a big way."

"Fuck . . . just when you thought it couldn't get worse . . ." Rozurial still looked a little pale, but mostly he seemed back to his usual self.

I'd let go of the guilt over last night, and now I just wanted to find the cocksucker who was responsible for charming me into that little episode.

"Yeah. And I have a feeling we're only probing the surface right now—" The sound of the front door opening put all of us on guard, but then Nerissa's voice rang out through the hall.

"Honey, I'm home!"

I hit the ground running as Nerissa burst into the kitchen, her tawny mane coiling down her shoulders. She looked tired, and was still in her business suit. My love was striking, statuesque, and her Amazon-like stature exuded a pheromone that drove me nuts.

She dropped her briefcase and held out her arms. I raced over and she caught me up, her soft, lush lips meeting mine. As I melted into her kiss, melted into her love and her passion, for a moment the world was okay, and all the ghosts were driven away.

Chapter 7

"I'm so glad you're safe!" My fears vanished as the warm smell of sugar vanilla filled my senses. I loved how Nerissa smelled—and when I was around her, I did my best to wrap myself in her fragrance because it made me feel loved and at home. Nerissa was still dressed in her suit from the conference—a tweed skirt that stopped three inches above her knees, and a tailored jacket over a baby blue button-down shirt. She had on three-inch spikes, which brought her up to Delilah's height, making her a foot taller than I was.

I floated up to stare at her eye level, then slowly reached out and kissed her nose. "We have problems. Did Iris tell you what went down?"

Nerissa nodded, sliding her big leather hobo purse to the ground. She shrugged out of her jacket and draped it over an empty chair, then kicked off her heels. "You mean about the ghosts and the doppelganger? Yes."

"Has anybody strange been hanging around you lately? We're feeling watched."

Nerissa stared at me for a moment, then looked around

the room at the mob scene that was our kitchen. She snorted. "Um . . . you mean anybody stranger than normal?"

"Dork." I tapped her nose. "Yes."

Nerissa dropped into the chair, leaning her head back. "I was at a conference with two hundred people. There were bound to be oddballs there, but nobody sticks out in my mind. Give me a few minutes to relax and maybe something will come to mind."

I leaned down and placed another kiss on her lips, then nuzzled her cheek. "Are you hungry?"

"Yeah, I didn't stop for anything on the way home. Bellingham is a long drive from here on an empty stomach." She let out a long sigh and leaned forward, eyeing the table. "Plate, please?"

Hanna handed her a bowl and Nerissa filled it with chili and sprinkled cheese on top, then piled three biscuits on the border. She slid into the empty chair next to Delilah and tucked her napkin in her shirt collar. Nerissa had expensive tastes and she was wearing a designer silk shirt—there was no way she was going to chance spilling anything greasy on it.

As she began to shovel the food in her mouth—my girl liked to eat—I glanced at the clock. "There's a Vampires Anonymous meeting tonight. I have to go. Honey, I know you're tired, but Roman wants . . . he asked if you'd come with me."

Nerissa tore her gaze away from her food to stare at me for a moment, but I kept my mouth shut and gave her a short shake of the head. I didn't want to discuss Roman's obsession with watching the two of us in front of everybody. I'd fill her in before we left, in private.

I looked around at the others. "Delilah, Camille . . . would you and Morio and Smoky come with us? Last night I met Roman on the Dream-Time and he said he'd ask around about Andrees. With any luck, he might have some information for us tonight."

Nerissa groaned. "I hoped we could just stay home." I winced as she added, "But since you have to go, of course I'll come with you. Let me take a quick shower first, after I eat, and change into something more comfortable."

"Don't show too much skin," I muttered.

She snorted. "Right, go to a VA meeting decked out for clubbing? I don't think so." And then, before I could say anything, she plunged back into her food.

After a moment, she stopped. "You know, the convention had a lot of people there but I did notice something, now that I think about it. There was one man—the first day I was there, every time I turned around, he seemed to be staring at me, but I didn't think anything of it. Guys do that to me. But when I think about it, he was at every meeting I had that day. I can't remember much about him except that he seemed nondescript. He wore glasses, had short hair, average height. About my age. If anything, he made me think of a librarian, but I was so busy focusing on the speakers that I didn't really pay much attention."

"Did he ever speak to you?" Morio leaned in. "Did he touch you? Touch anything you were carrying?"

Nerissa spooned another bite of chili into her mouth and tapped her biscuit on the side of her plate as she thought. "You know, now that I think about it, he did. There was one point later in the day, where I got into the elevator and he crowded in, too. It was full—there must have been ten people in there—and he scooted next to me and then, he lurched a little and caught himself on my shoulder. He apologized, and I didn't think anything of it, except that I was glad he hadn't grabbed my butt."

"Ten to one, he's spying on us and was scoping you out." Morio glanced over at Shade. "They'll be gathering as much info on us as we are on them. *They* being Gulakah's forces."

"I think you're right," Shade said. He turned to Nerissa. "You say you only saw him the first day of the conference?"

"Yes. I guess I thought he was only there one day. Like I said, I would never have noticed him if he hadn't been around me so much. In fact, I thought it was odd that he didn't introduce himself." She polished off her food and Hanna carried the bowl to the counter.

"He probably wanted to make sure you weren't meeting with other allies there. After the first day, he probably figured out it was just a conference, and not some clandestine plot." Shade leaned forward, resting on his elbows as he folded his hands together.

"You're probably right. Why do you think he was watching me?"

"Because you're aligned with us. You're Menolly's fiancée." Shade paused. "But he had to know enough about you and Nerissa to know she'd be at the conference."

I frowned. "Good observation. Who knew you were attending?"

She shrugged. "A lot of people. Everybody at the FH-CSI. You guys all knew. And a number of my friends. And of course, the conference organizers and anybody who had access to the attendee list."

"Hard to trace through, then." I was about to suggest Camille try scrying when the doorbell rang. Since everybody else was busy eating, I answered it. Lindsey Cartridge stood on the porch. By the looks of her flat tummy, she'd had her baby.

"Lindsey—we haven't seen you in several months. Come on in."

Lindsey was the director of the Green Goddess Women's Shelter for battered women, and she was also the high priestess of an FBH pagan coven of witches. While the magic of full-blooded humans differed greatly from magic like my sister and Morio used, it was still be a powerful force, and Lindsey was an advanced practitioner.

"I didn't mean to interrupt your meal," she said as I led her into the kitchen. In the brightness of the overhead lighting, she looked tired. In fact, I'd never seen her looking so worn out.

"No problem." Camille jumped up. "Here, sit down." She motioned to the rocking chair. "Are you all right? I heard you had your baby—how's everything going?"

Lindsey smiled and gratefully sank into the chair. "Everything at home is fine. Little Feddrika is growing like a weed. She's almost two months old now and is healthy and happy."

"Little *Feddrika*?" I grinned at her, making sure my fangs were reined in. I didn't like intimidating friends.

"Yes." Lindsey ducked her head, a silly grin on her face.

"I sincerely hope that Feddrah-Dahns doesn't mind, but we kind of named our daughter after him since he provided the charm that helped me get pregnant."

The fact that she'd named her daughter after a unicorn prince made me laugh. It just seemed so par for the course in our life. I clapped her lightly on the shoulder. "I don't think he'd mind. Do you, Camille?"

Camille had the same grin on her face. "No, Feddrah-Dahns would be pleased, and we'll tell him next time we see him. But what brings you here on such a rainy night? I get the impression this isn't a social call."

I had the same feeling, and a quiet sense of dread began to slip over me.

Lindsey hung her head. I could hear her pulse racing, and the scent of fear rose off her like a wisp of smoke. The smell of fear was a turn-on to a vampire, and it spurred on the hunger. But this time, it did nothing for me. Lindsey wasn't afraid of us. No, there was something else provoking her fight-or-flight response.

I decided blunt was better than tact in this case. "What's going on, Lindsey? I can smell your worry across the room."

She leaned back, resting against the headrest on the rocking chair. "I'm not sure, but there's something wrong. I can tell you that. I'm not sure how to describe it . . ."

"Start from the beginning." Smoky pushed back his chair. "That's usually the easiest."

I shook my head. The dragon could sometimes be a lunkhead, but he meant well. "Smoky's right, Lindsey. Just tell us the best you can."

Trillian and Hanna began to clear the table. Maggie let out a wail from Iris's room and Bruce went in to tend to her. He had a way with the gargoyle that none of us had expected and had taken over helping care for her.

"As I said, I had my baby a couple of months ago. I took about eight weeks off from leading the coven—three before having Feddrika, and five after—but they look to me for guidance and I decided it was time to take up the reins again. So . . . it was about three weeks ago that I started attending meetings again."

She paused to accept a cup of tea from Trillian, and a peanut butter cookie as he brought the tray to the table. "Thank you. I've been craving sugar lately and I don't know why. I never ate much of it before."

"Hormones?" Iris asked from the sink, where she was scraping plates and filling the dishwasher.

"No, I don't think so. Lack of energy. Which is a part of my story." Lindsey frowned as she bit into the cookie. "Okay, here's the best way I can describe matters. I came back to the coven, feeling okay. I mean, postpartum is hard, and yes, I'm tired from the baby and pregnancy and feedings, but the minute I took up leadership again, my energy began to vanish and I know it's not related to hormones, though everybody keeps saying it has to be. I checked with my naturopath and she says my hormones are right where they should be for this point. Also, I began to notice the same thing about my coven-mates."

Good. Lindsey had done all the practical things, which she should have. Now she was coming to us. Trouble was, we sure didn't have all the answers.

"Do you have any thoughts on what's happening?"

"I don't know," she said. "Even the strongest members of our coven, those who were always the most energetic, are hard pressed to muster up enough energy to charge the candles for ritual. We've been meeting the past three weeks as usual, but there's no . . . *oomph* there. And what's worse is that no one in the group besides me seems to give a damn. Maybe they're all too tired to care."

"I suppose I could try scrying for an answer." Camille was fairly good when it came to divination.

Lindsey let out a soft shrug. "I hope you have more luck than me. I did a reading, but my cards are wonky and won't talk to me the way they usually do. And my cards *always* talk to me. I'm worried and I wasn't sure where to go for advice. So I thought I'd come here and ask you."

This was more Camille's territory. I motioned to her. "Any ideas?"

Camille played with her cookie, breaking it in half and then dropping the pieces on the saucer. She looked perplexed.

"Do you know if this started in your absence, or around the time when you came back?"

Lindsey started to shake her head, but then stopped. "We met in the afternoon on that first Saturday I returned, and everybody seemed fine. We headed out on a field trip to a psychic fair being held in north Seattle. While we were there, we just hung out, got some readings done, bought crystals and incense and other doodads like that. You know, a peaceful, low-key afternoon. Then we broke for dinner and met up again that night for our usual meeting. And everybody . . . seemed different. Zonked out."

"So something happened between the fair and the meeting." Delilah grabbed a second cookie, and then a third. Shade reached over and gently took the third cookie out of her hand and bit into it. She growled at him, but then laughed. "Get your own damned cookie, *sweetheart*."

He snorted. "Share and share alike, *darling*."

Camille pulled a steno pad to her and began to jot down notes. "Maybe something didn't happen *between* the fair and meeting, but *at* the fair." She glanced over at Lindsey. "Where was this fair held? Who sponsored it? And do you remember anything odd at all about the day?"

Lindsey leaned back in the rocking chair as Bruce carried Maggie in.

"Our girl wants her dinner." He hefted her on his side—she was nearly a third as big as he was—and headed over to the playpen. But Lindsey stopped him.

"Can I hold her? She's so cute and such a little love."

As the woman took the gargoyle in hand, I could see the maternal glaze in her eyes. Mamas were mamas around babies, that was for sure. And it didn't matter whether the baby was a gargoyle or a kitten or human.

As Bruce deposited Maggie in Lindsey's arms, Lindsey snuggled her close. "The fair was held in the Westlake Community Hall. I'm trying to remember who sponsored it— usually I have a good memory but the past few months the hormones have played havoc with my thought processes." She frowned. "Something like . . . oh yeah, I remember. They called themselves the Aleksais Psychic Network."

"Are you sure?" Camille jotted down the name.

"Yes, because the name struck me. I'd never heard of the group before and decided we'd go check them out, get a feel for who they were. Most of the covens and psychics around here are networked to some degree. We have pages on Spell-Space, and forums, and whatnot to keep abreast of news in the supernatural community, as well as our own psychic community. We're not as networked as Portland, but we're getting there. If the group had been around for a while, I would have heard of them before."

"Did you meet any of their organizers?" I took Maggie from her as our baby girl began to get a little agitated. "Maggie, be good. I know you're hungry but you have to wait for Hanna to mix up your cream drink."

"Cweem—cweem! Want!" Maggie began to wail in earnest as I tried to pacify her by dangling my braids in front of her. Sometimes it worked, but this time Maggie's cries just grew more frustrated and finally, I set her on the table and scolded her. "*No, Maggie!* Stop crying. Either you behave or you'll go to bed *right now.*"

She stopped, cocking her head to one side. The ears gave her a lopsided look when she did that and I stifled a laugh. Even though she was cute, Maggie didn't like being laughed at when she was in one of her moods. She understood enough to know what I'd said, and so I kept my expression stern, and after a moment, the tears subsided to a coughing sob, and she sniffled pathetically.

"Yeah, you know how to work it, don't you?" I quietly hugged her again. By then, Hanna had prepared her bottle and took her in the living room, where Maggie wouldn't disturb our talk.

Lindsey shook her head. "I can hardly wait till my little Feddrika hits those years." She grinned. "But you're in for it a lot longer than I ever will be." Sighing, she said, "As far as the organizers go, yeah. I think we did meet one. Strange fellow, now that I think about it. He seemed . . . almost like he wasn't quite in this world. I didn't think about it at the time. I guess I thought it was because of the energy in the building from all the psychics, but now that I think about it, he didn't feel *real.*"

That could mean a number of things. "Not real, how?"

Lifting her teacup to her lips, she frowned and took a sip. "Not real as in . . . as if he were in disguise. He looked the part, sounded the part, but something felt discordant between his energy and his actions. Like an actor who hasn't got a full handle on who their character truly is."

That made sense. I glanced over at Camille, who nodded. "Do you remember his name?"

Lindsey munched on the cookie. "Hal Danvers? No . . . Halcon Davis. That's it. Halcon Davis, and I remember because I thought, gee—his name seems a lot like the word *halcyon*."

I jotted down his name. "So you went to the psychic fair and after that . . ."

"Malaise. That's what I'd call it. All members of my coven who went that day have been pretty much out of steam since then. Our rituals feel forced; we don't have the rhythm down that we did. At first I thought it was because of my pregnancy and how it had changed my body and energy field, that maybe I was infecting the others with some sort of fatigue. After checking with my naturopath, though . . . I don't think so. And, I had a dream."

"Dream?" Vanzir, who had been fooling around with Morio's laptop, stopped to look over at her. "What kind of dream?"

She leaned forward and set her teacup on the table. "Last night, I woke up in a cold sweat. I've been doing that off and on for the past couple weeks but couldn't figure out why. Anyway, for the first time in over a month, last night I remembered my dream, and it felt familiar, like I've had it before."

As we waited for her to continue, the energy began to thicken. Lindsey's eyes were wide, brilliant, and afraid. She slowly let out a long breath. "I dreamed that I was out of my body, attending some sort of ritual. I was standing there and looked down at my silver cord and—"

A pause. Another beat as she seemed to struggle for words, and the next moment, she was heading toward the floor. She hit the floor, her eyes rolling back in her head as her body began to jerk and twist.

"She's having a seizure. Stand back, give her room!" Iris immediately shooed everyone back and was on her knees as Lindsey writhed, her body racked by spasms. She began to froth at the mouth.

Iris rolled Lindsey on her side and called for a cushion. I raced into the living room and brought back a pillow off the sofa, which she slipped beneath Lindsey's head. Lindsey sounded like a frantic dog, her sounds chaotic and rough, almost like barking.

"Should I call 911?" Camille grabbed the phone, but Iris shook her head.

"Not yet—give me a second." Iris placed her hands on Lindsey's back, taking care to avoid the flailing arms, and closed her eyes, whispering something so low we could not hear her voice. A moment later, Lindsey began to calm, and yet another moment and she was limp, breathing shallowly, her eyes closed.

Trillian hurried into the hall bathroom and returned with two cool cloths, gently pressing one against Lindsey's forehead and the other behind her neck. After a moment, where Iris kept her hands pressed to Lindsey's back, our friend's eyes opened, and she moaned softly.

"What . . . what . . . ?" Confusion filled her face as she looked up at us.

"Shush, my dear. You had a seizure. Lindsey, do you have epilepsy?" Iris motioned to Trillian, who cautiously lifted Lindsey into a sitting position. Lindsey groaned and reached for her neck.

"No, I don't. I ache all over. What happened?"

"What's your name?" Iris took her hands and held them, rubbing them gently in her own small ones.

"I'm . . . I'm . . . Lindsey. That's it. Lindsey . . . Cartridge." Lindsey began to look alarmed.

"Very good. What day is it?"

"Today's . . . I don't remember. It's . . . um . . . oh—Tuesday. I don't know why I forgot. Today was the day that I was supposed to return to work, but I told them I'd be in tomorrow because I'm still tired." She grimaced as she rubbed her neck. "I hurt like hell. What the heck happened to me?"

"You had a seizure, Lindsey. Do you have blood sugar issues?" Iris felt her forehead, then gripped her wrist, checking her pulse. "You're clammy, and your pulse is racing."

Lindsey shook her head. "No, nothing like that. I've never had a seizure in my life." As Trillian helped her to her feet, Smoky brought a chair over and Lindsey weakly sat down. She leaned on the table, trying to shake off the attack.

"Do you remember what we were talking about before you lost consciousness?" I had a sneaking suspicion and wanted to see if it proved out. This was too much of a coincidence.

"You need to eat something. That took a lot of energy out of you. And drink the tea." Camille brought her another cup of tea, setting it in front of her along with another cookie.

Lindsey closed her eyes, breathing in the steam that rose off the cup. Iris moved behind her and, using a stepstool, began to lightly massage her shoulders. Lindsey leaned back into the back rub, sighing.

"I can't remember what we were talking about. Last I remember, I was telling you about the psychic fair." She pursed her lips, squinting, then again shook her head. "That's it."

"We were asking you about a dream you mentioned— one that woke you up in a cold sweat?" I didn't want to trigger another seizure, so decided to walk softly on the subject.

Lindsey cocked her head, looking confused. "I don't remember saying anything about a dream. I haven't been sleeping well lately but I'm pretty sure it's the baby causing it—she wakes up every few hours for a feeding, and I'm up off and on all night."

I debated whether to push further, but behind Lindsey, Iris gestured *no* so I left it at that. "Okay, we must have been mistaken. You've probably been overtiring yourself. I don't like you driving home by yourself. Let Shade drive you home and he can come back here through the Ionyc Seas. He's a good driver and will get you there safely."

Her mouth twisted and she looked like she was going to cry. "I know I came because I'm worried about my group. I can't remember everything we talked about—that scares me."

"That's common in seizures. Short-term memory loss. I'd

say go home, rest, and go to your doctor tomorrow and tell her you had a convulsion. We'll look around and see if we can find out anything that might be affecting your group. And Lindsey . . ." Iris paused.

"Yes?"

"It's not a good idea for you to do magic right now. You just need more time off to rest after giving birth." The look on Iris's face told me plainly that she was lying. Whatever might be going on, it plainly wasn't in Lindsey's best interest to be playing around with the astral realm, or with anything that might drain her energy any further.

Lindsey nodded, looking lost and bewildered. Shade helped her up and escorted her out. As the door closed behind them, Camille and I stared at each other.

"Am I going to be the one to say it, or are you?" She slumped back in her chair and looked over at Vanzir.

He shifted, darting glances between the two of us. "No way, I didn't do anything. And from what she described, no dream-chaser demon would act like that. Just too much doesn't track."

I snorted. "We aren't saying you're at fault, so chill. But it's obvious something's gotten into her dreams and also seems to have some control over her in the waking state. You can't call that convulsion a coincidence, not when she was about to spill the contents of her dream. We're just wondering if you've got any experience with other creatures roaming the Dream-Time."

Vanzir grumbled but seemed appeased. "I can do some research. Off the top of my head, though, it could be . . . oh, a number of freaks. Nothing I'm willing to bet on at this moment."

I glanced at the clock. Fuck. It was time to leave for the VA meeting. "I've got to go. Camille, Nerissa, I need you guys with me." I wanted one of the guys with me but, considering Smoky's temper, decided to play the better part of wisdom. "Morio, want to join us? Considering the crap we faced last night, the rest of you better stay home."

Iris returned to washing up. The guys began to grumble about being left home and I finally relented. "All right—one more of you can come along. Roz, you. Smoky—we need you here in case there's any more trouble. Trillian, too." That would leave the two biggest egos at home.

As we gathered our things and headed for the car, I realized I had a splitting headache. Stress. You'd think, being a vampire, I'd be immune to maladies such as that, but stress affected everyone, even the undead, though it hit us in other ways than the living. We wouldn't die from a heart attack if the stress got bad enough, but we could get a mite testy.

As the others shivered in the mist and rising fog that rolled across the lawn, I pulled Nerissa to one side. "I know you're cold, but I have to tell you something quick, before we get in the car. I don't want to tell the others—it might stir up an argument."

"What's wrong? Are you okay?" Nerissa lifted my chin, leaning down to kiss my nose.

"I met Roman on the Dream-Time. Um . . . he has a request. And it's just *that*—a request, not a demand." I hurried to say, not wanting her to think it was an order.

She squinted and pursed her lips. "I think I know what this is going to be. The same thing he suggested a few weeks ago, right?" Roman had been teasing us when both he and Nerissa were at the bar with me a couple of weeks back, flirting with both of us.

I kicked a rock across the drive. "Yeah, it's what you think. He suggested a threesome. He won't join in unless we ask."

"You really trust him to not get so excited that he leaps into bed with us and bites the fuck out of my neck?"

"Don't. Please don't." The memory of my fangs slipping into Roz's neck was still all too painful. I was going to have to tell her soon, as much as I feared doing so. Would she understand? Would she leave me?

"What do you want?" Nerissa stood back, her neck cocked to the right. "Do you want me to do it for you? To help you cement your position? I will, but quite frankly, I'm not that attracted to Roman."

I looked up at her, my heart melting. She meant what she said. She'd crawl into bed with Roman and me if it meant a boost for my position in the vampire community. And that made me love her all the more.

"I don't want you fucking anybody you don't want to—not even to help me. But you need to tell Roman yourself, so he'll believe you. He promised he'd back off if you said no." I paused, glancing over at the cars. Camille, Morio, and Roz were taking her Lexus. Nerissa and I would take my Jag. They were waiting for me to head out, to take the lead. I steeled myself and turned back to my love.

"I have more to tell you, and this doesn't concern Roman, but let's get a move on. We need to be at the VA in half an hour."

She nodded, uncrossing her arms, and followed me to the car. As we slid in and fastened our seat belts, Nerissa smiled a tired smile. "I love you, you know. Thank you, for not pushing the issue about Roman. I'll have to think about it."

"Save your thanks until I tell you about last night." I started the ignition and pulled out of the driveway, heading into the fog-laden streets. "Last night, I fed from Roz." And then, I told her the whole story.

After I finished, I shot a quick look her way. "Do you hate me?"

A brief pause, during which I felt a million years creep by.

Then, "Hate you? Why the *hell* do you think I'd hate you? You were under the control of a spell. You couldn't help it—it's not like you took a long look at Roz and went, *Gee, I'd love me some cock and blood. Gonna bite now.* Seriously, get real, Menolly. You're still so insecure about why I would love you, when you're a vampire? Can't you just accept that I love you because you are *you*? Because you're my sexy, gorgeous partner? I want to make you my *wife*, and you assume that I'm going to change my mind just because of a spell?"

Oops. I had some backpedaling to do and I'd better do so quickly. I glanced behind me. The others were close on our tracks and I couldn't just swerve off the road for a chat.

I tried to explain. "I don't want you afraid of me. It has nothing to do with me thinking you don't love me. It's about safety. I fed on Roz—I feel horrendous about that and I swear

I'll never do it again. But what . . . what if I fall under another spell? What if I attack *you* next time? I couldn't live with that, Nessa." There it was. My secret fear.

Nerissa made a little sound, like a cat, and then laughed. "So, what if I accidentally toss the broom to you and it hits you in the heart? Or what if I buy you a necklace without realizing it has silver in it? There will *always* be chances for us to hurt each other, but it's the same for any couple. You can't protect me from all possibilities. I'm not a little girl, and I don't need a mommy. I need my lover."

Relief flooded over me and, ignoring the others behind us, I pulled to the side of the road. Leaning over, I unlocked my seat belt and fastened my lips against Nerissa's, my tongue probing her mouth as my hands roamed over her body. Oh, how I wanted her. Right here, in the car, naked and under my touch. I wanted to run my fingers over her skin, to lower my lips to her breasts, to make her moan with delight. I wanted to hear her tell me she loved me.

She groaned in my mouth, her fingers slipping under my shirt. "Don't we have to get to the meeting?" Her whisper was low, regretful.

I slowly edged away. "I want you so bad. Roman's a fun playmate but there's nobody in the world I want more than you. Nerissa, how did I ever come to deserve you?"

She laughed. "Just lucky, I guess." And then, as I disentangled from her and fastened my seat belt again, she touched my arm lightly. "I love you. I love you more than I've ever loved anybody. Menolly, you're *the one*, you know. The only woman who will ever hold my heart in her hands. *I give you my heart.* I give you my *love*. I would give you my life if you needed it."

And just like that, my fears were quelled, and I held her hand, raising her fingers to my lips to graze them gently. "I never believed I could find love. Not once Dredge turned me. I never dreamed I'd be able to have a relationship, or love, marry, anything normal again. Thank you, for giving all of that back to me."

She sniffled. "You'd better get this car moving, before I

start crying. And Menolly—if it will help you with Roman, I'll do it. He's not offensive. But . . . if he gets rough . . ."

"If you decide to say yes, and he gets rough, I'll stake him through the heart." And with that, I pulled back onto the road, where the others were waiting, hazard lights flashing, and we headed for the VA meeting.

Chapter 8

The VA meetings were held in what had been Sassy Branson's manor, now known as the Seattle Vampire Nexus—the SVN.

When she'd died—when I'd killed her, to be exact—she'd left it to Wade Stevens, the leader of Vampires Anonymous. The mansion was to be used to help give new vamps a safe introduction into the life. Wade was a former psychologist who had chosen to devote his new life—as a vamp—to helping newbie bloodsuckers adjust. He helped them fit into society instead of turning into the monsters that made everyday citizens want to go all Buffy on them.

Wade and I'd dated for a while, but his mother had been a stumbling block—one I wasn't willing to skirt around. Belinda Stevens was every woman's worst nightmare of a potential mother-in-law. And, as we walked through the doors of the mansion, Belinda Stevens just happened to be lying in wait.

"Menolly!" Belinda hustled over. She was a short, stout woman whose upswept copper bouffant was lacquered with so much hair spray that it would take a brick to put a dent in it. Add to the picture a twang that placed her from the Jersey shore and a hideous pleather pantsuit in brilliant chartreuse, and she was impossible to ignore. But Belinda Stevens wasn't East Coast born and bred. I knew for a fact that she was a Seattleite.

Her beady little eyes latched onto me like I was a duck caught in the crosshairs of her shotgun. I'd rather deal with Gulakah any day over talking to Wade's mother.

"Menolly, how are you? I see you brought your girlfriend, isn't she adorable—I was telling Wade just the other day how much I missed seeing you around. I said to him, 'Wade, why don't you bring those delightful D'Artigo girls over for tea?' but he just brushed me off as usual. *So* like him—you know how it is—sons, they never listen to their mothers! We work and slave making a good life for them but then they just up and grow up. And the pity is I'll never see grandchildren—but I suppose that no one would believe that I'm old enough to be a grandmother—"

Even five minutes of her nasal yammering was enough to make me want to stake her. And to make it worse, she didn't need to stop in order to take a breath. "Mrs. Stevens—if you'll excuse us, I need to find Roman."

Her eyes glittered, but she opened and closed her mouth like a fish out of water a couple of times and then forced another toothy smile. "I believe Lord Roman is somewhere in the main meeting hall. How lucky you are to have forged such a powerful connection, my dear. And how *lucky* Roman is to have one of the *mighty D'Artigo sisters* for his consort." And with that, she turned her attention to another group of vamps who had just entered the hall.

I looped my arm through Nerissa's and dragged her into the main meeting room, Camille and the others following.

The hall had originally been Sassy's parlor and office and a drawing room. Wade had opened up the three rooms into one gigantic meeting space and now we had a lovely, elegant hall big enough to hold more than a hundred people. Which came in handy for the Supe Community Meetings, now that the Supe Community Center had been burned to the ground. They were in the process of rebuilding, but it would be several more months before it would be ready to open to the public again, and the SVN had opened its doors to help.

The room was filling up. Ever since Wade had opened up the Seattle Vampire Nexus and Roman had backed the group, vampires had flocked to the place. Vampires Anonymous had gone from being a small, insular group to having a countywide membership, and now groups were hiving off in other cities like Bellingham, and even as far as Portland, Oregon.

Roman had set Wade in charge of teaching a select group of leaders on how to approach their members. While he couldn't go out and turn a bunch of shrinks in order to have the knowledge base needed, a few doctors were willing to work with the vampires and train those geared toward the healing arts. We'd managed to form a connection with the medical community that was still tenuous, but growing. And they were willing to work with us to secure vampire rights.

Blood Wyne, Roman's mother and queen of the Vampire Nation—also known as the Crimson Veil—had sanctioned the Seattle Vampire Nexus and Vampires Anonymous as worthwhile organizations, and I had a feeling eventually she would order all new vampires to attend the meetings.

I still wasn't sure what she was up to. I'd never had the chance to meet the woman and wasn't sure I wanted to. Any mother who would turn her own children into vampires in order to keep her "dynasty" intact wasn't in the running for Mother of the Year. At least not in my book.

I glanced around the room. The hall was set up just the way it had been the first day I'd walked into a VA meeting. I hadn't wanted to go but Camille had tricked me into it, and I ended up glad I went.

The chairs were set out so that vampires' living family members were encouraged to sit on the side nearest the door. In case of emergency, it gave the breathers a fighting chance to get away. A table filled with cookies and coffee and soda offered the guests refreshment, and another table held bottled blood for members. Drinking from a living host during the meetings was strictly prohibited.

The seats were rapidly filling up. I recognized the

regulars—at least some of them. Brett waved at me. Forever caught in geek-land, Brett had been turned while young. I wasn't sure if he'd been in high school or college, but he'd been a nerdy, shy, comic-book-loving guy. After death, he decided to use his newfound vampiric powers to foster his superhero complex. And so Brett's alter ego became Vamp-Bat, and he'd saved more than one woman from being attacked in his nightly rounds through the city.

There were others—Albert and Tad, both Microsoft employees who worked the night shift. They'd kept their jobs and were actively working on the computer system for the Seattle Vampire Nexus, and the software was state of the art. The Supe Community Council had hired the pair to work with Tim Winthrop, the brains behind *their* computer network.

Of course, the most conspicuous absence was Sassy. The memory still stung. As if reading my mind, Wade swung up next to me and murmured, "Sassy would have been proud of what we've accomplished here."

I nodded, unable to speak. Sassy's death had hit me hard, especially since I'd been the one to cause it. But she'd strayed too far into her predator, and I'd fulfilled a promise I'd made to her. When I staked her, she was free to move on, and I'd seen her spirit leaving, with the young daughter she lost so long ago, and her best friend—Janet—who had been her faithful companion for most of her life.

Wade seemed to notice my silence. "It's okay, Menolly. You did what she wanted you to. You did what she couldn't. When the predator takes over, it's almost impossible for a vampire to walk into the sunlight on their own. Sassy's happy now. She's reunited with her daughter, with her best friend. You gave her freedom."

"I suppose I did," I said, hanging my head. "But why do I feel like I destroyed one of the best friends I could have?"

"Shush . . . it's over. You did what you had to. And sometimes, the right thing isn't the easy thing." He nodded toward the far corner of the room. "Roman's over there. He's talking to a few new members. They're awestruck, of course. You might as well be dating a rock star."

I snorted.

Nerissa, who had come up behind us, cleared her throat. "She may be *his* official consort, but she's *my* fiancée."

Wade grinned at her, the tip of his fangs barely showing. His spiky platinum hair was a brilliant contrast to his leather pants and button-down silk shirt. Wade was really quite cute, but I didn't envy his current girlfriend. Let *her* cope with his mother.

"Touchy, touchy." He laughed. "Roman knows perfectly well that you guys are engaged. He was mentioning earlier how well he thinks you suit each other."

I wasn't sure what to think of that, but I let it drop. "I need to ask the membership a few questions. We've got a missing OIA agent, and he was last seen around White Center. The fools sent him over here without checking what kind of an area they sent him into. While Andrees has a good head on his shoulders and can fight his way out of most situations, he's never faced down a gun before, or a low-rider full of gang members."

Wade whistled. "White Center? So not good. All right. I'll make sure you're first on the agenda so that people are still paying attention. They tend to drift off after about thirty minutes."

We took our seats and Roman made his way over to us. He was wearing the requisite smoking jacket—this time in deep purple—and a pair of expensive black jeans and black motorcycle boots. Beneath the jacket, the ruffle of a cream-colored shirt peeked out. His hair was loose tonight, swinging to his shoulders in perfect precision; whoever cut it was an artist. I repressed a laugh. Roman really didn't fit in with any crowd, that was for sure.

He leaned down and gently brushed my lips with a kiss, then reached for Nerissa's hand. She offered it to him, and he lifted her fingers to his lips and planted a firm, quick kiss on the top of her hand. He held it for a beat longer than necessary and Nerissa's breath quickened, then she pulled away.

"As always, it's a pleasure to see my beautiful consort, and her beloved."

Oh, he was courtly, all right, and the vampires around us

were drinking it in. Several of the women shot me venomous looks, and I realized that they coveted my spot. I knew why, but even though I enjoyed Roman's company, I would have happily given up the position, if I could have. I wasn't cut out for courtside manners or decorum.

Roman settled in beside me, and his retinue of guards—some ten strong—followed suit, surrounding us with their presence. They included my sisters, Morio, and Rozurial within their protective circle.

Camille was sitting on the outside, next to Morio, and I glanced down the row at her. She was eyeing the vamp next to her with a combination of wariness and curiosity. He was a burly man, wearing dark glasses, and the standard garb that Roman's contingent wore—black wraparound sunglasses, black turtleneck with the crest of Roman's house on it, and black jeans.

I leaned close to Nerissa and whispered, "Looks like we've stumbled into some beatnik poetry slam."

She snickered and covered her mouth with her hand, stifling a laugh. Roman glanced at me, amusement playing across his lips. He leaned over to whisper to both of us. "I happen to write poetry and if you two continue to make fun of my fashion choices for my bodyguards, I'll make you listen to it."

"It's not *Vogon* poetry, is it?" Nerissa choked out.

Roman slapped his thigh with a thunderous laugh. "I'm afraid I can't measure up to Douglas Adams's standard for greatness, my dear."

Just then, Wade took the podium. As always, he waved to the crowd and said, "Hi, I'm Wade, and I'm a vampire."

"Hi, Wade!" the crowd thundered back.

Row by row, one by one, every vampire in the room stood, took their turn, and—like the "wave" in a sports arena—echoed the call.

It came to my turn. "Hi, I'm Menolly, and I'm a vampire."

"Hi, Menolly!" The first few times, I'd developed a horrible case of the giggles when they'd echoed back to me, but now it was like an old shoe. While not fancy or flashy, the ritual was comforting.

As the meeting got under way, Wade had the secretary—my middle-aged daughter Erin—run through the minutes of the last meeting. I flashed her a smile and a wink. She had blossomed out the past month, and was coming into her own.

After the old business was finished, Wade said, "And now, Menolly D'Artigo has an urgent matter she wishes to speak to us about. Menolly—will you take the podium?"

I slid past the others in the row and stepped up to the podium. When renovating the mansion, Wade had had the construction workers build a three-foot-high stage in the front of the room in order for the speakers to be seen better. At my height, that was a good thing.

I tapped the microphone. "I won't take up more time than necessary, but I have a couple of urgent questions. If anyone has any information, please see me and my sisters after the meeting, or call us if you remember anything. The desk will have our phone number."

Pausing, I sought for the right way to approach the subject. "You know that my sisters and I are from Otherworld. We recently learned that a friend was sent over Earthside. He ended up in the White Center district of Seattle and has vanished. We're worried about him. His name is Andrees, and he's full-blood Otherworld Fae." I ran down a description of him and added, "If you have seen him, or heard of him, or if you see him, please let us know."

As a murmur went through the crowd—it always did after an announcement—I cleared my throat. "And on another subject, if anyone has any information on either the Aleksais Psychic Network, or someone by the name of Halcon Davis, would you please contact us. We just need to talk to them. Thank you."

I leaped off the stage instead of using the stairs, noticing that Roman had leaned over to whisper something to Nerissa. Hoping he wasn't pressuring her, I frowned and hurried toward them, but as I neared my seat, Camille held up her phone.

"Menolly, we have to book. We've got a problem." She was already making her way toward the door, the others following her.

I glanced over at Wade and waved, then at Roman, who nodded his good-byes. As we headed to the door, I wanted to ask Nerissa what he'd said to her, but that would have to wait.

The look on Camille's face was grim. "We can't take Nerissa with us—it's too dangerous."

My girlfriend might be a werepuma but she wasn't a trained fighter, and I wasn't going to put her in more danger than she already was just because she was my fiancée. But I couldn't leave her here alone, among a bunch of vampires.

Roman, who had followed us, said, "I'll make sure she gets home safely. You have my word."

I gazed into his eyes. They were unreadable. "You promise?"

"On my honor." He looked past me to Nerissa. "Do you trust me to escort you back to the house?"

She nodded. "It's all right, Menolly. I'll meet you when you get home. Considering what's going on, I don't want to sleep at my condo tonight. Be safe, love."

"I will. Don't worry about me." And with that matter resolved, I gave her a quick kiss. But I still fretted as I headed out the door.

"What's up?" We hit the street just as the skies opened up and a downpour started. The streets glistened under the fat drops splattering to the ground, and the ripples in the puddles shimmered under the street lights.

Drenched, Camille held up her phone. "Chase texted me—he said there's something going down over at the monastery."

I blinked. "Seattle has a monastery?"

She shrugged. "Well, it was a monastery at one time, that started out as an old mansion. A group of Buddhists took it over in the early 1950s. But in the late sixties, the monks abandoned it, claiming it was haunted, and they couldn't put the spirits to rest. Nobody really paid much attention, until recently, when the land was purchased by friends of Chase. They started renovations last month, I think. I gather this afternoon, all hell broke loose and they called Chase because they didn't know what else to do."

I had a nasty feeling that I already knew the answer, but had to ask. "Where is this mansion?"

Camille nodded. "You guessed it. The Greenbelt Park District."

"Fuck. Fuck, fuck, fuck. *Of course it is.* Of course it's in the *Greenbelt Park District.*" I kicked the curb and almost broke one of my toes. The toe didn't bother me—it would have healed up so fast I would have barely noticed it. But I'd scuffed my new boots and that was the icing on the cake. "Hell. I just bought these. Now look!"

The Greenbelt Park District was the most haunted district in Seattle. Somehow, the ghosts had taken over. We didn't know why they congregated there, but congregate they did.

We hurried toward the parking lot that Wade had built on the property.

I pulled out my keys. "It occurs to me that we should trace the roots of why the district is so overrun with ghosts. My first thought is that it's the fault of the rogue portals."

"That wouldn't make sense, though. The rogue portals are a recent occurrence. The hauntings have been going on for decades in that area. There must be something that pulls the ghosts there—that stirs them up." Morio headed toward the Lexus. Roz opted to ride with them again, too. "Camille will text you the directions."

Camille held up her phone in one hand while she opened the driver door of her Lexus with the other. "Already done. See you there, and drive carefully. The roads are slick with all the rain tonight." She, Morio, and Roz headed out first.

I followed. As I plugged the directions into the GPS, I was dismayed to see how close the haunted monastery—or mansion, or whatever it was—was to the underground lair that Charles, a vampire serial killer, had nested in. Yeah, definitely the Greenbelt Park District.

As I sped through the silent streets, following my sisters, I mulled over what Morio had said. He was right—with the hauntings going on for so many decades, there was no real way it could be Shadow Wing or the portals at fault.

Sometimes, an atrocity could scar the land, make it a haven for ghosts and spirits. When a series of murders or horrible acts took place in one area, the spirits could latch onto the land. Or, sometimes, the energy of the acts twisted and tainted it in some way. I didn't fully understand the concept—that was more up Camille's alley—but I knew that some places felt evil. More often than not, something horrible had happened there.

The Greenbelt Park District was shrouded in history. The buildings had a weathered feel to them; they were old stonework, gray and beaten down by the rains. The masons who'd worked on them didn't build a *development*—they had built one building at a time, to the specifications of the old money that had lived here. Even the buildings and houses that had been abandoned or let go had an aura of mystery to them, and a quiet, decrepit elegance.

Seattle was known as the Emerald City because it was rich in trees, and the Greenbelt Park District more than lived up to its name. Looming firs and cedars overhung the streets in the residential areas. A number of the shops were interspersed with old, crumbling apartment buildings. The neighborhoods still had people living in them, but a lot of the stores sat empty, and there was a deserted, uneasy feel to the streets.

Following Camille, I turned right on Foster. The street narrowed and I wove in and out around the few parked cars. They were nice cars, but older makes, and weathered as if the owners didn't have the money to keep them up. The ever-present trees crowded the streets, their branches leaning on power lines that stretched across the roads.

Three blocks more and the Lexus turned into a large circular turnaround, pulling through what had once been a gated drive. The gates hung open, half yanked off their posts. Up at the house, I could see lights glowing from within the two-story mansion, and Chase's car was already there, on the side of the drive away from the house. It sat alongside a black BMW and what looked like a silver Camry. The tires of the cars had rutted the road, and mud puddles sparkled under the glow of a series of lampposts.

I pulled in behind Camille and jumped out of the car,

hurrying over to her. "You feel anything?" I asked, staring up at the foreboding mansion.

Morio frowned, worrying his lower lip. "There are spirits. I can feel them from here. They aren't just in the house but on the grounds. In fact, remember Harold Young's place?"

"How can I forget? That was a house of horrors." I didn't want to remember. Some memories—some people—were better off being pushed to the past and left there.

"This is worse." Morio looked around at me, his eyes glowing. "This . . . is scary big."

Camille slid her arm through his and nodded. "He's right. I guess we should go in. I don't want to be out here when the ghosts begin to walk."

We headed across the drive, careful to avoid the ruts and muddy water, and dashed up the wide stairs leading to the veranda. A long porch ran the complete length of the house and curved to both sides. My guess was that it completely encircled the mansion, bound on the outside by a white—or what had once been white—banister. The steps creaked, a symptom of old age, and as we reached the door and knocked, I felt a give in the porch floor that strongly suggested it would soon be time to change it out for a new one.

The door opened. Chase was standing there. He silently stood aside, letting the others enter.

I paused, unable to cross the threshold. "You have to invite me in, Chase."

"Oh shit, that's right. Come in, please." He nodded me through and I was able to pass the invisible demarcation line. Contrary to popular rumor, the owner of the building didn't have to be the one issuing the invitation—just someone who was already welcome in the home. Nor were private residences off limits if they were used in a public manner—like a frat house, for example, or an apartment above a grocery, or a law firm housed in a home.

As I entered, it struck me that a lot of mansions were laid out in similar patterns. A grand staircase in the center of the foyer, a left and right wing off to the sides. But unlike Sassy's mansion, or even the grand hall of the Rainier Puma Pride, this one had seen better days.

Old paper that had once been a deep crimson, with ovals containing yellow pineapples in their centers, hung in strips, curling off the walls. It looked like the new owners were helping it along, but I could tell that—along the molding at the ceiling—it had started to peel on its own. The crown molding was worn, and I thought I saw mildew on one end. The staircase was badly in need of a makeover, the polish long gone from both steps and railing. The chandelier—whatever it had been—had been removed and it looked like a new one was ready to go up, sitting to the side in a pile of plastic wrap.

Camille raised her eyebrows. "Real fixer-upper."

"Looks like they're diving into the project." I turned to Chase. "Who are these people? You said they're friends of yours?"

He nodded. "Fritz and Abby Liebman. I've known Fritz from when we were in the police academy together. He decided to switch fields and go the lawyer route. Abby works from home. She's an artist and illustrates bird-watching guides for several major publishers." He nodded to the right of the stairway. "They're in the living room, waiting. Let's go."

We followed him down the dark hall until we came to an open door. As we entered, I noticed that one entire wall had been gutted, with the exception of a load-bearing beam. We were looking into another room, just as spacious. The wallpaper had been fully stripped; primer spackled the walls. The lights were hanging from the fixtures. A sander sat on the floor—which was stripped of its stain and polish—and so much dust filled the air that Camille and Delilah started to sneeze.

A woman leaped up from her place on one of the footstools that was covered by a tarp—all the furniture in the room was swathed in plastic. She was short, about five three, with short red hair. Sturdy, she looked like an athlete. She bobbed her head at us.

"Hi, I'm Abby. I'll get some lemonade. I forget just how bad the dust is in here—I guess I'm getting used to it." She started through a side door, then paused. "Chase . . . Fritz, would one of you come with me?" The quiver in her voice belied her nervousness.

Fritz stood up and dusted his hands on his jeans. He didn't look like a lawyer, but more like a lumberjack. But he had an easy grace about him and a winning smile. He glanced at us. "Let me help Abby and we'll be right back. Make yourselves at home."

As they left the room, we scouted places to sit. The furniture looked old and dilapidated, and I suspected that it had been here when they bought the place.

When Fritz and Abby returned, he was carrying a tray with glasses and a pitcher of lemonade on it, and she held a plate of cookies. But before they could reach us, Fritz suddenly let out a shout. From where I was sitting, I could see the imprint of hands against the back of his shirt, as he went stumbling forward. I leaped up as he hit the floor, the pitcher and glasses shattering as they bounced off the tray onto the hardwood.

"Fritz!" Abby shoved the cookies into Chase's hands and went down on her knees on the other side, fear washing across her face.

Glass was everywhere. Camille and Morio stood, holding hands and closing their eyes, as Delilah reached down to help Abby.

"Fritz, are you hurt?" I didn't see any blood, and he blinked, so he was conscious. But the shove had been pretty hard and I was worried that he might have broken a leg or arm.

He shook his head, struggling to sit up. I helped him avoid the shattered glass and lifted him up and over to the sofa, where he leaned forward, stunned.

"Damn, you're strong." He glanced up at me. "I'm okay. I think I am, at least."

Rozurial spied a whisk broom and dustpan in the corner and went to work sweeping up the broken glass after he used a drop cloth to wipe up the lemonade. Chase circled the room, on alert, but by now I could also tell he was trying to reach out, to use his burgeoning powers in order to help. Which maybe wasn't such a good idea.

Camille and Morio dropped hands and came over to sit on either side of Fritz and Abby. Chase joined us after scouting out the kitchen. Roz finished sweeping up the glass and put the dustpan on the table near the window.

"I told Chase I didn't know how to explain what's been going on but . . . I guess you got a firsthand glimpse." Tears rolled down Abby's face. "This has been going on for a month now, since the middle of February. We bought this house and closed on the day after New Year's. We've been coming over for a few hours at a time to work on it and . . ." Here, she paused.

"You said that you closed in January and that this has been going on for a month. That leaves a month in between. Did anything ever happen during that time? Maybe not so dramatic, but something odd or out of the ordinary?" Either something had stirred up their ghosts, or they had been slow to manifest.

Fritz shook his head, but Abby nodded.

"Yes, actually." She looked up at her husband, tears in her eyes. "I didn't tell you, because I thought you'd think I was tired and needed a vacation." She shrugged at us, apologetically. "I'm a workaholic. It's hard for me to be away from my desk, but renovating the house has been so interesting that I've been making time for it."

"What happened?" Fritz took her hands in his. "And you know you can tell me anything."

She leaned her head against his shoulder. "I came over here alone a couple of times, while you were at work. I was clearing out things and getting the house ready to start the renovation. The first time I was in here alone, I felt like somebody was watching me. I thought, no big deal—everybody feels that way at some point in their lives. Big empty house, unfamiliar neighborhood . . . you know. But the second time . . . I began to hear things."

"What kind of things?" Camille asked.

"Children laughing, like they were taunting somebody. And someone . . . a man with a deep voice, whispering to me. But when I'd stop to listen, the sounds would vanish. I thought my imagination was working overtime." She hung her head. "Then it got worse."

"Worse? How?" Chase was taking notes and so was

Delilah. Camille and Morio were listening. Rozurial had parked himself by the archway into the kitchen, and had put himself on guard duty, by the looks of his stance.

Abby raised her head. "Worse as in . . . I began to hear footsteps on the second floor. They echoed, like heavy boots. Another time I caught a glimpse of children playing in the yard but when I looked again, there was nobody there."

She accepted a tissue from Camille and wiped her eyes, then turned back to Fritz. "That's why I begged you to take the time off so we could get this place done together. It wasn't just because I'm in a hurry to move in. The house began to scare me. I can't stand the thought of living here now— *especially* with what's gone on in the past month."

"Why don't you tell us what's been going on since February?" Morio said. "And do you remember the day it started?"

Fritz, looking pale, nodded. "Yes, actually. I do remember because it was the day after Valentine's Day. We came over and were stripping wallpaper in this room when . . ." He hesitated.

"Tell him. Or I will." Abby pressed her lips together. I could read her energy clear as a book. She was fed up, and now that help was potentially at hand, she wasn't going to let it go by untouched.

Fritz shrugged. "It's simple, really. Whatever this ghost or spirit is, it tried to kill us."

Morio straightened up. "That bad? What did it do, exactly? We need to figure out what spirits we're facing."

Abby let out a pained breath. "Shortly before Valentine's Day, we started renovation. I'm not sure if that's what stirred up the spirits or not. As I told you, until then, the hauntings were limited to footsteps, laughter, stuff like that. But after we started steaming off the wallpaper and taking down the lights, the activity increased and we began having major incidents."

"What was the first? Wasn't that when the hammer flew across the room? Or did I miss something?" Fritz shivered.

"No, I think that was the first." Abby pointed to the ladder. "The hammer was over there, sitting on the top of the ladder, where Fritz had left it. He was taking a break—I'd made sandwiches—and as he walked toward me, the hammer flew across the room and missed him by just a few inches and hit the wall" She nodded to the opposite wall. There was an eight-inch hole in the drywall, exposing the boards beneath. "It almost put a hole through Fritz's head."

"At first, I couldn't believe it." Fritz crossed to the wall and fingered the hole. "By then, Abby told me about the noises—she heard most of them. I believed her, but part of me wanted to put it down to the creaking of an old house. Then, when the hammer came spinning by . . . the only reason it didn't hit me was because I moved a couple of inches to the right, just before it sailed past. It could have killed me." His dark eyes glimmered with fear. "After that, I couldn't ignore it. I had to admit something was going on."

"Poltergeist, maybe. What else happened?" I had learned far too much about ghosts over the past few months. It bothered me that I could name off as many types of spirits as I could.

"We took a break for a couple of days," Abby said. "I think we were both afraid to come back. But this house is ours and we couldn't just walk away. So a week later we returned. For two days it was quiet. On the third day, we decided to work on the attic. I hadn't cleaned it out yet, so we hauled several old trunks out of there. One belonged to the monks and contained a few old robes, and some documents. I've made sure they were sent to the Order. But the other trunk . . ."

"The other trunk contained the possessions of a little girl," Fritz broke in. "From babyhood to about age ten. When I opened the trunk, it felt like . . . almost like something slipped out of it—a shadow or something of the sort."

Abby nodded. "I felt it, too. As we started to carry the trunk down the stairs, something shoved me from behind. I dropped my end—I was at the front—and fell down the stairs. If Fritz hadn't held on to the trunk it would have come tumbling down on top of me."

"Right before she went sprawling, something cold swept past and I heard a man laughing. He had a deep voice. And then, Abby screamed and the trunk almost yanked me down the stairs when she dropped it. I thought . . . when I saw her lying at the bottom of the stairs, I thought she'd snapped her neck." He broke down, shaking his head as he rubbed his temples. "I thought she was dead," he whispered.

"I strained an ankle and fractured my little finger. But it could have been far worse." Abby picked up one of the cookies and bit into it. A crumb of chocolate stuck to the corner of her lip and she wiped it away. She had pale pink lips that curved in a lovely bow, and it struck me that she really was pretty. Her eyes were an arresting shade of blue that twinkled like marbles in the sun.

"What did you do after that?"

"I took her to the hospital, and we stayed away again until this week. Finally, we agreed that we weren't going to be chased out of our own home. I did some research and saw that you're supposed to use sage to cleanse energy. So we came back yesterday and smudged the house. Everything seemed to lighten. Then, we were up in the attic this afternoon when we saw a man."

"He was horrible," Abby chimed in. "We couldn't see his face, but he was angry—so angry. And he was watching me, and then . . . I don't know how to describe this but he . . . he . . ."

"He attacked her." Fritz's voice was harsh. "I couldn't move. It was like I was paralyzed. I was sitting on the floor, working on a light fixture and I looked up and all of a sudden, I couldn't move. I saw Abby go flying onto her back and something yanked her shirt open."

Abby began to cry. "Whatever it was, it tried to unzip my jeans, and I was kicking and trying to get free of it. My arms were pinned over my head. I don't how. He had to have four or five hands to do everything he was doing to me. I thought that it was going to . . . But then something different swept around me. The spirit let go and I felt him follow it—almost like he was chasing whatever the energy was. I heard a little girl laughing, and then a growl and then . . . then they were gone."

"What did you do then?" Chase asked.

"We ran downstairs—Fritz could move again—and

called you from the car. We only came back in when you got here." Abby looked around, terrified. "I can't stand this house now. I loved it so much when we found it, but now I hate it. We didn't know what to do, so we called Chase and he called you." She began to cry again, and Fritz wrapped his arm around her shoulders and kissed her on the head.

Fritz glanced up at me. "We're at our wit's end. We need help or sooner or later, we're going to die. Or lose our money when we walk away and abandon the house. The spirits here are out for blood. Our blood."

As he finished speaking, a low laughter filled the room, and then—all hell broke loose.

Chapter 9

※※※

"What the fuck?" I leaped up as a trowel—the kind used to apply putty—went flying past me. If I hadn't jumped out of the way, it would have sliced into my forehead. Not fatal for me, but it would definitely have put a dent in my skull.

Camille pointed. "There!"

As we turned, a dark cloud began to creep across the ceiling, a roiling black mist, churning and growing as it seeped out from beneath the moldings. Abby and Fritz stumbled back, terrified.

"Oh God, no, no . . . please, no . . ." Abby whispered under her breath as the cloud began to lower into the room, taking form.

Camille shoved her toward the door. "Run. You and Fritz get the hell out of here."

They stumbled toward the arch, but Abby screamed again. I whirled to see another cloud of mist entering the room. They backed up, Abby whimpering as Fritz grabbed her and pushed her behind him.

Chase was near them and he caught hold of Abby's arm and shoved her behind him, with her back to the wall. I was headed their way but stopped short. Rivulets of blood raced down the wall, thin fingers coming from nowhere. I could smell it—coppery and sweet and yet . . . there was something off-putting about it.

"Chase—Abby, get away from there." I motioned them away. They turned to see the crimson rivers flowing behind them. Abby stumbled forward; she'd almost backed into it.

"What the fuck is going on?" Chase's voice was hoarse.

Camille and Morio joined hands and, heads down, they whispered something under their breaths. I could hear the chanting—ancient and hollow. As they raised their heads, their eyes were shining with silver and purple light, and Morio let out a low laugh.

The black shroud of mist circled the room now, and out of it, a large male form began to take shape. I backed up as he came striding out of the cloud, all smoke and mist, with eyes that burned a vicious green. He was evil. I knew evil—on an intimate level because I battled with it daily. And this creature—this spirit—was evil to the core.

Chase tried to shield both Fritz and Abby. The blood pouring down the walls was thick and viscous, but it didn't set me to hunger, as the scent of blood usually did. Instead, it revolted me, turning my stomach.

Camille and Morio intercepted the figure striding toward us, hand in hand, like some baleful Jack and Jill. The look on their faces was as frightening as our opponent. Camille raised her left hand, palm out, and Morio his right.

> *From night to night, from dusk till dawn,*
> *From darkened shadow you have spawned.*
> *From what you are to what you once were,*
> *Let truth shine forth from under blur.*
> *Let illusion crack, let lies dispel,*
> *As your magic we bespell.*

As they incanted their spell, their voices echoed through the room and the spirit roared. A gust of wind raced through, fighting against the mist, trying to drive it away.

But the shadow was strong and fought back, a coiling

serpent ready to strike. The spirit laughed again, but there was an edge to the laughter—tempered with a faint hint of fear. As the tension increased, a noise like a whistling of metal against air startled me. I turned in time to see a screwdriver spinning through the air, aimed at Camille's heart.

She didn't see it, so rapt was she in the magic, and neither did Morio.

I screamed and launched myself, flipping head over heels to land in the path of the screwdriver. It struck me in the shoulder, driving me forward as I careened into Camille and Morio. Camille shrieked as they broke the spell and fell backward. I yanked the screwdriver out of my shoulder, a slow burble of blood following. Vampires bleed very slowly, if they've not been hit in the heart and dusted, and my wound hurt like hell but started to close immediately. I whirled, turning on the spirit that was still bearing down.

Their spell might be broken, but the results held. Now we could see the spirit in his entirety. He was male, about fifty, wearing a top hat and tails and a pair of dress trousers. His hair was shoulder length and straggly, and a leer on his face made me terribly nervous. I couldn't figure out why, and then it hit me. He had the same cold avarice that Dredge had. This man . . . spirit . . . had been a sadist. He was a *mean* son of a bitch. And death had not changed his nature.

He didn't stop but strode toward me. "Little girl. You're going to die." His voice was the voice of a hundred empty husks blowing on the wind. As his eyes lit up with delight, he reached out his hand toward me and a jolt ran through me, picking me up to send me sailing across the room.

I slammed against the bloody wall near Chase and the Liebmans. As I slid to the ground, I quickly ran my hand through the blood and brought it to my lips, tasting just a single drop, but not swallowing it.

"That's not blood! I don't know what it is, but it's not blood." I eyed the spirit, wondering how the hell to engage him. He hadn't hit me with anything physical, and I wasn't sure I could attack him.

Camille and Morio were back on their feet, and they clasped hands once again. The hairs on the back of my neck stood up. They were up to something and all I could think was, *Get the fuck out of Dodge*. I backed out of the way as they headed toward the spirit, heads down, gazes locked.

The spirit ignored me and went for them.

Abby screamed as a huge bronze framed painting that was resting on the mantel flew off and spun through the room at them, at a dizzying speed. Morio and Camille raised their joined hands and the picture bounced away, as if it had hit an invisible wall. It crashed to the floor nearby, the frame and glass splintering.

"Leave this house!" The spirit spoke again, his words echoing through the room. The lights began to flicker on and off, creating a strobe effect, and Fritz cried out and tried to cover Abby's eyes.

"Close your eyes!" He looked terrified. Abby was staring at the strobing lights, and a glint around her neck told me she was wearing a medic alert pendant.

Fuck. *Epilepsy!* I dashed around back of Morio and Camille, over to where Chase was trying to protect Fritz and Abby. Rozurial was fiddling with another one of his home-made bombs and turned, suddenly, sending it reeling toward the door. It exploded, shaking the house, and an odd rosy light appeared.

"Get them through! The ghost won't be able to follow you for a few!" He turned back to the spirit and raced forward, not getting in the way of Camille and Morio, but pulling out a bottle of water as he ran.

I didn't question, I just did. I swept Abby into my arms before she seized and motioned for Fritz to follow me. Chase pushed Fritz to get him moving, and at first I thought the detective was going to come with us, but he didn't. I didn't have time to get him out, too.

Fritz tried to yank open the front door but it wouldn't budge, so I slid Abby into his arms—she'd gone immobile—and turned back to the door. With one swift kick, I broke the lock and the doors swung open.

I took Abby from him again and ran through the door, followed by Fritz. Leaping, I cleared the porch and steps, landing on the sidewalk below. As I raced across the drive, Abby in my arms, a scream cut through the night. I turned around in time to see hands reaching through holes in the porch. They had hold of Fritz's legs. He was fighting them, trying to get away.

Opening my Jag, I laid Abby in the backseat, closing the door before I ran back to the porch.

Fritz was being pulled down into a swirling vortex that looked suspiciously like a portal, except that it felt different from any I'd encountered.

He held out his arms, grimacing. "They're hurting me!"

At that point, I saw that the arms reaching through the floorboards were taloned. Blood was staining his jeans. I leaped onto the railing, balancing as I tried to figure out what to do. If I stepped onto the porch, I'd be caught in the same mire. But there was no time to make plans, so I reached out, grabbing for his hand, and he held tight to my wrist as I pulled.

Whatever was on the other end was pulling just as strongly, and I had a horrible feeling I was going to lose him as I struggled to retain my balance, poised on the three-inch-wide beam that was the railing.

Just then, Chase appeared at the edge of the doorway. He stared at Fritz for a moment. Then, reality blurred and I thought I could see two Chases—one watching his friend get sucked down to his death. The other stepped out of his body and dove below the surface of the porch. I couldn't even begin to figure out what he was doing, but the next thing I knew, the creatures' grasps lessened and I gave one strong yank and pulled Fritz up and over the railing.

As we teetered on the edge and then fell to the ground, the "other" Chase returned to his body, and he gave me a thumbs-up and turned back to whatever was going on inside.

I helped a limping Fritz over to my car and bundled him into the driver's seat. "You know where the FH-CSI is?"

He nodded, stuttering as he tried to get out a "Y . . ye . . . yes . . ."

I pressed my fingers to his lips. "Shh . . . Here are my keys. Start the car and get your asses over there now. Ask for Sharah. Tell her exactly what went on here tonight. We'll be there as soon as we can."

As he started the ignition and pulled out of the driveway, I steeled myself, then turned back to the house. Whatever was going on in there, they needed me. And even though I really didn't want to go back in, I made a running leap and, when I landed on the top step of the porch, flipped over the floorboards and managed to careen my way through the open doors.

The whole house had gone psycho. And by that, I do mean the *house*. The walls were oozing with the bloodlike substance, and as I watched, large black scrawls of some language appeared across the ceiling, as if from some invisible charcoal pencil. There was a sickly green light flickering from within the living room, and, as much as I didn't want to, I ran headlong into the fray.

As I crossed the threshold, it was as if I'd entered a house of mirrors. The walls were distorted, and everything had a blurry look about it. I squinted, trying to clear my sight.

Morio and Camille were raising a circle of mist around them—it glittered and sparked and was thoroughly suffocating, making me glad I didn't have to breathe. Over in one corner, Chase was trying to coax someone out of a closet, and in another corner, Roz was plastered four feet up against the wall, arms and legs spread, unable to move.

The spirit had grown larger, looking more demonic, and I edged around to the side as he focused on Camille and Morio. They were headed toward him and he was waiting. But standing behind him stood a young girl. She must have been nine or ten, and she was holding a torn doll and weeping as she stared up at him, a mask of fear covering her face.

Who the hell was *she* and how had she gotten in here? I was about ready to skirt around him in order to get to her when I realized that I could see the chair on the other side of her—right through her body. Translucent and misty, she must also be a ghost. I edged a little farther beyond him, enough to see that an energy cord of the sickly green light ran from his tailbone to her, coiling around her neck. The bastard was keeping her tied to him!

I glanced at Camille—how to let her know about the girl's spirit without disturbing her concentration on whatever spell they were conjuring up? There was no good way and I didn't dare interrupt them.

But then, I knew what I had to do. I hurried over to Chase. He was peering into a closet, trying to coax someone out. I glanced over his shoulder and saw the vague outline of another child—a little boy. He, too, looked horrified, but he was only about four, and a sickening thud hit my stomach.

"Chase, I need you to come—maybe you can do something." I grabbed his arm and pulled him along with me. The spirit who was making a beeline for Camille and Morio ignored us as we passed by. He was gearing up to do something awful, and I didn't want to be in my sister's shoes when he let loose.

"What is it?" Chase stopped short when the little girl came into view. *"Oh no."*

"He's tied her spirit to his. Can you do anything?" I had no idea why I thought he might be able to help, but something inside urged me to let him try.

Chase licked his lips as he stared at the girl. "I might. But you have to be ready."

"Ready to do what?"

"When I give the word, throw yourself between the spirit and her. Are you willing to do that? It could be deadly." He looked frightened, but I could read the determination in his eyes. Chase hated it when anybody hurt a child—be the attacker corporeal or spirit.

I nodded. "Yeah. Go for it."

Chase reached out to the little girl. A flicker of energy oozed out from his hands, and the girl turned toward him, eyes wide. She reached out to him, then opened her mouth. A haunting scream echoed through the room.

The spirit, startled, whirled around. When he saw what Chase was doing, he roared—his anger shook the room, and pens and pencils and the cookie plate and anything else that wasn't nailed down started flying through the air.

Camille and Morio began a low incantation, driving forward as if they were plowing through a whirlwind or hurricane, one step at a time, their palms out, energy crackling before them.

A shriek caught me off guard. I stumbled back, turning to see Roz, still pinned to the wall, but now a knife was lodged in his shoulder.

I raced over to him and levitated up to eye level. As I grabbed the hilt—it was a kitchen knife, like a serrated tomato knife—and yanked, he let out a curse and I stuck the knife in my belt, not wanting it to become airborne again. I tried to pry him off the wall, but to no avail. Blood fountained from his wound but it wasn't in a vital area and, while it might sting, right now it didn't put him in danger. But if anything else aimed itself for him, he could be spitted like a rotisserie chicken.

Torn—Roz needed me to protect him, but the spirit was bearing down on Chase—I tried to weigh where I was needed most.

"Go, Chase needs you!" Roz struggled to move his head. "Menolly, you know he can't fight that creature!"

I glanced around. Things were still flying through the air, but Roz was right. Chase was the most vulnerable. I nodded and, wishing I could be in two places at once, raced back to Chase's side.

He and the ghost were playing tug-of-war with the girl's spirit, dragging her back and forth. She was crying, but no sound escaped her lips. I landed by Chase just in time to see a chair come flying across the room at him. I couldn't intervene directly—the legs were pointed in our direction and one wrong placement and I'd have a stake through the heart. So I dove for the detective, taking him down to sprawl on the floor.

His grasp on the girl broke and the spirit reared up again, his laughter shaking the walls. He lunged for the girl, a lecherous look in his eye, but at that moment, Camille and Morio sent a bolt of energy into him.

> *Spirits dance and spirits writhe,*
> *spirits toil, spirits tithe,*
> *Fire and ice, and spinning wheel,*
> *let your life to this sign be sealed!*

A fiery glowing sigil appeared in the air, crackling as it burned with a bright purple flame. A thousand howls of anger came rushing through the rune, and then a black, shadowy arrow broke through, aimed for the heart of the spirit. It pierced his back, driving through to the other side.

Camille made a sign with her free hand. The arrow developed barbs and as she jerked her hand backward, the barbs caught hold of the spirit's ethereal body and dragged him away from us.

Morio, grinning fiercely, drew another rune in the air with his right hand and it circled around the little girl, severing her connection with the spirit. She went rebounding back, hiding her face.

The arrow quivered and sparkled with the violent flames. And then—as the spirit let out an angry, frightened roar—the arrow exploded, taking him with it. A shower of sparks rained over the room, and the smell of ozone hissed and popped.

Our opponent was gone.

We stood there, staring at the devastated living room. Roz fell to the floor, along with everything else that had been hovering in the air.

The little girl looked up, fear filling her face, but then she saw that the man was gone and slowly walked forward. She cocked her head, looking first at Morio and Camille, then at me. Then she turned to Roz and regarded him with a serious look.

"You're okay now, honey." Chase knelt and opened his arms.

A smile broke out on her face. The closet opened and out stepped the little boy. The girl ran over to him and caught him by the hand, bringing him back to stand in front of Chase.

Chase waited, his arms wide, looking so sad and weary that I wanted to take him in hand, put him in his jammies, and tuck him into bed with a cup of hot cocoa. He continued to kneel as the girl and boy slowly walked into his embrace.

Tears were falling down his face now, as he slowly closed his arms around them, murmuring something I couldn't hear. And then, as they leaned against his shoulders, they slowly began to fade. In another moment, they had vanished in a shimmer of cleansing light, and we were alone in the house.

Camille and Morio dropped to the sofa, mute and spent. Roz was hurt. Chase looked weary beyond belief. And I . . . I was confused and had a horrendous headache.

After a moment, I slid to the floor. "What the fuck just happened here?"

Chase lifted his head. "Abby and Fritz—are they okay?"

"They took off for the FH-CSI in my car. They should be there by now. There were . . . there was a vortex on the front porch that almost caught Fritz. Arms reaching through to pull him down." I looked around at the destruction and mayhem. "Was it all just that one spirit causing problems?"

Camille shook her head. "No. We cleared him out, but there are more things here. Evil things, lurking. I can feel them. They're just biding their time, and we really should get the fuck out of here before they come after us. Because I don't know how much magic I have left in me tonight. That freaking perv was hell on wheels to get rid of. Thank you, Chase—you distracted him long enough for Morio and me to build our spell."

Chase stared at his hands. "He hurt them. When they were all alive. He hurt both of them and I think he killed them, too. He bound the girl to him and was chasing after the boy all of these years."

"How do you know?" I cocked my head. Chase's abilities were opening out. After he'd been injected with the Nectar of Life to save his life, abilities had been coming to the surface. We'd known Chase had psychic potential, and the nectar had thrown down the gauntlet.

He shrugged. "She told me. What can I say? I could hear her in my head—not so much in words, but I could . . . I know what he did to them." It was all he said, and it was all he needed to say. The tone of his voice told us the rest.

We struggled toward the back door. I didn't want to take another chance on meeting whatever was haunting the front porch. Somebody was tunneling up from a nasty-assed place, and right now the last thing we needed was another battle.

We came around the front and I looked back at the house. "Shit. Forgot to lock the doors." I grimaced.

"Hell, okay, I'll go back." Morio started back, but I shook my head.

"You guys stay right here. I can get across the porch without putting a foot on it." I hated levitating—I was by no means an expert, and more often than not, I ended up running into a wall. But it was better than trying to turn into a bat. My bat-girl abilities had a better chance of flubbing than Camille's Moon magic. *A lot better.*

As I floated up and over the porch, I glanced down. All I could see was floorboards, but they wavered and rippled. The vortex hadn't sealed itself. I slowly levitated through the front door and touched down, turning to slam it behind me and lock it.

The house creaked and moaned. I had the uneasy feeling the sounds weren't just from the floorboards settling. The pseudo-blood was still streaming down the walls, and while no knives hurtled through the air at the moment, as I walked through the living room, muffled moans and cries assaulted my ears.

"I should just get Ivana Krask down here," I mumbled to myself.

It would be a gamble—forming deals with the Elder Fae was risky business—but she did eat up ghosts. Sucked them right up in that bizarre vacuum cleaner of a staff she carried, and then took them home to plant in her spirit garden for torturing.

Frankly, as long as she didn't take innocent spirits, like the little girl and boy, I no longer cared what she did with the freak shows of the Netherworld. This was getting old. We'd been fighting spirits for too long, and I was getting really tired of playing ghostbuster to the demonic world.

As I neared the kitchen, the sound of a door slamming stopped me. I didn't want to turn around. I really didn't. But the door was right behind me. Either the front door, or a side door to what had been the parlor. Slowly, I peeked over my shoulder.

Mother pus-bucket... Instead of a closed door, I was staring at a demon. It had to be a demon, because it had coiling horns and dark blistery skin, and a feral grin on its face. And it was leaning against the doorway, watching me. This was no ghost.

I paused a half beat, trying to recover my senses, and then bolted for the door. The demon came after me, and he was *fast*. He was as fast as I was.

I screamed as I crossed the kitchen in two leaps and tripped out onto the back porch. I scrambled up, grabbing for the knob to pull it shut, but he was right there. His hand covered my wrist and he yanked me inside again.

I let out another scream and kicked him in the balls, landing a solid hit. He groaned and bent over but kept hold of my wrist. Good, he was corporeal. I could at least attack *this* freak.

He snarled, closing his grip on my wrist again, but seemed confused when I didn't scream. Instead, I tensed my arm and whirled around, dragging him with me to smash him against the wall. He let go as his horns pierced the drywall, entangling him. I laughed and pulled my arm away, spinning to kick him again, this time shoving my stiletto heel into his ass. I yanked it back, satisfied when blood began to pour out of his butt cheek.

"Home run!" But I knew when to back away. He was as strong as I was, and I had no clue what kind of powers he had or what kind of demon he was. I dashed out the door, slamming it behind me. As I jumped over the steps, landing in a crouch, I turned, sure he'd be hot on my heels, But he was standing there, staring at me through the window, making no move to follow me.

It occurred to me that maybe he *couldn't* follow me. Maybe he was somehow trapped within the house. If so, score one for us. If not, we'd find out sooner or later. I dashed around the front, back to the others.

"There's a freaking demon in there. I have no clue what kind but he's big and horny—literally—and I left him with a nice hole in his ass thanks to my heel. He's mean, though. Tough sucker."

As I leaned against Camille's car, we turned back to watch the house. The lights were running wild inside, strobing on and off in a dizzying cycle.

"I'd hate to have the electricity bill for that," Camille whispered. But as we moved to leave, there was another sound—a popping, or hissing, or something of that sort, and we slowly looked back.

The house was on fire, burning with a brilliant flame.

"Shit." Chase pulled out his phone and began to dial 911.

"Wait." I looked at him. "We can't let the firefighters go in there—the ghosts are in there, and the demon. Best thing is to just let it burn to the ground. Hopefully, the insurance will pay off and Fritz and Abby can find another house. Because they're never going to reclaim that one. It's too far gone."

Chase gave me a long look, then glanced at the house again. "You know that I can't . . ." He stopped. "Yeah . . . and if anybody asks, we weren't here to see it start, so we couldn't report it."

We waited, watching the house, for another ten minutes and then Roz edged across the street and, taking out one of his little specials, tossed it into the flames, then ran back to us.

"Duck!"

We turned to cover, just in time to miss the explosion. As the house roared to life with an increase in heat and flame, I knew there would be nothing left. Whatever Roz had used had magnified the flames. And there would be nothing to prove that the ghosts had been there, or anything else.

The fire marshal wouldn't find any concrete reason—so faulty wiring would most likely be blamed. So many of the old houses needed rewiring, and that had been a project on Fritz and Abby's list. Insurance would chalk it up to accident. And they would get their money and be able to move on.

After another five minutes, Chase called Yugi. By the time the fire trucks got there, the house had imploded and there was nothing left but gutted timbers and a burned-out shell. The basement was open to the rain, the main floor vanished among the flames. Chase talked to the fire marshal, and I'm not sure what he told them, but within a few minutes, we were ready to head out.

"Go home," I told Camille and Morio. "I have to get my car from headquarters anyway. I'll meet you later. I may stop in at the Wayfarer to see what's shaking there."

They nodded and wearily drove off, taking Roz with them. As I climbed into the prowl car with Chase, I glanced over at him.

"Okay, truth. What the hell were you doing with that little girl's ghost? I know you were trying to free her from the spirit, but how did you know what to do? And *what* were you doing?"

He shook his head. "I don't know, really. I don't know much of what I'm doing lately, especially when it comes to . . . magic? Psychic stuff? I really have no clue. I just feel this prompting inside and I can't ignore it till I do what it wants. I knew that I could untangle her from him, if I only had enough time. But it turned into a tug-of-war match. And then, after he vanished, I knew that I could help those kids over to the other side. All I had to do was hug them, pull them in, and they'd be free."

"And it happened." I leaned my head against the seat and closed my eyes. "Chase, you're all right. You know that, I hope."

He laughed. "Menolly, anytime you pay me a compliment, I pay attention. I know you don't bullshit, so I listen."

And with that, he fell silent and so did I. All the way to the FH-CSI building, the only sounds that passed were those of his breath, his still-beating heart, and the whir of the wheels eating up the road.

Chapter 10

~&~

After I made sure Abby and Fritz were okay, I glanced at the clock. I couldn't believe it, but it was still only around ten P.M., so I decided to pay a visit to Carter. He'd confirmed that Gulakah—the Lord of Ghosts—was definitely back in Seattle, but I wanted to know more about the Greenbelt Park District. And Carter would know its history.

I sped through the streets, worrying over the evening. By now, I was used to having to multitask battles as we connected the dots along the way. Even though Abby and Fritz's house of horrors seemed most likely related to the Greenbelt Park District activity, since the house was in that neighborhood, I couldn't help but wonder if somehow Gulakah had a hand in it.

As I waited for a stoplight to turn green, I glanced over at Galaxy—one of the newer clubs in town. It was on the corner of Broadmore and Wales, and Camille had told me it was frequented by mages and witches. At first I'd feared another Energy Exchange, but she and Morio had checked it out and, apparently, it was more of an FBH hangout for Earthside pagans to learn about Otherworld magic.

As the car idled, I watched a group of people loitering around the door. They didn't look particularly troublesome, but something seemed amiss. I rolled down my window and listened. Most clubs played loud music, and even from this distance, with my hearing, I could catch the throbbing beat. But the FBHs and the Fae hanging around the entrance seemed lethargic. Most were either leaning against the building or looking like they'd already reached the hangover stage.

The light changed and I crossed into the intersection, turning left. Carter's basement apartment was up ahead and I eased into a parking spot and hopped out into the misting night. As I pressed the key lock and pocketed my keys, I glanced around. Nobody was prowling the streets. Carter had a foolproof magical grid set up by local witches. It cost him a pretty penny but kept the area around his apartment, including the parking spaces, protected.

I clattered down the stairs and knocked at the door, once, then again. After a pause, I heard the sound of locks clicking and the door swung wide. For once, it was Carter himself who answered. He had great coiling horns and a brilliant shock of red hair that was tousled by the best hairstylist. When he saw it was me, he smiled and motioned for me to come in. He walked with a brace on his leg but was incredibly charming and charismatic.

Carter was part demon, part Titan. His father had been Hyperion, one of the ancient Titans, and his mother had been a demoness. He was one of a litter, and his father had taken over the parenting duties when Carter's mother abandoned her young. He was also one of the agents of the Demonica Vacana Society. They watched over demonic activity Earthside and recorded it. Whatever else they did, I hadn't a clue. Carter was a relatively tight-lipped demon, as pleasant as he was.

"Menolly, come in, come in. What can I do for you?" He gestured me to the overstuffed, Old World upholstered sofa. Carter had a penchant for all things opulent and ancient.

I glanced around. The cats were playing with some toy in the corner—it was a round track with a ball caught in it and cardboard in the center, and the three of them seemed terribly involved in a game of keep-away with the ball. They were still kittens, and Carter was incredibly fond of them.

"If you're looking for Tobias, he's no longer here." Carter glanced at me through long lashes.

Actually, I *had* been looking for Carter's gentleman friend but didn't want to seem nosy. Carter wasn't gay. Nor was he straight. I don't know if I'd even apply the term *bi* to him. Carter was . . . well . . . Carter, and he lived by his own rules.

"Lover's quarrel?" I winked. I felt like I could be myself around him—at least for the most part. Carter didn't fit into any one world, either.

He settled himself on the chair next to the sofa. "Tobias proved to be . . . unsatisfactory as a companion. And as a djinn, it was a given our tryst would run its course. They are simply not capable of sustaining anything long term except grudges. Apparently, he remembered one he had not yet put to rest. He left last week after I indicated that doing so might be in his best interests."

I nodded. Djinn were tricky and not to be trusted. We'd fought against one in league with Karvanak.

"I'd say I'm sorry but somehow, you don't seem too grief stricken." I wasn't very diplomatic and, with Carter, didn't feel that I needed to be.

He smiled faintly at me. "I'd say I'm sorry, too, but I'm not all that broken up over it. Fondness is about as close to love as I ever get for anyone, and even that wears thin. At least, most of the time." He stopped, toying with his glass of sherry, and I knew he was thinking about Kim, his adopted daughter.

"You miss her, don't you?" I leaned forward. "You did love *her.*"

A soft laugh, and then he saluted me with his glass. "Touché. But more than love. I trusted her, and she betrayed that trust. I gave her everything, I treated her like my own daughter. And she spit in my face." A cold fire raced through his eyes and suddenly, I felt nervous. We had no clue what Carter's full powers were; we'd never been privy to them.

I wondered . . . just what could a demigod do when he was pissed enough?

"Yeah . . . I get it." I decided it was better to backtrack from this line of conversation. "We had a problem tonight."

"What happened?"

I frowned, then said, "This touches on demonic activity, since I happened to see a demon, as well as some crazy-assed ghosts. We are dealing with the Greenbelt Park District again." And I told him all about our evening. "So, I want to know about the history of that area. I figured if anybody knew why it was so haunted, it would be you."

He considered the question for a moment, then motioned me over to his desk. "Let us see what we can find. I should be able to come up with some answers for you. That district has been a hotbed of activity for decades, and it seems to be getting worse."

"I keep thinking Gulakah has to have something to do with the ghostly activity there." I paused. "And what about the whole blood-running-down-the-walls thing? I tasted it. It was *not* blood."

"No, it wouldn't be blood," he said. "That would be a form of ectoplasm—although the term is a little misleading. I merely use it for expediency's sake. There's a form of electromagnetic energy that can manifest at times around ghosts and spirits. That it appears as blood is a parlor trick, usually played by malevolent spirits, to frighten mortals. You smelled blood but when you tasted it, it probably had an odd coppery taste—almost metallic, right?"

I nodded. "Yes, but not in the way that blood does."

"As I thought. Scare tactic and manifestation of a buildup of energy." He thumbed through a bookcase while I settled myself in a chair by his desk. After a moment, he hauled out two heavy scrapbooks and—acting as if they were light as a feather—tossed them on the desk, where they landed with a resounding *thud*.

"Can I ask you something?" It probably wasn't a good idea, but since we were being all buddy-buddy tonight, I decided to pry a bit.

Carter settled into the chair opposite me and turned on

his computer. "You may ask what you like. A question does not oblige me to answer. What is it you wish to know?"

As he took hold of the mouse, his gaze glued to the monitor, I felt an odd disconnect. He seemed so mortal at times, but then the glamour would lift and his power would shine through. I could feel it now, as he focused on searching through his databases. He was brilliant—probably genius level beyond any mortal on this planet, and I could feel a chilling shroud of intellect surrounding him. All of a sudden, I wasn't surprised that Tobias had left.

"If you don't want to answer, I won't be offended. How did you get the brace on your leg?"

He looked over at me, surprise washing across his face. "The brace? Why, I seldom think of it anymore. My leg was permanently injured when I was caught in the midst of a daemon uprising in the Subterranean Realms. I was there on business, and Trytian's father was just forming his rebel group. I got it into my head that I needed an adventure and joined them. We went against one of Shadow Wing's outposts. This was before he ascended to rule over the Sub-Realms."

"You were part of a rebel group?" It was hard to picture, but the more time I spent around him, the more he surprised me.

"Yes, I was. I signed on for a lark. It turned out to be a grueling battle, and hundreds on both sides died. I was maimed—my leg is twisted, but I survived. That was enough war for me. I was quite happy to retire back to my desk."

He snapped his fingers. "Here we go. I found something of the history of that area. I've never done much research into it, just documented what came past my inbox. By the number of entries I've logged, a great many evil deeds have occurred there in the past ten years. However, when we look back to the beginnings of the city, the district was . . . let me see . . ."

"If you say it was a graveyard, I'm going to break your computer." I grinned at him.

He raised his eyebrows and then winked at me. "Why, Menolly, you underestimate my loyalty to my technology. I'd have you down and pinned in no time."

I gaped at him, not sure what to say.

Carter chuckled. "A *joke*. I'd never threaten to stake you—I do not threaten death lightly. However, I do warn you. *Never* underestimate me."

"I won't." It was all I could think of to say.

"Good. Well, here we go. While yes, there was—and is—a graveyard there, that's not what I was going to say. The district was the site of one of the first mental institutions in the area. An asylum, really. This was back in the day when the insane and disturbed were treated cruelly. We're talking electroshock therapy, starvation therapy, and—because the owner was a thoroughly demented prick—plenty of abuse, rape, and murder made out to be accidental."

Holy shit. That would be enough to stir up unsettled spirits, all right. "How come this isn't common knowledge? The little I've read about the district doesn't mention a word about it."

"You think that sort of knowledge would be encouraged by the tourism council, or by residents looking to buck up their property values? No, the asylum—and it *was* an asylum, not a hospital—operated for fifty years before it burned to the ground one cold, blustery night." He gave me a smug look and began leafing through his scrapbooks.

"Fifty years of debauchery. Were operations all under the original owner?"

"No, the son took over about thirty years in. Like father, like son, so it seems." He paused, then turned the scrapbook so I could see the articles. "Here, it says that the hospital was in the center of the district, and the administrator owned five hundred acres buttressed up to the left of the asylum."

I stared at the pictures of the building. It loomed in black and white, stark and cruel and twisted. I could see that much through the photos.

"How did it burn down?"

Carter let me look at the article while he opened the other scrapbook. After a moment, he pushed it back.

"A group of patients managed to overpower their guards. They killed the administrator—the son—and went on to massacre a number of their fellow patients. Some escaped, but so many were killed. They took control of the asylum. At that

point, things aren't too clear, but it looks like one of their
worst patients—Silas Johanson, who was incarcerated for
being criminally insane—went down to the boiler room. They
aren't sure what he did, but the boiler exploded and a gas main
burst, and the building went up in a massive explosion."

I stared at the outside of the asylum. Even the pictures
dripped with fury and hatred and fear, and it was hard to be
sorry the place had burned to the ground, except for the people who had been caught inside the inferno.

"How many died?"

"Three hundred fifty-seven patients, twenty-five guards,
and two dozen nurses and doctors." Carter leaned forward
and stared at me from across his desk. "They said Silas complained about voices telling him to harm the other patients.
However, he was in there for killing his mother, father, wife,
and three children. He swore the devil made him do it, and
so they tossed him in there."

"Yeah, the devil gets blamed a lot for what people do."

"We demons get a bad rap. Occasionally you get a demon
who can control others through mind tricks, but we're not
Jedi and we don't go around forcing our will on others. Not
usually." His nostrils flared.

"But a ghost . . . a ghost can drive someone nuts, can't
they?" I thumbed through the pages recording all the activity at the Greenbelt Asylum. Time and again, I saw records
saying that patients complained about voices ordering them
to do things against their will.

"Perhaps, if the person is prone to control." One of Carter's cats jumped on the desk and he absently stroked her
long, fluffy fur.

"Aegean, right? Delilah and Camille told me."

"Yes, they are Aegean. This one is Roxy. The other is
Lara, and the third—a newcomer—I named Zhivago." He
paused to remove the cream-colored cat from his desk, then
returned to musing over the clippings. "I don't think this was
the beginning of the hauntings in that district, though it certainly contributed to it. But there has to be more. I will
research and let you know what I can find."

It seemed like that was plenty to me, but I didn't argue.

"Do you have the time? I hate to put you out." I genuinely liked Carter, though he frightened me sometimes. I think he frightened all of us.

He shrugged. "Time? What is time? I have more time than most of the world, my dear Menolly. I might as well fill it productively."

As I stood, I suddenly felt sorry for him. He seemed lonely, but I didn't want to say anything to exacerbate the issue, or—worse—to make him think I was interested. He was definitely attractive, and he'd take on a demon no problem, let alone a vampire. Maybe *that* was the problem. Whoever his partner was would end up being the vulnerable one.

"Do you ever . . . if you are ever in our neighborhood . . . We always have plenty for dinner." I wasn't sure what I was asking but he just laughed, softly.

"Oh Menolly, I do not travel much—not via modern conveniences. And I never *drop in*. I am an old-school gentleman when it comes to proper decorum, if you haven't noticed. It is only in . . . private . . . that I wear the ringmaster's hat." The emphasis told me all I needed to know about his personal preferences. As he stood, I hastily stumbled back.

Carter noticed, of course, and he held out his hand for mine. "Do not be alarmed. I am a gentleman with all of my guests. If I may speak frankly, my paramours, perhaps, are of another flavor. They must have a taste for the . . . exotic. But trust me, you and your sisters will only receive the most proper behavior from me."

As I gave him my hand, he brushed the top of my hand with a light kiss and pressed close to me, so that I could feel the steady pulse of his blood through his clothing. "Do not feel sorry for me, Menolly. I need no pity from anyone. I am content in my life, and I have my friends and lovers. Count yourself lucky you are among the former and not the latter." And with that veiled warning, he escorted me to the door and waved me into the night.

As I turned to my Jag, I let out a strangled cry and the door flew open again. "What is it? Are you all right up there?"

My eyes glazing over with anger, I whirled back to him. "No! Somebody keyed my Jag!" There was a long scratch gouged in the paint of my Jaguar, and I was pissed out of my mind.

Carter shook his head. "It can't be. I have the wards strong—wait."

He closed the door, and a moment later, when he came out again, the horns had vanished. I knew he'd simply cloaked them, but he made a striking-looking man without the head-gear. He made his way up the stairs, somewhat stiffly, but I had the feeling it was more for show than anything else.

"Well, obviously they aren't working right now. What the hell happened?"

Closing his eyes, Carter reached out one hand. After a moment, he let out a low guttural sound that could have been either a growl or a warning. Or both.

"I don't know, but the wards have been broken. I'll find out and call you. Something is on the move, and I don't like what it seems to be bringing to town." He slid his hand into his back pocket and brought out his wallet. "I'll pay for your car to be repaired, of course."

"No need." I didn't want to hold him responsible—I had assumed it would be safe because it always was, but it wasn't his fault the wards had been broken.

"Nonsense. Here's my accountant's card. Get an estimate and we'll make arrangements. I'll let him know. And Menolly . . ." He paused.

"Yes?"

"Be cautious and tell your sisters to be careful. There's mischief afoot. I'll call you tomorrow night with what I've found. Or your sisters. Either way, I'll try to have more information for you by then."

And with that, he nodded gravely, turned, and went back inside. I heard the tumblers of his locks click, and it occurred to me that if the son of a demoness and a Titan felt the need to lock his door, we were facing something very big, and very unhealthy.

The Wayfarer was jammed. Derrick Means, my werebadger bartender, was shooting out drinks as fast as the orders came in. He was working out really well. Derrick was talented, sober, and able to take care of troublemakers. And he knew how to use a shotgun.

Almost every booth was filled, and as I looked around, I wondered when we'd gone from being a moderately success-ful bar to a happening spot. "Vampire," by People in Planes, was playing on the jukebox, and several people were dancing.

As I took a closer look, I realized that there were a number of vamps in my bar. We served bottled blood—animal—for them, but I hadn't been very popular among the bloodsucker set and I blinked. When did this happen? I'd been so busy, I'd lost track of what was going on here. And then, as I passed through, waving at people, I heard their whisperings.

Roman's consort—she's here.

She doesn't look like much. I wonder what Roman sees in her.

Look at those eyes—you can tell she wasn't ever human.

I hear she's a lesbian—

No, she's bi. I bet Roman gets to fuck her and her girlfriend.

So *that* was it. Somehow I'd gained status—of whatever sort—because of Roman, and it was starting to play out in the bar. The continual ring of the cash register told me just how well we were doing, and as I took my place behind the bar with Derrick, he gave me a quick nod.

"Meni—we need more help." He had five orders in front of him and I took over two of them.

"Why didn't you tell me earlier?" I flipped a bottle in the air and caught it, pouring three straight shots of whiskey. As I set them on the tray for Chrysandra, she shook her head.

"We not only need a second bartender, but we need at least two more waitresses if this keeps up. Afternoon shift isn't too bad, but man, around five or six, the joint's started to jump." She slid the tray onto her hand and wove through the milling throng, deftly keeping her balance.

I worked quickly, taking the pressure off Derrick. "As I said, why didn't you guys tell me?"

"You've been busy, and we know that it's something big, though I'm not sure what it is. But this started about three weeks ago. I'm not sure what spurred the increase, but the Wayfarer is one of the hot spots now. And every room in the bed-and-breakfast end is booked up for the next four months. We've got reservations from OW up the wazoo." Derrick grunted and handed out another tray to Lena, a waitress I'd hired to help out topside, with room service for our overnight guests. I saw that they'd drafted her to the floor.

"Shit, I don't have time to interview. Derrick, you know anybody who's good, who needs a job?"

But even as I asked, a dark, swarthy vamp sidled up to the counter. "Roman says you might have some work for me?"

I'd never seen him before. "Who are you?"

"I work in Roman's household, and he suggested you might be able to use my talents. I've been bartending since 1885."

I snorted. "You don't look a day over forty."

He flashed his fangs, but there was a glint of laughter in his eye. "Good thing I was only forty-three when I was turned, and not eighty. I probably would have stepped into the sun if that had been the case."

I glanced over at Derrick. "You think you can work with another vamp around here? He'd have to be with you on the night shift."

Derrick shrugged as he poured out three martinis. "I'm the lead bartender, right? I've worked here for a while."

"Yes, you're the lead." I glanced back at the vamp. "What's your name? And you do know that I can—and will—check with Roman to make sure you're telling the truth."

He inclined his head. "You won't find anything amiss. My name is Digger."

I set down the bottle of schnapps I was about to pour. "Digger? Really?"

"I worked for a stint as a gravedigger in the twenties. Before that my name was Joe, but Digger stuck. And the Were need not worry. I won't try to steal his place, and I won't put the fang on him." Digger glanced around. "I can start right now."

"You don't even know how much I'd be paying you." I didn't like being pushed, and it felt like he was pushing. But

if Roman wanted him working here, I'd have to at least consider it.

"Roman said he'd pick up the tab for my work." Again the
fangy smile.

"Oh, he did, did he? I pay my own tabs," I muttered, but
Digger still caught it.

"Roman doesn't want the increase in business to unnerve
your staff. Think of my work here as a gift. *A present.*"

I knew that emphasis—it meant Roman wanted Digger
here, for whatever reason, and I'd play hell fighting the sug-
gestion. I decided Roman and I really needed to have a talk,
but now was not the time.

"Fine. Get back here. The rules: You follow Derrick's
lead. I don't want to hear about any problems from you.
Absolutely no drinking from any of the customers. I don't
allow any bloodwhoring in my bar. And keep your mitts off
my waitresses' tips." I slipped on an apron and hopped over
the counter. "I'll help Chrysandra for now."

Derrick motioned for Digger to step behind the counter
and showed him where everything was. As I began taking
orders, I took a closer look at the people who were hanging
out in the bar. A wave of vamps, yes, but also FBHs. And
then I saw fang marks on some of their necks. Oh *crap*, the
vamps had brought their bloodwhores with them. Delightful.
I absolutely refused to allow bloodsucking in my joint. I finished delivering my orders and told Derrick I'd be back in a
minute.

I hightailed it to my office, where I wrote up a quick
sign—I'd get a professional one made soon—that read, NO
BLOODSUCKING ALLOWED ON PREMISES. VIOLATORS WILL BE
DRAINED AND STAKED!

When I finished, I carried it out to a spot near the wall
clock, levitated up, and quite loudly pounded a nail into the
wall, then hung it up. Everyone turned to stare at me, which
was what I'd wanted. They'd see the warning sign better if I
made a racket and caught their attention.

As I lowered myself to the floor again, I caught several
dirty looks cast my way, but I just returned them with a
fangy smile. Everybody knew I wasn't above staking my

own kind. Hell, I'd staked my sire, a taboo among vamps, and now I was Roman's official consort, so they'd *better* watch their step. It suddenly occurred to me that I could get away with one hell of a lot. Of course, I wouldn't abuse the privilege, but . . . the fact might come in handy sometime.

The door opened and I turned to see Nerissa, wearing a long trench coat and heels. Shade escorted her in, then waved and headed back out the door.

I rushed over. "Is everything okay?" I pulled her into my arms, leaning up on my tiptoes to kiss her.

She wrapped her arms around me.

"Yeah. I just asked Shade to come down with me—he can drive my car home and I'll ride with you. Camille and Morio told me about what went down tonight. I just needed to reassure myself that you were safe."

Her voice was soft, her lips pressed close to my ear, and I caught a wave of her perfume and went weak in the knees.

"Come with me." I led her back to my office and shut the door, leaning against it as I turned. "I'm so sorry we haven't had much time together since I returned from Otherworld. Life's in such a jumble."

"Have you given any thought to our plans?" She dropped into a chair.

I sighed. I didn't want to discuss wedding plans right now. I straddled her lap. "I haven't had time. Why don't you just plan what you want and I'll be happy with whatever you choose for us?"

She let out an exasperated sigh. "I want us to plan it *together*. It feels like you don't really care." Pouting, she fluttered her lashes at me.

"Baby, it's not that—you know that I care. I want us to have a lovely ceremony, but I'm not good at planning these things. Camille and Delilah helped Iris with her wedding. I just showed up in what they told me to wear."

I stroked her hair back and kissed her lashes, trying to coax a smile out of her. When Nerissa was ticked, she could hold a grudge for days. And we'd already been through this five or six times already.

"Please don't be mad at me."

She ducked her head, then kissed my finger as I gently bopped her nose. "You just . . . I just want to think you're as invested in this as I am." As a tear slowly trickled down her cheek, I felt horrible.

"Sweetheart, you know how much I love you. If I could give up being Roman's consort, I would. For you, I'd do anything."

"*Roman* doesn't bother me. What bothers me is that I want you to be part of this—not just *show up*. I want you to be *part of my life*."

I cupped her chin and then slid into the chair beside her, taking her hands in mine. "Please, never think I don't want this. You *are* part of my life."

Nerissa shrugged, then sniffled. "Then why won't you tell me . . . I don't know. Can't you even decide what you want to wear to our commitment ceremony?"

I sighed, then leaned back. I liked clothes but Nerissa and Camille did my shopping, for the most part. They had bonded over fashion and makeup. But one look at Nerissa's tears told me it was time to step up, to actually make a decision.

"Okay, then." I closed my eyes, trying to picture myself at the ceremony. After a moment, an image began to shimmer into my mind. "I guess . . . I can see myself in a long violet gown, with a white cloak, and I want a bouquet of white roses and purple lilies. I want silver sandals, and I want you by my side. I don't care where we hold our ceremony, I don't care who is there, except that you're standing beside me to pledge your love."

I looked at her, then slowly raised her finger to my lips and kissed her ring. We'd exchanged bands a few months back.

She smiled, then. "You'll be so beautiful in that. My Menolly."

"If you want me to, I'll even wear my hair down for you." I'd started taking it out of the braids now and then, but somehow, it made me feel too vulnerable and I was always uncomfortable till Camille cornrowed it back. "I know you love it that way."

But Nerissa shook her head. "No. I'm pledging my heart

to you . . . and Menolly, your braids are part of you. But maybe you can change the beads out for sparkling silver ones? That would be lovely. Or green?"

I snickered. "Camille will be only too happy to help." Then, because I knew it mattered that I ask, I said, "What do you want to wear?"

Nerissa smiled through the tears. "I wanted to wait, to hear what you decided on. If you dress in violet, I'll dress in deep plum. Long, elegant. We'd better hurry the shopping, though. We don't have much time left. As far as venues, I'm afraid we've waited too long to book any place I can think of."

I stopped her fretting with another kiss. "Shush, my sweet. The perfect place will crop up and I promise you, you'll love it. You start looking for gowns tomorrow—I've told you what I want, and I trust your taste. But I do want you to promise me something else."

"What?" She sounded eager, and I realized how much my being part of the decision-making process meant to her. It really *did* matter.

"I want to throw all the pledge ceremony crap out the window and just marry you. I still have to be Roman's consort and I don't mind if you play with the boys. But we get *married*."

Nerissa gasped. Shifting in her seat, she asked, "But what about the logistics? You know . . . you're a vampire, I'm a Were. We talked about future problems . . . what about all of that?"

"Fuck it all to hell. Let's just stop dancing around vocabulary and you just fucking become my wife. *On our terms, in our way, by our rules.*"

And then, as she teared up again, I pulled her to me, my lips against hers. As I shifted, our kiss became deeper and she moaned in my mouth. She reached for my blouse, unbuttoning it from the top, and her hands sought my breasts. I didn't wear a bra most of the time, and so her fingers grazed my nipples, teasing me as she thumbed them and then pinched, hard. My clit started to ache. I wanted her, wanted to stroke her, eat her out, watch her come.

Standing, I reached for the buttons on my jeans, but she

slapped my hands away and slowly unbuttoned them one by one, then slid them down my legs, stopping at eye level with my cunt. I wasn't wearing underwear either, and she leaned in, tongued me quickly, a long slash of moisture against my aching fire.

"Gods, do that again." I started to kick off my jeans, but she stopped me.

"Wait." Nerissa slowly stood and opened her coat but did not take it off. She was wearing only pink panties, a garter belt, stockings, and a push-up bra. In her heels, she looked like some wanton succubus and I found it hard to keep from tackling her right there.

But she held up one hand. "Pull up your jeans."

"Why?" I looked around. "It's so loud out front that no one will hear us."

But as she shook her head, someone knocked on the door. She motioned for me to stay put and walked over to answer it.

"You can't answer it dressed like that—" I started to say, but she opened it, peeking out. A second later, she stood back and swung the door open.

Confused, I quickly buttoned my jeans again. But then my confusion turned to understanding as Roman stepped through the door. His gaze glittered as he first looked at Nerissa, and then at me.

"My limousine is waiting, ladies." His voice was like silk over satin, smooth and delicious.

Nerissa smiled, graciously, and tied the belt of her coat, wrapping herself up again. She slipped her arm through mine and kissed me on the lips, then the neck. "I'm ready, willing, and able," she said.

"I can see that, most delightfully." Roman's nostrils flared.

Nerissa straightened her shoulders. "I warn you. Menolly is my fiancée. And no matter what relationship you have with her, that will not change. She's going to be my wife. But she is only your *mistress*. Do you understand?"

Roman bowed, flourishing his hand toward the door. "Understood. And understand this . . . I would not change your relationship for the world. It would hurt both of you. I simply want to taste a part of it, to be a small part of it. Even if only for one night out of a thousand."

I still hadn't found my tongue as we walked out of my office and to the front door. I didn't know if I couldn't think of anything to say, or if I was afraid of *what* I might say. So I said nothing at all.

Chapter 11

✺✦✺

As we headed into the night, I suddenly realized what was happening.

"Nerissa, you don't have to do this. I won't let him coerce you." A slow panic was starting to rise. "I won't let anybody use you!"

"On the contrary, my sweet. Nerissa is the one who called *me*." Roman motioned to his bodyguard, who opened the door to the long stretch limo for us. He waited for us to climb in, watching me expectantly.

Nerissa stepped in and slid across the seat. She patted the place next to her and I climbed in. Roman followed and his driver shut the door. As we headed into the night, a funny feeling settled in my stomach. Butterflies? Moths to the flame? I wasn't sure.

I turned to Nerissa, ignoring Roman. "Are you sure? Are you sure you want to do this?"

She shrugged. "The only thing I've ever been sure about is my love for you. Men come and go—they're nothing to me." Pausing, she leaned around me to smile at Roman. "No offense, Roman, but seriously, pussy's my first love. But I think you're right. Since we have to share Menolly, we need to come to an understanding, and this may be the way."

Roman gave a little shrug. "No offense taken, Mistress Nerissa. As I said, I am content to watch. If you invite me to join, I'll be more than happy to oblige, but I would never pressure either of you to participate in something uncomfortable."

I closed my eyes and leaned back against the seat. This was so not how I'd intended to spend the evening. And I wasn't sure how I felt about the prospect. In fact, I was quickly reaching the point where I'd rather go fight a few ghosts than get through the next few hours.

We fell into an amiable silence. Roman offered Nerissa some champagne and she shook her head without answering. *Good girl,* I thought. *Keep your wits about you. Especially when dealing with someone as old and powerful as Roman.*

As we approached his mansion, I tensed, but Nerissa laid one hand on my arm and winked at me. She seemed almost . . . eager. Maybe I'd misjudged her desire? But no, she'd made it clear that she wasn't all that interested in playing with male vamps.

Roman escorted us out of the limo and his bodyguard walked us up to the door, where one of his servants met us. I handed her my coat—Roman was a stickler for decorum— and then Nerissa slipped off her coat, gaining a surprised look of delight from the maid. I moved closer to my girl, and then, pausing, I turned to Roman.

"As long as we're in your house, where there may be other vamps, I need a ribbon for her throat." I gave Roman a long look. "You know why."

He nodded, turning to the maid. "Bring a guest ribbon, please. I think . . . pale pink suits her."

As the maid slipped over to a sideboard and withdrew a long pink velvet ribbon, Nerissa gave me a questioning look. I took the ribbon from Roman and gently tied it around her neck with the bow to the right, making sure it wasn't too tight.

"What's this for?"

"Turned to the right, it means only the boys may ask

permission to play with you. I'm not letting any female vamps touch you. And it will also ensure your safety. It basically means you're my pet for the evening. I did this to Delilah once . . . when we raided the Fangtabula—this was before I was in love with you, Roman." I waited for his reaction. I didn't know if he knew about our involvement or not.

"So, you're the one who caused such an uproar. Why am I not surprised?" He shrugged, his gaze running from Nerissa to me, then back to her. "The ribbon looks lovely and yes, every vampire under my roof will respect what it means. I guarantee with my word."

As Nerissa stood there in her bridal-night get-up, a surge of possessiveness swept over me. I wanted to wrap her up in her coat and take her home. But she was here of her own free will, and I couldn't play protector all the time. I had to trust that she knew what she was doing.

Roman led us to a side room I'd never before been in. While I might be his consort, I didn't live under his roof, nor did I have leave to explore every room—and I didn't pry. I assumed there were things I didn't want to know about hidden behind those closed doors that protected Roman's life.

The room was filled with Roman's overindulgent penchant for Victoriana, to the point of being suffocating. But it was pretty, I'd have to give him that. Two fainting couches sat at right angles to an ornate coffee table, and the room was a mishmash of velvets and jacquards and brocades. In a way, he and Carter had a lot in common, but Carter was more minimalist.

Nerissa must have been reading my mind. "You certainly don't go for a minimalist approach, do you? How can you breathe in here?"

He laughed. "I have no need to breathe. And yes, I realize that my tastes are, perhaps, from another era. But this is my home, and so . . ." Shrugging again, he glanced at me and I could tell that this wasn't going quite how he'd planned.

She laughed and draped an arm around my neck. "No problem—I didn't mean to make you uncomfortable. It is lovely, it's just not my taste at all. I feel rather claustrophobic."

I blinked. Nerissa did her best to be diplomatic at all

times. I had no clue what was getting into her, unless she was trying to turn Roman off.

She leaned down and pressed a long kiss against my lips and I returned it, sinking into her soft, beautiful body. Her skin was soft as silk sheets, and I rubbed my face against her arm, unable to do anything but respond.

Roman cleared his throat and sat back. I looked over at him. He edged into a wing chair, his gaze fastened on us, his fangs slowly lowering. I met his gaze and did not see what I expected to see. I'd expected a haughty look, superior, but instead what I saw was desire. Hunger, but not predatory. *And loneliness.*

Faltering, I slipped my arms around Nerissa, kissing between her breasts, then kneeling to gently press my lips to her belly button. I stayed like that for a moment, until she reached down and took my hand, motioning for me to stand. She looked over at Roman and I guess she saw what I saw, because she softened. She leaned down and kissed my forehead, then my nose, then my lips, but chastely, as she stroked my cheek.

She turned to Roman and gave him a soft smile. "This is what you want, isn't it? You aren't just looking to get off on a threesome. That sort of thing bored you years ago. What you're looking for . . ."

He stared at her, his expression darkening. "Don't say it, girl."

It hit me like a ton of bricks. Roman had told me he was falling for me, and I'd warned him not to. He'd been married a number of times over the years . . . so many years. And he'd lost most of his wives to death—most of them hadn't been vampires. The ones that were, got bored and moved on. He wanted someone to be with, to the end.

"Roman, please . . . don't hope." *Don't make me hurt you. Don't make me tell you I don't love you.*

"I know," he said, slowly. "But . . . the two of you . . . you have something that perhaps I can touch, for even a moment. A flower, both fragile and yes, stronger than steel." He moved to stand, but then paused. "If you wish me to leave, I will excuse myself."

I looked at Nerissa. It was her choice. She stood silent, for a moment, then walked over, slowly, to Roman.

"Come." She held out her hand. He studied it a moment, then turned it over and brushed her wrist with a kiss. "Come with us."

As he stood, hesitant, she leaned in and kissed him on the cheek. "We can never give you what you want most, but we can give you the next best thing." She reached down, untying the belt of his smoking jacket and slipping it off.

I took off my boots, then pulled off my shirt and jeans. Naked, I crossed the room to the sofa where they were sitting. Nerissa lightly caressed his shoulder and he seemed at a loss for words—something that Blood Wyne's son never had a problem with.

As I slid onto the sofa behind him, spreading my knees to press my breasts against his back, I began to kiss his neck, his back, and wrapped my arms around his waist. He moaned lightly as I tickled his abs with my fingers, and turned his head to smile at me with those icy gray eyes. He kissed me softly.

Nerissa's eyes lit up and she knelt in front of him. She pressed her breasts against his legs as she reached for the zipper on his pants. As he reached down to run his fingers through her hair, she gently coaxed his cock to attention. He was thick, and pulsating, and Nerissa reached out and squeezed, hard enough to make him tense. As she lowered her mouth to the tip of his cock, I began to kiss his neck in earnest, not quite biting—we didn't dare do blood sports because of Nerissa—but nipping him enough to produce a ripple through his body.

Nerissa embraced the head of his cock with her mouth. Roman groaned again. As I watched her luscious lips and tongue began to work him, the fire began to grow within me. She was gorgeous, pale and pink against the darkness of his world, and all I could think about was tasting her.

I let go of him and slipped around to the front, where I sat on the floor in front of his chair. I tipped my head back so I was staring into her pussy, and then, leaning up, began running my tongue over her clit. Nerissa let out a loud sigh, her mouth filled full with Roman's girth. I began to tongue-bathe her, and slid three fingers inside the moist wetness between her legs. She squirmed against me, as she bobbed up and down on Roman's cock, moving faster and faster. Roman did not breathe, nor pant, and I wondered if that seemed strange to her but then again, we'd been together for a while now, and neither did I.

But then he clutched her hair with both hands, and I could see he was holding himself back, trying not to hurt her, and in another moment, as I fluttered my tongue over her clit, he came, loud and crying out. He pulsed in her mouth, and I watched as clear liquid ran down the sides of her cheeks. She swallowed, draining him dry, then turned to me, and I tipped her over on her back, on the floor, my head between her legs, holding her by the waist.

"Menolly, oh harder, please, harder." She was bucking, as I gave her what she wanted, what she craved.

I rose up, shaking my braids back from my face. "Baby, you love this, don't you?" As she cried out *"Yes,"* I went back down, coaxing her, cajoling her, bringing her to the verge and then hanging back. I slid two fingers inside her and she clamped down, squeezing hard as I tickled her G-spot until I got a response.

As Nerissa gave a little shriek, Roman swung around behind me and the next moment, he was thrusting himself inside me, hard and demanding. The feel of his cock filling me full, of his balls swinging against my ass, sent me soaring, and the knowledge that Nerissa's lips had been on him, that he'd been in her mouth, made everything that much more exciting. I worked Nerissa, worked her good, and as she came, shrieking, Roman came again, spurred on by her cries.

He rolled away, to the side, spent. As he lay on the floor, his head turned to the side as he watched us, Nerissa moved up to lay me back. She covered my face with kisses, as her fingers traced over my breasts.

And then, the world fell away, Roman included, as we focused on each other. Touching, teasing, persuading, tongue against skin, lips against breasts, legs entwining, her fingers tickling my stomach, until the room was filled with a sex haze so thick you could cut through it with a knife.

There was no end to me, no beginning to her. We moved as one, knowing each other so intimately, so intently, that every touch resonated through both of us, every kiss rocked the room. And then, the kindling caught a spark, and we were up, like a rocket, riding our passion. The world around us could have ended, and we would never have noticed.

I rested my head on her shoulder, still flush with the warmth of her love. Nerissa softly combed through my hair with her fingers, then traced down my arm to my hand, embracing it, threading her fingers between mine.

I murmured a soft *"I love you"* as everything came back into focus. And then I realized where we were. As I slowly sat up, Nerissa following suit, I looked around. Roman was gone.

"When did he leave?" He wasn't anywhere in the room.

"I have no clue." Nerissa stretched, a luxurious expression on her face. She wrapped her arms around her legs, hugging her knees to her chest. "This was . . . different. But not bad. Not nearly what I expected."

"Me either." I leaned against her shoulder. "How did you know?"

"Know what?" She shivered, and I grabbed a throw off one of the fainting couches and draped it around her shoulders.

"That Roman is lonely. I didn't see it. I had no clue. I thought he just wanted . . ." But I stopped. He'd made gestures before, said things that caught me off guard. Maybe I *had* known, but hadn't wanted to see it, because once something became apparent, it meant I had to deal with it.

"I think I knew at the VA meeting, when he was watching us. On the way home, we talked. He said . . . he started talking about our wedding, and that led to me asking about his weddings. He didn't say much, but then he looked at me and said, *'There can never be enough love in the world. I'm so glad Menolly has you.'* And he sounded lost, like a little boy out in the rain who doesn't know where his home is."

It was hard to imagine Roman saying that, but then again,

Nerissa was a counselor. She brought out the confidential side in people.

I nodded. "If I showed the slightest move to being his mistress instead of just his official consort, he'd jump on it." I stood, wrapping my arms around my shoulders. I really wanted a shower. Glancing at the clock, I saw that it was close to four A.M. We'd have to be leaving soon.

"I know he would, too. I see the way he looks at you. Menolly, honey, he doesn't want me. This was never about *me*. Which is why I suggested tonight. It's about what you and I have together, and what he doesn't have. He needed to see it for himself. To prove to himself that . . . that what we have is real. That he'll never come between us. But Roman, thank the gods, is too much of a gentleman to move in and force the issue."

I nodded. "Yeah, he is. Maybe he still has more feelings— emotion—than I give him credit for. Vampires tend to lose their humanity through the years. Some manage to keep it, but it takes nurturing. Roman's done very well, but I thought . . . I didn't think . . . he'd ever be interested in that side of life again. Sex is one thing . . . love, quite another."

At that moment, the door opened and a maid came in. She curtsied. "Lord Roman offered the use of his bath if you'd like to shower. He's indisposed, but he bids you take the limousine home, and he also asked me to give you this." She held out a box wrapped in gold paper, with a large bow. "He said to tell you that it's fragile, so please, be careful with it."

I slowly took the box and peeked at the card.

Menolly and Nerissa—please accept this token of my esteem in light of your coming marriage. I regret that I shall not be able to attend. But thank you, for an evening well spent. Menolly, I will always and forever remain your humble paramour.—R

"A wedding gift." I frowned, tapping the card against the package. "Let's go home and shower there. The Wayfarer is closed, so we'll just grab the Jag there and take off."

Nerissa looked like she wanted to ask something, but I

shook my head. I was getting a seriously weird feeling, and I wanted out of Roman's place. She gave me a nod and we hurried into our clothes.

The limo driver dropped us off by the Jag and waited for us to get in and make sure everything was in working order, and then he took off back to Roman's as we pulled out and headed home.

"What was it you wanted to ask?" I glanced at Nerissa as she leaned back against the seat. She was used to clubbing half the night, so I knew she wasn't too worn out, although she did look tired. But I sensed something was bothering her.

"We haven't even sent out invitations for our wedding. Roman passed, not even knowing when it would be. Why do you think so?"

That little fact hadn't escaped my notice, either. "I have no clue, and I'm not sure I want to. But . . . I'm thinking . . . I don't know. No, I don't even want to speculate. Roman could have a thousand reasons for saying what he did, and I'd rather not assume. It's dangerous to assume with vampires."

"Yeah, I suppose. Just . . . the energy shifted, babe. By the time we left, I was totally creeped out. What happened? And why? And why do I never want to darken the inside of his house again?"

I didn't answer as she turned her head to gaze out into the darkness. As we sped through the rain and mist rising off the asphalt, with the glittering rain splashing in the headlights, a dozen thoughts raced through my head, none of them pleasant to dwell on.

I went wandering in my dreams again, out on the Dream-Time, cloaked in mist and a burgundy hooded robe. I wasn't looking for Roman—in fact, I didn't want to see him at all for a while. Luckily, there were no official events coming up any time in the next few weeks.

As I skirted mist and rock, I tried to figure out why I was here. Sometimes I just dreamed, usually nightmares. And some days I slept in oblivion, blissfully unaware until the sunset called to me.

But when I went wandering out on the Dream-Time, there was usually a reason. I came to a boulder and sat down, waiting for some answer to come to me—a sign, or even just a tap on the shoulder.

The tap on the shoulder shocked the hell out of me, for two reasons. One, I really wasn't expecting it, and two, it was a *real* tap on the shoulder and Chase was on the other end of the finger.

"Chase!" I jumped up. "What the hell are you doing out here on the Dream-Time?"

He was wearing a pair of dark jeans and a sports jacket, and his hair looked tousled, as if he hadn't brushed it in a while. "I have no clue. Something must be wrong because I was sitting at my desk a little while ago and now I'm here and I have no memory of going home, or going to bed."

"Pull up a rock and sit down." I motioned to the space on the boulder next to me. At least, if I had to be stuck out here, I had company. "Can't you just wake up or something? I can't, but . . . you're human."

"Human with not so much elf in him?" He grinned. When I looked confused, he sighed and leaned back on his elbows. "Oh come on, you've been over here this long and you haven't seen Monty Python? The rat skit?"

Again, I shook my head. "TV is Delilah's department."

"Never mind; if I have to explain the joke, it's not funny." He sighed and then sat upright again. "I feel like I should be remembering something, but it's not coming to me."

"I know—only for me, I feel like I should be finding something out, and I have no clue what it is." I paused, then decided, what the hell, since we were here, we might as well shoot the bull. "How's Sharah?"

"About the same. Crying a lot. Throwing up a lot. She and Iris are getting together to talk all things baby. Oh, she asked me this morning to pass along the info that Siobhan Morgan has left for the Isle of Man. She and Mitch need to get over there early enough before the baby is due. They left last week."

I nodded. "I'm not down much with the baby thing, but I'm glad to hear she actually gets to do that. I can't believe it's been this long already since we helped her. That was a rough time . . . for both her and Mitch."

Last year, shortly before the fall equinox, we'd helped a friend who had been stalked by an enemy of more than a hundred years. Now she was off to the Isle of Man Selkie Pod to have her baby and to reclaim a royal lineage.

"I hope she comes back. I hope she doesn't stay there." I paused, then drew swirls in the mist with my fingers. "So much has changed."

"You can say that again." Chase kicked a loose stone on the ground. "For Siobhan. For all of us."

I wasn't bored, but I was getting confused. What the hell were we doing out here? Especially Chase, who should be awake, at his desk. I stood up and dusted off the back of my robe. It was also confusing—I didn't own a burgundy robe and had never even contemplated owning one. I could change my clothes at will out on the Dream-Time, since it was only my dream-self here, but I usually picked something that was more akin to my nature.

I turned back to ask Chase whether Carter had contacted him but stopped cold. Chase was slumped over on the boulder. I raced back to him.

"Chase, Chase!"

His head lolled to the side and I saw claw marks on his neck. Fuck! What the hell had happened?

"Chase, wake up! Can you hear me? Chase!" I shook him, pulling him up to a seated position, but he was out good.

"What the fuck do I do? Is anybody out here? Can anybody hear me?"

I didn't like calling attention to myself on the Dream-Time, but I couldn't wake up in order to get help, and it was obvious that Chase was in some sort of a crisis. I thought quickly. Who could hear me out here? And where was *out here*? I had no clue how to contact anybody.

Chase moaned and began to shake. I went down on my knees beside him and tried to take hold of him, to keep him from hitting his head on the ground. Logically, I knew that he wasn't here in body, but I couldn't help it—I had to do something. As he thrashed, I wondered what the hell was going on with him. Was there anybody on the way who might be able to hear me? If he was unconscious, maybe they'd send somebody out to the Dream-Time for him.

And then, I jumped as a crash sounded behind me. I whirled around, still holding Chase in my arms. A creature was aimed right at us. It was nebulous, as translucent as the mist itself, looking very much like a jellyfish. As it neared, I moved to place myself between it and Chase.

The thing paused, then moved to the right, several of its tendrils drifting out toward Chase. I moved with it, interfering with its goal. As one of the tentacles touched me, I felt a little spark but nothing more. Maybe it wasn't dangerous? Maybe it was just curious?

But then it moved to the left, more aggressively, and I had the gut feeling that if it reached Chase, he'd be in serious trouble. More than he already was. I launched myself and tried to land a strike, but my foot went right through it. I did, however, get a nice tingling shock down my leg. What the hell? It could touch me, but I couldn't touch it?

"Play fair, bitch!" I was darting now, as its tentacles swept this way and that, attempting to reach beyond me to grab Chase. He lay there, unconscious, paling as the minutes passed. Great, I was playing keep-away with a freaking jellyfish and Chase was the ball.

I was starting to run out of ideas, and the creature was growing more aggressive, when another voice rang out—one I recognized.

"Menolly!" Vanzir raced through the mist, toward me. He looked intact, however—solid in a way neither Chase nor I were. He had leaped onto the Dream-Time in body, not an easy feat. But, for a dream-chaser demon, easy enough, I supposed.

"Vanzir—help me! Chase is in trouble." I dodged again, trying to cover Chase's ass, but the jellyfish landed all its tentacles on me and sent me reeling. No more little shocks, but one long, intense racking pain.

As it sailed past me toward Chase, Vanzir launched himself, landing in its path. He held out his hands and tendrils appeared. They were wormlike, neon ribbons that filtered out from his palms, eerie and alive and writhing.

"Your powers—you've got your powers back!" I watched, mesmerized as the tendrils sank into the body of the jellyfish and began to feed on its energy. The thing shifted then, no longer a jellyfish but the vague shape of a human, though far more nebulous. No features showed, only gaping sockets where there would be eyes. But it was hungry, and it wanted Chase.

"You betcha, babe. Only I'm in control now—I no longer have the need to feed. But oh, it feels so good." He closed his eyes, cackling as he siphoned the energy off the creature. It began to shrivel and fade, and then was gone.

Vanzir turned to me. "Surprised to see you out here, babe."

"How did you know what was happening?"

"We were down at HQ, discussing a few things about last night. I went along to get out of the house, and I also wanted to drop in on Carter. He called for us to come over—he told us about your visit last night." He eyed me up and down. "Don't ever think about fucking with him, girl. He could tear you to bits and probably would. It may not show, but he likes it rough."

"He actually talked to you about that part of our conversation?"

"Demons stick together."

"Well, trust me, the possibility didn't cross my mind." I stared at him. "Get on with it. What's going on with Chase?"

"Anyway, we got a call from Sharah that something was going on and we headed over there. By the time we got there, Chase was unconscious. We could tell he was being drained. Somehow, he must have thrust his spirit over here to the Dream-Time. He's getting damned good at that. But I could sense something had latched onto him and was sucking away his energy. So I came over to see if the leech was on this side of the veil. Apparently it wasn't, but whatever that thing was, it was ready to feed, too." He paused. "What are you doing here?"

"I don't know, to be honest. Sometimes I find myself on the Dream-Time when I'm sleeping. I think, maybe, I came here because Chase needed me. Maybe he called me out here somehow. What the hell was that thing?" I looked at the wispy remains of the jellyfish creature, which was now a mere shadow, floating on the breeze.

"It sure as hell isn't something you'd find on a *Nova* special, regardless of what it looks like. It must be some sort of spirit." He paused. "It's not a Karsetii demon, but there was a similar feel."

I shook my head. This felt all too familiar. "Hungry ghosts?"

"Maybe . . . or maybe an offshoot of them. And ten to one, whatever it is, it's out and about thanks to Gulakah. By the way, I heard about your adventures in spookland last night. Delightful." He sighed. "Well, I'd better hop off the Dream-Time and see how Chase is doing. By the way, this— my powers returning? Very recent. The Triple Threat had something to do with it, though I'm not sure exactly what. But we'll talk about that later. Bye, wench. Sleep well."

Before I could stop him, he plastered a kiss on my nose, then winked and vanished, along with Chase. I stood there, staring at them as they faded, wishing I could wake up, too. As I meandered around the boulders, I wondered—had Chase really managed to call me out? I'd been able to keep that freak show tentacle monster from sucking his life force out until Vanzir had been able to get here.

And if Chase *had* summoned me, what the hell was he evolving into? Even the little bit of elf in him couldn't account for some of the changes going on. But then again, humans had their own type of magic, and we knew next to nothing about the rest of Chase's family.

As I stared up into the misty skies of the Dream-Time, I felt myself fading. The next thing I knew, it was sunset, and time to rise. I slipped from beneath my covers and once again, dressed to face the endless night.

Chapter 12

❦

As I entered the kitchen, it was eerily quiet. I looked around, but there was only silence. I'd never gotten up when some-body wasn't cooking something or eating something or arguing in the kitchen.

Worried, I headed into the living room, looking for signs that somebody might be around. The living room was quiet, too. Where the hell were my sisters? The guys? Iris? Maggie and Hanna?

A peek into the parlor showed it was empty, too.

"What the fuck?" I dashed upstairs, poking my head into Delilah's room. Nothing. As I slowly descended to the second floor, a sound from Camille's study caught my attention. I quickly opened the door. No one was around, but the Whispering Mirror was making noises.

I sat down in front of it and spoke the password. The mirror shimmered and—in place of the reflection of the empty room, since I couldn't see myself in mirrors—Trenyth's image appeared.

"Who's there? Menolly, is that you?" He squinted, staring at his mirror.

I nodded. "Yes, it's me. I'm sorry, the entire house seems to be empty and I have no clue where everybody went. I was just headed downstairs to look for them. What's up?"

He cleared his throat. "Quall and the others are headed by caravan to Rhellah. They arrived in Ceredream just in time to sign on for a caravan. They should arrive in Rhellah in a few weeks. I thought I'd just update you on matters."

I studied his expression. Since nobody else was around to shut me up, I decided to ask a few of the more indelicate questions I'd been mulling over. "Tell me the truth. Can we trust Quall? I know what you said in conference, but, seriously, we need to know."

Trenyth looked over his shoulder, then turned back to the mirror. "Don't trust him if you're alone with him. He's cruel, and he's vindictive, and he takes delight in the pain of others. But truly, he *is* on our side. He's out for his father's blood, and he's got the best reason in the world to back up Queen Asteria—he owes her his life and she made sure he knew that from the beginning. That's all I can say for now."

I nodded. "We've got problems over here. We're not sure if they're all tied together or not." But before I could tell him about what had gone down, he darted another look over his shoulder.

"I'm being summoned. Her Majesty needs me. I'll talk to you soon, Menolly." And with that, the Whispering Mirror went dark.

I stared at the mirror, seeing only Camille's study reflected behind me. Might as well go figure out where everybody was hiding. I dashed downstairs and did another run through of the house, but nobody was there.

Seriously worried, I headed out onto the porch and into the driveway. Most of the cars were there, and I could hear some commotion out back. I raced around the house, readying myself for a fight, but stopped when I saw the trailer parked in the back yard. Iris and Bruce's temporary home had arrived!

Smoky, Trillian, and Vanzir were hooking up wires and whatnot, and the door was open. I paused next to Vanzir, who squatted beside the trailer, installing what looked like a jury-rigged Internet cable.

"You guys might have left a note for me so I wouldn't freak out, thinking you'd all been captured or something equally hideous."

"Eh, we knew you'd figure it out pretty soon." He set down the wrench he was holding and stood, arching his back. "You get back okay from the Dream-Time?"

"Yeah. I was going to ask . . . so you *were* there? And Chase? How is he, and why isn't anybody there with him? What's going on? I expected a note, asking me to rush down to the FH-CSI. In fact, when I didn't find one, I was beginning to think maybe it really was just a dream."

He shook his head. "No, unfortunately. As for why no note, Camille asked me to send you down to HQ when you woke up. She's down there right now, with Delilah, Shade, and Morio. The rest of us are helping Iris get her trailer ready."

"Where's Maggie?" I looked around. "I can imagine how much help she's being."

"Hanna took her for a walk in her stroller. That woman thinks everybody should live on fresh air and exercise." He grinned, though. Hanna had managed to win over everybody in the house.

"Alone?" I glanced around. "What about—"

"No, don't worry. Roz is with her, and one of the elfin guards." He gave me a reassuring nod, which, coming from Vanzir, wasn't all that reassuring.

"I'll head out for the station, then." I turned to go, then, stopping, looked over my shoulder. "Say, are Roz and Hanna . . ."

"Have they hooked up?" Vanzir snickered. "I'm surprised it took you so long to ask. Let me put it this way, they've become friends . . . with benefits. I doubt if Hanna wants to involve herself emotionally with an incubus, and Rozurial knows better than to break her heart."

"Thanks. Just curiosity." As I headed back to the house, I felt unaccountably glad that Roz and Hanna had managed to find some sort of companionship together. Hanna needed someone to remind her she wasn't just a servant, and Roz . . . well . . . Roz just needed women who enjoyed his company, since there was no way he could have the one woman who seemed to have touched his heart since Zeus had turned him.

I reached the FH-CSI in record time, breaking every speed limit in the city. But luckily, no cops were on duty and traffic was light. As soon as I entered the waiting room, I caught sight of Delilah, Shade, Morio, and Camille. Delilah rose, letting out a little cry and reaching for me. I hugged her tight.

"What's going on? How's Chase? I got the news from Vanzir. Did he tell you I was there last night?" I took a seat next to Camille and leaned back. We didn't look to be going anywhere soon.

"Chase is . . . holding his own but he's still in a coma." Delilah pressed her lips together and stared at her feet.

"What happened? The last thing I remember is that Vanzir was feeding off some spirit that was trying to siphon away Chase's life force." Hesitating, I glanced over at Morio.

"It's all right, you can talk about it. I know what the hungry ghosts can do, trust me. You know I understand that. But these aren't the same thing. They're . . . worse, I think." He sucked in a deep breath and let it out slowly.

"They're definitely nothing to mess with. What I saw on the Dream-Time last night was like a monster in its natural form. If that was its natural form." I explained to them what had happened. "So what did Sharah say about Chase? Or is she too close to the situation to take care of him?"

Delilah frowned. "Mallen won't let her tend to him. For one thing, with her pregnancy, she's far too vulnerable should something go wrong. And if something happens to Chase, she's too involved and it might hurt the baby. Mallen's been keeping her busy tending to minor bumps and bruises from some of the Fae coming through here."

"Have you been in to see him?" I wasn't good with bedside visits, but Chase was our friend and I didn't like just sitting around.

"Mallen hasn't let us go in yet. He's . . ." Delilah broke off as Mallen entered the room. Elfin, he looked young, but probably was older than any of us except for the dragons. Mallen was well into his prime. He'd managed to settle into working with Sharah. He was making a home for himself Earthside.

"You can see him now. I haven't let Sharah go back yet. I was hoping, if you can sense anything . . . I'm at a loss for what's happening." He worried his lip, then added, "His body is fine—he's fit and healthy. But the seizures did take a toll on him, although I think he can recover. As far as the coma . . . that's our problem."

We stood and followed him. Sharah was in one of the rooms we passed, attending to a young Fae woman, who looked like she was ill. She glanced up at us and nodded, but said nothing as we passed.

Chase was tucked away in a private room near the end of the hallway.

I'd been through far too much to find hospitals depressing, but when we saw him, lying there, his eyes closed as his chest rose and fell with his steady, even breath, I felt cold and alone and angry. Chase hadn't asked for what had happened to him, and here he was, a pawn in a desperate game. Or maybe it was random chance. But I was getting sick of random chance. The universe had one hell of a nasty sense of humor.

"Oh, Chase . . ." Delilah slowly moved to his left side and took one hand, while Camille took the other. It felt wrong for Sharah not to be here, but I understood Mallen's reasoning. We had to protect her, at least until we knew what we were dealing with. I glanced over at Shade. "Is there any way you can figure out what happened to him?"

Shade motioned for my sisters to move out of his way. He stood by Chase's head and motioned to me. "Turn off the lights, please. I need shadow in which to work."

Making sure all I was turning off were lights, I flipped the switch. The room dimmed, with only the blinking of the machines monitoring his blood pressure and heart rate to light our way.

Shade placed both hands on the detective's head and closed his eyes. It was hard to see what was going on, but a light began to flow between his fingers—pale violet, the color of the Netherworld, the color of death magic, the color of shades and shadows and ghosts.

I moved a step closer to Delilah, and she reached out for me. I took her hand and felt the trembling fear flow off her. Morio and Camille had joined hands and were watching intently. We stood, silent, waiting, as Shade began to fade into the thin layer of smoke that began to rise around him. It was as if his body were breaking apart into minuscule dots.

Beam me up, Scotty. The thought appeared unbidden, and I would have laughed if we hadn't been facing a crisis. Delilah gasped and clutched my hand tightly. The smoke that Shade had vanished into was infiltrating Chase's body, filtering in through his nose.

"Shade's going in search of Chase's consciousness," Camille whispered.

She looked up, silver scarring the violet of her eyes. Morio's eyes were also gleaming. Shade's magic was affecting them, bringing them in tune with what he was doing. Delilah began to waver, and her hand fell away from mine. One moment she was there, and the next, a large, sleek, black panther with a jeweled collar stood beside me. Quickly padding over to the bed, she rose up, front feet planted on the bottom of the sheets. I stepped forward, ready to grab her back if needed, but she just watched.

Camille and Morio began to whisper a soft chant, so soft I could barely hear it. Mallen stood back, watching and waiting. I forced myself to relax.

> *In through the shadows, in through the shade,*
> *Slide through the inroads we've made.*
> *Enter the psyche, open the door,*
> *Your secrets will be secrets no more.*

As I watched, a slow shimmer of silver light appeared from their breaths, flowing over Chase like a wave, rolling out to cover him fully, to settle in swirling clouds around and over his body.

After a moment, a faint voice cried out from the mist.

"I'm lost . . . help me . . ."

It was Chase, and he sounded frightened and alone. Delilah, still in panther form, leaned closer, surrounded by the swirling mist as well. Instinct made me step forward, take hold of her collar, and gently pull her away.

"You can't help right now, Kitten. Let them work. Let Morio and Camille and Shade do what they can." I knelt by her and wrapped my arms around the big fuzzy neck and crooned in her ear. She seemed anxious—hell, I *knew* she was anxious—but she listened to me and lay down. I patted her back, stroking her fur and scratching her between the ears. I knew better than just about anyone what Delilah liked when she was in cat form, and it wasn't all that much different when she shifted into her panther form.

She rumbled a broken purr, then licked me on the face. I wiped the slobber off and kissed her on the nose. "It will be all right. We'll find him. Just give them time and space."

With a slight hiccup, she rested her head on her paws and waited. I turned back to the others. Morio and Camille were now by Chase's side, their hands pressed on his heart and his forehead. Shade was still nowhere in sight.

"It's waiting for me, I can't get past it . . ." Again, the faint sound of Chase's voice, echoing through the room, but it did not come from his lips.

I glanced around. Where the hell was he and how come we were hearing him? And what was the *it* he was talking about? Vanzir and I had munched the creepshow that was after him last night.

But . . . but . . . it wasn't the thing that had *hurt* him. What I'd seen—and Vanzir had destroyed—was after him over on the Dream-Time, but it hadn't touched him yet. I'd seen to that. No, something else actually got to him. And whatever that *something* was, it still had hold of him.

And then, I saw it—a motion, a whisper of something being forced out of Chase's nose. He began to breathe hard, and I motioned for Delilah to stay where she was as I took a closer look. Whatever it was, it was wispy and wraithlike, and I knew it wasn't Shade.

Camille and Morio turned their attention to it. They

reached out, their hands joined, and plunged them into the heart of the creature. An unearthly shriek filled the air and the spirit vanished. A moment later, Chase let out a loud gasp and smoke poured from his mouth. It flowed over to the side of the bed and out of the dim shadow, Shade stepped forth.

Chase coughed, harshly, and then moaned. Mallen rushed over to him and checked his pulse and heart, then smoothed his hair back as Chase's eyes fluttered open.

"Where . . . where . . ." His voice was ragged and hoarse.

"Quiet, Chase. Rest. You're safe now." Mallen injected something into his arm, and Chase fell back into a peaceful, deep sleep. Mallen looked up at me. "I've given him a sedative. He'll sleep for a couple of hours and then wake. The drug is mild and short-acting."

Shade looked pensive. His gaze fluttered up to meet mine, and he shook his head. "Not good. Delilah, we have need of you, my pet."

Delilah began to shimmer, shifting back into her normal form. As she stood and stretched, eyes wide, Chase murmured in his sleep, but he was calmer and seemed to be resting peacefully.

"What the fuck was the thing that came out of him? And what on earth were you doing?" She gazed at him. "Is this part of your Stradolan nature?"

Shade nodded. "Partially, yes, and partially from my shadow dragon heritage. Come, let's go talk in private, where we won't disturb him." He turned to Mallen. "Can you have someone set up wards, immediately? The entire building needs to be protected from the outer planes—the Netherworld, astral, Dream-Time, and etheric. There may be more ways for them to enter, but for now that should do."

Mallen didn't ask why, just nodded crisply. "Can you stay here while I summon more help? I don't want to leave him alone."

"Hurry, then." Shade sounded worried, and when a dragon—half or otherwise—was worried, it was time for all of us to be concerned.

Mallen hurried out. Delilah was holding Chase's hand.

Camille and Morio looked as worried as Shade and I wondered what the hell they'd figured out. As for me, I was busy watching the walls for any sign of bloody ectoplasm or flying objects. Life was just too spirited anymore.

A moment later, Mallen returned with several medics and someone who reeked of magic. As I stared at her, she flashed me a quick smile, and I saw the fangs descending. Fuck, she was a vampire.

Mallen nodded for us to leave, but I wasn't ready. I motioned for the others to go, but I hung back, sidling up to the elf and the vampire.

"So, you're one of my kind." I glanced up at her—she, like just about everybody else, was taller than me.

She gave me a brief once-over and shrugged. "We both drink of the blood, but otherwise, I wager we're nothing alike." And with that rebuke, she turned to Mallen. "You wish me to begin? Please ask *her* to leave."

My feathers ruffled, I stood my ground. "I'm not leaving a vampire in here with my friend until I find out just who you are and what the fuck you're doing here. If you don't like it, we can just take it outside and shake it up, sister."

She bristled, stepping forward. "Do not tempt me. Just because Roman made you his bitch doesn't mean that you can't have an accident. You stab your sire and sit in a place of honor? I spit on your hem." As she jabbed me in the chest with her finger, I smacked her a good one, knocking her back on her butt.

Obviously, she hadn't been expecting that. "I should rip open your neck." She jumped to her feet and straightened her dress.

"Try it. See how far you get. I've got the blood of one of the most notorious vampires in history running through my veins. You really want to fuck with me?" And once again, I reached out and shoved her back.

She was just about to launch herself at me when Mallen stepped between us. "Enough. Charlotine, please—the wards." He turned to me. "Come with me—no, stop now," he added as I began to protest. "She will not harm him, I give you my word of honor."

"Your word better be etched in gold." I followed him out of the room. "What the fuck are you thinking, letting a strange vampire hang out around an unconscious FBH? Are you serious?"

Mallen took hold of my wrists as I smacked him—lightly—on the chest. "I have never seen you so hysterical. What the hell is going on with you?" His close proximity left me smelling his clean, leaf-green scent. The pulse of his blood raced through his veins; the gentle rise and fall of his chest bespoke the beating of his heart.

"Mallen, back off. Please." I waited for him to move away and quietly willed my fangs to fold back up. This thirst I'd been feeling for my friends was disconcerting and I didn't like it. "Chase is our friend. Practically family. You bring a strange vampire—who, I might add, acts like a sullen bitch—into the room with him. Not only that, but she reeks of magic. And you wonder why I'm upset?"

"That's why she's here. She's going to set up the wards to protect him. She's a very powerful sorceress and she works in Elqaneve for Queen Asteria. She happened to be over here on a vacation and I called her in. She's old, Menolly, very old, and she can be trusted even if you don't like her bedside manner."

I shook my head. "You can't trust any vampire. Not even me—not fully. Fine, let her set up her wards. But do me a favor and get your ass back in there and keep an eye on her."

Before he could answer, I turned and left.

As I strode into the waiting room, Shade motioned me over. "I know what we're facing and why Lindsey's group is feeling so lackluster. *Bhouts.*"

"Bow-uts? I've never heard of them." I looked over at Camille to see if the name meant anything to her, but she looked as confused as I was. Morio, however, was looking grave.

"Of course—I didn't even think about them because they're rare. But it makes sense. Bhouts . . . demonic ghosts. They're not fully spirit, not fully demon. They're from the Netherworld but can be used by someone from the Subterranean Realms." Morio shook his head. "We'll have to walk very carefully on this one. I seem to remember legends of Japanese emperors summoning demons to control the empire. I think we're just skimming the tip of the iceberg."

Shade sat down, elbows on knees, pressing his index fingers together. "Bhouts aren't fully of the Netherworld, either. I don't think anybody knows where they originated but they're . . . they're in the same class as doppelgangers—creatures that are conduits. They can take control of their victim. In turn, they're controlled by their master. The master controls the bhout—and by extension, their victim. They can see through the bhouts' eyes and eventually gain control over the target."

"So, the bhout is an active force used to control another?" I wasn't quite clear on the whole thing, but whatever it was, it didn't sound good.

"Not exactly. The bhout is an entity. Bhouts, when directed, can be used to control others. But it gets worse. Bhouts focus on magical or psychic energy. They feed off the magical force, not the life force. If there is no master controlling the spirit, they can kill their victims by draining them dry. It will break the silver cord."

"The elfin guards! That must be what happened to them." It was beginning to make sense now.

"Yes. However, when someone's controlling the bhout, they can command the spirit to siphon off just enough energy to keep their victim alive and under their command. That thing in there was trying to pull Chase under its control. If it had succeeded, he would have woken up and gone about his business, but he wouldn't be under his own control."

"Crap!" Delilah jumped up. "Mind control, then? Via ghostly demons?"

Shade nodded, grimly. "That's about the size of it. The bhouts feeding on Lindsey's group seem focused on trying to control them, so they've most likely been summoned in. Chances are, someone's bringing in vast numbers of them and some get free—like the ones who attacked the guards."

Camille jumped up. "Lindsey was very tired. And her coven is, too. Could these things be directly controlling them at this point?"

Shade thought about it for a moment. "Possibly. But there's also another possibility. The bhouts must feed. Since someone is summoning them here en masse, then the spirits will need to strengthen themselves. Lindsey's group is well known, but the primary targets are probably more important, like Chase. He runs the FH-CSI, and his newly awakened powers are growing, making him an attractive target."

"So meanwhile, these things can eat their fill off the people of Seattle, both Fae and FBH." Camille fell silent, then paled. "What about Morio . . . me? What should we be on the watch for? Can they attack . . . well, I guess they can attack the Fae, can't they?"

"Yeah. They find them especially juicy, so to speak. I don't think they can attack dragons or vampires, so Smoky, Menolly, and I should be safe, but Iris . . . you, Morio . . . all of the Fae out in Aeval, Titania, and Morgaine's courts? You're all in danger."

Mallen joined us then. "Did you find out what was attacking him?"

Shade regarded him quietly. "No. But we should take him with us to watch over him now that he's feeling better."

I started to say something but then shut up. Shade had his reasons for lying.

Mallen narrowed his eyes, then shrugged. "If you wish, feel free. He's not in any physical danger."

We silently followed him back to Chase's room, where the detective mumbled groggily as we woke him up. "Come on, Chase, we need to take you with us." I turned to Delilah. "Get Sharah. She should come with us, too." I looked at her pointedly, hoping she wouldn't say anything to give us away.

But she seemed to understand and left without a word. A moment later, she was back with Sharah in tow, a confused look on the Elfin medic's face. As Shade and Morio helped Chase dress, we stepped out into the hallway. Sharah started to ask something, but I shook my head.

"Wait. Please, just wait and do as we say."

"Very well. Thank you, though, for saving Chase."

Again, I just nodded. When Shade and Morio appeared, Chase leaning on their shoulders, we headed out to the cars.

As we hit the cold, crisp air, Camille and Delilah shivered. I glanced at them.

"Put Chase in my Jag. Shade, you go with Camille and Morio. Delilah, can you take Sharah, please?"

While they arranged the drugged detective in the backseat of my Jaguar, I pulled Shade off to one side. "How do we know these bhouts haven't gotten hold of Sharah or Mallen?"

"We don't, which is why I'll have to check her out. But I don't want to alert Mallen, in case he's being controlled. It's odd enough for us to remove Chase from the hospital, but right now we've told him we don't know what's causing the problem. They may—or may not—believe us. But it buys us a little time. Now let's head out."

He was about to head over to Camille's Lexus when my phone rang. I pulled it out and punched the Talk button.

Iris's voice came breathless over the line. "Menolly, we have a serious problem here. Can you come home right away?"

"What's going on?" A cold fright took hold of my stomach. *Please, don't let demons be invading the land again.* They'd come through at one time and torn the place to hell and gone. Iris had been lucky to escape with her life.

"The backyard is filled with will-o'-the-wisps. Bruce and I are stuck in the trailer. Hanna's in the house with Maggie and Vanzir—he's watching over them. Trillian, Roz, Shamas, and Smoky are trying to figure out where they're coming from and what to do about them." She sounded frightened.

"Hang tough. We're on our way. Do you have any idea what brought them out or where they're coming from?" I motioned to Delilah before she and Sharah took off. Camille and Morio were still waiting for Shade.

Iris's voice was shaking. "No, they started to show about an hour ago and now, the yard is filled with them. Bruce and I had just come out to the trailer when they started appearing. I've dealt with them before. I know better than to go outside when they're out there—they're not good for pregnant women to be around. Bruce thought they were eye catchers at first, but I know the difference."

"We're on our way. And we're bringing a whole 'nother set of problems. Can you call the Wayfarer and tell Derrick I doubt if I'll be in tonight? And is Nerissa there?" Nerissa had gone to work, but I wasn't sure if she had returned to her condo or decided to spend the night at the house, and I hadn't thought to drop in and ask Yugi before we left the building.

"Nerissa? I haven't heard from her all day. I thought she might be with you. I'll call her now." She hung up on me and I quickly filled the others in on what we were facing.

"Will-o'-the-wisps? They usually don't come out in the cold—at least not this cold." Camille looked confused.

Will-o'-the-wisps belonged to the Fae family, pretty but tough little buggers. They were mean and dangerous, and we'd faced them once before. The results hadn't been all that pretty then either. They were also known as Corpse Candles, a delightful name.

"They're energy eaters," Morio said. "Remember when we found Aeval in the crystal, in the cave? They were after us because of our magic. The whole town seems to be overrun with psychic leeches of one sort or another." He let out a long sigh. "We'd better get a move on. I don't know what we're going to do, though. What can stop a will-o'-the-wisp?"

I frowned. "I have no idea. Maybe we should contact Aeval?"

Camille shrugged. "No phones out in Talamh Lonrach Oll. How can we get out there in time?"

I glanced over at Shade. We needed him here, and he wasn't keen on carrying people through the Ionyc Seas because of his Netherworld energy. Apparently it wasn't exactly a comfortable mix. But . . . Smoky . . .

"When we get home, you and Smoky immediately head out there through the Ionyc Seas. Meanwhile, I need to make a phone call." I didn't want to tell her I was calling Ivana Krask, because she'd blow up and argue with me, and we couldn't afford to waste time in a bitchfest.

"To whom?" Camille looked at me suspiciously.

"Never mind. We're rapidly running out of options. We've got a town overrun with ghosts, and now the will-o'-the-wisps are moving in. We need help. Just fucking trust me." I pushed her gently toward her car. "Go. And the minute you get there, you and Smoky head out."

"Menolly, be careful." But she shut up when she saw the expression on my face. "Fine. Meet you at home."

And with that, we split off to our cars. I glanced at Chase, safe in the backseat. How to get him to the house without the will-o'-the-wisps interfering would be another matter, but we'd deal with that when we got there.

I hit the steering wheel, angry, but at least I had enough restraint not to rip it off the column. "Why the fuck is this happening to us? Why can't we ever catch a break?" Not expecting an answer—and not getting one—I flipped open my phone and put in a call to Ivana Krask, the Maiden of Karask. It was the last thing in the world I wanted to do, but I couldn't see any other way out.

Chapter 13

Ivana Krask. To say she was a freak show was putting it mildly. One of the Elder Fae, she lived by her own rules and complained about the lack of "bright flesh," her chipper term for babies. Served raw. On a plate. Ivana also kept a little garden out back, a kitchen garden to which she confined the ghosts she so loved to torture. I had a feeling those were just the bare bones of her delightful antics.

She answered the phone on the second ring. What the Maiden of Karask was doing with a phone I didn't know, but some of the Elder Fae had tried to assimilate into society, if only to continue wreaking havoc on the world.

"Ivana? It's Menolly." I wondered if she'd remember me, but I needn't have worried. She remembered me just fine.

"Well, Dead Girl. What are you thinking of tonight, *meat on the hoof*?" Her tone was jolly. I must have caught her at a good time.

Rule One: Never ask the Elder Fae for favors. If you admit to asking their help, you're in their debt forever and they'll take it by the pound out of your hide.

Rule Two: Show respect. But never show fear if you want something from them. Fear would get you in deep shit.

Rule Three: Never welsh on your debts.

Rule Four: Never, ever turn your back on one of the Elder Fae.

All other rules were subject to the matter at hand. And when in doubt, throw the rules book out the window, and run like hell. Because if you have to ask what to do next, they're going to chase you down till you wish you were dead.

"Ivana, I thought you might be interested in striking a bargain. *If* you can produce results." I waited, knowing the inevitable response.

"*Bright flesh?* You have bright flesh for the bargaining?" Her hungry voice gave me the shivers, and even though I'd be considered the monster by most people, I knew very well she was by far and away worse than I could ever imagine being.

"No bright meat," I scolded her. "*Never* bright meat! But prime beef or plump chickens."

She sounded disappointed. "You are a harsh one, Dead Girl. But . . . I think I hunger for oinkers. A suckling babe of an oinker, if the deal be struck. But before I commit to such a deal, tell me what you wish to trade for."

I could have sworn I heard a shriek in the background. I did not ask who—or what—was with her, especially when she giggled.

"Can you dispatch will-o'-the-wisps? And we may have some ghosts for your garden." I watched the wording carefully. Elder Fae were worse than the djinn for twisting the meaning of words.

Ivana paused, and I could practically hear the turning of those nasty little wheels in her head. After a moment, she said, "Aye. I can suck up the Corpse Candles and spit them out through my teeth. They fear neither Younger Fae nor Elder Fae, but Ivana knows how to handle them. Bugger the nasty pests, they get in my garden at times and I shoo them away when I don't feel like dispatching them."

"So you *can* take care of them? We have a yard full of will-o'-the-wisps and we need to get them off our land."

I glanced at the clock. I had to get moving. I settled the phone in the docking bay and activated the speaker as I pulled out of the parking lot.

Ivana snorted. "I can take care of them. An oinker babe, suckling and plump, juicy and raw."

I groaned. Where the fuck was I going to find a suckling pig this time of night? But we had to have her help. "Fine, a deal struck. I will meet you in two hours at the edge of our land. We live—"

"Oh, *I know* where you live, Dead Girl. Never think I don't know all about you and your sisters. A deal is struck on a tentative bargain. But 'tis not set until we shake in person." The line went dead.

"Phone, off."

Disconcerted that she knew where we lived, I stared at the road.

Where the hell was I going to find a suckling pig? I'd have to have it when she showed up. And then, I remembered. One of the werewolves we knew kept pigs and sheep. It was late—too late for a social call, but I didn't have time to wait. I stared at my phone, trying to decide whether to call first. But that would give Frank a heads-up, meaning a chance to forbid me to drop over. Weres and vamps weren't always the best of friends, though we were doing our best to put some of the old animosities to rest.

I brought up Frank's contact info and checked his address. He lived about twenty minutes out of Seattle, and with the light traffic at night, I could make it there and back before Ivana met me at the house.

At times like this, I missed being able to let out a long sigh. There was something so satisfying about letting out a breath, *oomphing*, as it were. Oh, I could do it, but it required me to focus, rather than being instinctive, so it was pretty much a waste of time.

I missed that, just like I missed making noise when I walked, which was why I wore the ivory beads in my hair— they clinked, reminding me that I was still alive. And high heels clicking on sidewalks helped, too. There was an eerie silence that went along with being a vampire. No breath filling the lungs, no heart or pulse beating. Once I'd died and been turned, I began to realize how many sounds the living body makes, sounds that I never noticed, but took for granted. As a vampire, all the sounds of life within were silenced. Oh, we had blood in our veins, but it moved slowly, quietly, magically.

As I turned onto the exit leading to the freeway, I glanced at the clock. It was eight thirty. I hoped Frank would still be awake. He tended to keep farmer's hours—early to bed, early to rise. I knew that because we got my bottled blood from him, and from a few other farmers around, and sometimes I came out instead of my sisters to buy blood, meat, and eggs. I'd show up at five in the morning, and every time, he was fully awake, breakfast tucked away, coffee in hand.

When he slaughtered the meat, he'd drain the blood, sanitize it, and pop it in the freezer. Selling it to us brought him some extra cash, and supplied me with necessary sustenance.

I glanced over my shoulder and, seeing no one behind me, shifted lanes, speeding along at a good pace. Seattle was a bustling metropolitan area during the day, but in late evening, when there weren't any baseball or football games in play, traffic was fairly light. Afternoon rush hour tended to last from around three to seven P.M. After that, the streets were relatively clear.

The rain started up again, bouncing on the windshield in fat drops. I flicked on the wipers, then turned on the radio, running through the stations until I found the evening news.

There had been a murder in downtown Seattle—gangbangers roughing it up. And a policeman—no one we knew—had been hit while he was directing traffic around an accident. But the announcer said the cop would recover. I breathed a sigh of thanks. I didn't pray to the gods much. Oh, I knew they existed, but I had no truck with any of them. They'd never done anything to help me, and they'd done plenty to hurt others. But for the cop's sake, I whispered a simple thank-you to the powers that be. There was too much bad news in the world, and I was grateful for the good that we heard about.

My phone rang.

"Answer phone," I said. There were laws against holding a cell phone while driving—for good reason. While we might break a lot of rules, there were some laws we actually followed.

It was Iris. "Camille and Morio are home, and they're trying to do something about the will-o'-the-wisps but not having much luck. Menolly, I've tried to call Nerissa several times and she isn't answering. I tried both her home phone and her cell. I'm worried. This isn't like her."

I kept my eyes on the road, but my mind began to spin. Where the hell was she? "Iris, can you call Yugi and ask him if she showed up at work today? Then call me right back."

"I'll do that now." Iris hung up.

I wanted to turn around and go home, but now we needed that pig, and even though I was worrying up a storm, I had to keep going. Less than two minutes later, Iris called back. "Menolly? I talked to Yugi. He said that Nerissa was at work today. She told him she had some shopping to do this evening. I would think she'd be back by now."

I eased down my speed. "Not necessarily. A lot of the malls are open until nine, and you know that Nerissa can shop till the stores close. I think I know what she's looking for." Images of wedding dresses flashed through my mind. "If she's not back by the time I get home, I'll go out looking for her. But right now, I'm working on a solution to those fucking will-o'-the-wisps."

"What are you doing, Menolly?" Iris sounded suspicious.

"I've engaged help and she'll be there in about ninety minutes. I'm procuring . . . payment." I knew what Iris was going to say but there was no getting around it. She'd out me if I didn't out myself. "I called Ivana."

There was a brief silence, then Iris exploded. "Are you mad, girl? You contacted the Maiden of Karask, after we warned you against it?"

"She can suck down the will-o'-the-wisps as well as ghosts. You yourself said that nobody was having much luck—"

"Yes, but Smoky and Camille just left for Aeval's. What do you think will happen if the Queen of Shadow and Dusk comes here, and then one of the Elder Fae shows up? Don't

you realize what a terrible combination that is? The Elder
Fae detest the Fae Queens, and the Fae Queens have little
love for the Elder Fae!" Iris sounded horrified. "Menolly,
what were you thinking?"

"Listen, I'm tired about worrying who's going to piss off
who. Iris, I have to go. I'm coming up on my exit and need to
focus on the road. Phone, hang up."

The phone went silent. There'd be hell to pay once I got
home, but I'd deal with that later. Iris's hormones were in
full form, and she'd become a terror on heels. Well, not heels—
she was wearing flats now, and she was already starting to
show. Which made sense, now that we knew she was carrying twins.

I changed lanes and eased onto the exit ramp. Frank lived
just north of Mountlake Terrace, on three acres nestled in a
suburb. He didn't keep a large farm, but it was tidy and neat
and provided meat for his family as well as several friends.
Camille said he made the best sausage she'd ever tasted, so
we bought all our pork from him. Not that I ever would be able
to taste the meat, but at least the rest of the family loved it.

As for animal blood, what we bought from him wasn't
too bad. I never tasted antibiotics or hormones in it, like
some of the commercial animal blood on the market.

I eased off on the speed and turned onto the private lane
Frank lived on. There were plenty of kids in the neighborhood, including Frank's three daughters, and animals running around, so I edged along slowly. The street was lit by a
couple of streetlights, but it was still dim. As I pulled into
the driveway, I was relieved to see lights on in the house. I
parked and hopped out of the car, dashing for the door to
escape the rain beating steadily down around me.

As I rang the bell, a noise sounded inside, and then the door
opened to reveal Esme, Frank's youngest daughter. Around
eight—or what the equivalent would be among Weres—her
eyes went wide as she stared up at me. Her hair was curly,
held back in a ponytail, and she was wearing a modest
jumper and saddle shoes. Frank did not allow his daughters
to dress beyond their ages.

Esme called over her shoulder, "Da! Miss Menolly's

here." And then, she looked back at me and solemnly curtsied, her finger crooked in her mouth. "Da will be here in a moment."

"Thank you," I said, stifling a grin. She was too cute for words.

A moment later, Frank appeared. He opened the screen door. "Menolly, is something wrong? Did you run out of blood? Come in." I was touched by his concern. He could have forced me to stay outside, but instead he had assumed I needed help and allowed me into his household.

"Thank you, Frank. I'm sorry I came around so late. I wouldn't have, if it wasn't a matter of . . . well, not life and death, but we have a situation with will-o'-the-wisps and need your help."

"I have no clue on what to do about Corpse Candles, Menolly." He ushered me into the living room.

"Oh, it's not them in particular that I need help with. It's . . . well . . ."

I sat in the chair he showed me to. Frank's house was modestly decorated, tasteful, cozy, and homey. I smiled at the family photograph hanging over the fireplace. That was new, and they were a handsome-looking clan.

"What do you need?" Frank Willows was tall with broad shoulders. He had black hair with a shock of white through it, and thick lips. He *looked* like a farmer, and he was proud of his work. His wife worked in IT, but she seldom came out to speak to us. Frank was definitely the head of the household, as was common among werewolves, but we never saw any sign of abuse of power when we visited. And we'd never heard a word against his character.

I cleared my throat. "I need a suckling pig. Preferably still raw."

Frank stared at me. "That's your solution to an invasion of will-o'-the-wisps? I didn't know they liked pork." A smile escaped his lips.

"Well, yes, in a way. I've engaged one of the Elder Fae to come help us and she demands an 'oinker' . . . a suckling piglet. It's better to meet their demands rather than to try to circumnavigate them."

Frank's mirth quickly vanished. "You've called on the Elder Fae? Do you have a death wish?"

I shrugged. "I'm already dead, so that's rather moot. Seriously, I've worked with her once before and she was of great help. We can't seem to figure out a way to get rid of the damned things, and she can."

Tapping my fingers on the blue upholstery of the chair, I said, "I know it's a fool's venture, Frank, but we have a lot of worries right now, and we can't be distracted from our main tasks. A yard full of will-o'-the-wisps may not seem like much of a danger, but anything that interferes with our primary focus is an impediment."

Frank rubbed his temples. Most people didn't realize that he was part of the Supe Community Council, but he was. And he was one of the few who knew about the demon menace. He was quiet, always staying in the background, but he exerted a steadying influence on some of the more volatile Weres, and since Exo Reed's death, Frank had been assuming more power in the Council.

"Menolly, the danger has come to town again, hasn't it? I'm hearing rumors, especially from those who use magic." He looked at me, straight in the eye, ignoring the competition that act could bring up between Weres and vamps. "Don't tell me who or what—I don't need to know. But . . . should I be watching the farm more? Should I be calling on the shamans of the various clans and prides to make certain they're safe?"

I gazed back at the gentle giant. He meant well. He was sturdy and stalwart and brave. And that made him the perfect target for those wanting to hurt us. "Yes, watch the farm closely. Guard who comes off and onto your land. Don't let your children play alone. But Frank . . . as much as you might want to help, don't get involved until we ask you to. Stand back and let us take care of matters. If—and when—we call on you, know that it will be with direst need."

He regarded me carefully. "While you and your sisters and friends face the danger head-on?"

I lowered my gaze. "We've had too much collateral damage, Frank. I don't want . . ."

With a slight nod, he agreed. "Very well. I have a suck-ling pig you can take. It's frozen, but not cooked. But Menolly . . . if events grow dire, I have relatives to whom I can send my children. And I will fight as you need. The Wil-lows clan—we do not shirk duty." He stood. "Now, if you'll excuse me, I'll fetch the piglet."

I paid him for it, then before he could start out of the room, stopped him, lightly laying one hand on his arm. "Frank, if Shadow Wing breaks through, then no place will be safe. I'll remember your offer. Meanwhile . . . tend to your farm. Enjoy your children."

After he returned with the pig, I accepted the heavy gar-bage sack from him, peeking inside. Yep, one dead oinker. At the door, I swung around.

"Frank, for my sake . . . for yours . . . rescind your invita-tion. I never want there to be doubt or fear in your thoughts." I did this with a number of friends, and they had grown to understand.

He looked almost hurt, but then nodded. "As much as I like you, Menolly, you may not enter this house." And just like that, the invisible force field returned. Comforted, I tossed the piglet in the back of the Jag and roared off into the night. I glanced at the clock. Forty minutes until Ivana was to show up and the roadway was clear. Wanting nothing more than to get home and make sure everyone was okay, I sped through the night, my car a silent shadow.

As I pulled into the drive at home, the will-o'-the-wisps were running rampant. Globes of light danced around the area. They were pretty, and wouldn't bother *us* much, except for Iris and Sharah. They had a penchant for pregnant Fae and were especially dangerous to humans.

If they made their home here, they'd spread out and mul-tiply. They bred like rabbits—although we had no clue how they managed it. They were pure energy, as far as anybody knew. Not even the great Fae Lords could explain how they fit into the world. They were an enigma.

I jumped out of the car and raced inside. Glancing around,

I looked for Nerissa and, to my relief, saw her in the corner, amid a pile of loot she'd managed to secure from Nordstrom and Macy's and a number of stores.

"Oh, thank gods you're safe! Iris had me worried. I imagined all sorts of dreadful things." I stepped over the bags and boxes, almost tripping on a large box from Leila's Boutique, and leaned down to kiss her. "Why didn't you call?"

Nerissa smiled. "I didn't know all this was happening. I was out on several cases today and didn't even make it back to headquarters before I finished up for the day. I had no clue Chase was in danger."

I glanced around. "Where is Chase? Did you manage to get Sharah and him inside away from the will-o'-the-wisps without a problem?"

Delilah nodded. "Yes, though we had to fight them off. They swarmed and it was nasty. However, Iris and Bruce were able to get into the house during that distraction, so it wasn't all bad." She paused as Hanna entered the room, a tray in hand. Marion followed, carrying another tray. They were filled with tea and cups and cookies and what looked like homemade pastries. Marion's big cinnamon rolls from her café! I longed to be able to taste one.

As they settled the trays on the coffee table, Marion looked up. "I know now is not the best time, but I wanted to discuss something with all of you."

"What is it, Marion? Please, don't tell me the Koyanni are making a nuisance of themselves again?" We'd had enough of the rogue coyote shifters.

As Hanna began serving the tea, Marion wiped her hands on her jeans and sat down next to Morio, who was sitting on the sofa.

Marion was a coyote shifter, herself. She and her husband, Douglas, had been living with us for a month since their house and café had been burned to the ground by Telazhar's cohorts. After he'd gated in Gulakah, the Lord of Ghosts, Telazhar had headed over to Otherworld. Meanwhile, the insurance company had actually come through and Marion's café was being rebuilt, and she and Douglas were house hunting.

"No, no sign of any of the stragglers. What I wanted to tell you is that Douglas and I will be moving out until our house is ready."

Delilah jumped up. "Oh, no! Please, we don't want you to go. Has anybody said or done anything to make you feel unwelcome?"

"Not at all." Marion sipped her tea, and bit into a cookie. "But let's face it—you've got an army living here. There's not much room and we're intruding. We've had an offer that will keep me busy while we're waiting for the café to be rebuilt and we find a house to buy. Douglas has his job, of course, but I need to feel useful and there's only so much I can do here." She smiled. "So, it's a good thing all the way around."

"Where are you moving?" I couldn't imagine they had enough money for a hotel. There was no telling how long it would take for them to find a new home.

"We're moving in with Wilbur, to take care of him."

Morio choked on his cookie, while Vanzir spit out a mouthful of tea. The rest of us stared at her like she was crazy. But Iris didn't hold back.

"You're moving in with *Wilbur*? You have to be joking! Marion, are you out of your skull?" She stood up, hands on hips, her eyes ablaze and ready to scold. "Wilbur is . . . he's . . ."

Marion held up her hand. "Wilbur did his best to help with the Koyanni problem and in the process, he was terribly wounded. He's almost ready to go home, but he's going to need tending to until he gets used to his artificial leg. Douglas and I . . . we want to help. We can take Martin back to his home, then."

Wilbur was a necromancer on our side—or as close to our side as he was ever going to get. Crude and lewd, he had raised his brother, Martin the accountant, from the dead and turned him into a ghoul, the only way Wilbur could think of to keep his family with him. Marion was right, though. Wilbur had nearly been killed trying to protect our secrets. His leg had been crushed to the point of amputation. Now, he was about ready to go home.

We'd been keeping an eye on Martin for him, as much as we didn't like the thought. We kept him out back, in a shed. I wondered just how much Wilbur understood that Martin—the Martin he knew—was long gone and that the ghoul left in his place had very little to do with his brother.

"Are you sure you want to do this? Wilbur's not exactly pleasant company." I held Marion's gaze, and she smiled softly.

"You forget. I brought up three children. I serve people for a living. I need to be nurturing someone. Wilbur may be a pill, but I think we can manage him just fine." She leaned back. "I'm antsy. I'm used to running a café."

"What does Douglas say about it?" I somehow couldn't imagine her husband enjoying the thought of putting up with Wilbur and Martin on a full-time basis, even if it was just for a month or so.

"Douglas and I talked it over. He understands." She gave me a feral little smile, reminding me again of why coyote shifters were given a careful berth. Even those not part of the Koyanni tribe could be highly dangerous. Maybe they would get on with Wilbur.

I glanced at the clock. "I need to meet Ivana at the end of the driveway in a few minutes. I suppose Iris told you all what I'm doing."

"Yeah, she did." Delilah walked over to the window and pushed back the curtains. The will-o'-the-wisps were thick on the front porch. "We have to do something. Camille and Smoky aren't back yet, and we have no idea if Aeval will even agree to help. Do what you have to."

"So you'll back me up?" Delilah was the last person I'd expected to take my side, besides Iris.

She nodded, still staring out the window. "Chase is weak. The bhouts have invaded Seattle. Lindsey called again tonight—several of her coven mates have taken ill; they're very weak. One guess as to what's going on there. And we've got a fucking demon general out there who likes to play with ghosts. I'd strike a bargain with the devil herself if she could help us."

I nodded. "Everybody, stay inside. If anybody is going to

make a deal with Ivana, let it be me. I've dealt with her before. And better one of us be beholden to her than all." As I headed toward the door, I turned back. "Nerissa, you're staying here tonight. I don't care how much you like your condo. It's just too dangerous." And without waiting for her answer, I headed out the door.

Ivana was waiting at the gate when I dragged the suckling pig down the drive. I swatted the will-o'-the-wisps away like flies. They couldn't do much to me, but they were annoying, like fat fireflies on crack.

I didn't like judging on looks, but Ivana really was hideous, phasing in and out, shifting form as she stabilized. Her face was wide near the eyes, narrowing to a sharp point at the chin. Her nose was tiny and snubbed, and her face was nearly flat, except for the gnarls that covered her skin—burls of skin and flesh that dotted her face. When she smiled, it was worse—needlepoint teeth gleamed through thin lips, and she looked quite capable of eating plenty of *bright flesh*, as she called it. Though she dressed like a bag lady, her clothes belied her stature and power, and I stopped a respectful distance from her.

"Ah, young *vampyr* . . . so, Dead Girl, do you have my suckling oinker? My tasty treat for an evening's snack?" She smacked her lips and I shivered, revolted by the gleam in her eyes. Even when I was in my most predatory state, I didn't think I had that much bloodlust in me.

"I have it." I dropped the bag on the ground and pointed to it. "So, can you remove all of these will-o'-the-wisps from the land?"

She craned her neck to peek up the drive. "Aye, there's a fair lot of them but I can."

"Then a deal is struck." I held out my hand, dreading her touch. She clasped my fingers, and the tingle that raced through me was like a pure jolt of fresh blood. I gasped, shaking my head. "What was that?"

Ivana regarded me with a sly look. "I can make you *feel*, Dead Girl. I can make you believe you're alive again. If you ever want more, just come to my door and ask." And with a heady laughter, she peeked in the sack. "Suckling, yes . . . an oinker for the Maiden of Karask." Then, all business, she added, "Back off, meat on the hoof. Let me do my work. Indoors with you. This will not be a pretty battle."

I nodded and jogged up the path. I wasn't worried that she'd just take the pig and go. When the Elder Fae struck deals, they kept their end of the bargain.

As I swatted another swarm of the will-o'-the-wisps away, I heard a shriek—long and mournful—and looked back to see lights exploding as Ivana began to walk forward, her hand out as she poked the will-o'-the-wisps with her fingers and they dove into her staff with mournful wails.

I slammed the door behind me and hurried to the living room, where Delilah and Morio were pressed up to the windows, watching. Shade and Shamas were sitting next to Chase, who was bundled in an afghan. He weakly raised one hand. Iris and Hanna had taken the tea trays into the kitchen and were washing up, with Marion helping them. Trillian was reading a book; Vanzir and Roz were playing video games. Bruce was playing with Maggie and talking to Douglas. Nerissa was nowhere to be seen.

"Where'd Nessa go?" I didn't often use my pet name for her in public, but it just slipped out.

"She's in the parlor, sorting through the clothes she bought. I saw the gown she picked out," Delilah added. "It's so pretty."

I knew I should go in, should see what she'd found, but there was just too much going on to look at clothes. People were being hurt, we had a full-fledged invasion of the spooktacular kind, and I couldn't drag my attention away to weddings and vows and celebrations.

I was about to ask if anybody needed anything from the kitchen when the air shimmered and Smoky appeared, Camille under his arm. They stepped out of the Ionyc Seas, Camille looking tired and spent.

Travel through the etheric seas wearied most living creatures except for dragons and those naturally acclimated to the in-between spaces of the world. But even as they appeared, there was another shimmer and I backed away, startled as a tall woman dressed in black and purple appeared. She was luminous, with hair as black as gleaming coal, and silvery eyes.

As Aeval turned to view the lot of us, she let out a soft laughter. "And so, we seem to have a problem with will-o'-the-wisps, do we?"

Aeval—the Queen of Night and Shadow—was one of the three Fae Queens ruling over the sovereign Fae nation, and Camille's Mistress.

"What is this?" She turned toward me. "I smell the blood of Elder Fae."

"About that. Um . . . the Maiden of Karask is here. She's outside, swallowing up the will-o'-the-wisps." I wasn't afraid of much, but the Triple Threat happened to be three of the few exceptions.

Aeval stared at me with glittering eyes. "You foolish girl. Do you know what you've done?"

Just then, the door crashed open and Ivana was in the room. She stared at Aeval. "I thought I smelled the stench of the Night. Well met, Aeval. Well met. The last we clashed, I swore I'd kill you the next time we crossed paths. After I finish with my oath-bound task, I trust you'll meet the match?"

But Ivana had forgotten to close the door, and the next moment, the will-o'-the-wisps came pouring through, filling the house. Chase and Marion screamed, and so did Iris, as we were invaded by the Corpse Candles.

Chapter 14

~~~~~~

"Crap!" I scrambled over to Chase as the will-o'-the-wisps poured into the room. Iris, Hanna, and Marion were shouting from the kitchen, and Camille and Morio bolted their way, slamming the front door as they ran. Everybody was moving at once.

A flutter of wings and the whisper of siren songs, and Chase was up, unsteady on his feet, and moving toward a large cluster of the creatures. I tackled him, taking him to the ground. As we landed, I heard him groan. Great, I'd broken him, but it had kept him from heading into their midst. I just prayed that whatever I'd hurt wasn't anything major.

Bruce was shoving through the clamor, trying to get to the kitchen. He darted through the mayhem, his size a plus in this instance, and I watched him go as I sat on Chase, trying to figure out what the fuck to do.

Delilah snarled from the corner. She'd transformed into her panther self and was snapping at the lights. She wasn't getting very far, but I had to give it to her—my sister had grown a pair.

The next thing I knew, Ivana was hovering over me,

popping will-o'-the-wisps right and left. Aeval was in the corner weaving some sort of spell that seemed to be causing havoc with the Corpse Candles near her. As I watched, a fork of lightning rippled out from her fingers, catching hold of one of the globes. It exploded in a puff of smoke as several lightning strikes emerged, finding their way to other will-o'-the-wisps, and like chain lightning, explosions rattled through the room. A wave of shrieks echoed as the will-o'-the-wisps vanished.

Ivana, not to be outdone, struck again and again, and between the Elder Fae and the Fae Queen, they began to clear the house. The pair, ignoring each other, exited the house, and we watched from the window as they dispatched the invasion.

"Chase, are you okay?" I helped him up, glancing around in case any of the globes had been hiding, but they all seemed to be gone.

"I think I sprained my thumb. My left one." He held out his hand and I grimaced as I watched the flesh swell and turn a lovely shade of black.

"Sorry, dude. Morio, can you take him to find Sharah? She can splint it. We've got plenty of medical supplies."

As Morio led Chase away, I worried about what would happen after Ivana and Aeval finished their mutual destruction of the will-o'-the-wisps, but before I could go out and check on them—taking care not to get in the middle of their obvious spat—Vanzir stopped me.

"Let them hash it out. Don't get in the middle."

Thinking about the way they'd greeted one another, I decided to take his advice. "You're probably right." I brushed a thin layer of dust off his shoulders, then realized it was covering everything in the room. It seemed the will-o'-the-wisps left something in the way of remains, after all.

"Great, just what I needed. Faerie dust."

Just then Camille herded Iris, Hanna, Douglas, and Marion in. They looked no worse for the wear.

She motioned to me. "Come on, Delilah . . . Menolly. We'd better get out there and prevent the pair from killing each other." As we headed for the door, she hissed at me. "What the fuck were you thinking? You knew I was going after Aeval.

Don't you remember the tales Father used to tell us about the feuds between the Fae Lords and the Elder Fae?"

"Apparently not." And truth was, I hadn't. But now that she mentioned it, a vague memory of the stories—and horrific tales they were—filtered back. Enough so that I bolted for the door. "Let's go!"

As we headed onto the lawn, the clouds broke and the moon bathed the yard in her light. Camille paused, looking up at the silver crescent, soaking in the energy. I tapped her on the shoulder, and she nodded and took off again, following Delilah and me into the backyard, where Iris's trailer sat stark against the darkness.

Aeval and Ivana were standing there, and the yard was empty of will-o'-the-wisps. They were staring at each other, hostility oozing off them like the smell of rotten eggs.

"So, you have truck with the Elder Fae?" Aeval turned to Camille, her voice accusing. I had the feeling my sister was going to be in serious trouble for my decision, so I stepped up.

"No. Not Camille. This was all my decision. We needed help and I went to the only place I could think of." I glanced at Ivana. "Both of you, we owe you a de—" I stopped. I could not use the word *debt* around either one of them. So not a good idea. Even the word *owe* was a mistake. "We thank you both for your help."

Ivana laughed. "Dead Girl, you know your lore but not as much as you should." She turned to Aeval. "And so, the Night and the Morning have set up their courts again and now gird themselves with the mantle of Dusk. To what season will she rule? Neither Summer nor Winter—those are in the keep of you and Titania. But the *other* . . . *She* is not truly Fae. Not full-blood. You make a grave mistake and you know it."

Aeval regarded Ivana closely. "We are returned, yes. The Fae Queens rise again and we will surpass our former glory. We build an empire. The Dusk . . . she serves a purpose, for now. And so we are the Court of the Three Queens. And Camille studies with us, bridging Otherworld back to Earthside." She turned to my sister. "You are the hope of the future, in our Courts."

The Elder Fae let out a long sigh. "There is no hope for

the future. The old days are long past. The humans and mortals have razed our groves, have ceased to pay us homage. They no longer fear us."

With a laugh, Aeval shook her head. "They would fear you, Maiden of Karask, if they knew you truly existed. The day will come when they will know our power once again. But a great shadow looms, and first we must dispatch the danger. I shall not kill you this day, Elder Fae. Instead, I tell you this: Go to your brethren and warn them to gird themselves for war. For war is coming, and whether it be in this world or in Otherworld, if we choose to face the future, we must all battle against the darkness that would shroud it in fire."

Ivana regarded her silently, and I had a feeling that the two powers were speaking in silence.

After a moment, Ivana inclined her head. "Let our personal battle be at a truce for now." She turned to me. "Dead Girl, there is much you have kept from me. Though I will never forgive you for depriving me of my bright flesh, I am here, at your service, for deals when you need them. If your ghosties keep you awake in the night, you know my number."

And then, without another word, she slung the piglet over her shoulder and vanished into the darkness. Aeval watched her go.

"The Elder Fae were ancient when I was young. They are the backbone of this world. They live in the ages of the Harvestmen and the Hags of Fate and the Elemental Lords." She inhaled sharply. "The demons are on the move. I know they threaten Asteria, but there is little my people can do for her. Instead, we train. For war is coming. But do not expect it in the loud clamor of guns or swarms . . . instead it creeps silently, infiltrates by ones and twos. Shadow Wing is not stupid . . . like all demons, he will seek to corrupt, to gain allies. What better way to wrest control than to divide and conquer?"

Camille gazed up at the moon. "Asteria mentioned that the dark moon Priestesses of the Moon Mother are her sorcerers."

Aeval flashed her a mirthless smile. "The dark of the moon holds power over the unseen. The dark of the moon hides secrets. The veils grow thin during the waning half of the year. Moon Witch you are, and Priestess . . . but your true power resides in the abyss, in the purple flames of death. Like your cousin Morgaine, you, too, are a child of the dusk, my girl, trapped between worlds. Trapped between races. Trapped between the day and the night."

She moved away, gliding over the ground, her long trailing gown light as leaves whispering along the ground. "Camille . . . be ready. Beltane will come, and the dragons will fly. And the gods will rut. And you, you will ride at the helm of the Hunt—and you and your Priest will learn what it means to belong to the night. The will-o'-the-wisps came out because they live with the spirits, and the spirits are singing a bright song, as of late." And then, as the wind whistled by, she vanished as if she'd never been there.

We stared into the yard. The night was silent. There was nothing creeping out there that we could hear. Turning around, we filed back to the house.

We trailed back into the house with more riddles than we had answers for. As we dropped wearily into chairs, staring around at the others, it felt like we had no clear place to start.

"Where are we at?" Delilah asked. "What do we know? What don't we know?"

"We know that Gulakah is here in Seattle. We know that a bunch of demonic spirits—bhouts—are running loose in the city. We don't know if the two are tied together, but I'm thinking it's likely." Shade thumb-wrestled with himself.

"Carter told me that the Greenbelt Park District has been haunted for far longer than Gulakah's been around, but I'm betting it's an attraction for him, given the amount of ghostly activity there. And the activity has definitely stepped up the past few months. That may relate to the Lord of Ghosts being in town, too." I frowned. "What else?"

"We know that those who use magic are being attacked and drained. Lindsey's coven, Chase . . . and there are others, I'm sure. The bhouts seem to be responsible for that. If they're draining the energy from people, is it going directly to feed them, or their controller?" Camille scratched her head.

"Probably both. The bhout attacked Chase in order to possess him. Chase controls the FH-CSI." An idea struck me. "Think what Aeval said—Shadow Wing may not wage open war but come in through the back door. What would it mean if he could gain control of some of the more important members of society . . . those in charge?"

"Mind control . . . he could arrange anything, then. He could have the three of you deported or killed. But not all government officials have psychic energy," Smoky said.

"No, but enough must have latent powers to tempt him. We can't be certain that's his goal, but we better consider it." I pulled off my boots and socks and propped my feet on the coffee table. I'd painted my toenails—they were a brilliant crimson.

"Otherworld is on the brink of open war. Over here, the war is covert. The worlds are vastly different and call for different strategizing. Shadow Wing has to understand that, and so we're seeing the results of what was probably long-term planning." Trillian was sitting on one end of the sofa, Smoky on the other. Camille stretched out between them, her head on Trillian's lap and her feet on Smoky's knees. He rubbed her toes gently while Trillian stroked her head.

Morio sat on the floor next to them. "So two different fronts, two different battle plans."

"And my people—humans—don't know that nuclear weapons probably won't do a lot against demons, but you know the governments here would resort to that if they knew about this danger. Shadow Wing may be worried that they might be effective enough to make things difficult. He doesn't care if most of the world gets offed in the attempt, but he doesn't want his forces harmed. No, I'm guessing that he thinks it's better to infiltrate from within," Chase said.

I had to agree with them. "You're probably right. As far as we know, his attempts Earthside have been limited and will probably remain on the down low. However, should he make inroads in Otherworld, the sorcerers might be able to open enough portals to let the demons in that way. And from there, they can access the portals leading over Earthside."

"That's a horrible thought." Delilah shivered.

"Damned right it's a horrible thought. The influx of demons Earthside will be far greater once they gain a stronghold in Otherworld. My guess? Most of his outright efforts are being focused on Otherworld, while here, he's preparing the reception committee, so to speak." My feet hit the ground as I stood. "Mind control here can pave the way for them to come over from OW without a fight."

"Which means we need to find and destroy Gulakah and stop the war in Otherworld. Neither of which will be easy. We don't know where Gulakah is, Carter hasn't been able to locate him, and there's enough psychic mayhem going on in the city that—" Camille stopped as the phone rang.

Iris answered it. After a moment, she motioned to me. "Roman on the phone. Wants to talk to you."

I stepped into the foyer where I could hear him better while the others continued to talk. I was nervous—I hadn't spoken to him since Nerissa and I had left his house. "Hey . . . what's up?"

"Menolly, I have some information for you. I'm sorry to tell you that one of my guards stumbled over a dead body about ten minutes ago, out in Tangleroot Park. I think it may be your agent."

Fuck. Andrees? Dead? My heart sank.

"Crap. I didn't want to hear that. Andrees is a good man. I hope to hell it's not him." I paused. "You say Tangleroot Park? There's a rogue portal there. We've had one hell of a night so far and it's not even midnight."

"Do tell?"

I was about to tell him about the will-o'-the-wisps and the bhouts when call waiting beeped. I glanced at the screen. Carter. "I have to go, Roman. I have another call that I need to take. We'll get over there as soon as we can. Will you have your men stand guard over the body until we arrive and tell them not to touch it, please? We've got several situations going. I'll call you back as soon as I can."

"Talk to you in a bit, my sweet. My man's name is Standers,

by the way. He'll keep an eye on the body." He hung up, and I clicked over to Carter.

"Carter?"

"Menolly? I have news. I got a call from a compatriot in Portland, Oregon. Something seems to be amiss with the witches and pagans there. A lingering malaise spreading through the communities."

"That sounds all too familiar."

"Yes, doesn't it? I've talked to the witch who casts my wards. She's a powerful sorceress, not fully human, but I'm not going to speculate on what her other lineage might be. She said that a week or so ago, she started to notice her energy flagging. She didn't seem all that interested in talking to me, and I know something must be wrong."

"I know what's going on, Carter, but I can't talk right now. We found our agent, I think. Dead. We'll stop by after we get done in the park." I paused, then added, "Carter, things are starting to go down in a really bad way. Watch your back." And with that, I hung up and headed back into the living room to give Camille and Delilah the news.

The three of us, along with Shade, Morio, and Chase, headed out for the park. For once, I longed for the pull of the sun. So much had happened the past few nights that everybody was getting worn out, and I knew that Camille and Delilah were pulling long shifts with little sleep.

Morio offered to drive, so we took his SUV. Camille sat in front. Delilah and I were in the middle seat, and Shade and Chase sat in the back.

"Do you think that it's really Andrees?" Delilah asked after a moment, her voice cracking. "I mean . . . it's been a long time, but I really liked him. I always wondered what would have happened if I'd actually been brave enough to ask him out."

"I'm hoping it isn't him, but considering how stupid the OIA was, well . . ." I leaned back against the seat. "Now that we're on speaking terms with Father again, we really have to reorganize things over there. As soon as we have this situation in hand, we're revamping the ES side of the organization."

"That's what the FH-CSI was originally supposed to be," Chase said from the back. "But the OIA refused to talk to us. They fed us what they thought we ought to know, which wasn't much, and let it go. I had a list of operatives—before they pulled out—but half the time, it wasn't accurate."

"So, as we told Father, we're going to establish a new base of operations here. We're working for them on our terms now." Delilah grinned.

"We can turn the FH-CSI into what it was meant to be." I glanced back at Chase. "You like that idea?"

"Love it," he said. "I've been feeling overlooked and underappreciated since your people first came over—not by the three of you, but by your government. This would make me feel vindicated. I've done my best to hold things together for the visitors coming over from Otherworld, but it would be nice to have more support from your superiors."

As we pulled into Tangleroot Park, Chase grimaced. "I don't fancy a revisit to this area, but I'm game."

"You still have nightmares about old Spider-Hag?" Chase had been captured by one of the Elder Fae—a spidery freak show who intended to fatten him up and eat him. Luckily, her plans had been nixed and he'd escaped. We thought we'd destroyed her, but upon leaving the plane into which she'd dragged him, we weren't so sure.

"Her . . . Karvanak . . . the Tregarts. I count my blessings I'm still alive. I wouldn't be if it weren't . . ." He stopped, turning sober.

"For the Nectar of Life," Delilah whispered.

"I was going to say you three. But yes, the Nectar of Life, as well." After a moment, he changed the subject. "So, will you know your friend by sight?"

I gave him a nod. "Yes, we should. Andrees . . . we go way back. We took the same classes when we entered the OIA. Or rather, the YIA—we didn't originally work for the branch dealing with Earthside affairs. Before we were assigned to specific departments, every agent has to go through what you might call a basic training."

Camille turned in her seat, to stare over the back. "We joined the YIA before the portals to Earthside were opened up. Before we even really knew about them. The YIA—Y'Elestrial Intelligence Agency—took care of some of the worst criminal cases in Y'Elestrial's history. We tracked down the rogue vamps, serial killers, the worst of the worst."

Chase nodded. "I thought that might be what it was like. So you met Andrees then?"

"We met him in basic training, yes. What you would think of as the preliminary academic studies. Then he was assigned to Delilah's department. The YIA is divided up into a number of departments and the OIA started as a branch, then hived off to become its own division." I shrugged.

"Did you sign up because you wanted to come Earthside?" Chase had never asked us much about the time before we came over through the portals.

I hesitated, not sure of how to respond. "Not really. We were assigned to the OIA . . ."

"Oh, just say it. We were transferred to the OIA because of me," Camille's face clouded over. "My boss had been gunning for me for years because I wouldn't fuck him. I managed to make a huge bust—I brought in Roche, a serial killer who had been a member of the Des'Estar. That's when I met Trillian, in a nightclub I was scoping out."

"And that didn't cement your position?"

"My boss, Lathe, tried everything to get me to fuck him. He's a sadist. He liked humiliating women. When I tossed Roche's body at his feet, he couldn't deny me a raise and a commendation. Three weeks later, Dredge caught hold of Menolly. And after that, Lathe set out to make my life a living hell."

"You couldn't call him on sexual harassment?" Chase looked mystified.

"In Otherworld, sexual harassment isn't against the law. It's only an issue when the individual employer forbids it. Among the Fae, it can be a fact of life. Especially for a half-breed like me." She grimaced. "When the OIA opened up and they began recruiting agents, nobody wanted to join. Well, almost nobody. But Lathe, he 'promoted' me . . . and

I guess they figured they could get rid of all three of us at the same time. We were all assigned to the division."

Delilah let out a sigh. "They didn't like me because I was squeamish about roughing anybody up. I guess I've gotten over that little problem."

I laughed. "That you have, Kitten. That you have. And they wanted to get me off their hands. Having a vampire in the YIA was an embarrassment, but they couldn't just fire me, because it was their fault in the first place that Dredge caught me. Sending me into that nest with no backup—that would have been a nasty scandal, and I could have made things very messy for them."

"Sorry to interrupt, but we're here." Morio edged into the parking lot. "Be careful. We have no way of knowing what the fuck is lurking around. I don't even know what happened to the portal."

Camille opened her door and stepped out into the chill night air. "Aeval told me that she can't seal it permanently. The damn thing is growing stronger."

"Delightful." I glanced around the parking lot.

There was a black sedan parked nearby—presumably belonging to Roman's guard. No other cars in sight. The paths were no longer covered with snow, but the rain had started up again, a light drizzle that was more annoying than anything else. The trees were stark against the sky, black silhouettes rising up, towering fir and cedars overlooking the deciduous trees whose leaves were mere buds on the branches at this point.

I motioned to one of the paths. I could sense the vampire nearby. As we headed in that direction, I called out, "Standers? It's Menolly—"

I'd no more than said my name when he slipped out from behind a bush. He was average height, had been an FBH, but was now dressed in Roman's requisite uniform—black turtleneck and jeans. He wore the crest from Roman's house on his shirt pocket.

"Miss Menolly, thank you for arriving so promptly. The Master said you were on the way." He paused, looking at all of us. "Follow me, please. I've made sure nothing touched the body since I found it." And with that, he led us back along the path to where two firs stood side by side. We weren't far from the portal, and I noticed both Camille and Chase nervously glancing down the path.

"Back here, behind these bushes." Standers led us through the trees, onto the grass. It was spongy from the rain, and the scent of moss floated up, mixed with mildew and mushrooms and the sour tang of the earth. The woodlands were pungent in the Northwest, but they were also crisp. The smell of rain on cedars was one that I willingly forced myself to notice. It had a *wake-up* feeling to it.

The *drip-drip-drip* of rain splashing off the needles trickled down our cheeks and hair. I shook away a droplet that threatened to fall into my eyes and veered around the huckleberry bush. There, on the ground, a body splayed out, covered in dried blood and very, very dead. *Andrees.*

Camille and Delilah caught up with me, and then Morio, Shade, and Chase. Camille bowed her head as Delilah let out a little cry and covered her mouth with her fingers.

"Yeah, it's Andrees," I said, after a moment. I knelt beside the body on one side, while Chase knelt on the other. It was obvious by the state of his corpse that Andrees had been murdered. But the single gunshot wound in his head couldn't have caused the body to be so ravaged, nor did the cuts and marks on him look like an animal.

Chase stared at him for a moment, then said, "I think he was killed before the body was torn up. That's an execution-style gunshot—he was murdered and dumped here. Probably a gangbanger, by first look. But those cuts . . . they're made postmortem, I believe. I need to get Mallen over here."

He flipped open his cell phone and punched in a number. "Mallen, you're still up? . . . Get dressed, then. We need you down here at Tangleroot Park . . . No, no injuries—just one very dead Fae. Bring a forensics team. We're not dealing with death by natural causes here."

While Chase was on the phone, Delilah and Camille headed down the path. I tagged along, sliding in between them and slipping my arms around their waists. "I'm sorry. Delilah, I know you were closest to Andrees."

She nodded, a stark expression on her face. "He was a good man. He was a good agent. At one point, I really thought there might be a chance . . ."

"I know." I glanced up at Camille. "How are you doing?"

She shrugged. "Fine, I guess. Weary. Wishing we could catch a chance to breathe." Then, laughing faintly, she added, "You know what I mean."

"Yeah, I do." I stopped. "Do you hear that?"

We spread out and began to move forward. Something up ahead was making noise. A hum, or perhaps a faint pulse, thrummed lightly.

As we rounded the bend in the sidewalk, Camille let out a groan. "The portal, it's active again."

And it was. The portal, which was supposed to have some-one watching over it at all times, had been left unattended, and it was shimmering in the darkened night. It hummed with a faint tune, whispering melodies of spring and of invi-tations and of tea parties and tulips and a light wind on warm days. Even I could feel the invitation echoing out from it.

"Crap, they're at it again." Camille shook her head. "I wonder what Tra and Herne are up to?" Herne, the god of the forest, and his son Tra had been dancing around in there the last time they'd gone through, and the experience hadn't been all that jolly.

Delilah cleared her throat. "There's one way to find out."

"Oh no you don't!" I jumped in front of them. "Don't you dare. We have no idea what's on the other side, this time. Remember, Yannie Fin Diver is still there, and other, worse, Elder Fae."

Camille nodded, slowly. "Right. I wish to hell we could figure out why we can't seal it. Except the Elder Fae use it and their magic is stronger than even Titania's or Aeval's, let alone magic like Morio and I use."

We stared at the opening for a moment, as if we expected something to come through at any time. After a while, when nothing did, we returned to Chase, and to Andrees's body. There was nothing more we could do for him, and once more, with a heavy heart, the three of us whispered our prayer for the dead over his body, commending his soul to the Land of the Silver Falls, with Chase, Morio, and Shade standing at attention, heads bowed.

"What was life has crumbled. What was form, now falls away. Mortal chains unbind and the soul is lifted free. May you find your way to the ancestors. May you find your path to the gods. May your bravery and courage be remembered in song and story. May your parents be proud, and may your children carry your birthright. Sleep, and wander no more."

After that, we waited for Chase's team to arrive. I sat beside Andrees, far enough away not to mess with the crime scene, but close enough to keep watch. Camille and Delilah stood near me, a silent vigil.

I felt we owed it to him. He was one of our own—an OIA member who had done his job, and done it well. And because of the cruddy bureaucracy, he'd ended up being sent to the wrong place at the wrong time with no backup, and he'd paid for it with his life.

"Where do we go from here?" Camille shivered, pulling her jacket tighter.

"To Carter's. I didn't tell you this before, because we had to hurry over, but Carter called while I was talking to Roman. There are reports filtering up from Portland that some of the witches down there are being drained. And another thing I forgot to tell you. When I went to see him last night, the wards on his place were broken. He called his witch/sorceress today and she didn't seem to feel like talking about the issue."

"Crap. Then the bhouts are spreading out? We have to find out how widespread they are. If Gulakah is controlling them, and they spread to other parts of the country, he could be pulling the strings of a lot of very valuable puppets." Delilah pressed her lips together, shifting from one foot to another.

An owl hooted softly through the trees, announcing the arrival of strangers. It was Mallen, with a forensics team. As they took over, we asked Chase to come with us. He was still vulnerable to the demonic spirits, and we had to keep an eye on him. With heavy hearts, we headed out for Carter's apartment.

Chapter 15

As we neared the Galaxy club, I pointed it out to Camille. "You should check it out—I have a feeling the bhouts may have gotten in there. Just a hunch."

"No time like the present." She grabbed her purse. "Pull over and let me out. I'll go in and scope it out, and you can pick me up after you talk to Carter. His place is only a few blocks from here."

Morio swerved into a parking space and turned off the ignition. "Fine, but you are *not* going in there alone. I forbid it."

"I'll be fine—" she started to say, but he grabbed her wrist.

"*No.* Just, no. You will take Menolly and Shade with you. They can put down just about anything that happens. Meanwhile, Delilah, Chase, and I will go see Carter."

I repressed a grin, waiting for the blowup. Camille had three very possessive and alpha husbands, although Morio was the least volatile. When they tried to run her life, she usually exploded. But as they locked gazes, he leaned in, staring at her intently.

"Don't even *think* about arguing or I'll tell Smoky and Trillian and we'll all have ourselves a field day." Arching one eyebrow, he planted a quick kiss on her nose. "You hear me, wife?"

"Fine. I hear you." She let out a little huff. "Come on, you two." She slipped out of the car and—with no real time to argue—Shade and I followed her down the street to the club. I'd wanted to go visit Carter, but Morio was right. This was the safest arrangement.

"Your husbands have a firm hand with you." Shade moved to the outside of the sidewalk, and I moved to the inside so we buttressed Camille from both directions.

I laughed. "They have to, considering Camille's nature."

"Hey, what is this, Pick on Camille Day?" She rolled her eyes.

Shade shrugged. "I rather think it's called for with you at the helm."

Camille whipped around, glaring, but when she saw the grin on his face, she swatted him. "You're lucky you're my sister's fiancé, or I'd—"

"You'd what? I don't think you have room in your harem for another dragon." Again, the laugh, and a long wink. Shade had it going on, but he was totally devoted to Delilah and we knew it.

Camille shook her head, a disgruntled look on her face, but then she laughed. "Twit."

"Don't be so sure about that." I skipped ahead, dancing over the cracks in the sidewalk. "Camille's got a heart that keeps growing with every addition. But you're probably right. Smoky would put his foot down at another dragon, and I don't think it would be a pretty sight."

The easy banter felt a welcome respite after all the shit that had gone down, and by the time we reached the club, we were in a better frame of mind. Camille glanced at the few FBHs who were hanging outside and said nothing, but she gave me a look that read something was definitely wrong.

We entered the club and an instant wave of technopop hit us, loud and pounding the walls. But nobody was really doing much of anything. The people on the dance floor were lethargic, moving back and forth in a slow shuffle. Nerissa and I loved to go clubbing, but the feel of this club was one of quiet desperation.

The décor was olive green, purple, and silver. It wasn't the most coordinated set of colors, and the large room was scattered with tables and booths that took up valuable space. Whoever had laid it out sure didn't have an eye for interior decorating or for proper utilization of a floor plan. If I took control of this club, it would seat twice as many and have a bigger dance floor. All it required was some organization.

Camille leaned close. "The energy is fucked up here. Really fucked up."

"How so?"

"This is supposed to be a club for those who use magic? I'm not feeling so much magic . . . and what there is, feels tainted. Not as if they dabble in dark spells like sorcery . . . just . . . off."

We threaded through the crowd, heading toward the bar. Even at the tables and booths, people didn't appear to be having fun. They sat, drinks in hand, just staring around laconically.

"She's right. This is fucking creepy," Shade mumbled, glaring at a couple who were hanging off each other. "I feel like I'm in a zombie bar rather than one that should be alive with magic." He glanced around. "Even the few Fae I see seem . . . lackluster."

Camille slipped up to the bar, and we joined her. She climbed onto one of the stools and motioned to the bartender. He was lean and tall, and he set me on alert.

"What'll it be?" He slapped the bar towel over his shoulder and gave us a gaunt, hungry look.

"Coke, please." She tossed a ten-dollar bill on the counter. "Shade, what do you want?"

"Coffee, if you have it." He slid onto the stool next to her and I took the other side, waving off the bartender when he turned to me. As he moved away to get the drinks, Shade glanced around again, then leaned close. "Bhouts . . . I can sense them. They're thick in here."

The barkeep came back with their drinks, and Camille

waved away the change. "Keep it. Listen, this is my first time in. You usually have such a low-key clientele?" She turned on the glamour and the barkeep's eyes lit up.

He tilted his head, leaning across the counter. "Nah, not until lately. Usually it's jumping in here but the past week or so, things have been pretty quiet. Maybe everybody's studying for their second-degree tests or something." He stared at her, then over at me. "You're from Otherworld, aren't you? What are your names?"

I studied him for a moment. Shadow Wing already knew who we were. Gulakah knew us. There was no more hiding, no more skulking in shadows.

"I'm Menolly, and this is my sister Camille. That's Shade over there." I pointed to Shade, then flashed the bartender a glimpse of my fangs. When in doubt, intimidate.

He stared at me, and I could hear the pulse of his blood, the quick intake of breath. He was afraid, all right.

"Welcome to the Galaxy. Too bad it's not more active in here. I bet you girls could liven things up." He paused. "Do you want . . . we have bottled blood. Finest cow, pig, and . . ." Again, the pause. "Human, if you like."

Fuck me hard. It was against the law to serve human blood in bars unless you had voluntary bloodwhores right on the premises. Even then, it wasn't encouraged. I looked around, and he must have known what I was searching for.

"Bloodwhores stay in the back. We don't have many— don't get many vamps, but some of them prefer the blood of those who work magic." And his eyes took on a starry glaze.

I glanced at Camille, who seemed a million miles away, then glanced back at the bartender. "And you? Why are you here? Do you work magic?" I knew the answer already, but decided to ask anyway.

He shrugged and again, the hungry-jackal look returned. "Me? No, haven't got the gift. But I like being around the energy. I've got a thing for witches." And he again turned to Camille, his eyes practically jumping out of his head.

Just like the Faerie Maids, who were groupies looking for sex with the Fae, there were guys who went all horn-toad for women who had power, and witches were their first choice.

This guy would always be an outsider, but like a moth, he desperately craved to touch the flame.

"Yeah, well I'd put the tongue back in the mouth, if I were you. She's got three husbands and they're all strong enough to tear you to pieces." Shade leaned in. "Pay the lady some respect and quit talking to her boobs."

Camille jerked, as if she'd just noticed what was going on. "Um . . . I feel funny," she whispered to me.

"What's going on—"

Shade suddenly jumped to his feet, dragging Camille to hers. "Come on. We should get going."

Camille looked confused but didn't argue.

"What's going on?" I felt agitated, like ants were crawling over me. "Camille? Camille? What's happening?"

Camille started to waver, her eyes fluttering. Unsure as to what was wrong, I followed Shade's lead and grabbed Camille's other arm. We hurried her out of the club, pushing through the throng.

The minute we were out of the club, he tossed her over his shoulder and took off running up the street. I followed, easily keeping pace.

"What the fuck happened?"

"The bhouts have gained a stronghold in that place, and I sensed one trying to latch onto Camille. I don't know if we got her out in time, but we couldn't stay there or it would be feeding on her, like that one caught hold of Chase." He sat her down after we reached the intersection of Broadmore and Wales, and she leaned against the brick wall of the apartment building. We were only a couple blocks to the left from Carter's.

"Let's go. Carter lives up ahead. Can you carry her, or do you want me to?" It only seemed polite to offer him a choice whether he wanted to lug my sister that far, or whether I ended up doing so.

"I can go . . . I think . . ." Camille still looked confused, but she seemed to be snapping out of it. But when she took a step forward, her knees buckled and she started to fall. Shade swept her up in his arms and we took off at a jog. We were a block from the Galaxy when Camille urged him to put her down.

"I think I'm better. I'm still a little shaky, but I don't feel so light-headed." She stood, unsteadily, for a moment, then was able to walk with us supporting her. It took us less than five more minutes to reach Carter's apartment, all uphill. The Seattle streets were notorious for their grades, and walking in the city beat any treadmill for exercise.

Morio's SUV was parked outside. We navigated down the stairs and knocked on Carter's door. He answered almost immediately.

As we stumbled in, Morio, Delilah, and Chase were sitting in the living room, looking over some photographs and documents. Camille paused, leaning against the back of the sofa.

Carter seemed to notice something amiss because he hurried to the bar, where he poured her a brandy and pressed it into her hands. She gratefully took a sip and lowered herself to the seat beside Morio.

"What's wrong?" Morio looked her up and down, then craned his neck around to look at us. "What happened to her?"

"A bhout got to her at the club." Shade sat opposite. "I need to double-check to make sure it's not still attached to her. I couldn't do that out in the street, but we left the club as soon as we knew something was wrong. Camille, if you'll permit me . . . sit back and close your eyes."

She shivered. "Leeches—the damned things remind me of leeches. Fucking parasites. I'm cold. Carter, do you have a throw I could wrap around my shoulders? Even my jacket doesn't help."

"Certainly." He brought her a light throw that was hanging over a rocking chair. It had pictures of cats on it, along with plenty of cat hair, and she smiled as she wrapped it around her shoulders.

One of his cats—I could never remember which one was which—came up and jumped in her lap, kneading gently against Camille's chiffon skirt, but my sister didn't shoo her away or try to stop her. She just gently scratched behind her ears, and the cream-colored fuzzball curled up in her lap and began to snooze.

"I have a request, too, if you don't mind. I need shadow in which to do my best work. Can we turn off all but a dim light?" Shade slipped out of his duster and stretched, flexing his fingers.

Carter acquiesced, then retook his seat, watching with fascination as Shade lowered himself into trance. A pale haze of smoke began to rise around him, obscuring him from easy sight, and then he vanished into the fog, and it settled around Camille. The cat leaped off her lap and padded over to Chase, who gave her a long eye and grudgingly let her climb up on his nice black suit. Oh yeah, a lovely trail of cat hairs was going to follow.

As Shade engulfed Camille in his moving shadow, he swirled around her and then seemed to vanish into her body. Morio didn't look all that happy, but I tapped him on the arm and shook my head, and he relaxed. We waited, silent, Delilah leaning forward, a worried look on her face.

"I feel . . . so strange . . ." Camille said, her eyes still closed. "I can feel Shade working—moving through my energy field—but it's like there's more than him there. I can't explain it."

A few moments later, the smoke issued out from her mouth and she let out a deep sigh, as if she'd been holding her breath. The shadow drifted back over to where Shade had been sitting and re-formed into a cloud, from which he emerged, shimmering back into view, his eyes crackling with purple fire, a grave look on his face.

"Thankfully, the bhout wasn't able to fully attach to you, but it did siphon off some of your energy. You'll be particularly susceptible to them now, so you're going to have to work on some protection magic and wards to carry with you."

"Was it in the club? Or just hanging out in the astral?" I asked.

"I think a group of them are focusing on the club. They found a ready feeding source, although that won't last too long. Not at the rate they're draining the clientele there."

"Do you think the bartender is in on it?" I hadn't liked

him, he was a seedy little thing, but I didn't want to blame him for something that wasn't his fault.

Shade shook his head. "No, he doesn't have anything to do with it, in my opinion. I think he was as mystified as we were about why the customers are so lethargic. And, probably a bit disappointed, considering he's an energy whore." Shade turned to Carter. "I only know so much about these creatures. Do you have any information on them, since they're of both the spirit and demonic realms?"

Carter frowned. "I'll have to look in the archives. Meanwhile, Morio, why don't you fill them in on what I told you. I'll consult my files and be back in a few moments." He excused himself and retreated to his desk.

Before Morio launched into what Carter had been telling them, he took Camille's hands and held them tightly. "I should never have let you go in there. We should have thought about what might happen."

She shook her head. "We didn't know. We can't hesitate every time there might be danger involved. You know that. Don't you start acting like Smoky!" She looked ready to scold him but then dropped back in her seat. "I'm too tired to argue, so don't even start on me."

He looked like he wanted to say something, and a lock of his hair escaped his ponytail and trailed down the side of his face, stirring something inside me. I wanted to lick his face and sink . . . *Whoa, Menolly, back it up pronto.*

This was neither the time nor the place for these thoughts. In fact, there was no time or place that would be right for them. Enough was enough. There had to be a way to break the bond that had formed between us.

A thought struck me. "I'm so stupid," I blurted out.

Everyone looked at me, confused.

Flustered, I shook my head. "Never mind, just something I was thinking about." Talking about how I wanted to fuck my sister's husband wasn't going to add much to the conversation except tension. But it had suddenly occurred to me to ask Roman what to do. If anybody knew how to break a vampire-blood bond, he would. Why hadn't I thought of that in the first place?

Morio held my gaze. His nostrils flared slightly, but then he turned back to Camille, making sure she was tucked under the throw and that her brandy was refilled. When he was satisfied she was okay, he looked over at Delilah and Chase, and they nodded.

"Menolly, why don't you and Shade move over next to Camille so you can all look at these pictures together?"

We did, flanking her sides.

Morio took what had been Carter's chair. "Okay, here's what Carter found out for us." He motioned for Delilah to hand us the sheaf of photographs. "Reports have filtered up from Portland, Oregon, of bhout activity, but they thought they were just ghosts. They didn't realize that the spirits were demonic."

"We didn't either, at first," I said, glancing at the first photograph. It was taken with a special camera, and it had actually captured one of the wispy jellyfish-like creatures on film. The spirit was latching onto the aura of a woman sitting in a recliner with her eyes closed. "That's one of those things I saw on the Dream-Time. That must be its natural shape. But who took this? How did they get a picture of it, if the bhouts aren't corporeal?"

"One of the paranormal investigators down there used a special film he developed to see if he could figure out why she was languishing. And *languish* seems to be the word." Delilah handed me another piece of paper. It seemed to be some form that had been filled out, and when I glanced over it, I saw that it was a from the Oregon Psychic League, a paranormal investigatory outfit.

As I scanned the contents, it became clear that, at least down in Portland, the psychic community was better organized than up here in Seattle. They'd recognized the problem sooner than we had and had formed a task force to investigate.

"So she's a test subject who reported lack of energy, inability to concentrate, and a drop in her psychic energy that didn't seem normal?" I pointed to one of the fields. "Here it says she runs one of the bigger covens down there."

"Yes, and apparently the entire coven has been affected.

When they heard this from several groups, they wondered if something was systematically draining their energy. Hence the tests. That photograph is one of the results. The other pictures are of ghosts and apparitions. Apparently, hauntings have picked up there, too." Morio glanced over to the desk, where Carter waved for him to continue. "Carter checked with a few other major cities on the West Coast and nothing there, yet. So if this is spreading, it's only reached down the coast so far."

"Is there anything else?" We had too many pieces of the puzzle that weren't quite fitting yet.

"Yes, I've found more," Carter said, returning to us.

He held another folder of papers in his hand and motioned for Morio to stay seated. Instead, he pulled the rocking chair over and sat in it.

"I found more information on bhouts. I also just received a fax from one of my operatives in the Demonica Vacana society. I'd contacted him about Gulakah. But I also asked him about the bhouts, to see if he knew anything about how they're controlled and how to stop them."

"What did you find? Anything we can use?" Camille sat forward, still looking wrung out. "If this is what it feels like to just be grazed by one, I'd hate to know what the FBH pagans and witches are dealing with."

"They'll feel it in a different way than you, since the magical abilities of Fae and humans vary widely." Carter frowned, glancing at the clock. "It's one in the morning. Do you want to go over this now?"

I nodded. "I have a good five hours left till the sun calls me down. I'd like to hear what you found out instead of waiting until tomorrow evening."

He held up his hand. "Very well, but give me a moment." And he disappeared through the curtains that cordoned off the rest of his apartment.

As we waited for him, my phone jangled. I pulled it out and glanced at the text. It was from Nerissa. *Are you okay, and are you ever coming home?*

Shit . . . I knew she was feeling left out, even though she understood what we were facing. But she'd gone out shopping for our wedding and I hadn't even glanced at what she'd bought.

I frowned and texted back, We're fine. At Carter's. Camille had a run-in with a bhout. Be home as soon as we can. Go to sleep, will wake you up when I get there. Love you.

A few seconds later, she texted back, Love you, too. You owe me big, babe.

I glanced up. They were looking at me, quizzically. After a moment, I rolled my eyes and said, "Nerissa. She's pissed at me again and I don't really blame her. She went out and shopped for our wedding and I haven't had the chance to see anything she bought." I sighed. "I wish she could understand that it doesn't mean I don't love her."

Camille nodded. "She'll be okay. As long as you give her some input."

"Well, I told her about a gown I thought I might like to wear. Honestly, I was winging it. I don't know what I want—I always thought I'd like to wear something someone in our family made. Aunt Rythwar is a beautiful seamstress. But I doubt that's going to happen. I'm just no good at these things."

"Good at it or not, sometimes you just have to fake it."

Morio grinned. "You never fake it, babe." He leered at her and licked his lips, and Camille gave him a withering look but then laughed.

"This is neither the time nor the place for that." She pulled the blanket tighter around her shoulders as Carter returned.

He was carrying a tray with sandwiches and cookies, and a goblet of blood. "We all need something to eat."

I looked at the blood and realized that I was hungry. Accepting the goblet, I tried to drink it without spilling any. No sense in squicking everybody out. As I tucked a sandwich into Camille's hand and encouraged her to eat, Carter poured himself an aperitif of cognac and settled into the rocking chair.

"All right, here's what I've found. The bhouts aren't easily controlled—it requires a central, physical anchor to control them, and *all* of them are controlled through this anchor. Only the most powerful sorcerers or demons can control bhouts—they're strong-willed spirits and only the strongest of bindings can bend them to your will." Carter set aside one piece of paper and picked up another.

"Does the anchor have to be in the actual possession of the demon—or sorcerer—who's summoning the demons?" If so, we were screwed.

At least Carter had good news on that front. "No. In fact, the anchor for this sort of gate is far too big to carry around. It's more of a *place*, than a thing. In my opinion," he said, glancing over the page he held, "you're looking for a cave. A good-sized one in which to hide the operation necessary to open a gate the size of a Demon Gate. Not only that, but for what he's up to, it must be near running water—a stream or a creek rather than a pond." He looked up. "That may narrow your search."

Delilah frowned. "A cave? That indicates a place out of town. There are a few small cubbyholes in the city, but nothing the size of what you're talking about. Do you think that means Gulakah is hiding out of the city proper?"

Shade chimed in. "I know something of Gulakah, being from the Netherworld." He rubbed his hands together. "Gulakah was the Lord of Dreams, as you know, and was cast out into the Subterranean Realms for misusing his powers. He isn't the sort of demon who enjoys skulking around in corners. He likes to be honored, respected—though that came to mean through fear rather than love."

"So he's a ham. What's that got to do with it?" Delilah was getting punchy; she was listing to the side and looked like she might drop at any moment. Everybody needed sleep.

"It means this, my little pussycat. While Gulakah might have to do his dirty work in the dark corners of caverns, he's not one to stay there the rest of the time. He has to be the one summoning the bhouts. Telazhar is in Otherworld and you cannot be that far from an anchor to control your minions."

Carter slowly thumbed through the rest of his papers. "That coincides with the information I have here. Gulakah is, to put it mildly, pompous and egotistical. He needs to see the results of his havoc. No, he's in Seattle somewhere, except for when he needs to summon more creatures. He hasn't revealed himself yet, probably due to direct orders from Shadow Wing, but the time is coming when he'll slip up."

"Until then, what do we do?" Morio asked.

"Simple. Find the cave and destroy the Gate. However . . ." Here, Carter paused, shaking his head, "That's not going to be as easily done as said."

"What haven't you told us yet?" I could tell by the look in his eye that there was something else—something we weren't going to want to hear.

Carter winced, then shrugged. "All right, here it is . . . none of you are strong enough to destroy a Demon Gate of this magnitude. Morio and Camille don't even dare try—if they go near it, they'll immediately be attacked by the bhouts. There are few creatures who are immune to them."

Shade blinked. "Dragons, for one."

"Yes, dragons. And some demons. And . . . vampires. Very few others." Carter tossed the papers on the table. "If you send in a human with magical abilities, they'll be a target. Same with one of the Fae. Send in an FBH without magical powers and they'll be ripped to shreds as the bhouts send objects flying through their bodies. Because with the bhouts come ghosts of all kinds."

"Crap. So Smoky, Shade, Vanzir, Roz, and I can go after them, but Camille and Morio, not?" It wasn't a bad force, but it would have been nice to be able to wield magic against them.

"What about me?" Delilah sat up straighter. "I don't use magic."

Carter held up his hand. "No, Delilah—not a good idea. But even if the five of you do go after the gate, you won't be able to destroy it. You must have a powerful sorcerer to disrupt the field of the Demon Gate. And none of you can do it. It doesn't take someone quite as powerful as the conjurer of the gate, but none of you have nearly enough power to destroy it."

I sat very still for a moment. A thought was creeping into my head, and I really wished it would go away because it meant asking a favor from someone I never wanted to meet again. "How powerful?"

"Powerful enough to disrupt spirits—someone who's been working magic for a long, long time. Again, they cannot be mortal—unless they've been around a thousand years."

Anxious, I pushed myself to my feet and paced. "I might know somebody, but I have to make a call first. May I step into your kitchen, please?"

"Use my parlor." Carter ushered me into a small chamber off the living room. I'd never been in here before and was quite surprised to see a television set and a stack of DVDs. Movies of all sorts. I gave Carter a quizzical look.

"Movies? TV? You? *Really?*"

Carter flashed me a sheepish smile. "I have my moments, Menolly. You are very quick to assume, I've noticed. Perhaps that is one quality you should be working on." The rebuke was gently given, and I gave him one of those *what can you do* looks.

"I am what I am, Carter. I try, but . . ."

"But you enjoy jumping to conclusions; you leap first and look later, and I think that's just your nature, girl." He headed toward the door but stopped to look back at me. "I offer criticism only with the best of intentions. With your strength, and the fact that you are a vampire, it would be easy to act first and come to regret afterward. And I somehow think . . . regret weighs heavy on your shoulders when it makes its appearance."

With that, he exited the room. I stared at the door behind him. He was right. I had a great deal of power and strength, and it would be so easy to abuse it. I'd seen that lack of restraint in other vampires, and I'd seen the bloody results.

"Maybe you're right," I whispered to the closed door, before taking out my phone. As I punched in Mallen's number, I grimaced. I'd be waking him out of a sound sleep. But there was no help for it.

He answered the phone after three rings. "Menolly, charming. Do you realize what time it is?"

I'd never heard Mallen being quite so churlish before. "I'm sorry to disturb you. Is everything all right?"

He let out a long sigh. "No. We lost three patients today. We have no clue why they died—well, we do, but there's nothing we can do. Charlotine told me they were drained. Apparently, whatever it is, isn't just draining of life force that can kill, but also draining magical abilities and energy."

I held the phone to my ear, staring straight ahead. "Yeah, we know." I made a decision and filled him in on the bhouts. "The deaths began with the guards on our land."

"And they're likely to continue. We've got a full schedule tomorrow of people complaining of the same symptoms. I don't know what we're going to do. Sharah's having to slow down a little because of the baby. The pregnancy is taking a toll on her—she's got such a slight frame." Mallen usually wasn't this outgoing with information. It worried me because it meant things were on the downswing for sure.

"We may be able to stop this plague. We have some information that might just change things. But if we can find the core of the problem, we're going to need help in putting a stop to it. Apparently none of us are strong enough to do anything about it." I paused.

"What can I do to help?"

I swallowed my pride. "Your friend—Charlotine. You said she's a powerful sorceress? We need her. Will you talk to her and ask her to call me?"

Mallen chuckled. "Menolly, that's the last thing I expected you to ask."

"Me, too," I said. "Me, too."

Chapter 16

꧁ ꧂

By the time we got home, everybody had gone to bed. I'd told the others about Charlotine, and they agreed to give her a chance, but first we had to find the cave. Tomorrow, the others would start searching for a plausible spot where Gulakah was gating in the bhouts.

I peeked into the parlor. Nerissa was asleep on the sofa. Marion and Douglas were staying in one of Delilah's spare rooms—we'd put up an air mattress for them, and they and their cat, Snickers, had settled in. Delilah and Snickers got along surprisingly well, and she spent time in her tabby form chasing him around the house. He never fought back and followed her around with those big round moon-eyes, both when she was Tabby and when she was Kitten. Misty, Camille's ghost cat, got in on the act, and all three of them would go tearing around the joint, knocking things over and racing up the curtains.

I crept into the parlor and over to the sofa. Nerissa was snuggled beneath a thick comforter, and her long tawny locks fell across her face in the most winsome way. She might be a powerful woman when awake, but in her sleep she looked young and vulnerable. My heart melted as I softly sat beside her, stroking her hair away from her face.

"Sleeping beauty." I whispered softly so as not to wake her, she looked so comfortable. The boxes and bags were over in the corner and I decided to take a peek, stopping by the fireplace to stoke the fire. I didn't want to turn on the lights—that would wake her up—so I lit a couple of vanilla-scented candles.

Tiptoeing over to the pile of shopping, I settled myself in the center of all the goodies and started carefully picking through the bags. The first contained shoes—two pair in silver, one in Nerissa's size, the other in mine. Hers were stiletto pumps, and mine were strappy sandals with a platform heel. I smiled as I slid them back into the boxes and set them to one side.

The next box contained a rich plum halter-top gown, velvet and stunning, with a plunging V-neck. I held it to my face, the material soft against my skin. Nerissa would be so beautiful in it. Refolding it, I examined the next box. My dress. I let out a quiet "Oh" as I held up a silk gown. The neck was Grecian, while the arms attached from tiny bows on the top of the shoulders, creating a draped sleeve. The color was the color of spring lilacs, of pale lavender, and it would blouse gently at my waist, then fall in sheer layers to create a diaphanous effect.

For some reason, I felt a little let down and I didn't quite know why. The dress was gorgeous, but something nagged at me. However, Nerissa would never know that I felt this way. She'd only know that I loved what she found for me.

I slipped the dress back in the box and set it aside. The rest of the bags contained an ivory bra, garter, and stockings in Nerissa's size, and pale white in mine. Evening bags and jewelry rounded out her shopping spree, and as I stared at the finery around me, I suddenly felt horribly sad and, realizing what was upsetting me, I slowly walked over to Nerissa, kneeling down beside her.

"Nessa, baby? Wake up." I gently shook her awake, hungry for her lips as she woke from her drowsy state.

She glanced at the clock. "Three o'clock?" She pushed

herself to a sitting position, her knit chemise stretching over her rounded breasts. I soaked in the vision of her, her scent filling me full, making me so horny I could hardly sit still. Just the sight of her turned me on, and when she was tousled from sleep, even more. I slid up on the sofa next to her and wrapped my arm around her. She was warm and her skin was silky, and all I could think of was how much I wanted to kiss her, everywhere.

"I'm sorry," I whispered.

"For what? What did you do?" She kissed my eyelids, then nuzzled my neck. "I missed you."

"I'm sorry that I didn't go shopping with you. That I've been so lax on making plans. I saw what you bought—it's all so perfect. I love it all, everything. But I should have helped. I can't make it up to you, but . . . I'll help from now on. I want our wedding to be perfect." I paused, knowing that if I promised what I was about to, I'd better damned well follow through. "I'll find the place. And it will be beautiful. Do you trust me?"

Nerissa tipped her head to the side, a smile spreading across her face. "My sweet, I trust you. All I ever wanted was for you to take an interest in the planning. I know you're busier than I am and that you may not be able to get out as easily as I can—at least not when the shops are open. That's all I wanted—to know you cared."

She pulled me to her, her lips seeking mine. I slid into her embrace, the warmth of her heart beating gently against the silence of mine. As she kissed my eyes, my nose, my lips, my cheeks, I slid my hands down her sides, then reached under her tank to walk my fingers up her abs, up to the curve of her breasts, where I cupped them, reaching up to finger her nipples as they grew hard against my thumbs.

"I never get tired of your touch," she said, grabbing my wrist and pressing my hand harder against her. "Menolly," she whispered, her chest rising and falling as her breathing came harder. She leaned back, her hair trailing over the back of the sofa, and spread her legs. I reached for her panties, and she shifted, allowing me to slide them down and off.

I leaned in, kissing her bellybutton, trailing my lips down

toward the downy patch of hair between her thighs. Her thatch was trimmed in a delicate "V" and I lingered over it, nosing her gently, as she slid farther down, opening up more to allow me to fully explore her sex. I pressed my lips against hers, gently opening her up, tonguing the budding clitoris that I knew so well.

I'd always known that I preferred women—though when I was young, I thought I'd marry, and perhaps take a mistress on the side. But my first glance had always gone toward women. Camille recognized it before anybody, and one night she sat me down and asked me point-blank. Mother had been dead for some time, and Father was still oblivious, mired in his grief.

Back in Otherworld, loving someone of the same sex wasn't a big deal. The only time it caused problems was if you were of royal blood and expected to produce an heir. Then, you were expected to marry, reproduce, and, if you wanted, take lovers on the side.

As with Earthside, marriages among the royalty—and even some tradesmen—were more for convenience and economy than for love. Luckily I hadn't had to worry about that. We weren't royalty and, being half-breeds, the three of us weren't likely to be considered for important nuptials.

Nerissa moaned as I nuzzled, grasping her ass with my hands as I held her firm. With a quick, sharp cry, she came hard. I looked up at her, rubbing her thighs softly as she caught her breath.

She gave me a sleepy smile. "Your turn?"

I could tell she was tired, so I shook my head. "I'm happy just pleasing you, tonight. Truly. Curl up under the covers again." I snuggled next to her and she stroked my hair as I leaned my head on her lap. "You're my heart-mate."

"I know," she whispered. "And you are the only woman in the world for me. I can't imagine loving anyone else." A yawn escaped her and she blinked, sighing deeply. "What happened tonight? Everything sounded so tense from your texts."

It was almost four. I really didn't want to go over it all again. "You sleep, love. Ask them at breakfast and they'll tell you. Or Chase can fill you in. He was there with us last night. Meanwhile, I think I need some time to just relax and meditate before the sun calls me to sleep. Do you mind so much?"

She pulled the covers up around her neck and rested her head back on the pillow. "Not a problem, my love. So you like the wedding dresses?" Again, she yawned and sounded like she was already drifting off to sleep.

I kissed her on the forehead and made sure she was tucked in. "I love them. And I promise, I'll find us a lovely spot to get married in. Sleep now, and rest . . . and dream deep."

And with that, I blew out the candles. Nerissa was snoring lightly as I left the room, closing the door behind me.

Once downstairs, I made one last call for the night, to Roman.

He answered immediately. "Are you all right? Was it your friend Andrees?"

"Yeah, it was." We'd been so busy, I'd almost forgotten, but now the reality came crashing back and I wondered if we'd ever find out who killed the agent. "Chase thinks he was killed execution-style. But his body was maimed after death, and Mallen doesn't think it's by the same person who killed him. He was found near the rogue portal in Tangleroot Park."

I paused, staring at the print on my wall. It was a framed reproduction of Monet's *Water Lilies*. I loved it. The painting made me happy; it helped me focus when I meditated.

After a moment, I said, "Roman, I have something to ask you. I need to break a bond and I'm wondering if you can help me do it." I told him about what had happened with Morio and the blood transfusion that had saved his life. "I love Morio, but like a brother. I don't like feeling pulled toward him and I know that, even though Camille would understand, it would still strain the relationship. Plus, all I can handle right now is one fiancée and one lover."

He laughed. "Yes, I can see that. There is a ritual to break a blood bond that isn't brought about through turning someone."

"Do both participants need to be there?" I hoped not. If I could do it with as little fuss as possible, all the better.

"Actually, no. But you'll need to come to me. There are . . . delicate computations to make. I will need to call on someone. Can you come over around six thirty? Shortly after sunset?"

"Unless we find . . . well . . . what we're looking for. But I'll need to talk to my sisters first about what they've discovered during the day before I come over. Say seven thirty?" And with a few murmured endearments, I hung up. It had been a very long night, and all I could hope for was a sleep untouched by demons and ghosts and memories of the past. I pulled out my yoga mat and went through several of the poses that most relaxed me. My body didn't need workouts, but the routine comforted me.

Finally, as the sunrise began its siren song, I slipped under the covers and, thinking of Nerissa and how much I loved her, I slipped into an oblivious slumber.

As I entered the kitchen, I was greeted with the sight of a fox chasing two cats—one a ghost cat and the other, obviously Delilah. Snickers was curled up on the windowsill, asleep.

Maggie was in her playpen, clapping and shrieking. Iris was standing on a chair with an upturned pie on the floor at her feet, and Camille was chasing what looked like a giant rat around with a frying pan. A scorch mark in the wall told me she'd already tried magic. Then I realized the fox and the cats were actually chasing the rat, too.

"Whoa there, Tex!" I motioned for Camille to stand back, then stepped over the splattered apple pie and swooped down to grab up the rat, which promptly bit me three times before it turned a terrified face to me. It was kind of cute, actually, and it didn't look like it had rabies. I stroked its head and it slowly calmed down and settled against me.

Camille whistled to Misty, who jumped on the table and

shook her ghostly plume of a tail. Delilah leaped up with her, looking bereft at me, yowling her head off. Iris let out a long sigh as she held on to the back of the chair and lightly jumped to the ground. Morio—in fox form—whined at the door, and Camille opened it. He bounded out and ran off into the yard. At that moment, Hanna came in from the laundry room, a big basket of laundry in hand.

"My pie . . ." Iris knelt down by the overturned tin and began scraping the remains of the pie back into it. "Well, we'll have to make do with three pies instead of four. That means no third helpings." She tossed the pan on the counter as Camille brought over a sponge and paper towels.

Hanna stared at the rat in my arms. "What will you do with that creature? I won't have rats in my kitchen."

Iris cleared her throat. "*My kitchen*, thank you. At least until my house is built. But I agree. Menolly, you can't keep that creature in here and if you put it outside it will only invite its family in."

Delilah, who had been staring up at me with big round eyes, let out another yowl and then proceeded to make several odd chirps and noises. The rat chattered back at her. As we all stared at the pair, Delilah shifted back into herself.

"Put him out. He won't come back. I have his promise upon pain of chasing him down and making a meal of him. But he wants to be let out near the edge of the forest. He doesn't trust me not to make a dash for him." She shook her head, still staring at the rat with curiosity.

"Fine, I'll put the rat outside. Kitten, you stay in here." I headed for the door.

"While you're at it, see if you can find Morio. He was in a playful mood and I guess the rat set off his hunting instincts, too." Camille looked over her shoulder from where she was mopping up the floor.

As I headed for the door, Delilah said, "Oh, by the way, the rat's name is . . . well, to pronounce it in English, it would be Chaka."

"Chaka . . . Okay, come on, Chaka, let's go give you a second chance." I opened the door and, still clutching the rat, exited to the back porch, then out the door to the yard.

Clattering down the steps, I held Chaka to my chest and
jogged over to the edge of the woods leading to Birchwater
Pond. As I knelt down, Chaka looked up at me with his
beady little eyes and twitched his nose.

"You go. You go—do whatever it is rats do and don't
come back to the house. I can't vouch for Iris and Delilah's
self-control. Get it?" I waited, but the rat just twitched his
ears. "You don't understand a thing I'm saying, do you? Maybe
you understood Delilah, though. Either way, go on. Have a
good life. Eat lots of . . . garbage." I set him down and he
paused, looking back at me, then raced off into the undergrowth. For some reason I felt a little sad to see him go.

As I stood and dusted my hands on my jeans, I glanced
around. Now to find Morio. Where would a fox go? A sentient demonic fox, at that?

I was due at Roman's in a little over an hour, and I still
needed to find out what the others had discovered while I
was sleeping. The last thing I wanted to do was find Morio,
alone, out here in the dark. I knew he'd be down with me
breaking the bond between us, but I didn't want to chance
anything going wrong.

After a few minutes, I decided to hell with it and headed
back inside. The kitchen was back to normal and Iris was
sorting through some cookies to provide an extra dessert. The
guys ate like bulldozers, and my sisters weren't shy around
food either. The Fae needed extra food—we all had higher
metabolisms, even the half-Fae. While I no longer required
the hearty meals my sisters did, the food bill around here
was massive.

"I don't know where Morio is. Chaka is, however, off and
pursuing all things ratty." I looked around. None of the men
were in the kitchen, and usually at least one or two of them
were helping Iris and Hanna. "Where are the guys?"

"Morio's outside playing fox. Vanzir and Roz are down at
the studio, mending a leak in the roof. Shamas is at work—
he's on duty the next few nights. Shade's over at Wilbur's,
helping Marion and Douglas settle in because Wilbur's coming back home tomorrow. He took Martin with him and apparently was able to corral him into behaving. They're leaving

Snickers here until they get their own house because they don't trust Martin not to eat the cat. Smoky and Trillian are off getting takeout for dinner. Iris made dessert but we decided to forgo a big family dinner tonight in favor of Chinese." Camille set the plates on the table and Delilah put out the pies and cookies.

Iris added silverware, chopsticks, and a bag of paper napkins, while Hanna carried the laundry over to the rocking chair. Maggie was in her playpen, playing with her Yobie doll—it had Yoda's head and Barbie's body and was pretty beat up by now with plenty of teeth marks, but she loved the thing with a passion and we didn't dare take it away from her.

I looked around for something to do. Motioning to Hanna, I said, "I'll fold the towels. You go ahead and take a break. Make some tea or something."

"I will take my break when it's time to eat. There is so little work here compared to Hyto's cavern, I am not tired." Hanna was sturdy, from the Northlands, and she never shirked on helping out. She was around her late thirties, early forties, and seemed content. But, while she was friendly, she seemed to have a very strong sense of boundaries.

"That's okay—you don't have to be tired to take a break." I reached for the basket, but she stopped me.

"*No.* This is *my* work. Menolly, you have important tasks. You and your sisters battle evil creatures. My duties are to support and tend to you. You saved me from Hyto's grasp, and for that, I will serve you willingly." Her English was still broken, though every day it seemed stronger, but she spoke with strength and conviction.

"You aren't our servant, Hanna." I shook my head. "But if you want to take on the duties of housekeeper, we're happy to pay you. We pay Iris."

"Iris is your family. I am not. Payment is welcome, but I am your servant and I am content in my place. This is what I know how to do." Her voice dropped. "When I lived in the Northlands, before Hyto destroyed my life, my husband—he was stern. The house and gardens and children, all were mine to care for while he was off hunting. He loved his children, and he treated me with respect, but nothing was easy." She struggled with some thought, trying to put it into words. "I . . . I was born a warrior woman, and would have . . . preferred to travel unmarried to make my own way."

"Why did you get married?" Delilah asked.

"My father owed a blood debt to Thaylon's father. I was payment, as wife to his son. It was my duty to fulfill my father's honor, and so I did. Such are the ways of my people. Honor is sacred." She shrugged, looking over one of the towels that had a rip in it. "I will mend this."

"Did you love him?" I let go of the towel I'd been holding, beginning to understand her a little better. Hanna had been tight-lipped over the couple of months she'd been with us, but she was starting to open up, little by little.

"Love my father? Yes. Oh, you speak of Thaylon." She smiled with her eyes. "He was a good man. He never misused me. He was proud of our children. I suppose . . . yes, I came to love him over the years and we had a good life, until Hyto found us." A shiver raced down her, I could see it visibly, and she pressed her lips together and said no more.

We left her to her thoughts as she set down the towel to comfort Maggie, who had started fussing. I glanced at the clock. Six forty-five.

"I have to be at Roman's at seven thirty. Tell me what you found out, if anything, before I go." I straddled a chair as Iris fixed a pot of tea. Camille was drinking what looked like a megashot mocha from Starbucks. Delilah opened the fridge and pulled out the milk, pouring glasses for both herself and Hanna.

Camille took out a notebook. "Yeah. We found two places that fit the requirements and are near enough here that either might be the anchor for Gulakah. One is out near Snoqualmie. Another is on the way to Mount Rainier."

"Great, near Smoky's barrow?" Smoky had a barrow that was near Mount Rainier. At first we'd thought he'd co-opted it from Titania, but the size of the underground chamber that allowed him to change into his dragon self kind of put that idea to rest. It had been she who tried to wrest it away from him instead of living in the cave she'd been hiding in. I was a little fuzzy on how he got out from the barrow once he shifted because, hey, dragons were big. Very big. *So* big.

"No, a little farther up the mountain than that. An access road leads there. It's a ways out, but not out of the scope of possibility." Camille finished sucking down the last of her drink and poured the ice into the sink, then dropped the cup in the recycling bin. "The one near Snoqualmie is in the general area where we found the fourth spirit seal." She paused, glancing at Delilah. "I don't mean to bring up bad memories."

Delilah let out a short sigh. She wiped off the frothy milk mustache and shrugged. "Zachary is happier where he is now. And Chase . . . he's living with what Karvanak did to him. We can't dwell on the past. What happened, happened. We can only move forward."

"You've grown up so much, Kitten." I crossed to her, kissing her gently on the cheek. "You're right. We can't go back. We don't even have time to *look* back. So we have two possibilities? Have the guys checked them out?"

Iris shook her head. "They only came up with the information this afternoon. There's been no time."

"Smoky and Shade are going to check out the cave near his barrow, and then they'll check the one near Snoqualmie. They've promised not to do anything until we've all discussed what they find out. They'll leave after dinner. So we have a much-needed night of downtime."

"What about Andrees? Did the forensics team turn up anything on him?" It felt like we were leaving our friend in the dust, though we had nothing to do with his death. He wasn't even collateral damage, as far as I knew.

"Not yet. We contacted Father through the Whispering Mirror." Camille picked up one of the cookies and began to munch on it. "Where the hell are the guys? I'm hungry." She wiped her fingers on a napkin and let out a sigh, leaning back in her chair. "Andrees's family will be notified."

"And Father's moving ahead on our request to set up the Earthside headquarters the way they were meant to be. He wasn't all that keen on the idea, but for once, he didn't argue."

She leaned on the table. "Chase says that Andrees was killed by a bullet—and it has gangland execution all over it. Somehow, he pissed off somebody he shouldn't have and they took him out. We may never know who. The mutilation came later. Again, no idea what caused it. Not dogs and not even a cougar or bear."

"Elder Fae is my guess. Remember, the Bog Eater is running wild over here." I glanced at the clock again. "I have to leave in about fifteen minutes. Anything else?"

Iris spoke up. "Menolly, I wanted to tell you—"

I groaned. "No, please. You're not going to bitch at me again about Ivana? I did what I needed—"

Iris held up her hand. "No, no. I'm not. It worked out, even though I still think it's a mistake to meddle with them. At least the world didn't implode when she and Aeval met." She set a bowl of whipped cream on the table. "What I wanted to say was this: I'm glad you spent some time with Nerissa last night. She was much happier this morning and was going on about the wedding in a way I haven't heard her talk for the past couple of weeks."

I stared at my hands. "I wish I hadn't been so blind." I glanced over at her. "Has she been depressed for long? Do you think I damaged *us* permanently?"

Iris turned as the door opened and Smoky and Trillian walked through, carrying at least a dozen large containers of food. It looked really good, but one piece through my lips would make me sick as a dog.

Morio followed them through, his jeans and turtleneck covered with dirt and twigs, and his bag carrying his anchor slung over his shoulder. Youkai needed an anchor in order to turn back into themselves from their demonic and animal forms. Morio's was a skull. He slid the bag over his head and put it on the floor near the door leading into the pantry.

Iris glanced at him, then patted my arm. "No, dear. I don't think you did any permanent damage. But don't let her down on your promise to find a place for the wedding. That would be bad. Very bad."

I nodded, then headed toward the door. "I need to go over to Roman's. Don't do anything without me unless it's an emergency. I'll be home as soon as I can." As I passed Morio, I glanced at him and paused. I wanted to tell him what I was going to do. He *would* be affected. But really, I was just putting right what had gone wrong. Returning things to normal. So, instead, I quietly gathered my keys and purse and left.

Roman was waiting for me as I dashed through the rain and up the steps to his mansion. The maid who answered waved me in. She knew who I was and treated me with deference. All I'd have to do is tell Roman that she was rude to me and he'd have her killed. I knew that much, so I never, ever complained about any member of his staff being slow or making a mistake when they called me Melanie instead of Menolly.

I handed the maid my jacket—which I wore more for fashion than for need—and purse. "Here you go, Alice. Thank you."

She curtsied. "Yes, Miss Menolly. You're welcome, I'm sure." As she turned to put them in the hall closet, she added, "The Master is in his study, waiting for you."

I hurried into the study. I was fifteen minutes late, and Roman always got a little testy when he was kept waiting. I never complained about his OCD tendencies on the subject. He *was* the son of a queen, and he did have standards to uphold. But when I entered the room, he just held out his hands to me.

"My dear." He kissed me on the cheek, then pulled me into his arms and pressed his lips to mine. "I have the ritual set up for you."

I stepped back, not knowing how to ask what I wanted to ask. "Roman . . . before we begin. The other night . . . you and me and Nerissa . . . you vanished. Why did you leave?"

Roman's shrouded gaze held me fast. He did not blink, nor did his expression change. "I wanted to be a part of your life—in a way more than this. In a way more than your being my *official* consort." He cupped my chin. "Every time you talk about her, your face lights up in a way that I haven't felt since—since I was young and alive, and in love with a village girl."

My lips trembled. "What happened?"

"To the girl? Her father sold her to a passing horseman. I wanted to marry her, but her father hated my family. I arrived at her home too late. All I could hear were distant screams." He lifted his shirt and showed me the long scar on one side. "That's how I got this. Her father's men fought me, prevented me from following them."

"Oh, Roman. I'm sorry—"

"It's long past . . . she turned to dust when the world was still much younger. Even though my mother avenged me— she had the father strung up in the square and gutted him while he was still alive—I never forgave him. I searched for her, everywhere. But I never saw her again. Every night for months, I dreamed about her, screaming as the warrior rode away with her. I kept imaging what he put her through." He stared into the gas fireplace as it burned brightly, caught in his memory.

"What was her name?" I touched him gently on the arm.

He ducked his head, then shrugged. "I don't remember. But when I see you talk about Nerissa, the look on your face reminds me of her when she'd run to me, run to kiss me. And it makes me . . . nostalgic."

I nodded, finally understanding. Roman didn't want to break us up. He wanted to recapture the one time in his life he'd actually been in love.

"Roman, I . . ."

"Say no more. I accept what you can give. But never bring Nerissa back to my house unless it's an emergency. I cannot stand watching the two of you together." He turned away. "Now you'll think I'm weak."

"Never. I think that you are still . . . somewhere deep inside . . . human. For what it's worth, Roman, I do love you. As much as I can. Nerissa is my soul mate, but you . . . you and I share something I can't share with anyone else. That I *choose* not to share with anyone else." And I wrapped my arms around his waist, kissing his shoulder through the velvet smoking jacket.

Roman paused for a moment, then slipped out of my embrace, and when he turned back to me, he was a mask of gentility, smiling again, with no sign of the suffering I'd seen a few moments before.

"Shall we begin the ritual? I've everything ready." He led me to a door at the back of the room.

"This will break the bond between Morio and me without hurting either one of us?" I looked at him anxiously, desperate to trust him, afraid to trust him.

"Yes. Better you break it now, because if you slept with him, the bond would be unshakable. Or if you drank his blood. You haven't done either, have you? Tell me the truth." He paused, his hand on the knob.

"No. Nothing. A lot of stolen glances. A kiss or two. But . . . no blood since my blood first healed him. And no sex. I think that's why I fucked Roz the other night, and drank from him. I wanted Morio so much that . . . I used Roz as a substitute." I hated admitting that—I didn't like using my friends.

"I thought it was the doppelganger? A charm spell or something?"

I frowned. "I don't know, to be honest. Six of one, half a dozen of the other, maybe? The drinking—yes, that was the doppelganger. The sex . . . I don't know."

"Well, at least you've not muddled things up too bad. Come now, we'll break the bond and you will be free to go back to your old selves. However, he will retain the strength he gained from you during the transfusion. And he will retain the wild streak . . ."

I glanced at him. "I *thought* he'd become more feral since then."

"Oh, no doubt, my love. And that will stay with him. I'm sure Camille has noticed by now? Has she not said anything to you?"

I shook my head. "No, she hasn't. But she couldn't be unaware . . ." And with that thought in my head, I followed him into the room, ready to close out at least one problem in my life.

Chapter 17

❦

The room into which Roman led me was small and made me think of a shrine. It was laid out in an appalling shade of blue. Or rather than appalling, perhaps it was just overwhelming. I winced. The color itself was pretty—not sea green blue, but the glimmering blue of cobalt glass, so that I felt I was under the water in a swimming pool.

The room was simple, with a central console table, low to the ground, against the back wall. On that table rested a clear goblet, a large pillar candle, a small vial of—something— and a silver knife with a bone handle, along with a dozen red roses. The room was lit from glowing tiles in the walls. Two pillows rested in front of the table, the only other furniture. A white dress, simple and much like a Grecian tunic, hung on a hook on the wall.

"Change while I prepare for the ritual." Roman turned and left me alone.

I knew enough not to poke around the altar. I didn't want to muck this up in any way. I stepped out of my jeans and pulled off my shirt, and gracefully draped the gown over my head, tying the simple belt at the waist. It felt elegant and from another time. Looking around for a place to leave my clothes, I finally took them out of the room and put them in the parlor.

At that moment, Roman entered, wearing a long crimson robe, belted by a gold sash. A crown of gold rested on his head and his hair was loose, falling around his shoulders. He looked every inch a prince, and for the first time since I'd met him, the fact that he was the son of Blood Wyne hit home. My stomach thudded and I let out a little sound of surprise.

He seemed to notice. "Few have seen me in my court attire." He did not ask if I liked it, merely motioned for me to reenter the chamber and followed behind me.

As we entered the room, I waited for his instruction.

"Kneel on the pillow to the right."

I did. He closed the door and took his place opposite me. He looked so at ease, and I realized how little I knew of him and his heritage. Blood Wyne had risen again. Roman had talked about his mother, but had he told me everything about her? Had he been truthful about her intentions? And how could I find out?

"Do you know how the vampires came to be, Menolly?"

I shook my head. "No, I don't know. It's not something we learned in school, or that the OIA taught me when they brought me back to sanity." I'd told Roman all about that time period—the year of madness and my slow fight back to sanity.

"No one knows how long ago it happened, but it was before recorded history, long before the Great Divide. Humans had risen to sentience and reasoning. And a shaman from a village desired immortality like the Fae."

"But the Fae aren't immortal. Even the elves die. Even the gods die," I whispered.

"True," Roman said, "but the mortals didn't know that. Their life span compared to a Fae? A whisper on the wind. The shaman's name was Kesana. At least, that's the name we know for her. She decided she wanted the same immortality the Fae had. She went on a quest through the Dream-Time to find the answer, and instead she found demons . . . demons who fed off life energy."

"Like Vanzir? Dream-chaser demons?"

Roman shrugged. "No one knows. All we know is that they promised her life unending if she would allow them to merge with her soul. And so, she agreed. The ritual took her down into death. She died and was reborn in the same body—but she was changed. The aging process had stopped, and her hunger for blood was strong."

"The bloodlust . . ." I'd wondered how blood played into our mythology and background. Roman's story rang true.

"Yes, the bloodlust. Kesana found that the more she fed on others—on their blood—the stronger she became. And her shamanic abilities allowed her to learn how to pass along the curse. She learned how to turn others. But instead of the demons merging with her victims, a little part of her own force brought about the change. That is how siring was born. She is the mother of us all."

It made sense. Vampires were considered minor demons. "What happened to her? Kesana?"

"No one knows. She vanished somewhere into history."

"Do you think she's still alive?"

Roman shook his head. "I don't know. Truly. If so, she has to have changed. During some rituals, the ancient vampires call upon her like a goddess, but it's more rite than belief."

I considered this. It made sense—paying tribute to the mother of our species. "I've always wondered how we first began. But what does that have to do with Morio and me and our bond? Or does it?

"In a very limited sense, you sired Morio when your blood was transfused into him. That's what I'm trying to say—it's not your soul that sires your children, but your blood. *Change the blood and the bond is broken.*"

As I gazed at the knife and then back at him, what he was suggesting began to filter through and a wave of panic began to rise. "I don't want to go through the turning again!"

Roman reached out and caught hold of my wrists when I started to rise. "No, that's not what I'm suggesting. You can never die again unless it's the final death, so the ritual can't reenact your turning."

"I can't relive that." Panic had me fully in its grip now,

and I could barely hear what he was saying. All I could see were Dredge's hands and Dredge's blood and Dredge's knife and the darkness of the cave. Furious, I pulled away. "I can never go through that again."

Roman jumped up and pulled me into his arms, turning me so I had to face him. "Menolly, stop!" He used a command voice and I froze, suddenly aware of my surroundings again. "I would never ask you to return to that time, nor to do anything that remotely put you through what you've experienced. I am a cruel master, but I'm no sadist."

He leaned down and lightly kissed my forehead. "Girl, I've done things that made Dredge look like an amateur, and at times, I was vicious and cared for nothing but what I could wrest from life. But . . . I am wiser, and older, and the blood-lust has shifted into an aspect of my life that I control and use where appropriate."

Nodding, I forced myself to relax. He let go of me and led me back to the altar, bidding me kneel again. "Through this ritual, you will take on some of my heritage. In a sense, I will 'adopt' you, so you will no longer be fully Dredge's daughter. That will change your blood enough to break the bond between Morio and you, because he will have a bond with the blood in your veins as it is now. *Change the blood, change the bond.*"

"How . . . how do we do this?"

"Trust me. I cannot explain the ritual—you must walk through it. But I promise you, it will involve very minimal pain. And what you will gain from it . . . my dear, you will be not only the daughter of Dredge with his strength in your veins, but also my own, with my strength running through you, too. You will become one of the ancient vampires over time—strong and wise, I hope, and brilliant."

"I know this is a stupid question," I said, "but will this change . . . us? Will you still be my lover?"

He smiled, then, and the faint lines around his eyes crinkled. "Oh, it will alter our relationship, but you will still be my consort. Perhaps more so, because we will be blood bound. And before you ask, this should not affect your feelings for Nerissa. I promised you that I will not interfere with your relationship with her, and I won't."

I nodded. That was as much of a guarantee as I was going to get until this was over and done with, and I'd have to be content with it. I glanced at the door. There was still time to back out. "What happens if I don't break this bond?"

"Eventually it will draw the two of you together. It won't wear off, if that's what you're asking. And if he's soul-bound to your sister and blood-bound to you, it's going to create a strain on the youkai." Roman folded his hands on his lap, waiting.

I had saved Morio's life, but at what cost? Binding him to me was as bad as when we'd bound Vanzir's life to ours. Slavery of sorts. Erin had made the choice—she'd been almost dead and she'd chosen to enter the life, but for Morio, the choice had been made for him. And while I knew he was grateful for his life, he was neither vampire nor fully himself.

"If I go through the ritual, what will happen to him?"

"His blood will no longer call to yours. It's different when you sire someone. You sired Erin and you know how she responds to you. That's normal. But it's not normal for vampire blood to be given to those still living, and it sets up a sense of opposition in their nature. He will never be who he was before the infusion, but he won't feel torn between you and Camille once you undergo the rite."

I nodded. That was good enough. "If he won't be in danger from this . . ."

"He won't." His frost-covered eyes focused on me. "Make a decision, Menolly. You must choose. And this is the only time I will offer the chance. It is not something I take on lightly, either, because it will forever bind the two of us. Perhaps I will regret doing so, one day, but we cannot know the future."

I dropped my head back to stare at the shimmering blue ceiling and murmured, "Let's do it."

Roman stood, and, motioning for me to stay kneeling, he began to circle the room, arms stretched out.

"Ancient Kesana, Mother of the Blood, Daughter of Demons, hear me. As you first took the bloodlust into yourself, now watch as I transfer my blood to sire one already sired." He turned, softly gliding back to the pillow, where he knelt again. He took up the knife and held it up. "Blessed be the knife that brings the blood to the surface. Blessed be the blade that calls forth the life. Blessed be the edge that slices the skin. Menolly, take the goblet and hold it beneath my wrist."

Drawing back his right sleeve, he held out his wrist. I picked up the goblet and placed it under his arm, as he drew the blade across the skin, moaning as the silver bit into his skin. The cut festered, opening wide, and turned brilliant red. Blood bubbled slowly to the surface—when we bled, it was slow and viscous, flowing in a slow trickle rather than fountaining up like it did with mortals.

The blood splattered into the goblet, rich and red and smelling headily like wine to me. I watched, transfixed as Roman bled into the goblet. He squeezed his arm to encourage the flow, until the chalice was half-full, and then he turned his arm up and waited as the slice healed, which took about five minutes.

"Now, your turn." He handed me the knife and I gingerly took it, staring at the silver blade. Why we used silver, I wasn't sure, but I knew this was neither the time nor the place to ask. The gown I was wearing left my arms bare, so I stretched out my right arm over the goblet that he now held and sliced the vein deeply with the silver blade.

The pain of the silver hit me like a burning brand. I managed to catch myself before I cried out, as the blood began its trickling descent to the glass, mixing with Roman's. As I watched the drops fall, splashing against the crimson of his blood, a shiver ran through me and I tried not to think about what this would mean. Dredge was my sire, but I'd escaped from him and the distance had provided a buffer. But there was no distance between Roman and me.

When the goblet was almost filled, he motioned for me and I turned my arm upright, watching as the wound finished healing. I placed the blade back on the table as he set down the goblet and lit the candle.

The fragrance of ylang-ylang and jasmine filled the room.

Roman picked up the vial and opened it. A strange smell filled the room, heady and intoxicating, making me lick my lips. I wanted to ask what it was but forced myself to remain silent. He carefully tipped it over the goblet and dropped one . . . two . . . three drops of the coppery-colored liquid into the blood, then took the silver blade and stirred it. Corking the vial again, he put down the knife and picked up the goblet. Turning to me, he dipped his thumb into the blood and pressed it against my forehead.

"I anoint you in the name of the First Mother." Once again, he coated his thumb and this time he motioned for me to pull back the folds of the gown, exposing my chest. He pressed his thumb against my heart.

"I anoint you in the name of Blood Wyne, my sire and mother." A third time, and this time he pressed his thumb against my lips.

"I anoint you in my name—Roman, Liege of the Vampire Nation, Son of the Crimson Veil." He lifted the goblet to salute me, then drank half of it. Handing it to me, he nodded. "Drink."

I swallowed the blood and it tasted like spice, like cinnamon and cloves and fire and copper. As it bathed my throat, the room began to spin; slowly but surely, I swallowed my fear with the crimson nectar.

I'd been through portals; I'd been through death. I knew transition when I felt it. There was no going back now.

Roman stood and dropped his robe off. He was naked beneath it, and his scars were glowing in a way I'd never before seen. I could see every mark he'd accumulated during his thousands of years. He motioned for me to stand and I dropped away my gown. I glanced down, gasping as every mark Dredge had made on me began to glow and shimmer. I was lit up like I was covered with fireflies or glowworms. But for some reason, here—in this place—it didn't bother me.

Roman took my hand and as we stepped back, the altar table slid to the left, and a secret door opened in the chamber, revealing a dark passage. A booming of drums and music began to sound as Roman drew me into the passage. He sped up and I kept pace, suddenly aware we were no longer in the mansion but somewhere in between worlds.

And then a light shimmered at the end of the passage, and we raced toward it, bursting through into a wide meadow under the rain-soaked night skies.

Up ahead of us sat a mansion that dwarfed Roman's house. Painted in alabaster and gold tones, it was surrounded by guards, but they seemed to take no notice of us. They stood at attention, dressed in crimson robes, with gold-hilted knives at their belts.

We walked up the stairs, hand in hand, naked and glowing, and passed through the door as if we were ghosts. I glanced at Roman, but he seemed perfectly calm, as if he did this every day.

As we entered the mansion's foyer, he pulled me to the right, into a small room, which turned out to be a coatroom. It was the size of our living room at home. Roman handed me a plain white tunic and draped a red cloak around his shoulders, trimmed with gold ribbons and beading. I slid into the simple cotton shift, wondering again what I had done.

After we'd dressed, we walked out and toward the central doors. Roman took my hand again.

He gazed down at me, pausing for a moment. "You are about to be inducted into the Crimson Veil. You will be my heir and hence related to my mother. Do not flinch. Do not hesitate. There is no returning to who you were before you drank the blood sacrifice. Do you understand me, Menolly? Do not fail me."

As the significance of what was happening began to sink in, I could only nod. My only choice was to move forward.

"I do." Every fiber in my being screamed against obeying— not because it was the wrong thing to do, but because I hated submitting to anyone or anything. But sometimes, in life, we had to relinquish control to a greater force, in order to bring about a greater good. And I knew in my heart this was the right thing to do, even though I rebelled against the idea of supplication.

Without another word, Roman led me to the doors, and two guards bowed low when they saw him. We walked through, into the throne room.

The chamber was tremendous, as big as our entire house

at home, and it was filled with seats lining the sides, like a university auditorium. At the center and back sat a raised dais and upon that dais, a throne. The throne was built of black marble, and on the throne sat a woman dressed in gold with crimson accents. She was stately, with salt-and-pepper hair, and a face lightly marred by time. She'd probably been turned when she was around fifty, and she had been in good shape, from the way she looked. Her eyes were the same pale frost as Roman's, and his facial features mirrored hers.

Blood Wyne stood, her dress billowing around her, form-fitting on the top and spreading like a princess gown at her hips, shining gold threads interwoven with sparkling rubies that had been beaded in swirling designs. Victorian in design, the dress had a low-cut sweetheart neckline and a gothic collar that shrouded the back of her neck. Blood Wyne's hair was swept up into a high chignon, accentuated by a diadem of rubies and diamonds inset into gold.

Pale as the mist. Pale as cream, with no color to mar her lips or cheeks. Blood Wyne, Queen of the Crimson Veil, was as cold as a sculpture formed from ice and snow.

She waited for Roman to bring me up the steps leading to the throne, and as he knelt before her, I did my best to drop into a low curtsey without disgracing myself.

Blood Wyne gestured for us to rise. Roman let go of my hand and—motioning for me to stay where I was—lightly ran up the stairs to place a kiss on his mother's outstretched hand.

"Your Majesty . . . thank you for seeing me."

And then, the marble of her face cracked—just a little—and she smiled at her son. "Roman, we are alone with the girl. Don't stand on ceremony."

Startled by her forthrightness, I jerked my head up to stare at her. She gave me a wolflike smile. "What? You do not expect ancient queens to be understanding of the modern world? Your Fae Queens seem to be. Do not underestimate me, girl."

"Never," I said automatically, before remembering I should probably wait for her direction to speak.

But Blood Wyne just chuckled and sat back on the throne. "Rise, Menolly. So . . . you are my son's chosen consort. Turn and let me look at you."

Feeling like a prize cow, I turned in my simple white robe, wondering what she must think of me. I wasn't cut out for the court, and I wasn't about to wear billowing ball gowns or jeweled tiaras unless it was an official function for which Roman needed me to dress.

"Interesting. I like the fire in her eyes, my son." She spoke to Roman as if I weren't even in the room, but I wasn't feeling much like contradicting her. She turned back to me and held my gaze. I felt like a stake was piercing my soul and I couldn't move. I had a feeling she could hold any vampire hostage with her gaze, which meant her power was very real and very great.

After a moment, she let me go. "The eyes speak volumes, to mouth banalities. But cliché or not, it is a truth that we can read much by reading another's gaze. And I can read the truth in your soul, Menolly. You do not love my son, but you are fond of him."

I stammered. "I . . . I love him as much as I can, Your Majesty."

Blood Wyne shrugged. "Love is overrated. My son seeks it, but love leads only to tragedy and loss. Fondness, loyalty are much better emotions to nurture. And I see that you have loyalty—but to whom? To whom do you bind yourself, Menolly?"

I swallowed, not wanting to tell her about my family. Vampires could make terrible use of emotions and bonds to control others. But one look at Roman and I knew she already knew the answers. He was her son. He owed her loyalty and he probably told her everything.

"My sisters hold my oath, first and foremost. My family and friends. My oath to the elves and to my home city-state. My beloved. I will never betray them. And . . . I have a loyalty to your son, yes. As long as it does not interfere with my other allegiances." Sometimes, it was better to just have the facts out in the open.

Blood Wyne nodded, somberly. "I do not take oaths lightly, my young vampire. And neither do you, I see. I admire that. I would rather you placed my son first, of course, but breaking one oath to forge another is tantamount to being warlock, and I will not tolerate broken vows in the Crimson Veil. Best now you understand this."

"I do, and I agree." Relieved that she wasn't going to attempt to supersede my loyalties with her own, I began to relax, just a little.

"My son told me he was performing the ritual of re-siring with you, and why. Did he also tell you that at this point, I must accept you into our line in order for it to fully take? And that if I don't, you will be killed?"

I gasped, turning to Roman. "You didn't—"

His face a blank mask, he stared solemnly at me. "I did not know."

I wanted to rail at him, to send him flying down the steps in a fury, but this was not the best place to go postal. His mother could pick me off like a fly. Glaring at him, I turned back to Blood Wyne.

"He did not tell me about the latter part. He guaranteed little pain."

"Little pain does not mean the same thing as not being hurt. But do not fret. He did not know, either, because I chose not to tell him."

As she stood again, she seemed to grow taller, towering over me. I felt fear for the first time in her presence. I went down on my knees, as did Roman. "You have no clue what it means to be in the presence of the Crimson Veil."

Her voice echoed through the room, rebounding off the walls. As I peeked through my fingers, she aged, not in body, but in spirit, and her power reverberated through me. She was no figurehead, but truly a queen.

"Do you even *know* what the Crimson Veil is, my girl?" She leaned down and reached for my hand, and—unable to resist—I gave it to her. As she drew me up, I shook my head, stupefied into silence.

"Then come with me, and learn."

The throne room vanished and I found myself standing beside Blood Wyne in a crimson haze, a flurry of smoke and fog rippling like some bloody aurora borealis. The bloodlust raced through my body. I let out a moan, trying to stifle my instincts, trying to push the predator within back into the closet.

"Welcome to the Crimson Veil. It is the place all vampires come to, in the end. It was created when Kesana turned the world into her playground by accepting the demons into her soul."

The winds shrieked around me, calling me to feed, to hunt, to tear through the world and rip it to shreds.

"What is this place?"

"This is the core of the bloodlust, the source of our power, the only memory we have left of Kesana. This is the primal power of the vampire. Some say this is what remains of Kesana's soul."

"Why didn't I feel it when Dredge turned me? Does every other vampire know about this?"

She shook her head. "No, only those who've reached a great age and choose to end their life, or those brought as a guest. Menolly, you repress yourself. You spend enormous energy denying your nature, and that is more dangerous than accepting who you are."

As she whispered in my ear, a sweat poured over my body, and I hadn't sweated since I was turned. I glanced at the beads of perspiration and they were bloody drops, saturating the white gown that I wore.

"I cannot give in. It's too dangerous. I will not turn on my friends. I will not become a mindless hunter in the night."

"You do not have to," she whispered. "But you must accept what you are, fully, and embrace it. Any lingering shreds of doubt and regret must be swept away if you are to fully become the vampire you're destined to be. You are half-Fae, yes, and half-human, but you are *all vampire*. You feed on animal blood instead of keeping bloodwhores. Why?"

"Because it's vile—I do not want the responsibility for their lives in my hands. What if I make a mistake? What if I can't control myself? What if I hurt someone I care about?"

"A bloodwhore lives to serve."

"I will not keep a stable." I began to cry, bloody tears streaking down my cheeks. "I hate the very thought of it. I hate that Roman does it. I find it . . ."

"You find it an abomination? But you *do* feed on humans. You are no saint."

I wanted her voice to stop. Clasping my hands to my ears, I shouted back at her. "I feed on the scum—those who hurt and harm and maim . . . those who will never be redeemed because they are beyond all repentance."

"Then you are their judge and jury, Menolly, and yet you pass judgment on those who willingly give of themselves that we might live?" Blood Wyne grabbed me by the wrists and turned me so I faced the veil that rippled in front of us. "Very well, you do not wish to keep bloodwhores. But until you can plunge yourself into the veil and understand your true nature, you will always be running from yourself. Until then, you can never be a part of my lineage."

I understood then. She would kill me unless I walked into the veil. Terrified—*what would it do to me? what would I become?*—I tried to look away, but she shoved me forward.

"Step into your nature and learn. Or be destroyed. It is your choice."

Weeping as she ripped my robe away, leaving me naked, I stumbled forward. There was no more leeway. Either I stepped into the veil—embraced the unknown—or I let Blood Wyne destroy me.

"Promise me one thing." I turned to her, straightening my shoulders.

"You ask for favors, girl? Well, what do you want?" She did not flinch as she looked over the scars that shimmered on my body.

"Promise me that if I turn into the predator I fear, you will instruct Roman to stake me, and that my family will be informed." I held myself straight, looking her in the eye. Against protocol or not, I didn't care.

Blood Wyne nodded, slowly. "Deal."

I turned back to the Veil. It rippled like a waterfall, and, feeling like a dead woman walking, I held out one hand to touch the shimmering field. My fingers touched the edge and then, as I walked into the Veil—

—*The world fell away.*

Everyone and everything was gone, and there was only me standing in the midst of the energy as it undulated around me. I'd expected to lose my mind, to be held in the grips of the blood-hunger, but instead, my mind cleared and I shivered, suddenly feeling the cold for the first time in a long, long while.

A shower of cool rain washed over me, except the rain was as blood, and it trickled down my body in rivulets, finding the channels of the scars that lined my body. I watched it flow, and for once, the smell didn't set off the thirst. I was able to take it or leave it. I turned back, to ask Blood Wyne what this meant, but she was not there. Only the static of the Veil.

Power does not have to corrupt. You do not have to be afraid of your power if you are its mistress.

The thought raced through my mind and I frowned, not sure where it came from. I thought about walking somewhere, but there was nothing save for the waves of energy flowing around me, and I was a little afraid that I'd get lost in the currents if I moved forward.

To take control over your self, to master your powers, you must accept them, embrace them, and wear them with humility and with pride.

And there it was. On a gut level, I understood what Blood Wyne was saying, and I also knew where I fell short. I wasn't proud of who I was. I didn't revel in it except rare times when the bloodlust caught me up.

"I don't know how to be proud of what I am." I said it aloud, and my voice pierced the Veil, dancing through it with shattering effect. Shaken, dizzy from the constant movement that shifted around me, I said it again, louder. "I don't know *how* to be proud of my powers . . . Dredge turned me, and how can I be proud of a curse given by a monster?"

The Veil twisted, coiling as I began to scream. "I don't want to be proud of what he did to me! I don't want to accept what he did to me! I will not forgive him, nor will I give him credit!"

As my anger grew, the crimson strings of energy began to twist and dance in on themselves, and I fell to my knees, caught in the full fury of my anger and memories. "I killed him—I dusted my sire and I'm proud of that! So how can I ever, ever embrace what he did to me?"

And then, Blood Wyne appeared in the middle of the

Veil, and she knelt to take me in her arms. She lifted me to my feet, like she might lift a child, and lowered her fangs to my neck.

"You don't have to be proud of him. Because you are my son's daughter now, and mine. And we—we will make you dizzy with pride. Embrace me, and leave your former sire behind. Embrace my son."

Roman appeared, on the other side, and he also wrapped his arms around me, and in the midst of the Veil, they lowered their fangs to my neck and fed, and it was glorious and delicious, and I came hard and quick, and then, without hesitation, aware only of my own desire, I fed from them, first from Roman, and then from Blood Wyne. And then, filled to the brim with the heady energy that ran through their veins, I slid into unconsciousness.

Chapter 18

When I woke, I was back in the ritual room. Blood Wyne was nowhere in sight, and I slowly sat up, feeling like I had a hangover from hell. I winced against the light, but apparently Roman had dressed me again. I leaned my head between my knees, trying to sort out everything that had happened.

As I examined my feelings, I realized something had changed. I was still me, but I felt different. Something was missing, something that had been a part of me for thirteen years. And then I knew what it was.

The feelings of shame and anger were gone.

I thought about Dredge. The fury that had remained after staking him had faded, leaving only a vague numbness. I glanced at Roman, and my heart skipped a beat as I instantly fell to my knees.

"My sire . . ." Catching myself, I realized that I'd acted without thinking. And then I remembered the same look on Erin's face when I came into the room.

"Crap."

Roman laughed. "Different, isn't it? But it will fade to a distant thunder, my dear, especially since I didn't sire you the

usual way. It will dissipate faster than you think, though probably not as quickly as you'd desire." He paused, then added,
"But the bond between you and Morio is now broken."

I gazed at him, feeling something stir in my heart. Not
love, but a sense of devotion. Something I'd never felt for
Dredge.

I glanced at the clock. "Roman, I have to go . . ."

He nodded. "I know. We're done. There shouldn't be any
other aftereffects that I can think of." Taking my hand, he
helped me to my feet. "I wish you a good evening. And I'm
sorry about your friend, Andrees. I have a couple of my men
looking into this."

As I headed out of the room, my mind was racing. The
evening had been one huge unexpected whirlwind, but
really, walking out of the mansion, nothing had visibly
changed. But inside . . . oh, yes. The bond with Morio was
broken. But what kind of a bond had I taken on instead?

By the time I got home, it was going on eleven P.M. Everybody was in the kitchen, waiting for Smoky and Shade to
return from checking out the caves.

Camille, Delilah, and Iris were playing a rare game of
quarsong—an Otherworld board game. Trillian and Roz
were playing chess. Nerissa rifled through a flower catalog,
looking at bridal arrangements, with Hanna peeking over
her shoulder. Vanzir was playing his Sony PSP. Morio pored
over maps of the Snoqualmie area. Bruce was tickling Maggie on the floor. And they all looked up as I came in.

Morio did a double take, shaking his head as he stared at
me. "What happened to you?"

Camille stared at me. "I can feel it, too. Are you all
right?"

"I'm fine . . . actually better than fine," I said. "Go on
with what you were doing." I'd tell them about what happened later. Right now, I needed to process my thoughts.

Downtime in our world was rare. We needed to make
the most of it. I joined Bruce on the floor. He was playing
horsey with Maggie, who was hanging on to his back as he

lumbered across the floor, neighing every few steps. I laughed and pretended to be a monster trying to stop them. Bruce valiantly turned into a knight in denim armor, saving the fair Lady Maggie, who giggled and danced around happily, if a bit clumsily, her wings knocking against the cupboard doors.

Camille tossed the dice and counted out her moves, then drew a card. "Five . . . six . . . seven. Tangleweed catches you in the marsh. Lose a turn. Hell." She shrugged. "I'll refill the cookie plate while you take your turns."

As she stood, plate in hand, Morio pushed back the maps and sauntered over to help her. He glanced back at me, looking confused, but then he turned and wrapped his arm around her waist and kissed her cheek. She leaned against him briefly, and for a moment, I felt a slight twinge, but it faded and I realized that, while he was cute, he really didn't appeal to me. Which meant the ritual had worked.

With a silent thanks to Roman, I went back to Bruce and Maggie. She held her arms up and I lifted her, resting her against my chest.

Bruce stretched, then headed over to the table to watch the quarsong game. Camille returned to the table in time for her next turn, and Morio joined her. She picked up the dice as I carried Maggie over to the rocking chair and sat down, holding her to my shoulder, crooning a lullaby.

Trillian had just checkmated Roz, and Vanzir was winning whatever he was playing—that much was obvious by his shouts of *"Die, sucker! Eat it!"* when Smoky and Shade shimmered in from the Ionyc Seas.

As we all turned, the quiet peace broken by our anticipation, I gently laid the now-sleeping gargoyle into Hanna's arms and she carried her off to bed.

Smoky glanced at Shade. "We found it. We found the cave where they're gating in bhouts."

"Which one is it? The one near Snoqualmie or the one up near your barrow?" I tensed, hoping it was the former—nearer and easier to get to.

"Near Snoqualmie. There's a large Demon Gate set up in there. But we can't destroy it—none of us can. The magic is so powerful it nearly knocked me for a loop. And there are creatures there, guarding it—ones I've never before seen. They're demons, but again, their energy is also connected to the Netherworld."

"What do they look like?" Vanzir pulled out a piece of paper and a pencil.

"They were spindly, long-limbed, gray-skinned. Their heads were almost heart shaped, with large, luminous eyes and an almost insectlike torso. And they had round mouths with sharp little teeth in a circle, lining the entire mouth." Shade gazed over at Delilah, and he looked nerve-racked. "I'm a dragon—well, half-dragon—and I have to tell you, the energy they were giving off scared the crap out of me.

Vanzir stared at the sketch he'd drawn from Shade's description. "Are you sure about this? Are you *absolutely sure*? Did they look something like this?"

Shade looked at the drawing and nodded. "Yeah, that's a good likeness. Do you know what they are?"

"Yeah." Vanzir stared at the drawing. He shifted uncomfortably and then crumpled the paper and tossed it in the garbage. "They're degas. They originated in the Netherworlds but were sent to the Sub-Realms when they became too difficult to handle. They're wild and unpredictable. Even Shadow Wing wouldn't allow them in the armies because he couldn't control them. They're like savage animals and will tear anything to pieces that gets in their way."

"Then how are they being used by Gulakah?" If they were so dangerous, how was he able to control them? I wasn't up on my Netherworlds lore.

"Remember, he is the Lord of Ghosts. He can control beings that otherwise are uncontrollable. He probably summoned them and put them under a geas. They have to serve him until he—or someone as powerful as he is—breaks the spell. Which means we'll have to fight them." Vanzir rubbed his chin, thinking. "I'm trying to remember what their vulnerabilities are. In the Sub-Realms, we had to learn how to avoid them because they frequented the wastelands and the slum areas of the cities there."

Cities. I hadn't thought about the Subterranean Realms

having cities. I cocked my head. "Um . . . didn't think about cities there."

Vanzir grinned at me and winked. "Yeah, and we have inns and stores and ice cream there, too. Well, not so much the ice cream. There are four main cities that I've been in. Shadow Wing's city—at least his while he rules—is named Quenisten. It's beautiful, in a dark way—with gleaming towers of dark marble, and bronze domes rising over his palace."

Somehow, the thought that Shadow Wing was organized enough to have a palace, let alone live in a city, didn't make me feel any better. But it did seem like a fact we'd overlooked and really should make notes on.

"We'll discuss this fascinating topic a little later. For now, think hard. The degas . . . what are their vulnerabilities?"

"Let me remember . . . okay, they aren't affected by heat or cold much—the Netherworld is cold, and the Sub-Realms can be pretty hot. Neither extreme affects them. But, if I remember right, they're sensitive to water. And they don't like loud sounds much. They have extremely sensitive hearing. High-pitched noises can disable them." He stood, stretched, and headed over to the refrigerator.

The phone rang and I picked it up while the others began to discuss ways we could disrupt them. It was Mallen.

"I talked to Charlotine. She's agreed to help you but on one condition."

Great. Just what we needed. A vampire sorceress who was about to slap us with a request for a blood payment, no doubt. "What does she want?"

"She wants an audience with Roman." His tone told me everything I wanted to know.

Charlotine was looking to move up in the world over here, Earthside. And she saw me as the way to do so, even though she despised me. She couldn't get an audience with Roman by herself, so she'd wiggle her way in there through riding on my skirt's hem. The thought of hanging around a vampire who thought I should be toasted was disconcerting, especially since she was older and, most likely, stronger, than I.

But wait, a voice inside whispered. *Now you have Roman's blood in your line—perhaps not to the extent that Dredge's is, but Roman is your sire and he won't stand for any mis-treatment of you.*

"Fine. Tell her she's got it. But on my terms, and when she goes out with us, she fucking takes her orders from me and my sisters. If she so much as moves to attack any of us, she's stick-a-fork-in-me staked. Got it?" I was out of patience and out of options.

Mallen paused, then let out a long sigh. "Yes, I read you loud and clear. I'll have a talk with her. She's not free tonight. Will tomorrow night work?"

"That's fine. Tell her to show up here by six forty-five P.M. And tell her to bring her bag of magic tricks. We need her to destroy a Demon Gate. A nasty-assed fucking huge one." Before Mallen could say another word, I signed off.

As I turned to the others, I saw that they'd been listening to me. I'd been so deep in my thoughts I hadn't noticed. I explained my reasoning. "Charlotine's the only sorceress that we know who's powerful enough to bring it down. And she'll help us. I was just laying out conditions."

"So tomorrow night, we move?" Vanzir asked.

"Tomorrow night we move. There may be bhouts there. They won't be able to mess with Charlotine, since she's a vampire, but that means Morio and Camille have to stay here. And I think we should leave Roz, Trillian, Delilah, and Chase at home. Which leaves Smoky, Shade, and Vanzir—you're with me." I had no clue what I'd do if Roman refused to give Charlotine an audience, but I was pretty sure I could persuade him to do so.

"We can go through the Ionyc Seas. Less chance of being noticed that way." Smoky rummaged through the refrigerator. "Any thing left for a snack?"

Hanna quickly motioned him aside and pulled out bread and ham to make him a sandwich. "Let me do this."

"As you will. Thank you." Smoky was always careful to be polite around her. He looked so much like his father that Hanna still had moments where she cringed when he got irritable.

"What about tonight, then?" Camille yawned as she folded up the board game and put it away. She looked tired.

Everybody looked tired. Even I felt weary. The ritual hadn't been all that easy on me, and I still hadn't told them what had gone down.

"I have something to tell you all."

"Oh fuck, what now?" Delilah slumped in her chair, looking so forlorn I started to laugh.

"No, it's not bad. At least I don't think so. But it is going to affect me, and so you'd better know what's going down." And so I told them about the ritual and Roman, and breaking the bond with Morio, and the fact that Roman was now essentially my sire. When I was finished, the room was silent.

"Well, don't all talk at once." I let out a snort. "Nothing's really that different."

"Oh, really?" Camille turned. "You've bound yourself to him, you know? You were free of Dredge, and now you take on a sire that you didn't have to." She looked angry, but I could hear the edge of fear beneath her words.

"I had to do it—for your sake, for Morio's sake, and for mine." I turned to Morio. "Truthfully, tell me, do you feel pulled to me now?"

He shrugged. "No, and the difference was apparent the minute you walked in. It's a relief, actually. There was this pressure . . . I couldn't be around you and not keep noticing you. You were a distraction."

Camille lowered her eyes. "You know that I understood."

"He does, and so did I, but eventually things would come to a head. Morio, Roman said that having vampire blood injected into you like that will bring out your feral nature more. You've probably already experienced that."

"Yes, I have, but it's not so bad that I can't control it."

"Well, then . . . I did the right thing. And meeting Blood Wyne and finding out the origin of the vampires was interesting, to say the least. And informative." Roman's mother still freaked me out, but I had a feeling she and I would be interacting more as the years wore on.

"There's nothing to be done about it now," Smoky said. "She's made the choice and been through the ritual and there's no going back. But Menolly, next time, you might think about informing us before you decide to do something so drastic."

Iris wouldn't speak to me—she looked mad as hell, and I had the feeling that, as I had with contacting Ivana Krask, I'd royally pissed her off. She silently helped Hanna finish up the dishes and said her good nights, and she and Bruce went out to their trailer. The guys had worked up an alarm system so that if anything bothered them, we'd hear it loud and clear. Hanna began putting away the last of the dishes and making our evening tea.

I turned to the others. "Maybe you should turn in early. Get sleep. You'll need rest tomorrow night." I leaned against the counter.

"Yeah, you're right." Delilah gave me a quick kiss on the cheek, and then she and Shade took off upstairs, taking their tea with them. Camille and her men sprawled out around the table but stared quietly at their cups.

Nerissa turned to me. "Come with me, love. As long as I'm staying here tonight again, let's take advantage of the situation. I have some things I want to talk to you about."

That didn't sound good. The words *I want to talk to you* had never prefaced a comfortable conversation as long as I'd been alive.

We said good night to the others and trailed into the parlor. Nerissa pulled off her shoes and changed into her nightgown. I pulled off my boots, relieved to have an evening where I wasn't out chasing monsters.

She curled up with the magazine and handed it to me, opening it to a Post-it-marked page. "What do you think?"

I stared at the arrangement. White roses and purple lilies, surrounded by fern fronds. "This is beautiful. I love it. Is this what you want? Because I'd be quite happy carrying that down the aisle."

I racked my brain, trying to think of just what aisle we'd be walking down. We could get married here at the house, if necessary, but I didn't want that and I knew that wouldn't be enough for Nerissa. She deserved something special and I wanted her to have it.

"Why is Iris mad at me?" I put the magazine down and leaned back, watching the second hand on the clock circle round. There were so many things in this house I never usually thought about. For instance, the clock—it had been an antique, bought from Rina's store before the demons killed her.

How long ago it seemed that we'd first faced Bad Ass Luke, but in reality, only a year and a half had passed. But right now, it felt like a lifetime since we first discovered the demons were here, working for Shadow Wing. So much had happened since then.

"Can't you figure it out?" Nerissa pulled her legs up into a lotus position on the sofa. She draped the blanket around her shoulders. "Iris and you have a special relationship—a special friendship. She's terrified you're going to be so reckless you'll get yourself killed. And Iris doesn't want to lose you."

I stared at my feet, holding them out and wiggling my toes. "I didn't think of it that way. I know what I'm doing—"

"Bullshit. Most of the time none of us know what we're doing. We just stumble through the day, doing our best to get by without making fools of ourselves . . . without getting hurt. Or in our case—killed. So don't give me any crap about *you know what you're doing.* You're no different than the rest of us, even if you do sink your fangs into people now and then." She snickered, yawning so wide I could practically see her tonsils.

I stuck my tongue out at her, but after a minute conceded the argument. "I hate to lose, and you know it, but you're right. I guess I'm just feeling my way through, doing what I think is best, but we can't ever know until it's over."

"Now I have a question for you." She paused, looking almost embarrassed.

"What is it? You can ask me anything and I'll give you the most honest answer I can."

She leaned forward, resting her elbows on her knees. "Now that you're connected to Roman, do you think . . . will he use that to come between us?"

I ducked my head. "I talked to him about us. I asked him why he left during . . . well, our tryst. He told me that he thought he could handle it, but when he saw the way I looked at you, it reminded him too much of the one time he was truly in love. And that ended badly."

"In other words, he wants you to look at him that way. And by being your sire . . ."

"No." I wasn't sure why I was trying to protect Roman, but everybody expected the worst from him and so far, he'd been a great help to us. "He didn't have to help us—none of the times he has. He's under no obligation to us."

Nerissa bit her lip, and a worried look crossed her face. "Okay, then. Do you think this will affect how you feel about me?"

Realizing that she was feeling insecure and even a little jealous, I slid across the sofa and took her hands. "Listen to me. Like you told me the other night, *I love you. I want to marry you.* I don't love Roman, even if there is a bond between us now. I don't want to marry Roman. I trust him on his word that he won't try to come between us. Please, don't let your fear push you away from me. Because that's the only thing that can divide us—fear." I kissed her fingertips and, as tears slowly trickled down her face, I kissed those, too.

She met my lips and took me in her arms, and we snuggled, silently, for the next half hour. Finally, she yawned again.

"I have to get up early tomorrow. I'd better sleep."

"Rest, then, and don't worry. Please, it just tears me up knowing you're unhappy. I love the bouquets. And I'm working on finding us the perfect spot for our ceremony." As I opened the door, I paused and looked back. "Nerissa . . . I'd give up almost everything for you. I'd give my life for you."

She blew me a kiss, and I quietly slipped down to my lair, where I took a shower and pulled on a pair of the Happy Mokito Bat pajamas Delilah had bought me for Yule. A movement startled me and I looked up to see Misty jump on my bed. Unlike most living cats, Misty wasn't afraid of me, and she came parading up the blankets to crawl on my stomach. I let her lie there, petting the ghostly fur as best as I could.

After a while, with still several hours to go till dawn, I began mulling over places to get married. There were a lot of beautiful parks and mansions around the area, but most mansions were booked well in advance.

As I mused over wedding plans, images from home kept creeping into my mind. And then, *I knew.*

The shores of Lake Y'Leveshan, near Y'Elestrial. There were parks there that shimmered with dragonflies and flutternuts and singing torries. I could see it now—we could marry at the head of the lake, near the Erulizi Falls, which thundered down over the cliffs above. The splashing drops prismed the sunlight that sparkled through them, mirroring rainbows in a dizzying array across the water. It would be perfect, and Nerissa would love it. We'd have to get married after sunset, but she'd be able to walk the shores during the day, and the moonlight reflecting on the water would be almost as beautiful as the sun.

I grabbed a notebook and began making lists of things we'd have to do, and people we'd have to contact, and the logistics involved. I got so involved in the planning that I didn't notice how much time was passing.

As a deep tug began to yank me down to sleep, I realized it was almost sunrise. I set the notebook on my nightstand, and, giving Misty one final pat, I slid under my covers and into my dreams. And for once, they were simply that—dreams, filled with sunlight and laughter and images of my beautiful, lovely Nerissa.

Chapter 19

❦

Charlotine arrived on time. I didn't like her any better than I
had when I'd first met her. She didn't offer any pleasantries
to the others, but to me, she at least said hello. She seemed
more subdued than she had when I'd met her last.

Mallen sure knew how to pick them. I would never again
give his taste in friends much credence. Perhaps she wasn't
his friend, though, but just someone he had to call in for
work now and then. *That* I could believe.

We'd armed ourselves as best as possible. Because the
degas were susceptible to water and to sound, I'd had
Camille go out and buy high-pitched dog whistles for everyone going. Vanzir had assured me that would work on them
to some degree.

And Vanzir had rigged up some sort of sonic shrieking
device. I had no clue what it was, but it was battery-operated
and let out an alarm that would outscreech a Bean Sidhe.

Smoky and Shade had spent the day calling in favors and
were now the proud owners of several water-based spell
scrolls. Neither would let Camille even touch the parchment

they were written on. She'd still been complaining about it when I woke up from the day's slumber.

Thirty minutes past sunset, we were heading out. Smoky carried Vanzir and me through the Ionyc Seas, and Shade carried Charlotine, who had put up a mild fuss about it until I threatened to stuff her in a duffel bag and let him carry her that way.

We stepped out of the mists to find ourselves standing near the trail leading up to the cave. In this area, the woods were thick enough to get lost in. Thick enough to stash bodies in. Thick enough to hide a cave frequented by demons. The timber was tall and the hiking trails not for amateurs. Boulders dotted the trail, and small rocks, and loose branches that had blown off the trees during recent windstorms.

Charlotine moved closer to me and I readied myself for an assault—just on principle—but she merely crossed her arms, rubbing her forearms as if she were cold. "I find the woodlands over here disconcerting."

"They can be. The forests are wild and not very friendly. You aren't elf, are you?" I couldn't place her. She didn't look elfin, nor did she look Fae, but she came from Elqaneve.

"Perhaps because I'm not." She glanced to the side, and when I remained silent, she shrugged. "I was a sorceress from the Southern Wastes. I moved to the north because I grew weary of the constant sand. I was tired of the testosterone wars between the various sorcery guilds. I wanted a better life. So I offered my services to Queen Asteria, and she took me in."

"How did you become a vampire?" It wasn't a polite question to ask, but I wanted to know who we were dealing with.

"Come on, let's get moving." Shade took the forefront, and Charlotine and I fell in behind him. Smoky and Vanzir guarded the rear.

Charlotine lowered her voice as we moved along, skirting the roots that were growing across the path. "I chose to become one. I asked Raleesha, mother of a nest, to turn me, and she did."

I had never understood those who chose to be turned. Death wasn't something I embraced, but being a vampire seemed like stopping in time—I constantly feared stagnation.

"Listen to me, and listen good. You blamed me for killing my sire. And I did. But you chose the turning. I didn't have a choice. I was tortured and scarred all over my body. I screamed so loud I lost my voice. Dredge raped me to the point of where he ripped my genitals. And then, he forced the turning on me and sent me home to kill my family. *I didn't have a choice*, so don't you ever judge me again."

After a moment, she glanced at me. "I wasn't told the details. I'm sorry. Nobody should ever be forced to make the transition. I was wrong to judge you. But you judge me. Do you want to know why I made the choice?"

"If you want to tell me."

"I was dying. I developed Spindle's Fever. There is no cure, and it's a painful, fatal disease. I wasn't ready to die. I had so much to live for, and Queen Asteria trusted me. I talked to her about it. The only possibility for me was to make the change. She agreed, and called in Mama Raleesha, who agreed to sire me. And so, before the disease did any further damage to me, I died and was reborn."

Spindle's Fever was a wasting disease, and it mostly struck those who used magic. Nobody knew what brought it on, and though it was rare, it was feared among sorcerers and witches. Camille had mentioned it once or twice, but any worries she had about it she kept to herself.

"I guess . . . I can see why you made the choice." I liked to think I wouldn't choose the same path if I were in her shoes, but until you faced the fire, you never knew what you'd do. So I kept my judgment to myself.

Shade stopped and motioned for us to do the same. "The cave is through this patch of woods and a little ways beyond. The path winds around in front of it, and on up the mountain. Get ready."

Vanzir and Smoky moved up next to us. Vanzir pulled out his whistle and made sure it was fastened around his neck. "The degas can be attacked physically, unlike the bhouts, but they are strong and dangerous. Try the whistles first, to disarm them and make them easier to attack. But sound alone isn't going to take them out, so be prepared for one hell of a fight."

I glanced at the path. "Let's go. And Charlotine—you may have faced some nasty things in the past, but make no mistake, these are demons, and they won't give you a chance. Don't give them any opening."

She held my gaze a moment. "Right."

And so, Shade and I at the front, Charlotine and Vanzir behind us, and Smoky bringing up the back, we moved in.

We approached the cave off-path, shrouded by the undergrowth. The ground was soggy and wet, spongy with forest debris. The constant drip of the rain off the tree limbs set up an odd cadence, and I was grateful for it, because it would help mask any sounds we made.

As we reached the border of the undergrowth where it cleared out into a small opening around a cave, we edged in, watching. There was activity there; we could see it and feel it.

Charlotine leaned in. "Do you want me to scout it out? I'm good at bat form."

I frowned. I wasn't good at taking any form, and I envied vamps who could. "Fine, go. But don't do *anything* except look. Get back here in under ten minutes."

She shifted, effortlessly, and flew up and out into the night. As I watched her, something in me responded to the transformation and I found myself wanting to shift, too. But that was crazy. I never had the urge, and when I did, my results were less than spectacular.

But the urging became stronger and I tugged on Smoky's arm. "Listen, I'm feeling pulled to change shape."

"You don't do that." Smoky frowned at me.

"I know, that's why I'm telling you."

"Do you want to try, while we're waiting for her to return?" Smoky gave me a quizzical look.

I scratched my head. The tingling was stronger. "Yeah. I won't do anything stupid, but I want to give it a go." I stepped back, giving myself room to focus on shifting. It had never been easy, and though I'd managed to attain bat form a couple of times, I never managed to hold it for long. And my flying powers were pathetic.

But as I closed my eyes, it was as if a switch went on inside and I found my body fluid, a whirl of smoke and vapor shifting into another form. The next thing I knew, I was hovering above the ground, in bat form, looking down at Smoky, Shade, and Vanzir. I could barely see them, but I could sense them. I let out a series of clicks and as they bounced back, I was able to make out their presence a lot easier. *What the fuck!* I was a bat! I took a few turns around the area before settling back down toward the ground.

Usually, transforming back was just as difficult. I strained as the shift began but was focusing so hard that when it came easier than expected, I overshot and fell forward, kissing the ground before I managed to catch myself. Smoky grasped my arm and helped me up.

"What the hell was that?" Vanzir asked. "You've never done it like that before."

"Yeah," I said, keeping my voice as low as I could. "Maybe it has something to do with the ritual that I performed with Roman. He's incredible at shifting forms to bat and wolf." Roman had other powers, too, and I wondered just how much I'd inherited from him. Life was suddenly looking up.

Just then, Charlotine came flying back. She landed gracefully and shifted back into her form. "Ten of the demons you describe. And the Demon Gate is glowing. There must be someone in there activating it."

"Gulakah? Fuck. We can't face him." A wave of panic rose up inside. But we had to go in. We couldn't let this go on, and we couldn't just sit out here until the coast was clear. "Okay, what are we doing?"

Smoky and Shade looked at one another. "There's room enough out there for us to shift into our dragon forms. The degas are strong, but not strong enough to hurt us when we're as big as a house."

"That's only if we can lure them out. And what about Gulakah?" I looked at Vanzir. "You can't latch onto him, now that you have your abilities back, can you?"

"I can try, but I won't win. That much I guarantee you, and I'm sorry, but I'm just not feeling up to a suicide mission right now." He turned to Shade. "You know the most about Gulakah. What do you know that will repel him?"

Shade shook his head. "I can't think of much that I haven't already told you. There has to be a way to defeat him, but I don't know what it is."

"We can't defeat him," Charlotine said, "but I *can* repel him. I can cast a powerful circle to keep out demons. Sorcerers use it for summoning, in order to protect ourselves during the rituals. We also have a variant for repelling the demons. The spell will last for about ten minutes, which will give us the leeway to destroy the gate and get out of here."

"You're sure you can repel him with that ritual? He's a god, exiled from his home." I knew Charlotine was powerful, but powerful enough to repel a god?

She gazed at me evenly. "I can do it, but it won't hold for more than ten minutes. It might go for fifteen, but I'd have to be focusing on it, and you need me to disarm the gate."

"What do we do?" I didn't like being backup, but in this case, it was all about teamwork.

"You keep anything and everything away from me so I can do my job. Menolly, I need you with me. Up front. I may need some help. Let the others fight the demons that will be coming in." And for the first time, she gave me a faint smile. "I work better with vamps."

I looked at the others, who nodded their agreement. "I've got your back. So what's first?"

"I set up the circle and you guys lead Gulakah out here." She slid out to the clearing. Luckily, there was nobody out there, and she was able to reach an open area. She opened her pack and pulled out what looked like a bag of some powder. She began sprinkling it in a large circle around her. Shade noticed me squinting, trying to see what she was doing.

"Sulfur," he whispered.

After the sulfur, she took out yet another bag and made yet another turn with it. I tried to see what it was, but in the darkness, with only faint flickering lights from within the cave to see by, it was impossible.

"What's that?"

Shade inhaled slowly and grimaced. "Asafetida. Pungent as all get-out, and very useful in keeping baleful spirits at bay."

The third time she cast the circle, I didn't even have to ask. Shade volunteered the info. "Rock salt. She knows her stuff, all right."

After she finished with scattering the sulfur, asafetida, and salt, Charlotine pulled out a dagger—double edged—that gleamed with a wicked blade. She cast a circle—that much I recognized from what Camille often did—and though I couldn't hear what she was saying, I could feel the hairs on my arms raise. Then, she motioned for us to join her in the circle.

"All right. While we're in here, someone has to go lead Gulakah out so I can finish the incantation. We'll be protected from him while we're inside the boundaries until I repel him out of here. After he vanishes—and if everything goes all right, he should—then we move out. Menolly guards my back, and you guys take on the degas and bhouts. The bhouts can't get to Menolly and me, but the other demons . . . they can hurt us."

"So who goes out to lead the Lord of Ghosts our way?" I would have volunteered, but I'd already promised Charlotine to be her backup.

Vanzir started to say something, but then Shade spoke up. "I'll do it. He'll recognize my energy as being from the Netherworld, and it may spur him on. The rest of you wait here."

Smoky took his arm. "I'm full dragon; I'm less likely to be harmed if he goes on a rampage."

"No. You have the household to protect. I'll be all right. I can fade into the shadows and hide." He leaped out of the circle and headed for the cave before Smoky could say another word.

Smoky glowered but said nothing. We waited . . . one minute . . . five . . . and then a low reverberation shook the ground. I tensed, moving behind Charlotine so I wouldn't be in the way of her spell.

And then, in that point between *then* and *now*, Shade

came rushing out, with a blur on his heels—Gulakah, in full pursuit. Nine feet tall, reptilian in nature, the Lord of Ghosts towered over everyone around him. Weaving tentacles emerged from his head to dart this way and that, like horrendous living dreadlocks. Matte-black eyes and razor-edged teeth marred the muzzle-like face, and his skin glimmered with a dirty green glow.

Terrified, I stood my ground, but watching the demon general-cum-god bear down on us was testing my limits.

Smoky tensed, and behind me, I heard Vanzir gulp.

Charlotine held out her hand. *"Repel!"*

Her voice shook the clearing as a crackle of flame lit up the night. Gulakah froze in his tracks, a look of rage on his face as the crazy snakes on his head writhed furiously. Then the flame blasted through the air, framing him with a halo of brilliant light as thunder cracked the air. Gulakah let out a roar and, in a single blink of an eye, vanished. Charlotine didn't hesitate but leaped out of the circle and raced for the cave.

"Come on. We have to get inside and take care of the gate before he comes back!"

Following on her heels, I charged into the cavern. Smoky, Shade, and Vanzir flanked us, ready to meet the degas and bhouts who poured out of the entrance. Smoky jumped in front and read from one of the scrolls as Vanzir set off his supersonic screech machine.

A loud piercing wail broke through the night as a torrential rain began to pour, and several of the degas screamed and cowered back. The raindrops seemed to act like an acid on their skin. One, who got caught behind us and the opening, writhed on the ground, screaming as the water ate into his skin, steaming with every place it touched the gray, wrinkled flesh.

As we pushed our way into the passage, Shade going first, I chafed at not being on the fighting end of things. I didn't like being a bodyguard—I'd rather be in there kicking the shit out of the demons—but Charlotine reached back and grabbed my wrist, as if she'd read my mind.

"Stay with me! I need you."

"I'm here." We drove our way through the narrow passage that was lit from within the central cavern ahead. Two degas were crowding into the passage, and the nearest shrieked as Shade slammed his fist through the creature's chest. How the fuck he managed that, I couldn't see, but the demon fell to the floor and Shade kicked him aside and moved forward to the other, who, apparently, had *not* learned from his comrade and suffered the same fate.

We broke into the main chamber, stumbling through the rough-hewn opening. Two huge standing stones were lit up like a Yule tree, covered with fiery runes that ran up one stone, over the crosspiece, and down the other, like some demonic copy of Stonehenge.

The cave was teeming with demons. A mass of swirling energy filled the room as bhouts poured through the Demon Gate. I stared at the monolithic structure, dread filling every bone in my body. How many hundreds of the spirits had already come through?

Charlotine yanked me forward with her as Smoky, Vanzir, and Shade went to work on the degas. Smoky's nails lengthened into talons and he set to ripping through them, leaving a trail of bloody, eviscerated demons behind him. Vanzir held out his hands and the neon feelers came twisting out, latching hold of several of the creatures, who writhed, unable to break away, as he triumphantly fed. A haze of purple fire emanated out from Shade, forming a mist around him to engulf an invisible enemy. I only hoped it was the bhouts and not something else that had come through, as well.

As screams and groans filled the air, Charlotine and I approached the Demon Gate. She stared up at it, the first look of uncertainty on her face that I'd seen from her.

Frantically, she shook her head. "This is huge. I don't know if I can do it. I'll try, but this . . . this isn't just any Demon Gate."

"Holy crap. If we can't destroy it, what the fuck do we do?"

"I don't know. But the number of spirits pouring through this gate is legion. Hundreds must have come through. If we break the gate, we break the control that Gulakah has over them. But that's a big *if* . . ."

I frantically tried to figure out how much time we had left

before he could come back. "We have to move quickly and then get the fuck out of here."

Just then, one of the degas came racing in, directly aiming for Charlotine. I jumped between her and it and rammed my fist into its face. The damned thing was hard as a brick wall, but I was stronger than brick and managed to smash its face. It dropped where it stood, and I gave it a nasty kick for good measure.

Turning back, I saw that Charlotine had her hands against the left pillar of the gate, and she was moaning as she pressed against one of the runes. The flicker of fire swirled around her, and I realized she was attempting to infuse it with her own energy. Another demon was on her tail and I intercepted again, throwing it back against a third that was headed our way. The two began marching in on me again, and I kicked one in the face as I slammed the other to the ground.

Behind me, Charlotine screamed and I turned to see her vibrating, holding on to the massive stones as they began to quake.

"Get out of there!"

"I can't! If I do, I'll break the spell and it won't work." She held on, her face a mask of pain and fear as cracks began to appear through the stonework, racing up the monolithic structure like veins popping out on skin.

I glanced at the others—they were being inundated by the demons. Where all the demons were coming from, I couldn't tell, but the degas were swarming them and the swirl of energy around Shade snapped and crackled, as if he were a bug zapper killing mosquitoes.

A great creaking began to reverberate through the chamber, and I turned back. The monolith was breaking up; the runes were flickering and going out as the stonework crumbled into massive boulders, tumbling down around Charlotine.

"No! *Charlotine!*" I tried to dart forward, but the rumble of the rock slide drove me back.

"Get out of here! Go!" She shook her head at me, holding on, her magic disrupting the Demon Gate, turning it into an avalanche of stone and dust.

At that moment, a sound from the front of the cave made

us all turn. Gulakah was entering the cave—the spell had dissipated. He jerked his head to stare at Charlotine and the breaking Demon Gate, and with a roar, he charged toward her. I started to throw myself in front of him, but suddenly Smoky was there, pulling me aside, Vanzir beside him.

Gulakah reached Charlotine and I screamed again, trying to break free from Smoky's grasp.

"You can't stop him—he'll kill you if you do." Smoky held me fast, his voice both terrible and terrified. "We can't help her."

"Go, please, don't make my sacrifice for nothing!" Charlotine's scream echoed through the chamber, caught in the fury of the tumbling stones as the Demon Gate crashed around her. Gulakah stopped, unable to reach her because of the rock slide, but he stared at her and his eyes began to glow, and there was a horrific blast of energy as the entire gate went up in flames, taking Charlotine with it.

Smoky grabbed Vanzir with his other arm, and the next thing I knew, we were in the Ionyc Seas, the ripple of energy sending me into a tailspin. It wasn't the same as going through a portal, and it affected me in different ways because I was a vampire. The mist rippled around us, and I could say nothing, do nothing, save for press against Smoky and Vanzir as the dragon protected us from the mist-shrouded currents of energy.

I closed my eyes, pressing against his chest, unable to shut out Charlotine's screams echoing in my ears.

After an indeterminable amount of time, although it took only moments in the physical world, we stepped off the Seas into the house. As Smoky let go of us, I saw that Shade was already there.

Shell-shocked, I dropped into the nearest chair. I stared up at them, unable to say a word. Camille knelt beside me, taking my hands. Delilah, Rozurial, and the rest were also there, waiting for news.

"I didn't mean for her to get killed." I stared at Camille, clutching her hands in mine. "I didn't mean for her to die."

"I know . . . I know . . ." She glanced up at Smoky.

He let out a long sigh. "Charlotine gave her life to destroy

the Demon Gate. It was stronger than any of us realized."
Quietly, without embellishment, he explained what happened in the cave.

"I didn't mean for her to sacrifice herself." I grimaced, remembering the look on her face when she'd shouted for us to run.

Shade quietly knelt beside me. "She knew what she was doing. She knew the risks and she took them because she worked for Queen Asteria and she understood the dangers of letting the Demon Gate stand."

"She didn't expect to die." I gazed into his eyes, watching the remnants of the purple flame sparkle in them.

"None of us expect to die. Not really. We *think* we may not survive, but deep inside, we don't really believe it will happen. She could have fled and left the gate standing, but she chose to take it down. She's one of the fallen heroes of this war." He reached out, brushed the braids out of my face. "Remember her on Samhain, honor her memory, and you do her justice."

Swallowing my shock, I slowly nodded. "She didn't want to die . . . that's why she became a vampire. She chose the life. I thought her selfish, but now . . . I'm glad I didn't tell her how I felt."

Nerissa motioned for Shade to move out of the way and, as he did, she pulled me to my feet and kissed me gently. "You'd do the same. You'd give your life if it meant taking out something that dangerous. We all would."

I nodded, resting against her shoulder. She kissed the top of my head, rubbing my back gently as I collected myself. When I was able to focus again, we went into the kitchen.

Smoky, his clothes still white as snow in that bizarre natural-detergent way he had, quietly asked Hanna if she could supply a snack. Shade and Vanzir, who were both covered with dust and demon guts, went to take showers. I was pretty mucky myself, so Nerissa and I went to my lair, where I took a shower and she laid out my clean clothes for me.

"She sacrificed herself." I slipped into the jeans and turtleneck, then sat on the bed, staring at my feet.

Nerissa nodded. "Yes, she did. As you would, for the

greater good. You, Camille, Delilah—you've all gone into battle more times than I want to think about. You go, knowing each time it may be your last. You go because you have to, because it's the *right thing to do*. You go because you can't *not* go. Give Charlotine the credit she deserves. Don't think she was ignorant of the dangers. You told her exactly what you were facing. She knew what she was getting into."

I slipped on a pair of ankle boots, zipping them up. "We are so far from taking out Gulakah. He scares me in a way the other demon generals didn't."

"That's because he's a god. He's powerful, and deadly, and he's playing for keeps. The others . . . they were dangerous but not like this. I have a feeling things are going to get worse before they get better." She paused. "You don't think he has one of the spirit seals, do you?"

I shook my head. "No, I don't think Shadow Wing would entrust him with one. Gulakah could probably face him down and maybe win, with one of them. But Telazhar has one." I looked up at her.

"We won this battle—we put a stop to him using the bhouts to control the magic in the area. But we aren't anywhere near winning the war. I dread his next move. He's pissed out of his mind, Nerissa. And when a god's pissed at you . . ." I let the words hang. I didn't want to finish the thought.

"Yeah." She snuggled beside me. "I know. But for now . . . at least the gate is broken and I doubt if he'll try the same thing twice. He's not stupid."

"More's the pity that." I stood and stretched. "Come on, let's get upstairs. We've got a lot of planning to do. And a lot of research. Next step: finding a way to kill a god."

Nerissa looped her arm around my elbow. "No, actually the next step—we get married. Have you thought of a place yet?"

I smiled then. At least I could give her some good news on that front. "Would you believe it? I have. How would you feel about making a trip to Otherworld?" And, as we ascended the stairs, I began to describe the lake and the falls, and how beautiful it all was.

* * *

Over the next few days, we kept a close lookout for signs that Gulakah had started up anything new, but all was quiet. The ghostly activity in the Greenbelt Park District was still jumping, but a return visit to the Galaxy club and a talk with the owner about warding the place put a stop to the rogue bhouts—which were no longer under Gulakah's control. The patrons were back to their usual lively selves.

We warned Lindsey's coven about the spirits, and they were able to ward against them, too. Chances were, there were hundreds of the rogue magic-feeders around, but when they couldn't find a good source for energy, they'd scatter off to other parts. It was far easier to deal with a single bhout than with a thriving community of them.

Carter got in touch with the Oregon psychic community, and they, too, put up wards and were having no further problems. Camille was still trying to run down information on the Aleksais Psychic Network and the strange man who had followed Nerissa, but so far, we hadn't discovered anything about them, and the network itself seemed to vanish from sight after the Demon Gate was broken.

We were sitting around the table a couple of nights later, discussing what to do.

"Chances are, this Halcon Davis has gone underground for now," Camille said. "But we keep our eyes open because I imagine he'll be back, along with the Aleksais Psychic Network, and we don't want to assume the problem's over. Because we all know it isn't. Tomorrow's the equinox and we all know the holidays are volatile times in the spirit and psychic world."

"My guess is that Gulakah will take a while to regroup and plan. And whatever he's got coming next will be as bad as or worse than the bhouts." Shade was straddling one of the benches near the table.

"That's my fear, too," Roz said. "We need to find out as much as we can about him during the next few weeks."

"I can make a trip back to the Netherworld and see what I can dig up there," Shade said.

"And I'll talk to Carter and go hunting through the Demon Underground." Vanzir leaned his elbows on the table, staring at the cookies he'd stacked in front of him. Delilah reached over and snagged one and he smacked her hand, gently.

"So your powers have come back?" Smoky stared at him. He was still hostile toward Vanzir, but there had been no outright spats over the past month, and I hoped things were calming down between them.

Vanzir glanced up at him. "Go ahead and finish what you're thinking: And I have no soul binder around my neck. Right?"

Smoky pressed his lips together but kept his eye on the dream-chaser. Camille poked him in the side and shook her head. I knew that look. It said, *Quit being an ass, my love.*

"Speaking of the equinox," Nerissa broke in. "Tomorrow night's coming quickly. When do we leave for Otherworld?"

"We go at sunset—the minute I wake up. Father will be waiting for us, along with Trenyth. I wish everyone could come, but Shamas has to stay and help Chase. And Hanna . . ."

"I will stay and watch the house. There will be guards here, and all will be safe. Besides, I am not ready to return there. Too many memories." She waved a dish towel at me. "Do not think of trouble."

Camille was opening mail, and she looked dejected. "The wetlands next door? The owner has told our lawyer somebody's already put down an offer and he's taking it. This sucks." She looked crestfallen. "Want to make a bet we'll get stuck with lousy neighbors?"

The disappointment must have showed on Delilah's and my faces, because Hanna immediately brought over another batch of chocolate chip cookies. "Here, sugar is good for disappointment."

"Thanks," Delilah said, dejected. "I really wanted to buy up that property. Over five more acres, along with four acres of wetlands and the pond? We could have done so much with the area."

"Cheer up." A tendril of Smoky's hair rose up to stroke Camille's face. "I know the owner. I think you'll like her."

"Who? *Hotlips?*" She gave him a withering look.

"Heavens preserve us from that. No, love. *You.*" And he began to laugh as the rest of us stared at him. The room erupted as Iris began dancing around with Maggie. "I bought the land and had it put in your name, my love."

Camille jumped into Smoky's lap, covering him with kisses. "Do you really mean it? Thank you! Oh, bless you."

"Well, I have not yet bought you a wedding present and it was time. We've been married for almost a year. This will do?" The big galoot of a dragon looked up, winking at Delilah and me. "And I do not mind if you share with your sisters. Or the rest of our family."

I shook my head. "Oh, good gods. You, Smoky, and Morio's anniversary will essentially be the same day as Nerissa's and mine."

"You're right," Camille said, laughing. "Shade, when you and Delilah get married, make it on October twenty-second, so Trillian and I can share our anniversary with you guys."

After the celebration following Smoky's announcement, I glanced at the clock. "I'm going downstairs to pack. And to meditate." I kissed Nerissa good night—she was sleepy and needed to rest up for the trip tomorrow—and headed down to my lair. In the midst of sadness, it seemed strange to be celebrating, but I was grateful for the respite.

But as I arranged myself on my yoga mat, I couldn't help but send a silent prayer Charlotine's way. She'd helped us win the battle. We wouldn't allow her death to be in vain.

Chapter 20
❧❦❧

The trip to Otherworld went smoothly. Even Iris had no problems with the portal—it didn't seem to affect pregnant women, except to make them terribly dizzy. We'd gone through the one in the Wayfarer, which led directly to Y'Elestrial.

Father was waiting for us, and Trenyth with him, as we arrived just after sunset. As Trenyth came forward, holding out his hands to me, I took them and smiled softly.

"I'm so sorry about Charlotine. But she . . . she saved our butts."

He ducked his head in acknowledgment. "As you said when you talked to us through the Whispering Mirror. Not to discuss business on your wedding day, but I thought you'd like to know that Darynal and the caravan are safe. So far, all things are going as planned. We should know more in a few weeks, once they've established themselves in Rhellah."

The thought that, to the south, the sorcerers were grouping like a pack of feral wolves hit home. For the first time, I realized there was no safety—*anywhere*. Oh, if we moved to the Dragon Reaches, we'd be safe. The demons weren't stupid enough to take on the entire world of Dragonkin, but we couldn't just leave Otherworld and Earthside to the hands of Shadow Wing.

"Good," I said. "We need to be kept abreast. We're working on the reorganization for the new Earthside headquarters of the OIA. It will be housed at the FH-CSI, but properly this time. Now that we're in charge, we can do so much more with keeping the lines of communication open."

Trenyth gave my hand a little squeeze. "That's a good thing. Now, put talk of business away. It's time to focus on your celebration."

Hard as it was—the future loomed dark and dreadful, like a gathering storm—I turned my attention back to Nerissa. She had never seen Otherworld, and now I saw it again through fresh eyes—through her vision.

We'd left Shamas, Bruce, and Vanzir at home—they'd volunteered to stay and watch over Maggie and the house. As much as I wanted our little munchkin with us, we felt it was safer to leave her at home. But Chase—with his broken thumb—and Rozurial, Shade, Morio, Smoky, and Trillian had come with us. And, of course, Iris and my sisters.

The carriages were waiting, and as we climbed in and began our trek through the crowded, bustling city, Nerissa laughed with delight.

"It's so beautiful, and so different. As noisy as the crowds are, it's quiet. No planes, no cars, no buzz of electricity . . ."

"But the magic hums brightly here," Camille said, laughing with her. She, Delilah, and Iris were in the carriage with us.

Eye catchers lit the streets, and I noticed the roads were actually clean. Apparently the usual beggars had been put to work sweeping the cobblestones, picking up litter, and cleaning the stables and streets of the manure left behind by the horses and animals. Tanaquar had instituted a work-for-food program, and even though she'd used our father and tried to cause trouble with us, I had to give it to her—taking the homeless off the streets and giving them jobs for food and simple shelter was genius.

We clattered along, the horses' hooves beating a staccato tattoo against the cobblestones, and as we went, Nerissa kept

pointing out the unfamiliar trees and flowers and the archi-
tecture that was unique to Otherworld. I let her ramble, loving the animation in her face and the delight in her voice.

"I wish you could see this in the daylight. But you will.
I've arranged for us to stay a couple days. Father has rented a
safe house for us, with a lair for me, and I'll be safe while
you explore the city with Camille and Delilah."

"But what about work—"

I shook my head. "I talked to Chase. You have the next
few days off. And we all need a break. The men will be
going home except for Smoky, and we'll stay here and visit
Father and maybe . . . maybe look up some of our old friends.
If any of them are left after the civil war." I didn't mention
that we'd had very few friends when we lived here before.

The trip across town to the lake took the better part of
two hours, but by nine P.M. Earthside time, we pulled into
the park surrounding the Erulizi Falls. Here, the trees were
just beginning to bud, the tiny leaves green and sparkling
with dew. It had rained during the day, but now the stars
were out and the soft whisper of raindrops dripping to the
lush grass below was calming. The night was chilly, but not
cold, and I saw that my father had set up tents for us to relax
and dress in.

The falls . . . the Erulizi Falls were one of the most beautiful places I had ever been in Otherworld. Wide, though not
tall, they covered a cavern in which a goddess supposedly
lived. Women brought flowers to her all through the summer
in supplication for her blessings on their homes and love
lives—for Erulizi was a goddess of passion and joy. Water
thundered over the top, sparkling in the light of the crescent
moon as it rained down on the lake below, concentric rings
rippling out along the surface of the lake.

I remembered the festivals from my youth spent here, on
holidays—they were some of my happiest memories.

Today, Y'Elestrial had already had its public spring equinox festival here by the falls, but tonight, we would have
ours, and perhaps, if she willed it, if she was in a good mood,
Erulizi would see fit to bless our wedding.

Nerissa walked out to the edge of the lake, staring over

the expanse. "I could get used to this," she said, turning to me. "I could get used to living here. Just . . . so you know."

I understood what she was saying and wrapped my arm around her waist. "Maybe one day, we'll have a home in both worlds."

"I'd like that," she said.

"What about your condo? Are you keeping your condo now that you're moving in with us?" We'd figured out that if she slept during the night, and I during the day, there was no real danger to her sharing my bedroom.

While the basement couldn't be expanded, Smoky and the men were adding on an extra sitting room upstairs, just for us. The parlor would no longer be Nerissa's home away from home and she wouldn't have to sleep on a sofa, or on a cot in Delilah's spare room.

"Renting it out. We might as well have the rental income coming in." She inhaled deeply, then slowly let it out, shaking her head as the breeze ruffled through her hair.

"I have a surprise for you. I hope you don't mind." I turned around and motioned to the carriage that had drawn near. "I invited someone to the wedding."

Nerissa turned in time to see Venus the Moon Child jump out of the carriage. The werepuma shaman, who was now one of Asteria's Keraastar Knights, hurried over to throw his arms around Nerissa, planting a big kiss on her cheek. He turned to me, and I allowed him to do the same. The smell of puma sweat clung thick to him.

"I'm so happy for you, Nessa." He clapped her on the back. "And you, too, Menolly." He lowered his voice, glancing over at Delilah, who hadn't noticed him yet. "Zachary sends his love. He didn't think it would be a good idea for him to show up—there's just too much water under the bridge, you know. For him, at least. But he's happy, and he can run free here."

"He's in puma form all the time now, isn't he?" Zach had made the final transformation to his full puma shape, eliminating the paralysis that had claimed him from battle.

"Yeah, but we talk a lot, and he's got himself a gorgeous wildcat of a girlfriend. She's pregnant and they're expecting a fine litter of cubs."

I left Venus and Nerissa to catch up and headed across the meadow to start dressing. Nerissa would dress in the other pavilion, helped by Delilah. When I reached the tent I found that my father had arranged a surprise for me, as well.

As I entered through the linen canvas, I found myself staring at Aunt Rythwar. She was standing beside Iris and Camille, who was weeping for joy.

"Auntie!" I rushed over to her, throwing my arms around the courtly Fae, who stood taller than even Delilah, with the same jet hair as Father and Camille, and crisp blue eyes. She wrapped her arms around me and held me tight.

"Menolly—my sweet little niece. Let me look at you." I stood back, obediently, as Aunt Rythwar made me turn for her. "Your beautiful hair, it is . . . most interesting. But you are, as you always were, my lovely niece. Daughter of my brother, so today you wed?"

I was having a hard time choking back my tears. It was as if Mother had come back to be with us—I'd never expected to see Aunt Rythwar again, yet here she stood, in a sparkling silver dress.

"We have so much to catch up on, but . . ." I glanced at Camille. "What time . . . ?"

"You need to dress. Aunt Rythwar will be here after the wedding, and tomorrow night, as well, so hurry and let us dress you."

"Camille's right. Shed your clothes." Iris was standing next to Camille, waiting for me. She gazed up at my aunt and I had an odd feeling that the surprises weren't over with.

Camille handed me the box containing my wedding dress, as eye catchers floated everywhere to produce soft, illuminating light.

"We have another surprise for you," Camille said. "Nerissa was in on this one. In fact, it was her idea, once she knew that I had . . . well . . . you'll see."

"I'm not sure how many more surprises I'm up to."

"Just open the box, will you?"

I slowly untied the ribbon and lifted off the lid. There, in the box, I found, not the wedding dress Nerissa had bought for me, but instead, a vision in white. As I held up the dress, I let out a choked cry.

"You didn't . . . I didn't know you had this!" I held up the flowing ball gown. It was a princess's dress, with long sleeves and a sweetheart neckline with beaded bodice, and the skirt was chiffon covered with tulle and lace. Every movement made it shimmer.

"*Mo'denasey* . . ." Aunt Rythwar clapped her hand to her mouth. "Your mother's wedding dress. You still have it?"

Camille was crying now. She nodded. "I saved it when war broke out. I kept it with me all this time, in the back of my closet. I knew I could never fit into it, and I thought maybe for Delilah, but she's too tall. Then I talked to Nerissa and she loved it so much . . . so we took it to the alterations woman and she shortened for you. It should fit, though. Mother was petite, like you."

A wave of sorrow and joy and amazement washed over me and I burst into bloody tears. Iris handed me a red handkerchief, which made me cry even more—it was the one Sassy Branson's ghost had left for me when she faded into the afterlife with her daughter and beloved Janet.

"I can't believe I actually get to wear Mother's wedding dress. It never occurred to me to even think that would be a possibility." I gazed at the gown, my heart warming like it hadn't in a long time. "Thank you . . . *oh, thank you.*"

After I'd dried my eyes and made sure my hands and face were clean, I let them help me try it on. The seamstress had been spot on. It fit like a glove, though it was still a little long, but I didn't care.

Iris went to unbind my hair and I stopped her.

"My braids are part of who I am, but you can put them up into some pretty design, can't you?" I was resisting the urge to cry again. I didn't want to bloody up my dress, so I kept the handkerchief ready.

She did, while Camille fixed my makeup. "I wish I could take a picture of you. I wish we could take wedding pictures of you and Nerissa, but . . . we've got the best thing." Iris grinned. "Are you ready for another surprise?"

"Another? I seriously don't know if I can take it." I hated to admit it, but it did bother me, the fact that we could never have a wedding photo. Nerissa insisted it was okay, but I knew she was disappointed.

"Just a minute." Camille opened the flaps of the tent and motioned. A moment later, Father came through.

He stared at me, letting out a little sound, and tears sprang to his eyes.

"Please, don't mind that I'm wearing Mother's dress . . ." It would just kill me if he yelled at me about it.

But he merely choked out, "You are so incredibly beautiful, my daughter. Your mother would be proud. This makes it like . . . she's almost here with us."

I ducked my head. "I wish she could be."

After a pause, Camille said, "Well, the rest of us are. And we'll have to do. Father, why don't you tell her your surprise? I almost spilled the beans."

He shook his head. "Your vernacular never ceases to amaze me." Then he turned to me. "I told you I had a gift for you. When I found out you were engaged, I began to search for someone with talent. As a wedding gift, please allow me . . . I hired an artist to paint the two of you. He's brilliant, and does quick work, and tomorrow night, you and Nerissa will sit for him here, by the lake. He can work all night long and then be able to finish up over the next few days on his own. So you'll have a wedding portrait."

I stared at him, uncertain what to say. Finally, because I was almost out of words for my feelings, I just said, "Thank you . . . so much."

"I just wanted you and your wife to be happy." He glanced around. "I'd best be getting to my post. I'll see you at the altar, my daughter."

Before he could turn, I jumped up and grabbed his arm. "I really mean it, Father. *Thank you.*"

"I know . . ." He ducked out of the tent as Camille tugged on my arm, yanking me back into the chair.

"If you do that again, I'm going to stick a mascara brush in your eye." Scolding or not, she was smiling, too.

When we were ready, we headed out of the tent. There, by

the side of the lake, our father waited. As befitting his office in Y'Elestrial, he would be legally able to preside. And since we were married in Otherworld, our marriage would be counted as legal over Earthside—that had been a mutual agreement when the portals first opened up. Marriages on either side of the fence would be recognized.

As I waited, the flap to Nerissa's tent opened and she stepped out, gorgeous and glowing in her plum-colored gown. Her eyes lit up as she saw me.

Camille pressed a bouquet of white roses, deep purple lilies, and sparkling green fern fronds into my hands. Delilah handed Nerissa her matching bouquet, and then the two of them, along with Iris and Aunt Rythwar, joined the men who were standing near the lake, where my father waited.

Venus, who was escorting us to the altar, stood between Nerissa and me. He crooked his arms, and we lightly rested our hands on his elbows as we waited for the signal to begin.

As the drummers began to beat out a rhythm, an elfin singer began to chant in the night, and we moved forward, step by step, until we were standing in the circle of roses that surrounded Father. The dais behind him held a glimmering array of candles and the handfasting cord.

"We stand in the presence of Erulizi, Goddess of the Falls, Mother of Passion, as we join these women in marriage under the watchful eyes of the Moon Mother."

He paused as Delilah stepped forward and took our bouquets, as Camille wrapped our hands with the handfasting cord.

I glanced at my beloved Nerissa, whose smile was as brilliant as the silver moon overhead. "Are you happy, my love?" I whispered.

"More than you can ever know." She grasped my hand tighter.

I shivered as I realized just how much I loved her and what a huge step we were taking. But there was no doubt in my heart that we were meant for each other. Men came and went, but Nerissa and I would endure.

My sisters and I would continue the fight. Friends would enter our lives, and some would leave—either in tragedy or for other adventures. But we would continue, as our family of choice grew.

A whiff of untahstar tree caught my attention, and I realized that yes, I truly was happy to be home—if only for a few days. This was where my life had begun, where it had ended, and where it had begun again. Now, I was reclaiming my joy and ability to love in my new life, with the woman I loved.

As the ceremony continued into the night, I caught my father's gaze. And for the first time since I'd been turned, the look he gave me welcomed me back into his heart. It might be fleeting, it might be fragile, but for the moment, we were a family again.

CAST OF MAJOR CHARACTERS

The D'Artigo Family

Sephreh ob Tanu: The D'Artigo Sisters' father. Full Fae.

Maria D'Artigo: The D'Artigo Sisters' mother. Human.

Camille Sepharial te Maria, aka Camille D'Artigo: The oldest sister; a Moon Witch. Half-Fae, half-human.

Delilah Maria te Maria, aka Delilah D'Artigo: The middle sister; a werecat.

Arial Lianan te Maria: Delilah's twin who died at birth. Half-Fae, half-human.

Menolly Rosabelle te Maria, aka Menolly D'Artigo: The youngest sister; a vampire and *jian-tu*: extraordinary acrobat. Half-Fae, half-human.

Shamas ob Olanda: The D'Artigo girls' cousin. Full Fae.

The D'Artigo Sisters' Lovers & Close Friends

Bruce O'Shea: Iris's husband. Leprechaun.

Carter: Leader of the Demonica Vacana Society, a group that watches and records the interactions of Demonkin and human through the ages. Carter is half demon and half Titan—his father was Hyperion, one of the Greek Titans.

Chase Garden Johnson: Detective, director of the Faerie-Human Crime Scene Investigation (FH-CSI) team. Human who has taken the Nectar of Life, which extends his life span beyond any ordinary mortal, and has opened up his psychic abilities.

Chrysandra: Waitress at the Wayfarer Bar & Grill. Human.

Derrick Means: Bartender at the Wayfarer Bar & Grill. Werebadger.

Erin Mathews: Former president of the Faerie Watchers Club and former owner of the Scarlet Harlot Boutique. Turned into a vampire by Menolly, her sire, moments before her death. Human.

Greta: Leader of the Death Maidens; Delilah's tutor.

Iris (Kuusi) O'Shea: Friend and companion of the girls. Priestess of Undutar. Talon-haltija (Finnish house sprite).

Lindsey Katharine Cartridge: Director of the Green Goddess Women's Shelter. Pagan and witch. Human.

Luke: Former bartender at the Wayfarer Bar & Grill. Werewolf. One of the Keraastar Knights.

Marion Vespa: Coyote shifter; owner of the Supe-Urban Café.

Morio Kuroyama: One of Camille's lovers and husbands. Essentially the grandson of Grandmother Coyote. Youkai-kitsune (roughly translated: Japanese fox demon).

Neely Reed: Founding Member of the United Worlds Church. FBH.

Nerissa Shale: Menolly's lover. Worked for DSHS. Now working for Chase Johnson as a victims-rights counselor for the FH-CSI. Werepuma and member of the Rainier Puma Pride.

Roman: Ancient vampire; son of Blood Wyne, Queen of the Crimson Veil. Menolly's official consort in the Vampire Nation and her new sire.

Rozurial, aka Roz: Mercenary. Menolly's secondary lover. Incubus who used to be Fae before Zeus and Hera destroyed his marriage.

Shade: Delilah's fiancé. Part Stradolan, part black (shadow) dragon.

Sharah: Elfin medic; Chase's girlfriend.

Siobhan Morgan: One of the girls' friends. Selkie (wereseal); member of the Puget Sound Harbor Seal Pod.

Smoky: One of Camille's lovers and husbands. Half-white, half-silver dragon.

Tavah: Guardian of the portal at the Wayfarer Bar & Grill. Vampire (full Fae).

Tim Winthrop, aka Cleo Blanco: Computer student/genius, female impersonator. FBH. Now owns the Scarlet Harlot.

Trillian: Mercenary. Camille's alpha lover and one of her three husbands. Svartan (one of the Charming Fae).

Vanzir: Was indentured slave to the Sisters, by his own choice. Dream-chaser demon who lost his powers and now is regaining new ones.

Venus the Moon Child: Former shaman of the Rainier Puma Pride. Werepuma. One of the Keraastar Knights.

Wade Stevens: President of Vampires Anonymous. Vampire (human).

Zachary Lyonnesse: Former member of the Rainier Puma Pride Council of Elders. Werepuma living in Otherworld.

GLOSSARY

Black Unicorn/Black Beast: Father of the Dahns unicorns, a magical unicorn that is reborn like the phoenix and lives in Darkynwyrd and Thistlewyd Deep. Raven Mother is his consort, and he is more a force of nature than a unicorn.

Calouk: The rough, common dialect used by a number of Otherworld inhabitants.

Court and Crown: "Crown" refers to the Queen of Y'Elestrial. "Court" refers to the nobility and military personnel that surround the Queen. "Court and Crown" together refer to the entire government of Y'Elestrial.

Court of the Three Queens: The newly risen Court of the three Earthside Fae Queens: Titania, the Fae Queen of Light and Morning; Morgaine, the half-Fae Queen of Dusk and Twilight; and Aeval, the Fae Queen of Shadow and Night.

Crypto: One of the Cryptozoid races. Cryptos include creatures out of legend that are not technically of the Fae races: gargoyles, unicorns, gryphons, chimeras, and so on. Most primarily inhabit Otherworld, but some have Earthside cousins.

Demon Gate: A gate through which demons may be summoned by a powerful sorcerer or necromancer.

Dreyerie: A dragon lair.

Earthside: Everything that exists on the Earth side of the portals.

Elqaneve: The Elfin lands in Otherworld.

Elemental Lords: The elemental beings—both male and female—who, along with the Hags of Fate and the Harvestmen, are the only true Immortals. They are avatars of various elements and energies, and they inhabit all realms. They do as they will and seldom concern themselves with humankind or Fae unless summoned. If asked for help, they often exact steep prices in return. The Elemental Lords are not concerned with balance like the Hags of Fate.

FBH: Full-Blooded Human (usually refers to Earthside humans).

FH-CSI: The Faerie-Human Crime Scene Investigation team. The brainchild of Detective Chase Johnson, it was first formed as a collaboration between the OIA and the Seattle police department. Other FH-CSI units have been created around the country, based on the Seattle prototype. The FH-CSI takes care of both medical and criminal emergencies involving visitors from Otherworld.

Great Divide: A time of immense turmoil when the Elemental Lords and some of the High Court of Fae decided to rip apart the worlds. Until then, the Fae existed primarily on Earth, their lives and worlds mingling with those of humans. The Great Divide tore everything asunder, splitting off another dimension, which became Otherworld. At that time, the Twin Courts of Fae were disbanded and their queens stripped of power. This was the time during which the Spirit Seal was formed and broken in order to seal off the realms from each other. Some Fae chose to stay Earthside, others moved to the realm of Otherworld, and the demons were— for the most part—sealed in the Subterranean Realms.

Guard Des'Estar: The military of Y'Elestrial.

Hags of Fates: The women of destiny who keep the balance righted. Neither good nor evil, they observe the flow of destiny. When events get too far out of balance, they step in and take action, usually using humans, Fae, Supes, and other creatures as pawns to bring the path of destiny back into line.

Harvestmen: The lords of death—a few cross over and are also Elemental Lords. The Harvestmen, along with their followers (the Valkyries and the Death Maidens, for example), reap the souls of the dead.

Haseofon: The abode of the Death Maidens—where they stay and where they train.

Ionyc Lands: The astral, etheric, and spirit realms, along with several other lesser-known noncorporeal dimensions, form the Ionyc Lands. These realms are separated by the Ionyc Seas, a current of energy that prevents the Ionyc Lands from colliding, thereby sparking off an explosion of universal proportions.

Ionyc Seas: The currents of energy that separate the Ionyc Lands. Certain creatures, especially those connected with the elemental energies of ice, snow, and wind, can travel through the Ionyc Seas without protection.

Koyanni: The coyote shifters who took an evil path away from the Great Coyote; followers of Nukpana.

Melosealfôr: A rare Crypto dialect learned by powerful Cryptos and all Moon Witches.

The Nectar of Life: An elixir that can extend the life span of humans to nearly the length of a Fae's years. Highly prized and cautiously used. Can drive someone insane if he or she doesn't have the emotional capacity to handle the changes incurred.

OIA: The Otherworld Intelligence Agency; the "brains" behind the Guard Des'Estar.

Otherworld/OW: The human term for the "United Nations" of Faerie Land. A dimension apart from ours that contains creatures from legend and lore, pathways to the gods, and various other places, such as Olympus. Otherworld's actual name varies among the differing dialects of the many races of Cryptos and Fae.

Portal, Portals: The interdimensional gates that connect the different realms. Some were created during the Great Divide; others open up randomly.

Seelie Court: The Earthside Fae Court of Light and Summer, disbanded during the Great Divide. Titania was the Seelie Queen.

Soul Statues: In Otherworld, small figurines created for the Fae of certain races and magically linked with the baby. These figurines reside in family shrines and when one of the Fae dies, their soul statue shatters. In Menolly's case, when she was reborn as a vampire, her soul statue re-formed, although twisted. If a family member disappears, his or her family can always tell if their loved one is alive or dead if they have access to the soul statue.

Spirit Seals: A magical crystal artifact, the Spirit Seal was created during the Great Divide. When the portals were sealed, the Spirit Seal was broken into nine gems and each piece was given to an Elemental Lord or Lady. These gems each have varying powers. Even possessing one of the spirit seals can allow the wielder to weaken the portals that divide Otherworld, Earthside, and the Subterranean Realms. If all of the seals are joined together again, then all of the portals will open.

Stradolan: A being who can walk between worlds, who can walk through the shadows, using them as a method of transportation.

Supe/Supes: Short for Supernaturals. Refers to Earthside supernatural beings who are not of Fae nature. Refers to Weres, especially.

Talamh Lonrach Oll: The name for the Earthside Sovereign Fae Nation.

Triple Threat: Camille's nickname for the newly risen three Earthside Queens of Fae.

Unseelie Court: The Earthside Fae Court of Shadow and Winter, disbanded during the Great Divide. Aeval was the Unseelie Queen.

VA/Vampires Anonymous: The Earthside group started by Wade Stevens, a vampire who was a psychiatrist during life. The group is focused on helping newly born vampires adjust to their new state of existence, and to encourage vampires to avoid harming the innocent as much as possible. The VA is vying for control. Their goal is to rule the vampires of the United States and to set up an internal policing agency.

Whispering Mirror: A magical communications device that links Otherworld and Earth. Think magical video phone.

Y'Eírialiastar: The Sidhe/Fae name for Otherworld.

Y'Elestrial: The city-state in Otherworld where the D'Artigo girls were born and raised. A Fae city, recently embroiled in a civil war between the drug-crazed tyrannical Queen Lethesanar and her more level-headed sister Tanaquar, who managed to claim the throne for herself. The civil war has ended and Tanaquar is restoring order to the land.

Youkai: Loosely (very loosely) translated as Japanese demon/nature spirit. For the purposes of this series, the youkai have three shapes: the animal, the human form, and the true demon form. Unlike the demons of the Subterranean Realms, youkai are not necessarily evil by nature.

PLAYLIST FOR *SHADOW RISING*

I write to music a good share of the time, and so I always put my playlists in the back of each book so you can see which artists/songs I listened to during the writing. Here's the playlist for *Shadow Rising*:

AC/DC: "Hells Bells," "Rock and Roll Ain't Noise Pollution"

Adam Lambert: "Mad World"

Air: "Napalm Love," "The Word 'Hurricane' "

AJ Roach: "Devil May Dance"

Amanda Blank: "Make It Take It"

Asteroids Galaxy Tour: "The Sun Ain't Shining No More," "The Golden Age," "Sunshine Coolin' "

Avalon Rising: "The Great Selkie"

Awolnation: "Sail"

Beck: "Nausea"

Black Sabbath: "Paranoid"

Blue Oyster Cult: "Godzilla"

The Bravery: "Believe"

Celtic Woman: "The Voice"

Cobra Verde: "Play with Fire"

David Bowie: "I'm Afraid of Americans"

Depeche Mode: "Dream On"

Eels: "Souljacker Part I," "Love of the Loveless"

Fleetwood Mac: "Gold Dust Woman"

Foo Fighters: "All My Life"

Foster the People: "Pumped Up Kicks"

Gary Numan: "Cold Warning," "The Hunter," "Stormtrooper in Drag," "Hybrid," "Down in the Park," "Cars (Hybrid version)," "Dream Killer," "Voix," "Are Friends Electric," "Dead Son Rising," "The Fall," "When the Sky Bleeds, He Will Come"

Gorillaz: "Every Planet We Reach Is Dead," "Dare," "Stylo"

Hives: "Tick Tock Boom"

Lady Gaga: "I Like It Rough," "Paparazzi," "Born This Way"

Ladytron: "I'm Not Scared"

Lou Reed: "Walk on the Wild Side"

Madonna: "4 Minutes"

Marilyn Manson: "Rock Is Dead"

Metallica: "Enter Sandman"

People in Planes: "Vampire"

Puddle of Mudd: "Psycho"

Rob Zombie: "Living Dead Girl," "Mars Needs Women"

Róisín Murphy: "Ramalama (Bang Bang)"

Saliva: "Broken Sunday"

Seether: "Remedy"

Soundgarden: "Fell on Black Days," "Superunknown," "Spoonman"

Stone Temple Pilots: "Dead & Bloated"

Sully Erna: "The Rise"

Tori Amos: "In the Springtime of His Voodoo"

U2: "Vertigo," "Elevation"

Ween: "Mutilated Lips"

Woodland: "I Remember," "Morgana Moon," "Blood of the Moon," "First Melt"

Yoko Kanno: "Lithium Flower," "Run Rabbit Junk"

Zero 7: "In the Waiting Line"

Dear Reader:

I hope that you enjoyed Shadow Rising, *the twelfth book in the Otherworld Series, as much as I enjoyed writing it. The world is ever expanding with each book, and so many possibilities have opened up for the coming books. Next up in this series: Camille's book,* Haunted Moon, *which will be book thirteen, coming February 2013, and after that,* Night Vision, *book four of the Indigo Court Series, will be out in July 2013, before we come back to Otherworld for Delilah's book.*

I'm including the first chapter from Haunted Moon *here to give you a sneak peek. For those of you new to my books, I wanted to take this opportunity to welcome you into my worlds. For those of you who've been reading my books for a while, I wanted to thank you for revisiting the D'Artigo Sisters' world once again.*

Bright Blessings,
The Painted Panther
Yasmine Galenorn

"Just breathe in, slow . . . That's it. Now, out in one, two, three." Morio's voice was low in my ear as he knelt behind me, leaning down, his hands on my shoulders, magic tingling through his fingers, into my body.

I sat cross-legged on the floor, wearing a filmy black dress, my arms extended to the sides. In my left hand, I balanced an orb of obsidian. In my right, I grasped a yew wand, carved with intricate symbols etched in silver.

"Now, focus on the spirit. Keep your gaze on it." Again, the soft whisper of his voice caressed my ear. We were in tune, my youkai and I, sitting in a flaming circle outside under the night sky, in a long-forgotten graveyard. The borders of the circle were ablaze with magical fire—the purple crackle of death magic—and I was doing my best to control it, struggling to multitask the spells we were working on.

We were in a small cemetery, one shrouded with disuse and neglect. The smell of earth hung pungent in my nose, and a scuttling of bugs across the ground made me shiver, but I forced myself to ignore them. I had to forget they were there as I stared at the spirit hovering in front of me. It was luminous in the night, rising above us, spiraling up from the skull that rested on the ground by my feet. I had no idea who the ghost had been, or why it was here, but only that I must break through its barriers and destroy it, setting it free to rest, or— if it would not go willingly—sending it into oblivion.

I gathered the rush of energy Morio was feeding me. The rumbling power twisted through my body, a radiant heat, a purple flame, urging me onward. The tingles sparked through my body, crackling through muscle and sinew as the power grew, buoying me up with it until it spiraled me out of my body.

Looming large before the spirit, I struggled to keep control of the fire—both of the flames forming the Circle and of those bucking through my body like a horse unwilling to take a master. Morio was feeding it through me faster than I'd ever been able to take it before. I lowered my head, searching for the key. And there . . . hiding behind a wayward spark, *there it was.* All magic—all energy—had a key, a signature. Control the key, control the force.

Reaching out with my mind, I latched onto the signature and, after a momentary struggle, the flames flared up. At first they resisted my control, but then they let go and quit fighting me. As they gave in to my will, they evened out, building in me like a backwash, ready to surge forth at my command.

The spirit seemed to sense my intention and shrank back, wailing, as I raised my palms to it, willing the roiling fire to blast through my body.

"Go, go now or I will destroy you," I whispered.

The spirit would not move but instead shrieked and aimed for me, its lifeless sockets staring at me.

"I command you to depart this realm."

Again, nothing, but it was planning something nasty, that much I could feel. I sucked in a deep breath and forced my palms forward, toward it.

"Death took you once, let death take you again." And then I summoned the release word. *"Atataq!"*

The sound of the fire roared through my ears, soaring with the pulse of my blood. It carried me with it, rising like a purple phoenix as it blotted out the moon. I swung astride its back, riding it like I might ride a lover, the rush of orgasm claiming me as the flame shrieked down, diving for the spirit. I came hard and sharp as the fire knifed through the ghost, exploding it into vapor. As the spirit vanished, the phoenix began to turn its head. *Oh shit*. It was looking at me like I was its next target.

Through my lust-crazed haze, I heard Morio shout, "Control it! Take control or it will go after you next!"

Quickly, I brought my attention back to the key, struggling to regain my hold on it. The phoenix paused.

"Bring it back now. Damn it, do what I say! Roll the power back *now*—there . . . you've almost got it." Morio's voice was abrupt, but I knew he was just worried about me.

I shook my head to clear my thoughts, beginning to rein in the power, reeling it back. I worked it, coaxed it, stroked it, and finally demanded that it retreat and—after a struggle, it listened, receding like a tide, rolling back to the ocean from which it had come. The phoenix turned back to face the silent night and then vanished in a bright flash.

Polished and cleansed by the flames, my body felt as if a fine dust of ash coated its every nerve. As the wave of death magic reached my crown chakra, I let go, and Morio took over, siphoning it back out of me into the sky, releasing it to the night, back to the haunted moon overhead.

Exhausted, I collapsed. Morio leaned over me, his eyes gleaming in the night. His long black hair hung straight, and I longed to run my hands through it, to feel the silken strands between my fingers. I wanted to pull my Japanese lover, my husband, between my legs, and quench the fire that had built within me.

"Do you know how much I want you?" he whispered. "Do you know how hungry for you our magic makes me?"

"Show me, my love. Show me," I whispered, ready to take him right there inside the circle of flames. But just then, my cell phone rang. It was in my purse, which was sitting just outside the circle. The ring tone played out "Demon Days" by the Gorillaz, which meant it was Chase. Which meant it was probably important.

"Fuck." I pushed myself up to a sitting position. "Get that, would you?"

Morio opened the circle, stepping over the flames as he did so. He grabbed my phone out of the purse and answered. "Hello? . . . Morio." After a moment, he motioned to me, his expression shifting from lusty to solemn. "Here, you need to take this. I'll start gathering our things and disband the circle."

"Bad?" I didn't want to hear. I really didn't.

But he just nodded. "Bad." And that was that. We were out of Circle, back to a reality I wasn't ready to face yet. But the fact was, our reality was growing more and more deadly with each week that passed.

"Camille?" Chase sounded out of breath. The detective was physically fit, so that in itself worried me.

"What's going down? Where? And how bad?" I didn't spare any words. Phone calls like this were always terse.

"Robbery at one of the graveyards. And we have a handful of zombies running around. As well as a bloatworgle."

"Robbery? What the fuck are they stealing—and are the zombies doing the looting?"

Chase growled. "*No*. There's more to it—I can't explain now . . ." He paused, and I could hear him panting. So not a good sign. Chase was in great shape for an FBH—full-blooded human. Or rather, an FBH with a tiny hint of elf in his long-distance background.

"Dude, are you okay? You're worrying me." I didn't like worrying about our friends because it had become an all-too-common theme. Collateral damage in this demonic war had hit us hard, and all too often as of late.

"I'd be fine if I weren't hiding out from a fucking zombie who's on the loose with the munchies for my brains. Or anything else it can latch onto. I'm playing hide-and-seek with it in Wyvers Point Cemetery, and unfortunately, I'm not the one doing the chasing."

"Let me guess . . . the cemetery is in the Greenbelt Park District?" If I never heard of that area of Seattle again, it would still be too much.

"Yeah . . . Fourth and Hyland Streets. Get over here as soon as you can. And can you call the others?" He was whispering now. "Two of my men are somewhere in the graveyard, but I don't know where. We're all on the run. Tell you more after you get here and help me get the fuck out of this situation."

I punched the End Call button and turned to Morio, who had quickly been gathering all of our things. "We've got another graveyard to pay a call on, and we'd better hurry or Chase is going to be on the dinner menu. Zombies, and a bloatworgle at the very least."

As Morio tossed our ritual gear into the back of my Lexus, I called home. We were closer to Wyvers than my sisters, so we'd get there ahead of time. But we'd also expended a lot of energy tonight on our magical exercises, and I knew that we—or at least I—couldn't take on a full force of undead miscreants without help.

I quickly filled Delilah in on what was going down. "Get over there, now. We're facing a bloatworgle, several zombies, and who knows what the hell else."

"Menolly's at the Wayfarer. We can call her if we need her once we're there. I'll bring Smoky, Shade, and Vanzir." Delilah punched off and I texted her the location.

Sliding into the driver's seat, I clicked my seat belt shut. While I waited for Morio, I grabbed a candy bar out of the glove compartment and scarfed it down. I desperately needed the energy after working the magic we just had, so I polished off the chocolate caramel and then went for a protein bar. By then, Morio was swinging into the car, and I took off as he slammed the door.

"I guess we couldn't expect the quiet to last for long." Morio pulled his hair back into a ponytail and yanked off his short kimono. Beneath it, he was wearing a pair of tight black jeans that curved around his butt in an oh-so-flattering way. As he fished a deep blue turtleneck out of a backpack, I managed a glance at his glistening chest. Morio was buff— not a muscle man, but definitely buff. I got wet just looking at him. One of my three husbands, he was Japanese, a youkai-kitsune—loosely translated, a fox-demon, though he wasn't the kind of demon that we were fighting. Together with Smoky, my dragon, and Trillian, my alpha lover and Svartan, we made quite the quartet.

We'd been in a refreshing lull over the past five weeks, since shortly after Menolly and Nerissa got married. And we'd savored every minute, using the time to bone up on our fighting techniques and magical skills, to stockpile weapons, and to hunt down as much information as we could on Gulakah, the Lord of Ghosts.

Unfortunately, that information didn't amount to a hill of beans. We'd also done our best to keep tabs on what was going down with the impending war in Otherworld. So, when I thought about it, we really *hadn't* had any downtime, per se—just a short break from the continual fighting we'd been embroiled in for months now. But that short break had meant the difference between being run ragged and having a little breathing room to regain our equilibrium.

Morio finished changing into the turtleneck and fastened his seat belt as I took a turn a little too sharply.

"Try to keep at least two wheels on the road, babe." But his eyes twinkled as he also dove into our stock of candy and protein bars. "We're probably going to be there about ten minutes before the others. So let's take stock of what we have to fight with, other than magic."

"I have a short dagger. I've started carrying it with me wherever I go. It's strapped to my thigh. So there's that much, but against a bloatworgle? Not going to be all that much help." I felt better carrying a weapon now, even if it was more of a pacifier than anything that would do much damage. "I left the Black Unicorn horn at home, of course. I didn't think we'd need it tonight."

About a year ago, I'd received a gift—the horn of the Black Unicorn—along with a cloak made from his hide.

The Black Unicorn was the father of the Dahns unicorns, and like the phoenix, he reincarnated every few thousand years, shedding his old body. Eight or nine horns and hides were rumored to exist, and I possessed one set. Any number of sorcerers and havoc mongers would have torn me limb from limb to get them—the artifacts were incredibly powerful—so I was cautious where I took them and who knew about them.

Near the autumn equinox, I'd earned the right to call myself a Priestess for the Moon Mother, undergoing a terrifying and heartbreaking ritual with the Black Unicorn. We were now bound in a way that I could not verbalize.

"Yeah, I don't think you want to expend the power of it on a few zombies and minor demons." Morio sorted through his pack again. "I can take my demonic form, of course, and make quick work of a few of them. I also have a blade in here." He held up a curved dagger that looked wickedly sharp. "How are you on magical energy? Did our practice wear you out?"

I gauged my energy level. I was tired; we'd been practicing a higher-level spell than I'd ever tried to cast before—one to destroy or dispel spirits. Ghostbusting, if you will, through magical means. And while I still felt amped up from the energy that had been pouring through my veins, I couldn't guarantee my accuracy if I had to actually start slinging around energy bolts and release spells.

"I can manage a few things, magically, I think, but seriously—don't count on my spells not backfiring. In fact, I think 'backfire' could easily be my go-to game tonight. And speaking of night—why the fuck do these things always happen at night when we're just about ready for bed? Why not in the morning, when we've gotten some sleep, had breakfast, and are good to go?" I swung the car left, onto Wyvers Avenue NW. The Greenbelt Park District wasn't all that far from home, from the Belles-Faire area where we lived. Wyvers Point Cemetery was on the border between the two.

"They do, but it seems that ghosts prefer the night. Just like vampires. Or maybe there's just too much activity in the daytime so they don't come out as much. Whatever the case, I suggest we take a break from the magic with this crew. And you, be careful. If you've only got a dagger, you're set up as an all-too-appealing target." He picked up my bag. "Are you sure you didn't swipe anything good from Roz last time you were poking around in his duster? No firebombs or anything?"

I grinned. Morio knew me, all right. Rozurial, an incubus who lived on our land and who had become enmeshed with our family, wore a long duster à la Neo from *The Matrix*, and the thing was filled with everything from wooden stakes to magical bombs to a mini Uzi. Although, now that I thought about it, last time I looked, the Uzi had been replaced by a magical stun gun we'd managed to liberate from a sorcerer's bar that we'd managed to make bite the dust. Literally. There was nothing left of the building except a pile of toothpicks.

"Nah. I tried to snag some stuff from him yesterday, but he caught me with my hands in the cookie jar and threatened to tell Smoky I was prowling through his pockets. You know what Smoky would think of that."

A dragon, Smoky was possessive and he didn't always get the joke. He shared me with Morio and Trillian because that was just the way things were. He seemed comfortable with the situation, but that was the limit of his generosity regarding my attentions, and he'd already thrashed Roz once for a misplaced hand on the butt.

Morio snorted. "He's always and forever going to be a big galoot. You know it, and I know it, and we just have to love him for who he is." He laughed, then sobered. "So, we have two daggers and my bad-assed demon self. And your potentially self-destructible magic. Sounds about right. I'll do my best to engage the creeps, and you try to rescue Chase from wherever he's hiding."

"Sounds good to me." I had worn a pair of my granny boots. They were stilettos, definitely not made for running, but I'd had plenty of practice. I hadn't expected to be out in the field tonight, not like this.

As we came to Atlas Drive, a small side street forking off from Wyvers Ave NW, I veered onto the darkened road and slowed down. We were no longer in a purely suburban area—the foliage was a little more tangled, the surroundings a little more rural. It was harder to see. The night was dark, the streetlights few and far between, and while it wasn't terribly chilly, the moon had gone into hiding behind a patch of clouds. In the Seattle area, there were only sixty-some days a

year that were totally cloud-free, and today—this evening—
wasn't one of them.

As I slowed the car, edging along the dark street, the tangle of branches overhead reminded me of our forests back in Otherworld. We were nearing Beltane, the sexuality and fertility festival celebrating the gods and the rut of the King Stag, bugling for his mate.

The leaves were starting to burgeon out on the trees as life sprang again, urged on by the growing length of the days and the warming of the soil. I could feel the push as the roots buried themselves deep in the ground. My body wanted to stretch out with the leaves as they reached for what sun they could find. The ferns were lush again, and the grass vivid green, and the days were hovering mostly in the low sixties, but the rain that came down wasn't the bone-chilling cold it was in winter.

We arrived at Wyvers Point Cemetery and I eased into the parking lot, parking in one of the slots nearest the wrought-iron gates. Why did cemeteries always come outfitted with cast and wrought iron? It burned me—it burned all of us who had any significant amount of Fae blood in our veins. Steel we could handle. While steel had a great deal of iron in it, somehow the process of its creation altered the makeup of the iron just enough to make it possible for us to handle it. Being half-human made it even easier for my sisters and me.

I parked the car and turned off the ignition, making certain my keys were zipped into the special pouch I kept around my neck when I needed to leave my purse in the car. I glanced over at Morio.

"We'd better get out there and find Chase and his men before they get pummeled." I leaned over and pressed my lips to my youkai, and the heat from his body stirred me even as he stroked my face.

"Be careful, babe." His eyes glimmered with brown and topaz, and I could feel his demonic nature coming to the surface. "Keep your eyes open."

"You do the same. The ghosts almost took you from me

once. I won't let it happen again." I ran my finger over his thin mustache and goatee, then lightly tapped his lips.

With that, we locked the car behind us and headed up the sidewalk, on alert for the ghosts and the bloatworgle, and who knew what else.

Wyvers Point Cemetery had been let go to ruin. I doubted if there were any graves here newer than from fifty years back, and while the grass had been mowed, the weeds tangled thickly along the walkway and the trees needed a good trimming. Some of the cedar branches were sweeping the ground, and here and there I saw limbs that had been bowed and snapped by the force of the winter snows and winds. Whoever was in charge of maintenance needed to clear them out, but I had a feeling that was low on the priority list for the groundskeepers here.

The path was open to the sky until we approached the gates, and then, directly through the wrought-iron bars, the trees closed in, shading the sidewalk. There were no lights to illuminate the way, and I shivered. An incredible sense of isolation and loneliness emanated from the land. The more I studied death magic with Morio, and the more intensive my training was becoming with Aeval and Morgaine, the more I tuned in to the nature of the land, and the more connected I was with the environment over here, Earthside.

I was becoming accustomed to the shadowed nature of the woodlands and the secretive feel that most of the wild places held. Otherworld might be more upfront with the magic, but here, roots ran deep, and so did grudges and longings and long-remembered animosities. The sacred places of this world would not give up their anger at being paved over, nor conquered in the name of religions, and the ley lines were very active, and very powerful.

"This place is one of the forgotten places." Morio glanced around, a solemn look on his face. He pinpointed what I'd been feeling but unable to put words to. "The graves and their occupants, long left alone to brood and to remember their deaths without anyone to grieve them."

"You feel it, too? I sense betrayal coming from the cemetery."

As I walked through the gates, which Morio swung open for me, I shivered. While death and spirits were becoming common fare, something about this place unsettled me and I didn't trust it. Didn't trust anything within the boundaries of this graveyard. It wasn't so much anger, but cunning and the sense of being watched, and stalked.

"Something's been watching us since we stepped out of the car."

"I know. I sense it, too." Morio's voice was light, and low, but beneath the gentle tone I could hear a warning. "On second thought, I don't think we should split up—"

A hoarse shout to our left, through a copse of cedar, cut him off.

"That's Chase!" I started for the voice, even as a pair of zombies broke out from behind a large patch of wild brambles to the left. "You deal with *them*. I'll go find Chase."

Morio quickly transformed into his full demon form. Eight feet tall, with a muzzle and glowing topaz eyes; his hands and feet were still human, though matching the rest of his size. His clothes transformed with him—I wasn't sure on the how or why of it—but he'd never gone all Hulk and ripped out of his shirt and pants yet. He had one hell of a tail and used it to balance himself as he lunged for the undead.

I wasn't too worried about him. Morio was ruthless when necessary. And so I headed in the direction from which I'd heard Chase calling. As I ran across the lawn, praying I didn't hit a gopher hole with my heels, I happened to glance up at the moon shining down. She was waxing overhead, the Moon Mother was, and now her light pierced the veil of clouds and hit me full on and I felt a surge of energy as she bathed me in her magic.

"Chase? Chase?" I called his name lightly as I approached the thicket of cedar and slowed. Putting my senses on full alert, I reached out, seeking his signature. Chase and I had formed some sort of magical connection, though what it was neither one of us yet understood, but there was some meshing of energy that had happened between us and we were able to find each other when we needed help. He'd found me from the astral plane when Hyto had captured me, and now . . . I could sense where he was . . . *hiding*.

I paused, holding out my hands. A tingle turned me to the left, and I followed it, ducking beneath the low limb of a vine maple growing in the shadow of one of the cedars. And then, I heard a noise. A snuffling, like some beast or pig hunting for truffles. Stopping, I tried to sense whether it was friend or foe.

A whisper echoed on the wind.

"She comes, the moon's mistress comes . . . she will not harm, she can help. She can make our home safe again as we tend the spirits in the garden . . ."

"But will she help us? And who is the human-not-so-human? He is frightened. The wayward ones seek him."

Taking a deep breath, I slowly broke through the undergrowth. "Who are you? I can hear you."

There was a shift and a blur raced by, then—hesitating—turned back. "Priestess?" The voice was wary.

"I am a Priestess, yes. Of the Moon Mother." I glanced around, looking for Chase, but could not see him. He was near, though, my senses told me that much, and he needed my help. "I'm looking for my friend—the human-not-so-human. Can you tell me where he is?" I wasn't even sure if we were speaking aloud, but the words were there, hanging in the air.

"Priestess . . . you are from the other side?"

At first, I thought that the creature—whom I still could not see—was asking if I was a spirit, but then I realized what it meant. "Yes, I'm from Otherworld. Who are you? Show yourself to me."

Slowly, as if shedding layers of an invisible cloak, a creature appeared before me. He—and for some reason, I knew it was a he—emerged from the shadows. About four feet tall, he looked like he was made of leaves and branches, vines and twigs. He reminded me of the walking sticks that inhabited the insect world, only his face was long and his chin pointed, and his eyes were slanted ovals, and on his face, a mere hint of nostrils. A crown of ivy wove around his forehead, and he wore a cape of moss and lichen.

"Are you of the Elder Fae?" I had never seen a creature like him, not even back in Otherworld, and he fascinated me. The closest I could think of would be Wisteria, the floraed who'd joined forces with the demons in her hatred of mortal-kind.

He cocked his head to the right. "No, I be not Elder Fae."

And then I knew what he was. "You're an Earth Elemental!"

"I am. I am of the land itself. I am guardian of this boneyard. And now, the bones are walking, where they should not be walking. Unnatural magic is afoot and has evil intent." He glanced around and motioned, and another one of his kind appeared from the shadows. They moved like leaves on the wind, like walking trees.

Honored—Elementals didn't appear to just anybody, especially since a number of witches tried to summon them up in order to control their movements—I curtsied.

"I know. My friends and I are here to help put the bonewalkers and the wayward dead back in their graves. But I must find my friend, before the zombies and demons harm him. Can you take me to him?"

I waited, forcing myself to be patient. And patience wasn't one of my virtues. But when dealing with Elementals, patience was key. Especially Earth Elementals, who tended to move cautiously until they were certain of their course, at which point they could surge forth like an earthquake or landslide.

After a moment, during which they exchanged chattering noises that sounded like sticks rattling, he turned toward me again. "Your friend is in the clearing directly beyond this thicket. He is hurt. If you will clear the wayward ones, we will not forget your help. We guard the bones of this space, and they should not be abroad. Bones are for memories. Bones are to feed the earth and the worms. Bones are not meant to be walking above the ground without flesh and soul attached."

"You're right about that," I whispered, as I started past them.

As I passed by, the Earth Elemental caught my wrist in his hand. A heavy, laden sense of gravity sank me to my knees. "You are young in the world, still. There are ancient powers waking from their slumber. Some are beneficial. Others hunger from the depths. Be wary, Priestess: Not everything that answers to the moon will understand the changes wrought in this world. The Mother is ancient, and some of her children nearly as old."

And with that, he let go and I stumbled forward. I tried to get his warning out of my head, but the words rang in my ears as I pushed my way through the cedars to yet another clearing—the graveyard itself.

And there was Chase, propped up on a tombstone, looking petrified as a zombie slowly made its way toward him. That was one saving grace of the zombie brigade—they couldn't move very fast. They shuffled. They scuffed along. Granted, once they reached you, if you couldn't get out of their way, you were toast unless you could totally destroy them. But given you were in an open space and not obligated to destroy them, you could usually run away.

Now ghouls were different from zombies. They were faster, even though they were also animated corpses. And far worse, they absorbed life energy as well as eating flesh, and so were doubly dangerous.

But Chase didn't look like he was going anywhere soon. He was leaning on the tombstone, one foot raised. In one hand, he held his Glock 40, even though he knew bullets were no real use against the undead. Chase was good with a gun—deadly accurate—but the bullets wouldn't stop what was coming our way.

He glanced at me as I headed his way. Six two, with dark hair cut in a slight shag, he was swarthy with olive skin, dark eyes, and a suave look to him. He was muscled, but lean. Right now, he mostly looked like he was in pain.

I hurried over to him, eyeing the zombies as I crossed the open swath of grass, past dilapidated headstones that were breaking apart, they were so old and weathered. The zombies were near enough to worry about, but we still had a few minutes before they'd reach us.

I cut right to the point. We didn't have time for small talk. "Can you walk?"

"I stepped in a pothole and twisted my ankle. I managed to hobble over here, but I think I'll seriously fuck it up if I try to set my weight on it." He winced but pushed the pain aside and nodded to the oncoming undead. "What about them? You can't carry me, woman."

"You'd be surprised what I can do. I'm half-Fae, remember?" But the truth was, I *didn't* think I could manage to carry him. I could outrun him, outwalk him, and probably fight him down to the ground, but I wasn't Delilah with her athletic frame, and I wasn't Menolly with her vampiric strength. "Put away the gun; that's not going to do any good and one of us will end up getting shot."

He tucked it back in the holster. "I didn't think it would help, but I was feeling vulnerable, you know? From now on, I'm carrying an armory, like Roz."

"It wouldn't fit in your suit jacket, babe." I began to edge away from the gravestone. The nearest zombie was getting too close for comfort, and still no sign of Morio or the others. I had to do something. "Hide behind the tombstone. I don't want you getting hit by any backfire from this if it goes wrong."

Chase knew well enough by now that when I said *duck*, he'd better move. Fast. And duck he did—crouching down behind the marker as I called down the energy of the Moon Mother. There were enough clouds that I was able to find the key for lightning, and I summoned it through me, praying that I'd have the energy to direct it without causing massive damage to either Chase or myself.

As the familiar tingle ran down through my crown chakra, into my arms and down through my fingers, it felt like my muscles and aura were being infused by a huge jolt of caffeine. I began to shake—yeah, I was too tired for this, but there was no choice. I could run, but Chase couldn't, and I wasn't going to leave him alone to get attacked by the zombies.

As I took aim, focusing the best I could, I let loose with the energy bolt. The blast ricocheted out of my body, flaring out in the darkening sky. It wasn't a fork of lightning. Instead, the spell spread out, blanketing a wide swath of grass and gravestones instead of just pinpointing the walking dead. It reminded me of a floodlight, suddenly lighting up the night.

But the energy caught the zombie and knocked it on its ass. The creature went flying back, landing hard, giving us precious time while it was trying to reorient itself and struggled to its feet again.

Meanwhile, I heard something coming at us from the left. I swung around in time to see a goblin, wearing full leather armor, leading a band of at least twenty other goblins at full tilt.

"What the fuck? *Goblins?* Chase, get your gun back out. It may do some good against them." Meanwhile, exhausted from the energy bolt on top of everything that Morio and I had already done earlier, I fumbled for my cell phone. I needed reinforcements and fast, or Chase and I were going to be mincemeat.

But before I could extract it from the zippered pocket that also held my keys, the goblins were on us. I yanked out my dagger and engaged the leader. As I swiped, desperately trying to focus, Chase let off a volley of bullets and two of the goblins went down, though they weren't dead.

Panicking, I lunged for the goblin's head and my blade connected with the flesh, plunging through to bounce off the bone. I didn't have the strength to drive the blade through his skull. As he lurched back, taking my blade with me, I scrambled to summon up as much energy as I could. I might be able to manage one more energy bolt. But as I dodged, trying to evade my attacker, a blur roared past me, and the goblin went flying. I blinked, trying to see what the hell had just happened.

And there, standing between me and the goblin horde, was Smoky. And he was *pissed*.